Nutmeg + Mistletoe

T.L. MARTIN

CONTENTS

WELCOME TO CINNAMON GROVE

Where Ambition Meets Obsession.

Most of my stories—and all of your favorite heartbeats—live right here in **Cinnamon Grove**. It's a place of manicured lawns, high-stakes power plays, and the kind of secrets that only come out after dark. From the elite offices of the city's most powerful men to the private sanctuaries where they finally meet their match, this is the world of the **Black Wife Effect**.

Whether you're following Timantha and Will's unbelievable journey to the altar, or fell in love with Sanctuary where you met Jax and Dash, all roads lead back here.

Visit **TLMartinWorld.com** to explore the map, find your favorite hangouts, and dive into the stories that turned this quiet grove into a billionaire's playground. Use the QR Code below to sign-up for Cinnamon Grove's official Substack newsletter!

Welcome to the Grove. I'm glad you're here.

PART ONE
Marlow

O kay. Before we dive in, let's get one thing straight — this *is* a Christmas love story. A beautiful one, in fact.

But, before we get to the part with the magic and mistletoe, we need to go back. Because what started as something silly and downright *ridiculous*, somehow managed to unravel the lives of four people in ways none of us saw coming.

I'll go first.

PROLOGUE
Marlow

One month ago in Las Vegas

I knew it. I *knew* it! I fucking *knew* it!

I'm standing outside one of Las Vegas' newest and most exclusive clubs, where I'm supposed to be celebrating my childhood best friend's bachelorette party. Champagne, dancing, bad decisions—the works.

But, no. Instead of partying, I've been pacing the damn sidewalk in stilettos, because my phone has been blowing up with call after call from an unknown number.

Finally, after the sixth one lights up my screen, I cave and answer.

And who is it?

My *ex*-boyfriend's childhood best friend.

You know the one. The one he swore up and down was *just a friend*. The one who always said, "babe, it only looks like we're close because we grew up together," every time I made a comment about how she was always around. The one he *gaslight* me about her not liking me for a year because, according to him, I was "just jealous" and "insecure" and only a truly mature woman could handle their friendship.

Yeah. That one.

She's pregnant.

And because life is apparently a soap opera, *Young and the Dickless*, she's decided to call me and tell me about it.

Her whiny, high-pitched voice oozes through my speaker. "I'm really sorry you had to find out like this, but I just feel like...women should stick together. You know?"

"Sorry!" I yell into the phone. "Were you sorry the countless times you were offering your vagina up to my boyfriend, you cantankerous cunt?"

A group of guys stumbles past, bumping into me. One of them smirks, clearly clocking my mood. "Chill out, babe. This is Vegas!"

I roll my eyes. "*So* helpful, that one," I mutter under my breath sarcastically.

I am not normally this feisty, nor would I ever curse someone out while standing in stilettos on a sidewalk. But sometimes a girl hits her breaking point. That moment where she realizes that playing nice, smiling through the bullshit, and being the "good girl" has gotten her *exactly* nowhere.

And let's be clear: I'm supposed to be having *the* weekend to end all weekends. One last wild, unforgettable, maybe-regrettable hurrah before I trade in tequila shots and spontaneous decisions for early mornings and professionalism. Because next week, I start my new job with the Atlanta Strikers Soccer Club.

So really... what better place to make a few questionable, possibly life-altering decisions than three thousand miles from home?

Jillian's still yammering through the phone. "Okay, I don't know what a... a cantankerous is, or whatever, but—"

"Save it, Jillian. You didn't call me out of sisterhood or solidarity or whatever fairytale bullshit you're selling yourself tonight. You called to gloat. To tell me you finally got what everyone already knew you wanted—you got Jeremy. Congratulations. May the four of you live happily ever after."

She gasps. "Four? I'm not having twins!"

I let out a cold laugh. "It's cute you think you're gonna break him up with his mama!"

Then I hang up. Hard.

Jeremy. *What a dumb name, anyway.*

By the time I weave my way back inside and find my friends, I'm already halfway into a bottle of tequila I picked up off of a waitress. No glass. No lime. No shame.

I simply gave the nice lady five hundred dollars and told her to leave the Don Julio with me.

The four bridesmaids and bride-to-be are huddled near the VIP booth, eyes widening as I approach, phone in one hand, bottle in the other. I've been angry texting them the whole time I was stomping around the casino floor, like we were playing some deranged game of Marco Polo.

"Hey, sweetie," Alaya says carefully, stepping toward me. "So sorry about Jeremy."

The other bridesmaids chime in behind her. "Yeah, girl. So sorry!"

I tip the bottle back, taking another long, defiant swig. "I hope he gets ass cancer!"

"Easy there," Alaya says, voice half soothing, half concerned.

"Fine! Dick and ball cancer. Is that nice enough for you?"

"Jesus, Marlow!" I hear from behind me.

I take another swig, wiping my mouth like a drunken sailor. "Well, it's a little dick, so it won't be much of a loss to society!"

Sarah eyes the bottle in my hand, her brows shooting up. "Um... anyone else notice she's drunk half of that already?"

I hiccup again, clutching my drink like it holds the answers to life. "And why is it—*why*—that women always settle for the guy with the little dick?"

"Can we stop saying *dick* so much?" Sarah hisses through her teeth, her smile frozen and eyes darting around. "People are starting to think we're prostitutes!"

I wave her off like she's missing something big and mind-bending. "We think—*we think*—if we accept a man as he *is*, with his little edamame-looking penis, he'll be grateful. He'll *worship* us. But no! He goes and knocks up Jillian. *Jillian!* The canker cunt!"

Alaya, calm and dressed like an off-duty goddess, leans in with her best preschool teacher voice. "Hey, Marlow? Since tomorrow's my wedding day, and you're my maid of honor and all, why don't you go back to the villa and lie down, sweetie?"

Translation: you are seconds from being immortalized in a viral TikTok meltdown, and we cannot have that.

"I'm just saying, Laya! With a name like Nelson, he better have a good di–"

Sarah pours more tequila down my throat, stopping me before another *dick* flies out of my mouth.

Then, seemingly out of nowhere, tears come. Hot and fast.

"I was finally going to introduce him to my dad, Laya!" I blurt, my voice breaking on the words.

She pulls me into a hug, rubbing my back. "I know, sweetie. We all know how hard it is to bring someone home to Daddy."

Harder for me than most.

I'd been dating Jeremy for a year before even thinking about introducing him to my father. Because my dad sniffs out men like Jeremy in a heartbeat. The ones who talk a good game, who charm their way in with no intention of settling down. The ones who only want to get in my pants. Daddy's words.

And he would've been right about Jeremy.

Because, let's be real—it takes a player to know a player. And my dad? He's one of the best.

Not in a sleazy way. He's not out here lying to women or spinning some fairytale. If anything, he's brutally honest.

Every time he meets a woman, he lays it all out there—he married the love of his life years ago, and now that she's gone, he has no intention of falling in love again. And somehow these women eat it up. The honesty. The no-strings-attached vibe. The man could sell sand in a desert. It's no wonder I suck at relationships.

Whenever I ask him—usually after we've split a bottle of wine—how the hell I'm supposed to find love when he's the example I grew up with, he always says the same thing. That I shouldn't overthink it: *"Find the man who's honest. The one who can't live without you. Find the one who gives you their whole heart without question. That's what you wait for. That's what I had with your mother."*

Then he reminds me he's still being honest with these women he goes out with today, which is why he feels no guilt about his bad boy image and the fact he'll never settle down again.

I usually roll my eyes because only men could get away with that logic.

I say my goodbyes to the bride squad, promising Alaya I'll be back in time for her sunset wedding tomorrow—hopefully minus the tequila still coursing through my veins and the simmering rage that's clinging to me like bad perfume.

"Go sleep it off," Alaya says, giving me one last hug. "You'll feel better tomorrow."

Sarah leans in for a hug. "And hey—no drunk-texting Jeremy, ok?"

I hold up three fingers. Then burp. "Scout's honor."

As I'm weaving my way through the casino toward the car queue, I pull out my phone and shoot my dad a quick text.

Me: *Heading back to the villa to sleep off tequila. Have fun tonight but not too much fun. I'm not bailing you out of jail...again.*

A minute later, the three little dots pop up.

Daddy: *The hooker said her pimp will bail me out.*

I laugh to myself and slide the phone back into my clutch. Pretty sure he's joking.

It's nine p.m. on a Saturday night and I'm wearing the *cutest* Crash Steele dress I had made especially for this weekend.

The bodice is pure art. It's strapless, with intricate black lace that curves in all the right places, hugging my body like a second skin. The layers of soft, inky-black tulle float out from my hips in an asymmetric sweep that hits mid-thigh. It's sultry, dramatic, *perfect* for a night out in Vegas.

I *should* be out partying, dancing, giving my best friend the biggest, wildest send-off before her wedding. But no.

Instead, my night is currently being ruined by a man who has never—not once—given me an orgasm.

The audacity.

As I round the corner near one of the side entrances, I pass a guy standing behind a branded pop-up table, a big neon sign flashing *SightUnseen* above his head.

He's calling out to people as they walk by, waving a clipboard in one hand. "Sign-ups open now! Condensed version of the show! Ninety minutes to meet the love of your life!"

I slow my steps, curiosity tugging at me.

He spots me immediately. "You look like someone who is ready for love!"

I arch a brow. "SightUnseen? Isn't that the reality show where people date through pods and end up engaged without ever seeing each other?"

"That's the one! This is the fast-track version," he says with a slick grin. "Ninety minutes in the pods. If you both make it through, you can either take a weekend getaway or go all in, get married, and win a million dollars if you stay married for a year. And hey—we've had some success stories!"

I cross my arms. "But we don't *have* to marry the person at the end of the night, right?"

He shakes his head quickly. "Of course not. It's just a fun social experiment. But you never know—sometimes love shows up when you least expect it."

Love can show up when you least expect it.

Sure, it sounds cute in theory—but what would I even know about that? About what love really looks like? What it's supposed to feel like?

It's not like I'm one of those girls who grew up chasing after her father's approval or wondering why he wasn't around. I had my dad. We've always had this weirdly close, open kind of bond—one where nothing's really off-limits. We talk about everything, probably more than most fathers and daughters do. But even with that, if I'm honest, there's still a gap in my understanding of romantic love.

Because outside of the way he talks about my mom, I've never actually seen a man love someone. I've never watched my father fall—never caught him dancing barefoot in the kitchen late at night, wrapped around a woman he couldn't get enough of. I've never seen him swept up in real romance.

So yeah, I had my dad. But I've never had a man model what true devotion looks like. What it means to choose someone—every day, without fail.

What if there's something I could actually learn from this little experiment?

I glance at the clipboard.

The tequila is definitely still working its magic, because this sounds ridiculous. Crazy. Utterly insane.

And yet... maybe insane is exactly what I need tonight.

I let out a breath and grin. "Screw it. Sign me up."

The guy leans in a little. "Okay, here's how it works," he says, grinning. "You'll start by meeting at least three different people, speed dating style. You won't see them—there's a screen between you. Just voices. You'll get fifteen minutes with each one to ask whatever you want, get to know them a little."

I cross my arms, tilting my head. "And if I hate them all?"

He chuckles. "You gotta talk to at least three. But if someone catches your attention, you can extend the session. Stay in there longer if you want."

I nod slowly, curiosity piqued despite myself.

"Then, at the end of the speed dating round," he continues, "if you and one person both choose each other, you get ninety minutes together in the pod. No distractions. Just the two of you."

"Do I get to see him then?"

"No. Not until the end when you decide if you'll stay together."

"And after that? If we decide to stay together?" I ask, arching a brow.

He flashes another grin. "At the end of the ninety minutes, you've got options. You can get engaged, get married right here on the spot—Vegas, after all—or walk away. No strings, no pressure. But if you last the entire time in the pods, you both win a trip to a destination of your choice."

I blink, processing.

I cannot believe I'm even considering this.

Me. Type A. Full-blown control freak. The high school senior who once cried in the nurse's office because she had the flu and was about to ruin her perfect attendance record—one that dated all the way back to kindergarten.

This has to be the most idiotic, unhinged, out-of-character thing I've ever let myself even *think* about doing.

And yet... I find myself saying, "Alright. Let's do it."

Chapter One
BLACK BERRIES & MOLASSES
Eslin

One month ago in Las Vegas

A pack of young socialites teeters past, all long legs and designer smiles, clearly on the prowl for a high-roller to take home. I slip onto a barstool at Ink—*the* hottest, most exclusive hotel to hit the Vegas Strip. Where the lighting is low, the drinks cost more than rent, and no one here is trying to play it subtle.

I'm usually not the type to approach a man. Or make the first move.

But I've decided while I'm in Vegas, I'm going to be bold. *Brave.*

Because if there's ever a place to rewrite the rules—the very rules I've spent a lifetime living meticulously by, the ones that kept me steady, safe, and striving just to make it to the life of my dreams...It's *here.*

I take a seat at the far end of the bar, where there's a guy nursing a drink like it's whispering every secret it knows. He's got that look—somewhere between lost puppy and down right lost. Or maybe it's something else entirely. Whatever it is, I'm curious.

"So, you get ditched by your friends too?"

The club hums with the kind of low thrum that's more seduction than sound. Velvet booths. Gold lighting that makes the crowd gleam like they belong on a magazine cover. You don't just wander into this place. You either know someone or *are* someone.

And this man looks like he checks both boxes.

He glances up, eyes catching mine. There's a flicker of recognition there, but I'm certain we've never met.

"I'd normally be here with my daughter," he says, voice low and rough. He pauses, gives a quick glance around, then lets out a sigh. "But...she's no longer here."

My hand flies to my mouth. Before I can think, my other hand lands gently on his wrist. "Oh my God, I'm so sorry for your loss."

He barks out a laugh—deep, rich, and so unexpected I jerk back a little.

"Oh goodness, no. She's not dead. She abandoned me for some bachelorette party madness or whatever she's got going on tonight."

Relief floods me, warm and fast, and before I can stop it, a laugh bubbles out. "Thank God for that. So, you're here for a wedding?"

He leans back in his chair, lazy and controlled. One strong arm drapes over the back of the barstool, the other cradling his glass with an ease that's far too practiced.

"Begrudgingly," he says, voice like smooth whiskey. "Emotional support puppy duties. I don't really do weddings, but it's the daughter of a family friend and my daughter refused to come unless I did." He lifts one shoulder. "So, here I am."

The therapist in me perks right up, curiosity sharpening. "Why don't you do weddings?"

He holds my gaze, eyes dark and unreadable, the air between us suddenly thicker. He studies me for a long, weighted beat, like he's peeling back a layer to see if I'm safe. And then—slow as sin—a smile tugs at the corner of his mouth.

"Because I haven't been to one since my wife died. Over twenty years ago."

Honesty. I can get into it.

I tilt my head, my expression intentionally unreadable. "The nerve of her. Up and dying on you like that."

My humor has always skewed a little dark—blame the New York City foster care system. Or maybe it's just baked into my DNA. I've never fully decided where I land on the whole nature versus nurture debate.

He chuckles and my chest does an odd little flutter. Go figure—he's a weirdo like me.

"Yeah," he says with a crooked smile. "Some nerve. Who the hell does she think she is?"

I arch a brow, matching his tone. "Well, lucky for you, there are about a thousand psychics on this strip. Want to go channel her? Ask what the hell she was thinking? Get some closure once and for all."

He grins, lazy and playful. Then he shrugs. "Already did. Apparently the angel Gabriel's hotter than me."

That earns a smile from me. And before I can help myself, I really *look* at him.

He's got a maddening kind of confidence that doesn't need announcing. It's just there. Unapologetic. The silver threading through his thick, slightly unruly hair isn't a surrender to age; it's a statement. One that says *earned every damn strand*.

His face is all sharp edges and sun-warmed skin—the sort of ruggedness that speaks more of afternoons spent under the sky than boardrooms or camera flashes. A beard, perfectly unkempt with salt and pepper roughness, lines his jaw. It makes my fingers itch.

But it's his eyes that really undo me. Deep blue to contrast his dark hair but steady and knowing, with just the faintest glint of amusement. They hold mine a beat too long and his gaze is one of those that sees through your first three layers without breaking a sweat.

Still...there's something about him. Maybe it's everything about him. All of it completely, dangerously enticing.

And—given the kind of experience I'm sure he has on me—without a doubt, a very bad idea.

I finish the remnants of the drink in my glass before slamming it back down on the bartop. "I haven't seen this angel Gabriel, so, I'll just take your ghosts' word for it."

He cocks a brow, eyes twinkling. "As in..." He's absolutely fishing for a compliment.

I roll my eyes, but the smile's already tugging at my lips. "As in, you're definitely sexy."

He grins, cocky and pleased. "You *have* to say that."

"Oh yeah?" He's baiting me into more conversation and because of those eyes and that smile, I bite. "And why's that?"

"Because I'm the devilishly handsome older guy who's about to ask the woman way out of my league if I can buy her a drink."

I tilt my head. "Am I *said woman* in this scenario?"

"Yes." He deadpans. "Try to keep up." Then, with that same playful straight face, he adds, "And since you're going to inevitably turn me down, you would've done me the simple kindness of calling me sexy. Your good deed for the day."

"I won't turn you down," I say quickly, eyes locked on his, voice just a little lower. Breathier.

He doesn't break eye contact. Just offers his hand, palm up. "Grant."

I slide mine into his. "Eslin."

"Besides, Eslin," he says with a wicked grin, still holding onto my hand. "You'd totally make my ghost jealous."

Do Black girls turn red when they blush? Because *my goodness,* my face is on fire.

"That's the nicest thing anyone's ever said to me," I manage, grinning while regretfully pulling my hand away to brush back a piece of non-existent stray hair.

"That you're so hot you'd make my dead wife jealous?"

I throw my head back and howl. "Did you really just *say* that?"

He shrugs, all casual. "Does it bother you that I'm weird? A little dark?"

I shake my head, eyes dancing. "You actually just got ten times sexier."

He beams. "Hey, Eslin?"

"Yeah?"

"Want to go for a walk?"

I smile, slow and sure. "I'd love to."

Chapter Two

CHAPTER TWO: CANDLELIGHT & CONFESSIONS

Grant

One month ago in Las Vegas

This woman is out of my league.

She walks in like she owns the air around her. All poise and edges, like the room bends just slightly to watch her move.

Her skin catches the low light—rich, smooth, the kind of beauty that isn't fair, not in a place like this. Not for a man like me. Thick, long, dread locs tumble down her back. And those eyes—sharp, knowing, framed by lashes that could cut a lesser man down with a single look.

She's dressed in a soft and elegant halter dress, wrapped high at the neck and bare at the shoulders, the fabric hugging curves that don't need an introduction. No loud colors, no flashy jewelry. She doesn't need it. This woman turns heads because she's *her*.

And I've got no business wanting her. Hell, I've got no business looking at her.

But I can't stop.

I don't bother wasting time waving the bartender down—just settle the tab with a flick of my card. Then I glance at Eslin. "Ready?"

She nods, a little too eagerly, and damn if that doesn't hit somewhere deep. The way she looks at me—open, curious, like I'm something worth discovering.

Historic artifacts usually are.

I'm hit with it fast and hard—this woman is exactly the type I've been drawn to lately. Young. Gorgeous. All that effortless energy, the kind that burns hot and never stays. Just temporary enough to make an old bastard like me forget every promise I've made to behave.

But then again...I've heard the saying plenty—*Black don't crack*. So as I fall into step beside Eslin, I'm sending up a silent prayer to whoever's listening that she's older than she looks.

Because deep down, I already know this woman's about to turn my entire damn world on its head.

As we weave through the crowd toward the exit, I glance back and catch her falling a step behind—her petite frame no match for my longer strides. So I slow, reach my arm back without thinking.

She takes my hand—no hesitation. And like that, I lead us out of the club, her hand steady in mine. When we hit the sidewalk, lights flashing, The Strip alive around us...I don't let go.

And we walk. No plan. No destination. Just her hand in mine, the two of us moving through the night like we've got nowhere else we'd rather be.

"You mentioned your friends ditched you in there?" I ask, breaking the quiet between us—not awkward. Just easy.

She jumps a little, like I pulled her from some thought. "Huh? Oh. Yeah. Sorry. My friends are here for a girls' weekend, but I'm not the type to spend all day doing touristy crap just to get dressed up and do more of it at night. So...they left without me."

I smile. "Forgive me for saying so, but I'm kind of glad they did."

She squeezes my hand—just a little tighter. "Yeah... I'm kinda starting to feel the same."

"You know, being from New York, I'd normally punch you in the face for being so presumptuous about holding my hand."

I chuckle, giving her fingers a playful squeeze. "And why haven't you punched me yet?"

She flicks those gorgeous brown eyes at me, then turns her gaze back to the path ahead. "I don't know, Mister. Something about you...feels good."

"I bet a lot of things about you feel good," I shoot back. *Way too fast*, before my brain catches up to my mouth.

Her lips twitch. "Easy there. You'll have me believing you've got ill intentions."

I lean in just a little closer, voice dropping. "Trust me...if I did, you'd know it."

"Well, if you do," she says, all smooth. "I certainly hope you let me in on those intentions before the night is over. Lots of things I could do with you."

I groan, dragging a hand down my face. "Please. Don't say things like that."

"Like what?"

"Things that make me want to discover what *lots* could entail. I'm actually trying to behave." This woman has no idea the danger she could be in.

She throws her head back, laughing. A rich, warm sound hitting me straight in the chest.

"*Pity,*" she teases, shaking her head, eyes sparkling with nothing but trouble.

We walk a few more blocks, her hand still tucked in mine, when she suddenly lets out the loudest squeal.

"O.M.G. Shut up!" she shouts, yanking me by the hand toward...Jesus Christ. A *van.* And not the sleek, professional kind either. There are likely no nice watches in there, no knock off Gucci bags or even Nike's spelled with an M—no, this thing looks one broken taillight away from being featured on *Dateline.*

Across the side, some half-faded letters read: *Psychic Readings.*

"You cannot be serious," I say, staring at it like it might bite.

"I am *absolutely* serious," she beams.

"I don't believe in psychics."

"Neither do I!" she fires back. "That's why it'll be fun! Come on, let's just do it for the fun of it."

I just told her I was enjoying getting to know her, but this is taking things in a direction I didn't intend.

I pictured us finding a quiet restaurant, slipping into a booth, spending the night wrapped in candlelight and confessions—soft smiles, shared stories, slow, dangerous chemistry building with every glance.

Not this.

I glance around, then back at the van, then at her—who's practically vibrating with excitement. "You do realize there are entire documentaries about women disappearing after getting into vans exactly like this, don't you?"

She throws her head back, laughing. "Well. I can give you three reasons why that's *not* happening tonight."

"Oh yeah?" I smirk. "Let's hear 'em."

She lifts her hand, ticking them off with her fingers. "One: Black women don't go missing in these situations. Kidnappers know we talk too damn much. They'd throw us back within ten minutes."

I bark out a laugh. "Valid. And two?"

"Two: I'm not one of those sweet, bubbly types who lights up a room and offers strangers the shirt off her back. I'm selfish as hell and I've had a resting bitch face since I was four."

"Duly noted." I nod, grinning. "Three?"

"And three..." She flashes a wicked smile. "I've got this devilishly handsome older gentleman with me to protect me."

That does it—I'm laughing again. Hell, I've lost count how many times this woman's made me laugh tonight.

"Fine," I say, shaking my head. "Let's go get our palms read or whatever ridiculous thing this is."

"Yay!" she squeals, tugging me toward the van like we're about to waltz into a five-star spa.

And damn if I'm not following her willingly—like *I'm* the unsuspecting woman who's just been lured in with promises of tacos and a nap out the back of a van.

Eslin knocks on the van door. No answer.

"Welp! We tried. Want to grab some food?" I say, but she doesn't back down.

"Don't be scared, Grant! They probably just have music blaring or something. The strip is loud!"

I watch in pure disbelief as she jiggles the back door handle of the van like she's unlocking her own damn apartment.

"Why are you so *committed* to being murdered tonight?" I whisper-yell.

She laughs again, bright and reckless. "Oh hush!" she calls, just as the door pops open with a groan.

"Esl—" I bark, reaching for her back to pull her the hell out of there. But my hand meets nothing but warm, bare skin—smooth, flawless, kissed by the God's hand—and fuck me, that's a dangerous distraction. I should be walking in the opposite direction right now. I'd ruin her.

But instead...I follow her.

Inside, the van has been converted into some kind of makeshift psychic den. Heavy velvet drapes hang along the walls, trying—and failing—to hide the rusted metal underneath. A low table sits in the center, draped with a deep purple cloth, a cracked crystal ball perched on top. String lights run around the ceiling, their soft yellow glow flickering just enough to make everything look vaguely mystical.

A beat-up velvet sofa—probably stolen from an old casino lounge—sits against the far wall, its cushions mismatched and sagging. The air smells like incense and cheap wine.

There's a woman—or what *might* be a woman—curled up on the ragged sofa, out cold. Eslin clears her throat.

How polite she is as we break and enter.

I swear to God, my pulse kicks up like we're about to wake a sleeping bear. The longer I look, the less sure I am if this is a man or a woman.

Suddenly, the figure startles and jerks upright. "Welcome to SheSeesThings Incorporated."

Original.

"How can I—" She coughs, loud and gravelly—like she smokes six packs of cigarettes and a handful of Swisher Sweets a day. Definitely a woman. "—help you?" she finishes.

"We would like—" Eslin starts sweetly.

"To leave you to your rest, miss," I cut in fast, trying to redirect this train-wreck before it really gets rolling.

Eslin swats my shoulder—playful, but it actually *hurts*.

"Oh! My boyfriend is so silly!" she chirps. "We'd like a reading!"

The blow is softened with her calling me her boyfriend. *I can get into character for this.*

"You're in the right place!" the woman beams. "Only, I no longer do *readings* on the account I gave my life to Christ last week. So, I'll just be giving you prophetic *insights*." She says.

"Oh really?" Eslin says, raising a brow.

"Yes. My life coach says I will be more marketable that way."

"How insightful. Our psychic has a life coach to help her see things."

"I'm Shavonne," the prophetic seer continues, "But you can call me Linda!"

I lean down, close to Eslin's ear. "This is already shaping up to be *very* enlightening."

She giggles—and hell, I'd pay a million dollars just to hear that sound again and again.

"Have a seat!" Shavonne—*Linda*—instructs, waving toward the saggy sofa.

We sit. I'm already regretting this.

Linda lumbers over to a battered cash box. "Alright. It's five hundred for your prophetic insights tonight."

"Five hundred?" I damn near yell. "So you're robbing people out of this van too, huh?"

Before I can so much as stand, Eslin slides her hand into mine, tugging gently. I glance over—and there it is. That face. Eyes wide, lashes fluttering, pure damn trouble wrapped in silk and curves.

I groan, scrubbing a hand down my face. "You should win an award for that level of trickery."

She just grins, victorious.

Linda continues. "Now...I can't guarantee results. And by staying, you agree this is legally binding. You can't sue me."

My brow shoots up. "*Charming.*"

She points to an ancient-looking camera propped in the corner. "And you consent to being recorded."

Christ. This just keeps getting better.

The reading...insight begins. Linda starts tossing out vague statements: *Someone from your past is trying to reach you. You've recently experienced a big life change. Someone new is entering your orbit.*

It's generic, but somehow we're both laughing. Because, honestly, it could apply to *anyone* in Vegas tonight.

Then everything shifts.

One second we're chuckling under our breath at the vague, fortune-cookie nonsense she's been spouting. The next—dead silence.

Linda's head tilts, her eyes narrowing, gaze locking on me like she's just tuned into a different frequency. Like she's hearing something no one else in this van can.

I feel Eslin still beside me, sense the air thicken between us.

Linda blinks slowly, then leans forward, voice low, still gravel rough. "You think you 'bout done? Waiting?"

The words slam into me like a gut punch.

Jesus.

I freeze.

It's what my Maddy, my wife, used to say. Every time we were out on the boat, just the two of us. I'd want to stay out there all damn day, chasing one more cast, waiting for one more fish. And when she was ready to head back—without fail—she'd glance at me, a smile in her voice, and say, *You think you 'bout done?*

Her way of telling me I had about fifteen minutes before her patience wore thin.

No one else knew that. No one.

For a beat, I can't move, can't breathe. The weight of it slams straight into my chest, knocking the air right out of me.

Eslin's watching me. I can feel her gaze on me—steady, curious, concerned.

She knows *something* shifted. But she doesn't press, doesn't speak. Just sits there, tense and quiet, reading me. Or at least trying to.

Before I can even gather myself, Linda's head tilts again. That eerie calm settling over her features as she turns toward Eslin. Her voice drops again. This time, it's as if she's connecting with something deep inside of Eslin.

"Some people," Linda starts, her voice almost as if she's getting emotional. "Some people stay, my child."

Eslin stiffens beside me. I feel it, sharp as a blade. Her hand tenses slightly against her thigh. The lightness from moments ago? Gone.

Neither of us laughs now.

We just sit there, caught in a stretch of silence that feels heavier than the walls around us. Both of us processing what the hell just happened—what was said, what it meant.

I don't know what those words meant to her. And she sure as hell doesn't know what they meant to me.

But somehow, without saying a word, we both know—*Linda hit something.* Something personal. Something meant for each of us, and only us.

And that unspoken truth hums in the air between us, thick and impossible to ignore.

When we finally step out of that van, the air outside hits like a slap—breeze sharp, the lights too bright, too loud. But none of it cuts through the weight hanging between us.

We walk a block in silence, our steps falling in sync, like it's been decided without a word.

Then, finally, Eslin exhales, her voice soft. "That was...interesting."

I snap my gaze to her. "I know, right?"

A slow smile ghosts across her lips. "I'll show you mine if you show me yours..." she says, playful, like we're two kids hiding under the bleachers.

I stop abruptly. A couple behind us stumbles, forced to break apart and shuffle around. I don't move. Just turn and look her straight in the eyes.

"You're asking me to share what those words meant?"

She lifts a shoulder, casual, but her gaze is anything but. "The way I see it, we'll probably never see each other again. Two strangers who shared one crazy, wild night. Who got to know something real about one another. Something deep. No strings."

I swallow. "And we're just supposed to...what...walk away? After a night like this? After sharing something so...intimate?"

She tilts her head, her smile softening. "What happens in Vegas..." She leaves it hanging in the air. No need to finish. We both know.

What happens tonight—whatever we decide to do—stays here.

And the player in me, the man who's built a lifetime on these kind of *one perfect night* moments, should be all in. No consequences. No morning-after regrets. Just one night with this incredible woman, and then done.

Usually, I wouldn't think twice.

But looking at her now... I don't want it cheap. She's not cheap. You can tell from a mile away.

So if this is all we get—one night—I'll give her the truth. Me. Every raw, unpolished part of it. And then I'll walk away.

What happens in Vegas, right?

I take her hand again, threading my fingers through hers. No words. Just us again.

And we start walking.

I've always been bold when it comes to women. I don't play childish games. No fishing with imaginary bait, waiting to see if they'll bite. I ask. Once. And if I'm given consent, granted access, then I take it the rest of the way. No hesitation. No apologies.

And tonight?

All I want...is to *know* Eslin.

Not her body. Not first.

Just her. The woman behind those eyes, behind that laugh. The woman who's already under my skin and doesn't even know it yet.

The Strip blazes behind us—neon signs pulsing, music thumping, the chaotic heartbeat of a city that never sleeps. But the farther we walk, the thinner the crowds become. The lights grow softer, more scattered.

The night shifts. The city that never tires...starts to feel like it's winding down. Like it's giving us this space, this moment, just for us. And walking deeper into the quiet, it's as if the whole city knows—some things deserve to be heard in the dark.

"I grew up in foster care. New York City," Eslin begins, her voice steady, but there's something behind it. I squeeze her hand.

"Don't do that, Grant."

Her words make me jump. "What?"

"Don't pity me. Don't start looking at me like I'm—"

I cut her off by leaning down and brushing a kiss against her cheek. Soft. Intentional.

"You're fierce. A force. I wouldn't dare see you as anything less."

She smiles, slow and a little breathless, her gaze locking on mine. I can see it—the way her breath is caught somewhere between her chest and her libido.

And even though it's clear I've knocked her off her game a bit, her hand stays in mine as we keep walking.

"I'm suddenly unsure of what I was—"

"You were telling me about the upbringing that made you a woman I'm ready to change my entire life for after only a few minutes in her space," I confirm. Because I, one hundred percent, mean it.

She lets out a soft, musical laugh, shaking her head. "Okay. Charmer. Keep it up and whatever happens here will follow us home..."

"Which is where?" I press, voice low, teasing.

She smirks. "Not yet. I want to stretch this out a bit. I don't know if I trust you to know where I live."

I chuckle. "You were about to share some pretty heavy stuff, miss. I think we need to pause and reevaluate your definition of trust."

"That's different," she says, with a playful protest.

"How so?"

She lifts a shoulder, the motion graceful and unhurried. "We made a pact. It's sort of an adventure for us."

My brow instantly shoots up. "A pact, huh?" I echo, intrigued.

"Yes. Try to keep up," she teases, and Christ—I bite the inside of my cheek to stop myself from dragging her into the nearest alley and tasting every inch of that fire she's been tempting me with all night.

I bet she tastes like black berries and molasses.

"And, if I'm honest—" She continues.

"Please be honest. This is a safe space," I say, voice sweet.

She glances over, something vulnerable flickering in those eyes. "To share these secrets with you and then walk away, knowing we shared this night and these stories, and then never seeing each other again? It's the most romantic thing I've ever experienced."

I rub my thumb across the top of her hand, voice dropping. "And to think, the night isn't over yet."

"It's only just beginning."

We stop in front of a 1950s-style ice cream shop—chrome-trimmed windows, glowing neon sign. The kind with a wraparound red leather bar, polished silver stools lined up perfectly. A relic in a city that keeps reinventing itself.

"Wanna share a banana split with me?" I ask, grinning.

She beams. "I thought you'd never ask."

We step inside, the place humming with old jukebox tunes and the soft clink of silverware.

At the counter, I let her order. I'm expecting the usual—nuts, whipped cream, maybe a cherry.

But Eslin? No. She starts rattling off toppings like a sugar-fueled mad scientist—gummy bears, crushed cereal, rainbow sprinkles, bits of candy I've never even heard of.

I blink at her, stunned. Who the hell is this woman?

And why am I tempted to spend the rest of my life discovering *everything* about her?

We settle onto the stools, splitting the monstrosity she's created, and I can't resist.

"So... those words. What did they mean to you?"

She takes a slow breath, eyes thoughtful.

"My mom lost custody when I was a baby," she says quietly. "I grew up in foster care. We didn't have much. But she loved me. She never stopped trying to make our family whole again."

I take a bite of ice cream to avoid the inevitable softening on my face that she will interpret as pity. Which is the furthest thing I feel for her. The exact opposite.

"When I was five, she lost track of me in the system. But I never stopped hoping she'd find me. And from what I remembered about her, something inside me knew she didn't stop looking."

I stay quiet, listening.

"She finally did. When I was graduating college." Her voice softens, the weight of it clear. "We became best friends after that. More like sisters than mother and daughter."

She pauses, swallowing hard. "Before she passed, she...well, she read me like a book. She saw how guarded I was. How hard it was for me to even let *her* in. And then she said—" her voice catches, and she collects herself, just like Linda had— "she said, 'Some people stay.' And that I didn't have to be so afraid of letting people get close. That anyone has the potential to become family."

I'm stunned.

"How do you think Linda knew?" I ask, voice low.

She looks at me, eyes shining. "I think you know, Grant."

"I most assuredly do not know."

She laughs. "Prophetic insight!"

"Clearly," I reply, chuckling with her, taking another bite of ice cream.

I take a breath, knowing it's my turn.

And for the first time—outside of those brutal, useless thirty days I spent in 'grief group'—I talk about Maddy. Really talk.

"She was my everything," I start. "The love of my life. After she passed, I tried the whole group therapy thing. Thought it might help. But all it did was make me more bitter. More resentful toward a God who'd take her from me and from my daughter when she still had so much life left. I wanted to murder my eyeballs every time someone cried about *hearing* their spouse's voice down the hall when they knew they weren't there."

Eslin's gaze softens, her hand resting lightly on mine.

"Group therapy isn't for everyone," she says gently. "There's more than one way to work through grief. You just have to find the *thing* that won't let it fester inside you."

I arch a brow. "And how do *you* know that?"

She smiles knowingly. "Let's just say I've had my share of rounds in the therapy chair."

"Noted." I grin. She's still holding pieces of herself close. I respect that.

The chords to Journey's *Don't Stop Believin'* start to play over the jukebox, and Eslin's face lights up—just like it did when we first stumbled across the psychic. The same spark, the same wild little glint in her eye that told me the second I was in her company, the whole world instantly got a little lighter. A little louder. And a hell of a lot more fun.

As the song plays in the background, Eslin leans in closer, her voice playful but curious. "If your life were a movie, what would be the first song on the soundtrack?"

I glance over at her, watching the way the neon light catches the shimmer in her eyes. She's asking like it's casual, but I can feel her trying to read my answer before I even give it. I take a beat, actually thinking it through, which is a hell of a lot more serious than I usually take questions like this. Finally, I smirk. "*Bohemian Rhapsody.* Queen."

Her eyes widen with amused approval. "Dramatic choice, Mister."

"That's me." I shrug, giving her a crooked grin. "Dramatic. A little unpredictable. A few moments of pure genius. Definitely way too long and full of questionable decisions that make you wonder what the hell I was thinking."

I pause, watching her bite back a smile, that little dimple threatening to give her away.

"But you get it. Get them—Queen and other people like us." I add softly. "Because even when you're faced with something a little too crazy that was never meant to be tamed or contained in this world...it's uniquely *them.*"

And for a moment, it's clear I'm not just talking about the song.

"You've given this a lot of thought," she says, but it's more statement than question.

"Not really, actually." I shake my head, my voice low. "Not until you just asked me. I just thought about the song that makes me feel the most like me...and blurted it out."

She tilts her head, studying me in that way she's been doing all night—like she's reading all the words I haven't said yet. "You don't strike me as the type of man to just blurt things."

She's not wrong. I'm not a man who blurts. I never have been.

In my world, you don't survive like that. You stay guarded. Controlled. Calculated. People are always watching, always waiting—looking for weakness to use as leverage. So I keep my circle small. My cards close. My emotions closer.

But somehow, with her...she sees straight through it. How does this woman see me the way she does and we've only just met?

From the moment I spotted her at the club tonight, I knew she wasn't like anyone else in the building.

There was something instantly familiar about her—recognizable in a way that made no sense, because I knew for sure we'd never met before.

And now we're talking like we've done this a hundred times, and I'm sitting here like some awkward teenager who doesn't know where to put his hands or how to handle all these big, messy feelings that came out of nowhere and hit me square in the chest.

It's dizzying. Completely unexpected.

And I want more.

She laughs, tipping her head back. "Fair point." She taps her chin thoughtfully. "Mine would be *Sophisticated Lady* by Natalie Cole. Except I'd swap out the knee-length dresses for jeans and sneakers most days."

I lean in slightly, dropping my voice just low enough to make her blush. "I don't know, Es... I wouldn't mind seeing the dress version every now and then."

Her cheeks flush, and that smile—God, *that* smile—damn near knocks the air out of my lungs.

She flashes me a playful, wicked little wink. "The dress version ain't nothin' to sneeze at, either" she teases, her voice smooth like honey with just enough edge to make my pulse spike.

I suck in a sharp breath, battling my brain and my libido like they're two heavyweight fighters in the ring. She's been toying with me all night—throwing out these playful jabs, suggestive remarks, practically daring me to cross that line.

But I can't. Not yet.

I want to enjoy her company a little longer. Get to know *her*—beyond the sparks, beyond the heat—before I risk stepping into something we can't undo.

A woman like this comes around once in a lifetime. And if you're lucky—*damn lucky*—maybe you meet someone just as rare a second time.

And with that knowledge pressing at the back of my skull, I have to suppress every single thought running through my mind.

Like how easy it would be to buy out this entire little ice cream shop, kick everyone out, lay her out across the countertop and explore all the toppings that would taste even better on her skin.

The problem is...I don't know how to say any of that without sounding like the ancient, dangerously cautious man I'm starting to feel like.

So I take the safest route, letting my lips curve into a slow, controlled smile. "I'm sure the dress version would drive a sane man crazy. No doubt about that at all."

Eventually, the ice cream's long gone, and we find ourselves wandering, walking again, words flowing easy between us. For hours.

We talk about life. About loss. About the things that scare us and the things that set us on fire. But somehow, we never share anything personal that could actually identify us. No last names. No real specifics. Just two people floating in this perfect little bubble we've created.

It's romantic. Intoxicating, even.

But it's also torture—knowing that when the sun comes up, we might go back to being strangers.

How could anyone meet this woman and not instantly want her close? Not just for a night. Not just for a moment.

Forever.

She pulls out her phone and glances at the screen. "It's nearly 4:30 AM," she says, eyes wide but still sparkling with that same playful grin.

I let out a quiet laugh, shaking my head. "Wow. I can't believe we've been doing this all night. I haven't done anything like this in..." I pause, actually thinking about it. "Honestly? I don't think ever."

"*Whaaa?*" she gasps, feigning shock. "You've never picked up some random Black lady in a club, walked around the city all night, and talked 'til the sun came up?" She shakes her head like she's genuinely disappointed.

I meet her gaze, steady. "I've never met anyone like you."

She narrows her eyes, smirking. "You've gotta get out more, Mister."

I lean in slightly, my voice a dangerously low tamber. "Sunshine, I've been to more countries than I can count. I've sat at tables with some of the world's most impressive people. And I can assure you" I pause, letting the words settle between us, "*you* are one of a kind."

She's fierce, sharp, quick, always ready with a comeback. But closeness? Eye contact? That throws her just a little. Knocks her off balance in the smallest, sweetest way.

And I decide, right then and there—*I like having this effect on her.*

"Wanna get some breakfast?" she asks, her voice light and playful, but I can hear the tiny edge behind it—she's trying to steady herself, trying to reclaim a little control after I've clearly rattled her.

"My treat," she adds, wiggling her eyebrows, throwing in just enough sass to pretend she's still the one in charge.

"Fine," I smirk, letting her have her little reprieve.

But I'm not done with you, Eslin.

"But just so we're clear," I continue. "I'm ordering the biggest stack of pancakes they've got, and you better not pull one of those '*oops, I forgot my wallet*' stunts when the bill comes."

She gasps, clutching her chest dramatically. "Sir, I am a woman of my word!"

"For your sake, I hope so. I take my pancakes very seriously."

She laughs. "And you're absolutely sharing."

"I will bite your finger if you come near my pancakes, woman."

"You promise?" She purrs.

And just like that, my pants twitch. Because ordinarily, yes. Yes, this would be a promise. A prelude to a night that begins with licking and biting and sucking—*stop it!*

Eslin tugs me into a small diner, the bright lights and clinking dishes snapping me back to reality—just in time to catch my thoughts before they drag me down a path paved with nothing but destruction and debauchery.

A path I was *dangerously* close to following because...you should really see this woman.

The hostess at the all night diner we walk into immediately leads us to a booth and Eslin is walking ahead of me.

"I'm going to need you to stop making comments like that. Tempting me. I've been on my best behavior for you tonight," I murmur under my breath, just loud enough so she can hear me.

Her head snaps back to me, not missing a step as we follow behind the hostess. "I really wish you wouldn't have told me that."

I narrow my eyes. "Why?"

We sit at the booth that is at the back of the diner and the hostess announces that she'll be back with water for the both of us.

"Because," Eslin whispers, staring me deep in my eyes. "I've sort of got this thing for bad boys."

My ears, and something else, perks up. "Oh yeah? Any particular reason why?"

"Blame it on my wayward upbringing and a lifetime of daddy issues."

"Lucky me," I say playfully.

She shrugs. "Except, you're on your best behavior or whatever, so..."

I suck in a tortured breath. "I did say that, didn't I?"

"You did. And now you have me curious about what I'm missing."

I lick my lips. "You know what they say about curiosity?"

She raises a brow. "That it killed the cat, right?"

I lean in, making sure only she can hear me. "Yes, but not before the cat was licked, sucked and played with."

"Mmm," she moans. "But you're on your best behavior."

I shift in my seat. "I am."

"Again...pity."

And I can't hold it in anymore. I do the thing that I rarely do—I blurt something out.

"How old are you, Eslin?"

She blinks, a little surprised by the question. But then answers without hesitation. "Thirty-one."

And with that answer—my entire world crashes down around me.

"Why? How old are you?" she asks, her eyes narrowing just a little, reading me.

"I'm forty-six," I say, voice steady but firm. "Fifteen damn years between us."

She tilts her head, unphased, and flashes me a mischievous grin. "That *is* significant. But again..." she playfully points to herself. "*Daddy issues!*"

I can't help it—despite everything swirling in my head, I smile and shake my head. She's impossible not to smile at. Impossible to resist.

And that might just be my biggest problem.

Yeah, she's grown. Mature beyond her years. Sharp, grounded, knows who she is. No question there. But the moment I heard her say her age, something inside me shifted.

Through ordering food, the easy flow of playful banter, even the flirtation that keeps skimming dangerously close to that invisible line—we keep talking, but I can't stop the loop playing in my head.

The gap. Not just in years. In life. In experience. She's closer to Marlow's age than she is to mine. And suddenly, I feel every single one of those fifteen years press heavy on my chest.

Then the ugliest thought creeps in—one I can't shake. What if the reason I'm so drawn to her has nothing to do with *who* she is... and everything to do with what she represents?

Young. Temporary. Easy to lose.

The very things I've clung to, to keep from wanting something real with anyone after Maddy. Exactly what I promised Marlow I'd stop chasing.

Finally, I can no longer hide my expression. "Why does it look like you've seen a ghost?" Eslin asks. Her voice is gentle, but her eyes are sharp. Intuitive.

I try to laugh it off, but the sound is hollow. Forced. "My daughter's just a few years younger than you."

She frowns, thoughtful. "And the age difference bothers you?"

I drag in a breath. "Me? No. Her? Definitely."

She studies me for a beat, her gaze piercing. "And you don't want to fracture your relationship with her for something that—"

"—should stay in Vegas," I finish for her.

She doesn't argue. Doesn't try to convince me otherwise. And damn if that doesn't make me respect her even more.

When the check comes, I refuse to let her pay. But true to who she's been all night, she slips a wad of cash onto the table and insists on covering the tip. Stubborn.

The young ones usually are.

We walk again, quiet but connected, the streets slowly waking around us. We're near the hotel and club where we first met when the first light of dawn creeps in. The Strip softens beneath the sunrise—Vegas shedding its shine for the day.

And then... she lets my hand go.

In that moment, I know.

After the best damn night of my life, I have to let *her* go too.

No phone number. No first or last kiss. No empty promises.

Just... *goodbye.*

CHAPTER THREE: CUPCAKES & CROISSANTS

Eslin

Present day

"Move in the summer!" they said.

"It'll be easier!" they said.

Well, the next time I see any one of my so-called friends who told me it was a good idea to move to the freaking *South* in the middle of July, I'm going to slap the taste from their mouths. All of them. On sight.

I wanted a change of pace. Hell, a change of life. So when my college friend, Maxine, called, telling me the Atlanta Strikers were looking for a team therapist and performance coach—someone to help get their players' *heads right* before the soccer championships next year—I didn't hesitate. It sounded like the perfect fit.

And since Maxine's boss just so happens to be married to one of the owners of the club, well, the door practically flew open for me.

Is friendship nepotism a thing? Because if it is, I one hundred percent condone it.

Sure, most of my experience has been with high-performing executives. But with a doctorate in psychiatry and years of therapy work behind me, stepping into the world of elite athletes wasn't exactly a stretch.

And the perks are exactly what you'd expect when you land a role in a professional sports organization.

The job came with a sleek new apartment—completely covered by the team—in one of the ultra-exclusive Fury buildings. Word is, the waitlist runs close to ten months, and landing an apartment in this building requires a background check just short of a full-blown FBI investigation.

It's one of those sleek *work, play, stay* buildings—designed so you never really have to leave unless you want to. The first few floors are all glass-fronted boutiques, coffee shops, high-end fitness studios, and a couple of restaurants that are so exclusive they don't even bother with reservations.

Above that are office spaces—modern, open-concept, floor-to-ceiling windows, the kind of corporate playground where execs in designer suits power-lunch and close million-dollar deals.

The top floors are where the luxury apartments sit—secure elevators, concierge service, rooftop pools, private gym, the whole works. My unit has views for days, smart everything, and finishes so high-end I had to Google a few of them to figure out what they were and how they worked.

It's basically a vertical version of a dream life. And somehow...it's mine now.

I overheard one of the movers say it was practically impossible to get into this place. But apparently when one of the owners of the Strikers makes a call, suddenly, I'm VIP.

It's a far cry from how I've lived in New York. And I'm not even talking about my foster care days. Even with a multi-six-figure job, life in the city wasn't exactly affordable. Hustle in, hustle out, paycheck gone.

So when the offer came—more money than I ever thought I'd see in my lifetime, a place to live, and the chance to actually *save* something for once—I didn't hesitate.

Oh, and did I mention they paid off my student loans?

Who the hell says no to that?

The movers have just left the final box, and I stand in the middle of my new apartment, spinning around slowly, barely able to believe it.

I made it. *To this part of life.*

The good part.

I've never been one of those people who thought they didn't deserve nice things. I was raised with enough good sense—and enough fight—to know my worth.

But if you'd asked me back then when this moment would come, or what it would even look like, I wouldn't have had an answer.

I just *believed* it would come. That somehow, all the bad, all the ugly things I've had to endure in this life would eventually stack up to something good. Something that made it all worth it.

And standing here now, I know two things: it was *absolutely* worth it. And I'm never going back to where I came from.

Cue the theme music.

Ladies and gentlemen, introducing *that chick.*

Who gon' check me, boo?

I grab my phone and FaceTime my best friend—the same best friend who's been trying to convince me to move to Atlanta for *years*. And then the moment I finally do? This heffa up and moves to Canada. The betrayal.

"Babe!" she answers, all bright-eyed and cheerful like she didn't just abandon me for maple syrup and snow.

"Hey, babe! I made it!"

"OMG! Your very own *Fury* apartment! What are you waiting for? Show me around!"

"Quit bossing me around, skank!" I laugh, flipping the camera and starting my impromptu tour.

First stop: the kitchen. All clean, modern lines, sleek white cabinetry with matte black hardware, marble waterfall island big enough to host a cooking show.

"Girl, look at this kitchen! I don't even cook that much, but suddenly I wanna bake croissants & cupcakes from scratch or something," I say, panning the camera slowly.

Next up: the living room—floor-to-ceiling windows with a skyline view that looks straight out of a movie, soft neutral-toned sectional, glass coffee table, gold accents, built-in shelves already calling for designer coffee table books I don't own, *yet*.

"Gorgeous," Maxine gushes. "All those clean lines and beautiful finishes. So many different surfaces for you to—"

"Don't say it," I breathe out, already shaking my head because I *know* where this is going.

"So many surfaces for you to get your *back blew out!*" she yells, cackling.

"Eww!" I scream, clutching my chest dramatically. "I cannot *stand* you! I am a lady, after all!"

"Yeah. Being a lady is why your va-jj is sending up smoke signals to every penis it comes within five feet of," she chides, wagging her brows.

I gasp, flipping the camera back around so she can see my face. "*The disrespect!* When are you coming back to Atlanta to pack up the rest of your stuff?"

She's wiping a tear from the corner of her eye, laughing so hard she's practically wheezing. "Probably not until closer to the holidays. We've got a ton going on with Eli's business, and I'm training my replacement for Timantha's company from here, so, there's really no rush for me to come back."

"I still can't believe Timantha didn't kill you for quitting!"

Max went on a road trip to Canada for a romance novel conference and somehow ended up stranded there for a week.

And apparently, that's all it took. Because in true romance novel fashion, this woman managed to get herself swept up in a full-blown small town love story—complete with a sexy Black lumberjack who spoils her rotten and looks like he walked straight off a book cover. And even though I will hold my suspicions for later, Max is also sporting what's starting to look dangerously close to a baby bump.

She told me while she loved being a boss and a badass back home, life in the Rockies gave her a kind of peace she didn't even know she needed. A different pace. A softer kind of happiness.

"Why would Timantha be mad at me for leaving? I found her an amazing replacement who's working out brilliantly!" she says, flipping her hair like the boss she is.

"I guess you're right," I say, flopping down onto my ridiculously soft new sofa.

"Is it weird? Living in a new city?"

I let out a slow breath. "Yes. But also it's no different than moving to a new home. I'm used to it. I treat it like an adventure."

"I love that," she says, her voice softening. "And I love how you always manage to find the positive in everything."

"It's the only way I know how to be," I shrug.

She sighs. "I miss you. And I'm sorry I moved the second you finally decided to come to Atlanta."

I wave her off, grinning. "It's fine. If I had a big, sexy Black-ass lumberjack taking care of me, I would have left you too."

We're both still laughing when her voice softens, turning a little serious.

"So... let's promise to get together for the holidays?" she says.

"Which one?" I frown, tilting my head.

"How about Thanksgiving? Eli doesn't really celebrate it, so we'll probably be down there."

"Okay! It's a date," I grin, my cheeks practically hurting with how wide I'm smiling. Just the thought of seeing her again already feels like home.

Because for me, home has never been a place.

It's always been people. The right people. The ones who feel like safety, like ease, like *belonging*.

I've lived a lot of lives. At one point, I was convinced I was going to work in tech—mostly because every guidance counselor I ever had drilled into us it was the one field that would *always* be in demand.

So I came down to Atlanta for a cyber security certification course at North Kensington University.

That's where I met Maxine.

She was the first real friend I ever had who introduced me to the glorious hot mess that is chili cheese Fritos—yes, with actual chili and cheese *squeezed straight into the bag*. It was ridiculous. It was delicious. It was the moment I knew we'd be friends for life.

And even though it's July, we immediately start a shared Pinterest board for our Thanksgiving menu—because why not be *extra*—and start pre-planning where she and Eli will stay when they come down.

After a flurry of ideas, recipes, we finally say our goodbyes.

And then?

I do the one thing I've always wanted to do in my very own, brand-new, luxury apartment.

I run around screaming at the top of my lungs, jumping on every single couch and bed like an over-caffeinated kid at a sleepover.

Because this is mine. And I'm going to enjoy *every damn second of it.*

CHAPTER FOUR: HOT DADS & HAT TRICKS

Grant

"We have a new midfielder starting next month, we just need to work out some visa issues and then he's good to go." Xavier announces, proud of himself for making a team choice that doesn't come with any baggage.

We had no business owning a soccer club. None of us did.

Will's got his hands full running a venture capital empire, Xavier practically breathes the financial services world, and I've spent years building my fortune, flipping struggling companies and stacking real estate like poker chips. Not one of us needed a sports team. Hell, none of us had the time for one.

But then there was one night with too many drinks, too much bravado when an old, foolish childhood dream started to sound like a good idea. And because we're all too stubborn to back down once we put something on the table, it steamrolled. Fast.

Now here we are—three billionaires who should've known better—owning a professional soccer club. And it's no longer just a vanity project. It's something with teeth. Something that could be incredibly rewarding or blow up in our faces if we can't get this damn team in line.

Right now, the Strikers sit at a frustrating 9-13-5. More losses than wins, but just enough points in the standings to keep them technically alive for the playoffs. The talent's there — a roster full of players who could easily turn the tide on any given night. But consistency? Discipline? That's where it all falls apart.

We've got at least five players who could be called up to play for their national teams next year. That kind of exposure — being able to say we've got Strikers represented on the world stage could bring in sponsors, press, international eyes. If only we could get them to act right long enough to make it happen. Because if we don't? It won't just be a bad investment. It'll be a public disaster. And in our worlds, reputations are everything. The clock's ticking and we all know it.

"Did you run that midfielder selection by Coach Jones?" Will asks, leaning back in his chair. "Last time I made a team decision without looping him in, the man had donkey shit delivered to my doorstep."

Xavier just smirks. "I'm not scared of a little prank. Besides, I *did* talk to him. I wouldn't dare make a final decision without his buy-in."

Will slumps, defeated. "It was more than a prank. I *stepped* in it."

My head snaps to him. "You stepped in donkey shit?"

His eyes go wide with pure trauma. "*Yes!*"

Xavier chuckles, but then leans forward, tone sharpening. "And this is exactly why we need to get this team in line. From the coach down to the players, we've got a behavior problem. If we don't get it under control, we're going to look like we've made the worst investment of the century. This team needs to produce. Needs to *win*."

I raise my hand to jump in but Xavier barrels on, cutting me off with a grin.

"*Win* matches, Grant. *Outside* of the ones they're winning in jail when they get arrested for indecent exposure!"

"Which brings me to *you*," Xavier says, voice sharp and pointed.

"What about me?" I frown, already not liking where this is going.

"How are things coming with bringing Marlow up to speed? Getting her trained to take your spot as one of the owners?"

I lean back in my chair, exhaling slowly.

Earlier this year, something shifted in me. After God knows how many hours spent haggling with agents, smoothing things over with publicists, and juggling my own damn family dynamics, it hit me—this is all I've ever done. Work is all Marlow's ever seen me do.

And to her own damn demise, she wants to follow in my footsteps.

My kid wants to run a business. But not one of my real estate companies. Not the world of flipping and selling companies I've built from scratch. No—she wants this one. The Atlanta Strikers. The one where no one in our collective circle really knows what the hell we're doing.

We went round and round about it. Me trying to convince her that this life, this team, it's no life for a twenty-seven-year-old woman. Her firing right back that this is exactly what I've prepared her for.

Somewhere in between her scathing arguments about how *I'm* the one less mature than her—and the very real threat of blackmail in the form of canceling my beloved Sunday dinners that she and I have every week—I gave in.

My kid always did know how to play to win. Maybe she won't be so bad at this at all.

"She's doing well," I say, keeping my tone steady. "She's been sitting in on management meetings, attending practices to get familiar with the team, and meeting with sponsors and vendors to learn the ins and outs of our contracts and merchandising process."

Will nods, looking genuinely impressed. "All good things."

"And what about *you*?" Xavier presses, eyes narrowing.

"Again...what about me?" I ask, though I know what he's likely referring to.

"Are you staying out of trouble? Being on your best behavior?"

Ah, *that* part of the deal.

That was the other side of the blackmail. The part that came from my so-called best friends. They hadn't exactly been thrilled about me grooming Marlow to take over my spot. And with the club already drowning in scandals—on and off the field—the last thing they wanted was to add *my* antics to the headlines.

So they made me give them six months. Six months to train Marlow, get her ready to take the reins. But *also* for those six months? No scandals. No late-night photos of me and a few women partying in some senator's pool. No parading a new date that's half my age to every charity event. And absolutely no sleeping with an opposing coach's ex-wife and posting pictures of her on social media to troll him the night before a game.

In other words...they wanted me to be someone I haven't been since my wife was alive.

For six whole months.

And if I didn't, it wouldn't just be my reputation on the line. It would jeopardize Will's. Xavier's. And worst of all—Marlow's.

So here I am. One month sober and on my *hot dad behavior*. Though this feels more like a hat trick than anything else because I can't believe I'm actually pulling this off. One month into playing the part of the responsible, well-behaved father and businessman. One month post-Vegas. One month since meeting—and saying goodbye to—Eslin.

And damn if she hasn't been haunting me ever since.

I haven't touched another woman since that night. Haven't even wanted to.

Which is saying something, considering I'm a card-carrying member of The Supper Club—Cinnamon Grove's most exclusive spot for incredible food and...well, let's just say *dessert* can take many forms there. I've never had a bad night in that place. Not once.

Until two weeks ago.

I walked in ready to do exactly what any red-blooded guy with a broken heart and too many pent-up fantasies would do—get Eslin out of my system. Preferably with a little help from a few of my favorite fellow female members.

Except...yeah. My brain was in it. My body? Not so much. No amount of charm, chemistry, or well-timed dirty talk could fix the problem.

The issue wasn't them. The issue was me. Or more specifically, *him*.

Down *there*.

Total no-show.

Which is completely insane and so not like me!

I barely touched her. *Barely*. But somehow, that was enough.

One night. One woman. And now she's lodged under my skin so deep, I can't shake her.

I clear my throat, dragging myself back to the present. "And while we're on the subject..." I pause, take a long sip of my drink, trying to summon what little courage I've got left.

"The new team therapist and performance coach?"

Will nods. "Eslin Saunders. She came highly recommended by Timantha's former assistant."

"Right," I say carefully. "But what I haven't told you is..." I start to ramble. "Remember I told you about that night in Vegas? The incredible woman I met?"

Xavier's brow furrows. "Yeah?"

"Well... funny story..." I laugh nervously. "That woman was... *is*... Eslin Saunders."

Xavier's chair scrapes back. "*The fuck?* You *fucked* the team therapist already?" he practically shouts, jumping up to pour himself another drink.

"Keep your voice down! And no! I didn't touch her, remember?"

"Okay, fine." Xavier glares. "But why the hell are we just now hearing about this?"

Two days after Eslin and I parted ways, Marlow and I were on a plane back to Atlanta when the email came through from HR—one of those generic onboarding announcements about a new team hire. The therapist.

I barely glanced at it at first. The name caught my eye—*Eslin*. Unique, sure. But it still could've been anyone. We never exchanged last names, so seeing, *"Welcome our new team member, Eslin Saunders,"* didn't immediately raise any red flags.

It wasn't until I scrolled down and saw the attachment—her team photo, fresh from HR's onboarding checklist—that everything slammed into place.

It was *her*. The woman who had flipped my world on its head in Vegas.

I had to sit there, trapped on that damn plane for four hours, with Marlow beside me, while my stomach bottomed out and my head spun, pretending like everything was perfectly fine.

I didn't know how the hell I was going to tell Marlow. She was the one who made the hiring decision—her first big move in this new role. The last thing I wanted was to step in and make her feel like she'd screwed it up before she even got her footing. I wasn't about to take that from her.

Which made the idea of telling Will and Xavier that much harder.

Because if there's one thing these two don't tolerate, it's me *complicating* things. And this? Complicated as hell.

I let out a long sigh. "I was waiting for the right time to tell you. Hell, it's been a month. Part of me was hoping she'd change her mind and not take the job."

"*Grant!*" Xavier swears. "I swear to fucking God! If you screw this up, screw with her—"

"You don't have to worry about it." I raise both hands in mock surrender. "Not only did I make you both—and Marlow—a promise, I told Eslin the night we met we couldn't be anything. Because of our age difference and my commitment to my daughter."

Xavier exhales hard, visibly relaxing. "Well, you should've *led* with that."

I look between them—two men who've had my back longer than I deserve. "You have my word," I tell them, voice reassuring. "I'll keep things *professional* with Eslin. No lines will be crossed."

Will watches me for a beat, then nods. Xavier still looks like he wants to throw something, but eventually exhales and leans back in his chair.

"My focus is Marlow," I continue. "Preparing her to take my place, making sure she's ready when the time comes. And whatever I can do to help this team get to the championship, I'll do it. You both know I'm in."

They nod again, and I can visibly see the tension as it starts to ease.

We wrap the meeting, papers shuffled, chairs scraped back. But as I stand, gathering my things, a sharp ache tightens in my chest.

Because for the first time since Maddy, I'm going to have to deny myself something that—for once—feels *real*.

Something that could actually make me happy.

And nothing else has done that for me in a very long time.

Chapter Five

CHAPTER FIVE: HUMBLE PIE & PEPTO

Marlow

We're in one of the conference rooms this morning, and once again, I'm in the hot seat. This time it's for training.

Karmen, our head of publicity, is across from me, walking me through another round of media training. Basically, it's a crash course in how to handle yourself when the cameras are rolling and the mics are still on. How to sound polished without sounding fake. How to sidestep questions you don't want to answer, and how to pivot the conversation to what *you* want to highlight.

It's like learning a new sport—only instead of goals and assists, you're scoring points with soundbites and saving yourself from a PR disaster with a well-timed smile.

Karmen makes it fun, though. She's sharp, quick with examples, and has me laughing between takes. Still, it's a lot to remember.

She leans forward, her tone warm but firm. "If the question feels too pointed or dips into anything legal; deflect. Pivot to something safe—team progress, community involvement, player development. You're not obligated to give them anything they can twist into a headline."

I nod, taking it in. "Smile, answer what I can, and don't get trapped."

"Exactly." She grins. "And if you get stuck, just say you'll have to consult your team and follow up later and buy yourself some time."

Since I started my training as one of the owners of the Strikers a few months ago, it's been brutal. There's no sugarcoating it. There's so much to learn—league policies, team operations, financial structures, sponsorship deals.

Endless rules, both written and unspoken, and a web of politics so tangled you need a map just to navigate a single conversation.

Every day there's something new, something I didn't know I needed to know. And the stakes are high. One misstep and you're not just risking a bad headline—you're risking the trust of an entire organization.

But despite how hard it is, it's everything I've always wanted. Everything I've been working toward, whether I admitted it to myself or not. The truth is, my dad groomed me for this. Not intentionally, not out loud. But from the time I was old enough to sit at the kitchen table and listen to him talk business, this world started taking shape in my mind.

He prayed I'd never want it—prayed I'd choose something simpler, something safer, something that didn't weigh so heavy. But that was never in the cards. Especially after losing my mom. Dad didn't know how to raise a daughter any other way than to raise her like him. And now here I am. Drowning some days. Thriving on others. And loving it all, even when it terrifies me.

I wrap my session with Karmen, and as I gather my things, I shift the conversation. "How are we looking on those partnerships? Specifically with groups focused on getting more women and girls involved in the sport?"

Karmen's eyes light up. "Really strong momentum. The new marketing director you hired has been planning some amazing activities that are giving me so much to work with from a publicity standpoint. The camps, the after-school programs, the back-to-school drives—it's all been getting a great response. And it's exactly what we need."

She's right. I've said it from day one: if you want to grow a team in this city, you've got to get the moms on board. They control the households; the husbands, the carpool schedules, the weekend plans. When we engage with them, we engage the community.

Karmen continues, "We've also lined up some fantastic holiday events with organizations across the state, starting with Thanksgiving."

"Wow! So early? It's barely August."

Karmen snorts. "Um, this is actually late! But since you pulled the trigger on so many other things, we had to give it a shot. It'll boost our image and give us a lot of positive visibility."

"Perfect. Keep me in the loop if you need my support on anything."

I glance down at my watch and feel a small jolt. Almost time.

"I need to head down to reception," I say, standing. "It's Eslin's first official day. I want to be there to greet her."

Karmen snickers. "Right and, sorry I couldn't do anything about the outfit!"

I flip her a middle finger on my way out of her office.

I groan inwardly.

I'm the type of person who plans *everything*. It's in my DNA. I hate surprises, and I really hate when things don't go the way I pictured or planned. So I prep. I build in backup plans for my backup plans.

Which means, naturally, I had this whole day mapped out—every detail, right down to what I was going to wear.

I ordered a gorgeous suit from one of those chic online boutiques. It looked stunning in the photos—sleek, off-white, modern but not stuffy. Perfect.

But this morning when I got it back from the dry cleaners and put it on, it took all of three seconds to realize something was off.

It wasn't off-white. It was pink.

Pepto Bismol pink.

And of course, I didn't really *see* how pink it was until I was already running late.

No time to change. No time to regroup. And even though Karmen normally has extra clothes in her office, she decided to have everything sent out for dry cleaning today.

So now, here I am, heading to meet my new team therapist and first official hire looking like a bottle of gas relief.

Still, it's not even close to the most embarrassing mistake I've made since joining the front office.

Like the time I confidently strode into the locker room after a huge win, clipboard in hand, ready to give a little *you killed it out there, boys,* speech! What no one told me was the press had already been let in.

Cameras were everywhere, interviews were taking place and most of the players weren't even dressed.

I walked straight into a sea of towels, bare chests, and more dicks than I ever wanted to see in a professional setting.

Worse, one of the cameras caught my reaction. Eyes wide, face frozen, and—God help me—locked right onto the monstrosity of Luca Chidubem's chubby.

This pink suit has *nothing* on that twenty-four-hour Threads debacle.

But in my defense, the man's penis was unethically big. I couldn't look away!

I own every mistake. Every challenge. And when I get knocked down, I get back up and face the next day. Today, it means facing my very real fear of being mistaken for Buckhead Barbie. Bright pink and all, I'm walking in with my head high and making damn sure Eslin feels welcome.

Chapter Six

CHAPTER SIX: GIRL POWER & STUFF

Eslin

Neither of us looks old enough to be doing these jobs. My new boss is a stunning brunette with long, dark hair, olive skin, and the kind of flawless complexion that screams she's not a day over thirty.

But hey, I'm thirty-two and still get asked where I earned my degree every time I remind someone to call me *doctor*, so who am I to judge? Honestly, I'm proud to work for an organization that empowers women like this.

She's *really* girly, though. Girly in a way that makes me pray she never wants to hang out.

"It's such a pleasure to finally meet you in person," Marlow says, wrapping up the formalities now that we're alone in her office.

Which is gorgeous, by the way.

"Likewise!" I reply brightly. "And, can I just say—mad respect for being the boss at your age? I know it's probably not PC to point it out, but seriously, you're killing it."

Thankfully, she grins—clearly taking it as the compliment I meant. "I appreciate that! It wasn't easy convincing my dad to give me a shot, but I kept reminding him that if I were a man, it wouldn't even be a conversation. He didn't have much to say after that."

"Valid!" I agree.

"So, how are you settling into Atlanta?"

"It's beautiful here. Humid, but beautiful. I lived here for a summer once, but never really had the chance to explore. It's been fun getting to know the city."

"I love that!" she gushes. "Have you made any new friends yet?"

How do I explain? I don't just *make* friends. They have to grow on me—naturally. No forcing, no pushing. And so far, I haven't let anyone close enough for that to happen since moving here.

"No, not yet! I've just been busy getting my place together," I lie smoothly, because let's be real—I moved in with seven boxes and four suitcases. Not exactly a ton of unpacking to do.

"Well, you and I are going to be great friends," she declares.

Oh, yay. Pretty sure that's an HR violation or something.

"There aren't exactly a lot of women around here, you know?" she adds.

I let out a nervous laugh. "Right! Girl power and all that!" I say, pumping my fist in mock enthusiasm.

I promise I'm not some mean girl or anything. I'm just...weird.

And what I've learned in my short time on this earth—and my long stints in random people's homes—is that weird isn't exactly widely accepted. People like fun but not too quirky, smart but not too intimidating, different but only in the ways they can easily explain to their friends.

So I don't let a lot of people get close.

Not close enough to see the weird.

She slides a sleek black leather folder across the desk—emblazoned with the Atlanta Strikers logo and my name.

"This has all your electronic key cards for the building, gym, and cafeteria. You get five hundred dollars a month for meals on campus, plus a fifty-percent discount if you spend your own money."

"Love it."

She beams proudly. "That was one of the perks I fought for when I came on board. I also pushed to add daycare for employees."

"Nice! Do you have little ones at home?" I ask, noticing a framed photo on her desk but unable to see the picture.

She waves a hand. "Oh, goodness no. But just because I don't have kids doesn't mean I can't support those who do."

I shake my head, impressed. "How am I seriously impressed and we only just met?"

"Oh, you know," she says with a playful wink. "Girl power and stuff!" I laugh, loving her callback.

She stands from her desk, and I can't help but smile at how cute and petite she is in this bright pink suit. "Let's get you a full tour of the facility."

"Good thing I wore my sneakers!" I say, proudly pointing down to the fresh pair of red and black AF-1's I just picked up to match the team colors. I also want to find anything else to stare...look at...other than her *really pink* outfit.

"Nice kicks!" Marlow flashes a somewhat nervous smile. "If only I would've gone with the dressed-down look today."

I laugh a little too quickly, already praying she doesn't ask *the* question. "You're the boss! I'm sure a suit is expected." *Please don't ask me how you look. Please don't ask me how you look.*

She narrows her eyes, tilting her head like she can see me dodging in real time. "Eslin Saunders. If you're going to work here—and if we're gonna be friends—you have to be honest with me."

I freeze, blinking. Calling us friends already is a bit presumptuous. "Okay?" I say, wondering where she's going with this.

"I look like a bottle of Pepto Bismol, don't I?"

I nod furiously, finally exhaling. "Girl! Like a pack of pink bubble gum!"

"Wasn't what I envisioned but I'm rolling with it", she quips back. We both crack up, full-on belly laughing.

"Okay, see? That's better! Ice officially broken. Now, come on, I'll show you around."

We step out of her office and into a sleek, modern hallway lined with framed jerseys and team photos. The pride of the Atlanta Strikers is practically built into the walls, even though it's still a relatively new soccer club.

First stop: the team offices. She leads me into a wing bustling with energy—PR, marketing, operations, coaching staff. Open-concept, glass-walled conference rooms, bright workspaces filled with the kind of people who *look* like they belong in a high-profile sports organization. Young, sharp, a little *too* good-looking.

"This is where most of the day-to-day magic happens," Marlow says. "If you ever need anything—team schedules, travel plans, media stuff—someone in here can make it happen."

I nod, taking mental notes.

"But I keep one of those open door policies so feel free to stop by my office with any questions too."

Next, we head down a wide staircase that opens up to the heart of the facility—the players' floor.

"This is where you'll probably spend most of your time," Marlow says. The space is massive. Floor-to-ceiling windows overlooking the practice fields. The vibe is luxe but functional. There's a lounge area with plush seating, a café stocked with every imaginable protein bar and smoothie, and a media room outfitted with big screens for game reviews.

Marlow points out the locker room. "State of the art. And smell-proofed, thank God."

I grin.

Then the gym—no basic treadmill situation here. We're talking Olympic lifting platforms, cryo chambers, hyperbaric pods. It's the type of place I would imagine athletes actually *want* to be.

Hell, I can barely lift a five pound weight but I'd love to spend some time here.

Finally, she stops in front of a wide glass door near the gym. "And this," she says, swiping her badge, "is your office."

I step inside and my jaw practically hits the floor.

It's huge. Way bigger than I expected. Damn near bigger than my first New York City apartment. One entire wall is glass, offering a view of the gym and practice fields. A plush sectional sits in one corner, with a sleek desk positioned front and center—modern, clean lines, high-end everything. Built-in bookshelves, a stocked mini-fridge, even a coffee station.

"Wow," I breathe, running my hand over the polished wood desk. "This is... incredible."

Marlow beams. "Told you we take care of our people."

She's not kidding. I'm officially blown away.

"Take your time getting settled in. Today is your official first day but since the team is gone for an away match, things will be quiet so you can take your time getting up to speed with everything."

I nod. "Got it. Thanks."

"Your laptop's been loaded with the latest HIPAA-compliant therapy software, and the team's files are already pre-loaded," Marlow says as she gestures toward my sleek new setup. "I went ahead and added photos of each player to their profiles, along with some notes on a few... let's call them *behavioral challenges* we've been dealing with. Your job is to figure out why they are the way they are—and help channel that energy back into their game."

I frown. "Funny. Xavier Darcy made it sound like my job was just to get them to stop screwing around and win more games."

She laughs, light and knowing. "Spoken like a true man. Please—take your cues from me."

I nod. "Will do."

Before I can brace myself, she pulls me into a hug. *Oh! Ok.*

"Welcome to the Atlanta Strikers. I really hope you love it here!" she says, and her warmth actually feels genuine.

"Thank you so much for the opportunity. I won't let you down."

"I'm sure you won't."

She starts to head out, but pauses in the doorway. "I mean, I'll know you're doing a good job by how well my boys perform on the field."

"With the world watching," I mutter under my breath, dread curling in my stomach.

"No pressure, though!" she calls cheerfully over her shoulder, then disappears down the hall.

I settle into the plush leather chair and pull up to the chic, modern desk. The oversized computer monitor flickers to life, prompting me to scan my fingerprints.

"Fancy," I murmur to no one, pressing my thumb to the reader.

Once I'm logged in, everything is exactly as Marlow promised—files, software, player profiles, all cleanly organized. My curiosity wins out and I click straight into the team files.

The first profile that pops up: Caleb Martinez, right wing. The notes describe him as fiercely competitive—so much so he's prone to explosive outbursts during practice and matches.

Multiple incidents of yelling at teammates, berating refs, and, on more than one occasion, punching lockers hard enough to break skin. Emotional regulation: *major work needed.*

Next: Matteo Santos, striker. On paper, he's a star—lightning fast, instinctual, technically gifted. Off the field? Shy to the point of isolation. Doesn't bond with the team, refuses to engage in group activities, avoids eye contact in team meetings. Trust and confidence issues flagged.

I click again. Malik Thompson, midfielder. The word *volatile* is bolded at the top of his notes. Known for going head-to-head with coaches, storming off the field, and ignoring strategy in favor of showing off. Rumors of deep-seated authority issues dating back to his academy days. Definitely one to watch.

I scroll down further, pulse ticking up a notch when I hit the next name: Luca Chidubem, center back.

Ah. The *cute one.* The reason the Atlanta Strikers suddenly have a spike in female fans. Social media's been having a field day with him—#CaptainChidubem trending more often than not.

I glance at his profile photo and can't help but smirk. The resemblance is uncanny—he's giving serious *Aaron Pierre meets Michael Ealy energy.* Smoldering eyes, chiseled jaw, the kind of grin that's equal parts charming and dangerous.

But charm won't keep him on the field.

I figure, since he's from Europe, he probably calls it the *pitch*—something I only know because I binged *Ted Lasso* while cramming for my new job.

He's poised to become team captain, a role he should excel in, given his leadership instincts and natural presence on the field. But the file tells another story. Focus issues started surfacing after a team trip to Vegas a few months ago. Since then, he's been making *solo* trips back—sometimes flying out between matches for what most assume are all-night parties and drinking binges. "Lacks discipline" is flagged multiple times in bold.

I blow out a breath and click to the next file: Croix London, goalkeeper.

Class clown. Resident prankster. The notes practically read like a rap sheet. Multiple minor arrests for stunts that went too far—one involving spray-painting an opposing team's bus, another ending with him zip-tying a teammate to a goalpost.

Charismatic and well-liked, but with zero impulse control. He's labeled as both *a team asset and a potential liability*.

I lean back in my chair, letting it all sink in.

No pressure, I think wryly, Marlow's words echoing in my head. The world will definitely be watching. And from the looks of it, I've got my work cut out for me.

Chapter Seven

CHAPTER SEVEN: CAFFEINE & CONVERSATIONS

Eslin

I t's Thursday morning, and somehow, I've almost survived my first week as the new therapist and performance coach for the Atlanta Strikers. *Almost.*

The week's been a blur of HR meetings, sexual harassment trainings, insurance enrollment forms—basically all the fun stuff that screams *Welcome to Corporate America, now sign here, here, and here.*

Oh, and the reporters. Can't forget them. A couple nosy ones cornered me in the hallway yesterday, asking what a *girl* was doing telling *men* how to play soccer. Because clearly that's what a performance coach does. I smiled sweetly and told them I had about as much business doing that as I did telling their wives that size isn't everything when they come to me complaining about their husbands' *shortcomings.*

That shut them up.

Across from the building where I live, there's a coffee bar called HollyDates. It's known for celebrating every holiday—all year round. I'm told it really comes alive during the big ones, but even today, the place looks like a greeting card exploded inside.

I push open the door, and it feels like I've walked into *MerryHallowKwanza Day.* Christmas lights, Halloween pumpkins, Fourth of July bunting, and about ten other holidays are all represented in some chaotic harmony.

"Happy Holidays! Welcome to HollyDates!"

"Hey, Holly!" I call.

"Hey, girl!" she calls back from behind the counter.

Holly's the owner—and my new caffeine dealer. We're friends now, mostly because she keeps me supplied with coffee.

Sometimes twice a day. She also insists on calling me *girl*, which I let slide. Coffee buys a lot of tolerance.

"So how's your morning been so far?" she asks, pulling out a cup.

"Better once you make me a Frosted Candy Cane Macchiato," I say, grinning.

Holiday-themed drinks are also served year round here.

"Coming right up!"

Ahh, the day's looking up already.

"Has business slowed down now that we're past the Fourth of July holiday?"

"Yes, thank heavens!" My favorite barista says, her long locs tied back, her whole vibe pure Lisa Bonet—earthy, cool, effortless. "I was actually able to close the bar down for a few days and rest. We made so much money, I could finally breathe."

"Oh, good!"

She slides behind the counter, pulling the ingredients for my usual.

"So, how's it been living in that fancy Fury building now that you've been there a couple of weeks?"

"Honey! It's out of this world luxury! I honestly had no clue concierge services for grocery shopping and laundry were even a thing!"

"When Logan Fury's name is on it, you don't need much of an imagination. Everything's at your fingertips in those places.

"And how would *you* know?" I ask, leaning in, lowering my voice conspiratorially.

She hands me my drink with a sly smile. "I may have had a night or two with a certain tenant," she says with a wink.

"You little hussy! Spill it!"

She shakes her head, laughing. "No, seriously. I can't. NDA."

"You had to sign an NDA for a booty call?"

She shrugs, casual as can be. "Rich people are weird."

"You can say that again."

I say goodbye to Holly and step out onto the sidewalk, phone in hand, scanning for my driver.

Another perk I managed to slip into my contract. Growing up in NYC, I never really *had* to learn how to drive, and after a few failed lessons and one time where I sort of rear-ended an old lady on foot, I figured—why start now? Having a driver just made sense.

I spot the town car parked a few yards down, engine idling. I'm about to head toward it when something catches the corner of my eye.

A man.

Not just any man.

Him.

At least...it looks like him.

Salt-and-pepper curls, a little longer on top, the kind you want to run your fingers through. That signature low, five o'clock shadow that somehow makes him look even more dangerous in daylight. And a suit. Damn. Dark, perfectly cut, hugging all the right places.

My heart jerks hard in my chest. It can't be him. It's not possible.

I didn't tell him where I lived—that I was moving to Atlanta. I *know* I didn't.

Did I?

I rack my brain, tracing back to that night in Vegas. No. No way. I was too careful. Too guarded. I didn't even give him my last name.

There's no way he could know.

Right?

But now? Now, he's striding out of the building across the street. My building.

Shit.

Panic flares, stupid and irrational, but real. Before he can turn his head my way, I duck behind a man walking past, moving way too fast for my heels to keep up.

And in my haste, my entire coffee tips forward, straight onto his suit jacket.

"Oh my God, I am *so* sorry!" I gasp, grabbing for napkins from my bag, blotting uselessly at the mess. "I will absolutely pay for cleaning, or—"

The man holds up his hands, surprisingly good-natured about it. "It's fine. Good thing I live upstairs." He tilts his head toward my building.

Of course he does.

I manage a sheepish smile but don't offer up the fact I live there too. I don't know him like that!

As soon as he disappears inside, I spin on my heel and march right back into HollyDates.

Holly looks up from the espresso machine. "Forgot something?"

"Girl," I say, breathless, leaning on the counter. "You will *not* believe what just happened."

I launch into the story, the words tumbling out before I can stop them. The night in Vegas. The man—Grant—who changed everything for me.

How we'd spent the whole night together. Walking, talking, laughing, like we'd known each other forever. How it wasn't just the chemistry—it was him. The way he listened. The way he saw me. The way he opened up without hesitation, like it was the easiest thing in the world. The way he held my hand, like I was his.

"By the time the sun came up, I was falling for him. Hard."

"Aww!" Holly swoons.

"But before we could exchange numbers—or even full names—he pulled away. Said he couldn't. That I was too close to his daughter's age and it didn't feel right. And just like that, he was gone."

She places a hand over her chest. "Heartbreaking!"

"And now I'm almost certain I just saw him—or someone who looks *exactly* like him—walking out of my building."

Holly's eyes widen. "Wait. You think he's here? In Atlanta?"

"I don't know," I say, running a hand through my locs. "But if that *was* him...it looks like we live in the same building!"

She lets out a low whistle. "Or he and his wife live there."

"No," I snap, too fast, too firm. "He told me he was a widower. It's more likely he was there visiting a woman. Because apparently, he's also a player."

"Ahh! A bad boy," she teases, waggling her brows.

"Ugh! What if he *is* seeing someone? How awkward would it be if I lived in the same building as one of his whores?"

She leans back, stretching her neck. "Easy, killer."

I have no right to feel jealous. None. But something about the thought of him with another woman makes me want to chew glass.

A man I've never even kissed.

A man who's ruined me for everyone else...because of the way he loves his daughter. Because of the way he made me feel seen.

Wanted.

CHAPTER EIGHT: ENCHILADAS & OTHER DRUGS

Grant

I am a glutton for punishment. A foolish, idiotic man.

When I found out Eslin wasn't backing down from the job—that she was, in fact, starting right after the Fourth of July—I might've insisted we offer her one of the corporate apartments.

In my building.

It's a small detail I conveniently left out when I updated Xavier and Will. No need to invite scrutiny where there doesn't need to be any.

Because it doesn't matter. I won't touch her. I won't make a move. I just wanted her...*close*. Even knowing full well I can't have her.

What can I say? I'm an addict.

Eslin is my drug.

I'm nearly two months sober now. Two months into what I've dubbed my six-month sentence of good behavior. I can't afford to screw it up. I can't afford to be selfish, not when my daughter is depending on me.

My driver pulls onto Peachtree, weaving through mid-morning traffic on the way to my next meeting. I pop open my laptop to knock out a few emails. Just as I start typing, a text notification flashes on the corner of the screen. I click the message app on my computer so I don't have to dig my phone out of my pocket.

Marlow: *I'm thinking enchiladas for Sunday dinner. Thoughts?*

Me: *I'm thinking delicious, but glad I sleep alone.*

A second later, her reply comes through—a string of laughing emojis.

I type back: Can't wait to see you.

She's been killing it lately. Grinding every day, learning everything she can about this team and the sport. I've basically been putting her through my version of bootcamp—making sure she knows the game, the players, the business side, all of it.

If I'm honest, it's probably the prep I should've done before I signed up to take over this mess in the first place. If I had, maybe I would've made a different choice.

I lean back in the seat, laptop still open but my attention drifting.

I'm not happy I sleep alone, but that's one of the new lies I tell myself. The one I sell to Marlow, too. That this time alone, my good behavior sentence, is good for me. Healing. Healthy.

But the truth is, all it's done is remind me how much I miss my wife.

Maddy.

Not just her—though I'll miss her for the rest of my life. It's everything we shared. The companionship. The laughter. The way she got my jokes before I even finished them. Movie nights. Lazy days on the boat. All the things we said we'd do more of once Marlow was off to college.

I miss it all.

And not only do I not get Maddy...I don't get Eslin either.

So I do the only thing I can...I watch. I wait. I dream.

A man can dream can't he?

***

The week flies by faster than I expect, and somehow, it's already Sunday.

Marlow's in my kitchen, sleeves rolled up, dark hair piled high on her head as she preps dinner—enchiladas, her new specialty. I'm leaning against the island, drink in hand, watching her with a small smile.

"You look just like your mother, you know that?"

She pauses mid-chop, a pile of fresh cilantro under her knife. She smiles softly. "So, I'm told."

Her mother was a storm—half Sicilian, half Italian, a force you never saw coming until it was too late. And Marlow? She's cut from the very same lightning.

"How've Xavier and Will been treating you? They still playing fair?"

I've had her shadowing just about everyone in the front office—publicists, the sponsorship team, even squeezing into meetings with Will and Xavier. Total trial by fire. But that's the point. If she's going to thrive in this world, she's got to see it from all angles. No sugarcoating. No surprises. And I've made damn sure she's going in with her eyes wide open.

She tilts her head, thinking it over. "Hmm… Xavier's knowledgeable but tougher than you with his expectations. Will's letting me tell him what I need to learn from him. Two very different leadership styles, but I appreciate both."

I take a slow sip of my drink. "But you'll tell me if they're too hard on you?"

She exhales dramatically. "No, Daddy. Because I'm a grown-up who handles my own problems. Like you taught me."

"By slashing a fucker's tires if they hurt you?"

She laughs, shaking her head. "*Or* by having a conversation?"

"Fine," I mutter. "But I will murder for you."

"I know, Daddy."

"Speaking of murder. The guys on the team being respectful?"

She groans. "Oh my God, enough! Let's talk about you. How's your dating life going? Met any quality women lately?"

She set me up a few weeks ago on some popular dating app—Caché Elite—an exclusive thing for executives and professionals. My profile's there, face blurred, bio carefully worded. I've got a pile of matches, but none that hold my attention. I only checked in the first place to see if Eslin had a profile.

She doesn't.

I shrug. "I'm more focused on getting you up to speed than speed dating, munchkin."

She rolls her eyes. "Stop calling me that. I'm twenty-eight."

"Nope. It's my right as your father. Nicknames are forever."

"You're impossible."

"And you're my favorite."

Dinner is incredible. She serves up the enchiladas hot out of the oven, perfectly sauced with melty cheese, sides of spiced black beans and cilantro-lime rice. The tortillas are crisp on the edges but soft inside, packed with slow-cooked chicken and roasted green chilies. I make a mental note to ask her to cook this again next week.

Halfway through the meal, she narrows her eyes at me over her glass of wine.

"You know," she says slowly, "you really should get back out there. You can't still be hung up on that woman from Vegas."

My stomach knots, my fork pausing mid-air.

I mask it with a quick smirk, take another bite, stalling just long enough to pull it together.

Because the truth? Of course I'm still hung up on her. On that night. On *everything* about her.

But I can't say that. I won't. Not when Marlow's orbit is so close to Eslin's now. A few loose words and she could be one step from figuring it out.

So I wave her off, casual. "I'm just busy right now. Plenty of time for dating later."

She studies me for a second, suspicious. But finally lets it go, returning to her plate.

I exhale, quiet, the weight of the unspoken truth settling heavier in my chest.

If she knew...if Marlow knew who Eslin really was to me—what she means to me—everything would unravel.

She'd never trust me again.

She wouldn't look at me the same way.

And I'm not sure I could stand to lose that when I've lost so much already.

CHAPTER NINE: TEQUILA & CURTAIN CONFESSIONS

Marlow

That one night in Las Vegas

This is stupid. Right? Of course it is.

No woman who graduated top of her class at North Kensington, spent a year backpacking Europe, and can recite every line of *The West Wing* in order would voluntarily enter something called a *pod* and expect to walk out with a soul mate.

An STD? Maybe.

A hangover? Most definitely.

But a soul mate?

"So... are you dating anyone?" the first guy asks.

I blink. "I'm sorry?"

I look around at the setup—dim lighting, plush seating, and a weirdly cozy scent that smells like warm vanilla and that one night I spent in an Amsterdam hostel. *Don't tell my dad.*

It's meant to feel intimate, romantic even, but the pod gives more "emotional detention" than "love connection." It reminds me of those sad, windowless metal trailers schools used when they ran out of space—smelled like anxiety and Lysol, lit with an artificial glow that made everyone look vaguely ill.

It's cramped. Claustrophobic. The air feels too still, too heavy. And the "curtain" separating me from the stranger on the other side is barely thicker than a hotel shower liner. I can hear everything—every breath, every shift, every creaky lean—and I suddenly feel like I've signed up for a glorified hostage situation. Only instead of ransom demands, I'm being promised *true love* if I can emotionally connect with a stranger through this adult-size pillow fort.

But hey—at least I have tequila.

I glance at the bottle I insisted on bringing in. My emotional support beverage. The producers thought it was cute. I thought it was the only way I'd survive this circus without committing a felony in front of witnesses.

Let the trauma bonding begin.

"Like, are you single right now?" My date clarifies.

I take a long, slow sip from my bottle. "I'm sitting in a pod. Talking to strangers through a curtain. What do *you* think?"

He laughs, like I'm flirting. I am not.

"I mean I feel like, if I meet the right person in here, my girl at home would have to understand, you know?"

He sounds like he mixes his cocaine with his creatine.

"I'm sorry—what?"

"The heart wants what the heart wants."

I grab the bottle and take a much larger gulp.

By the time guy number two starts talking about how his ex is still his best friend, and guy number three asks me how I feel about polyamory "in theory," I start plotting my escape route.

I distinctly remember the guy out front saying I only *had* to *meet* three of the men.

But then—then comes number four.

His voice is low, slightly rough. Warm. Like velvet and smoke and some kind of accent I can't quite place.

He clears his throat before speaking. Doesn't launch into a cheesy pickup line or ask me what my sign is. Just says, "You sound tired of this."

I laugh, maybe too loudly. "What gave me away?"

"You sighed when I sat down."

"Maybe you just sat down hard."

"Maybe," he says, and I can *hear* the amusement in his voice. "Or maybe this whole thing feels a little ridiculous. And you're smarter than most of the people in this room. And you're trying to figure out if this was a mistake."

I blink.

I *pause*.

Because... okay. That's not a terrible read.

"What makes you think I'm smarter than most of the people here?"

"You didn't laugh at that guy who said he'd leave his girlfriend for the right stranger in a pod. You told him to go to therapy."

"...you were listening?"

"I was waiting." He pauses and I nearly throw my panties across this partition when he says, "For you."

Oh *damn*.

Danger.

I sit back, bottle in hand, smiling for the first time all night since I sat in the pod.

"Okay," I say, leaning back with a smirk. "Now, you've got my attention."

"Only now? What did it for you?"

I pause, the corners of my mouth curving despite myself. "I'm not sure. Something about you," I say, softer. And for some absurd reason—I blush. "I can tell you're different."

"And I can tell you have a beautiful smile."

"How do you know I'm smiling?"

"Your voice changes when you do. Gets warmer. Softer." I hear the shift of his body on the other side of the curtain, the faint rustle of fabric. "I'd even bet the beautiful American girl is blushing right now."

Geez, how does he know? Can he tell my panties are wet, too?

I'm no stranger to men. I've dated plenty. Had a very questionable semester during sophomore year in undergrad. *Again, please don't tell Daddy.* I've been around the block—hell, I've probably mapped half of it.

But this. What I'm feeling, experiencing, through a goddamn plastic divider?

This isn't some guy.

This is a man.

And whether it's the tequila talking or my libido making executive decisions without me, one thing is certain—I don't want to date anyone else in this ridiculous excuse for a dating experiment.

I want *this* one.

"Have you done anything like this before?" he asks.

"Never. You?"

"No. Closest I came was signing to a new football team sight unseen."

I laugh. "Ha! Pun intended?"

"What?"

Right. He's not American. The joke doesn't land, and before I can continue, we speak at the same time.

"Tell me what you look like, Americana."

"Where are you from?"

"You first."

"Why me?" I ask, playing coy.

He doesn't answer. Not with words. Just lets the question hang—like he's waiting, like he knows I'll fold. And I do.

"What do I look like? I'm not very tall. Five four, give or take."

He makes a sound. A moan? Approving. "Do you wear those high heels, Americana?"

"Are you really going to keep calling me that?"

More silence. More heat.

I let out a sigh. Because this isn't my show. It's his.

"I do wear heels," I admit. "I work around a lot of men and—" I pause because did he just *growl*? "And they tend to take me more seriously when I'm closer to their eye level."

"If you were mine," he says, no hesitation, no doubt, "I'd keep you too fucked and too fed to give a damn what other men think."

My breath catches. My thighs tighten.

He says it like a threat without my permission. Like he's already claimed me and is just waiting for the rest of the world to catch up.

Waiting for me.

And suddenly, this stupid pod feels like the only place in the world I want to be.

That—or on top of him. I can't decide.

My brain is trying to act right, trying to be logical, but my body is already halfway to "fuck it."

I shift in my seat, the plush cushion sticking to my thighs like even *it* knows I'm hot and bothered.

"You're really confident for someone I can't even see," I say, trying to regain some kind of power.

"Not confidence," he replies. "Certainty."

Jesus. Did I just come?

"Are you always like this?"

"Like what?"

"Certain."

"Never before."

"And right now?"

"I'm certain I want you."

And just like that, I forget my name.

CHAPTER TEN: HYPE GIRL & HI, DADDY

Eslin

I'm in my office, perched on the edge of my chair, watching Luca Chidubem across from me.

He's leaning back, long legs sprawled out, that usual cocky grin toned down to something softer today.

For the past couple weeks, we've been working on his focus—exercises to help him lock in on the field, keep the outside noise from bleeding into his game. Visualization drills, breath work, mindfulness techniques. And it's been paying off. Big time.

"So," I say, notebook in hand. "How did it feel scoring the winning goal last match?"

He flashes a grin. "Felt fucking brilliant." His British accent wraps around the words, confident and smooth. "Didn't hear a damn thing once I was on the ball. Could've been in a stadium of ghosts for all I knew. Just me and the pitch."

I smile. "That's exactly what we've been working toward. Keep channeling that. The noise doesn't exist unless you let it."

He nods, running a hand through his curls. "Appreciate it, Coach. Feels like I've finally got my head straight out there."

"Relationship issues can impact us in so many ways, Luca. The important thing is to learn how to leave what serves the game on the field, and what doesn't—off."

During one of our sessions, he'd admitted it. A woman had him losing his footing. Mentally, emotionally. The kind of distraction that could cost him everything he'd worked for—his focus, his edge, and possibly his shot at the opportunity of a lifetime.

He hadn't shared much detail, not yet. But enough for me to know this wasn't just some casual fling. Whoever she was, she'd gotten under his skin.

Now, it's my job to help him pull that focus back where it belongs. Before it's too late.

We wrap up, and after he leaves, I settle in to check emails.

One subject line jumps out at me: Back to School Drive – Biddy Mason Charter School.

I click it open—Marlow's arranged for the team to participate in a community event at a local school. One of her newest projects to strengthen the Strikers' presence in the community and give their PR a solid boost.

I glance through the details, check the time on my screen, then push up from my chair. On the way out, I grab a protein bar from my drawer and head for the elevator, thumbing the button to take me up to Marlow's office.

I've always hated having to do events outside of work. Never understood the need to be around people all day, only to turn around and find more reasons to hang out with them after hours.

I don't like people seeing *all* sides of me. There's work Eslin—and there's after-hours Eslin.

And those two? They should never meet. And sure as hell shouldn't be in mixed company.

Marlow's at her desk, typing furiously. She looks up when I knock. "Hey! What's up?"

"I had a quick question," I say. "For the Back to School event—what should I wear?"

Another reason I hate attending functions outside of work? My love for sneakers and t-shirts. I never know what to wear.

I'm not the girl who gets dressed up every day, counting down the minutes until she can grab the latest pair of heels everyone's obsessing over.

I'm the sneaker-wearing, jogging suit-loving chick who'd choose a Starter jacket over a fur coat any day of the week.

Marlow grins. "Team jersey and jeans are fine. And your locs are effortlessly gorgeous, so your hair will only enhance the look."

I laugh. "You always know how to hype a girl up."

"Just the truth," she says, standing to grab a file from the cabinet. "And who knows, maybe you'll even snag a man while we're at the school!"

She pauses, eyes sparkling, clearly letting her imagination run wild.

"Maybe a strong, sexy gym teacher...or an English teacher who'll *read* to you. I hear teachers know how to talk you through it," she adds with a wicked grin.

I gasp. "Marlow, you *freak*! And to think I thought you were all buttoned-up and proper when you interviewed me."

She laughs, waving me off. "Oh, please. With my father? I've seen too much debauchery to be a prude—or anything close."

She flips through the file, then looks up. "Can you believe it's already been a month since you started working here?"

"No," I say, shaking my head. "Time is flying."

"We need to celebrate surviving the first month," she says. "Drinks Friday?"

"Absolutely."

I guess I don't mind hanging out with Marlow outside of work. She can be just as feisty as me and turns up like she's straight out of my borough in NYC. She's a pretty dope woman, and we vibe pretty easily.

I push to stand, turning toward the door—

And barrel straight into someone. Solid. Warm. Familiar.

Grant.

I freeze.

He's right there, inches away, those sharp eyes meeting mine with that same pull they had the night in Vegas. The air between us snaps tight. My heart's racing, pulse pounding loud in my ears.

Marlow comes around the desk, beaming. "Daddy! Perfect timing!"

Daddy. The fu–

"This is Eslin, the team therapist and performance coach I've been telling you about. The one you always seem to miss whenever you're here!"

Grant extends his hand and I extend mine back.

We can't know each other. We can't react.

I swallow hard. "Hi, Daddy—"

Shit.

"I mean... hi, Mr.—"

His lips curve, that smile doing dangerous things to my insides. "Mills. Grant Mills."

"Mills?" I look between him and Marlow as the pieces rapidly form and explode in my brain. "Grant Mills. Marlow Mills." I breathe out.

She has the same last name.

"Because... you're her dad."

My boss's dad.

Holy. Shit.

CHAPTER ELEVEN: CONFRONTATIONS & SALUTATIONS

Grant

L unch with Marlow is awkward.

I'm a mess trying not to think about Eslin too much and the adorable way she took the news. That I'm Marlow's father.

Marlow doesn't notice I'm distracted. I'm playing it off well enough—years of practice will do that. But I can barely focus on a damn thing she's saying.

I almost laugh to myself at Eslin's reaction to seeing me. And fuck, it was good to see her. To feel her pressed against me, even if it was by accident. Even if it only lasted a second.

Until today, I've been doing so well. So damn well. I've kept my distance. Stayed in my lane. Avoided Eslin like my life depended on it.

Hell, maybe it does.

I know her schedule. When she leaves for work each morning. The hours she's with patients. When she usually comes home. Hits the gym. Every detail.

I made sure I knew.

I'm not a stalker—far from it.

It was the only way to keep my distance. The only way to avoid crossing paths... reaching for something I know I can't have.

But today she changed her routine.

And she walked right into me.

I didn't even have time to react.

Well. Other parts of me sure as hell reacted. But she didn't give me the chance to say anything more than my name. She barreled past me like her shoes were on fire and stomped straight down the hall in the opposite direction.

And now here I am, sitting across from my daughter, trying to pretend I'm not rattled. Trying to pretend like my blood isn't still pumping too fast.

One brush of her body against mine and every carefully constructed wall I'd built these past two months cracked straight down the middle.

I take a sip of water. It barely touches the heat burning through me.

Fuck.

I've missed her. More than I was ever willing to admit.

And now I haven't got a clue how the hell I'm supposed to stay away from her.

Because one look, one breath in her space, and I already know—*I'm fucked*.

"Daddy! Did you hear me?"

Marlow's voice pulls me away from the pointless thoughts swirling in my head.

I blink and clear my throat. "Sorry, honey. There's an email I just remembered I forgot to send," I lie.

She rolls her eyes. "Always working."

"Hey—you and your new partners practically castrated me, making me behave. You had to know a few things about me were going to stay the same."

"Yeah, but not while we're out for lunch on such a rare occasion! This is *my* time with you!"

"Well, it's kind of hard to turn work off now that you've entered this world. Honestly, I'm fascinated by how quickly you've picked this up and taken it on."

She beams, practically glowing. "Aww! Thanks, Daddy! That's why I'm so proud of what we're doing in the community to turn the team's image around. Working with the PR team has been the best thing for me. I get to find creative ways to use my passion for making the sport more inclusive for women while helping the team's public image."

"That's impressive, Low. I'm really proud of you."

Her mother was the same way. Could champion any cause she believed in and make you fall in love with a porcupine if you talked to her long enough. Seeing Marlow channel those same gifts—seeing her do exactly what Will and Xavier have been begging for—makes me think this might've been one of the best ideas for everyone all around.

Even if it did take weeks of convincing from Marlow.

We wrap up lunch and I walk Marlow back to her office, already knowing exactly what I'm going to do next.

I check my watch—*perfect*. Eslin doesn't have another appointment for thirty minutes.

I catch the next elevator down and stalk toward her office, my stride purposeful. Every step, my pulse kicks harder.

Where all these testosterone-filled kids get to see her every damn day.

Get to sit in front of her. Hear her voice. Smell that honey and vanilla on her skin.

It's a wonder I've lasted this long.

My heart's pounding now—fast, hard—the closer I get to her door.

And then, I'm there.

She's seated behind her desk, typing. She doesn't look up right away. But then her fingers still, mid-keystroke. Like she *feels* me. Senses me standing there.

"Did you know?" she asks, voice even, eyes locked on the screen.

And I know exactly what she means.

"No," I say, voice rough. "Not at first. I found out the day I left you in Vegas."

She stays focused on the screen, refusing to meet my gaze.

I step inside, taking in the room. It's beautiful—soft tones, warm lighting, sleek, modern touches that suit her perfectly. The space feels calm. *Grounded.* The same way she makes me feel.

But I'm anything but calm right now.

My mind is racing. My body tense.

I want to tell her this wasn't some game. That I would never set myself or her up like this.

I wouldn't dare torture myself by hiring the one woman I can't have. The one I want more than my next breath.

The one I'm dying to lay across that desk and devour until she's trembling, breathless, begging me not to stop.

But I can't say any of that.

She stands, unhurried but intentional, rounding the desk. For a beat, I think she's going to reach for me. My breath catches, hope stupidly flaring in my chest.

"Es—"

"Your daughter," she cuts in. "Is fucking amazing. She's brilliant, and funny, and kind. She's everything I've ever wanted in a friend."

"I know. She's—"

"My boss," Eslin finishes sharply, her gaze finally snapping to mine.

I swallow hard. "Painfully aware," I murmur.

Her arms fold across her chest, her posture all steel and self-control. "And I would never betray my ethics for some *fling* with a guy I met once in Vegas."

The word hits like a punch. Fling.

Ouch.

Because it was never that to me. Not for a second.

I nod slowly, forcing the words out. "I understand. I would never ask you to betray your values or ethics for me, Eslin. I respect you too much."

She exhales, shoulders sagging slightly. "You've been avoiding me, huh?"

A humorless laugh escapes me. "Like you wouldn't believe."

"And that was you...on the sidewalk that day?" she asks softly.

I nod again, no point in pretending. "Yes. You were outside of HollyDates. Wearing a burnt orange suit."

Her lips twitch, something fragile flickering across her face. "Good memory."

"Impossible to forget."

She hesitates, fingers fidgeting—tangling and untangling like she's trying to hold something in or delicately unfold it.

"Do you...do you live in my building, too? Or were you visiting one of your *friends*?"

I meet her gaze head-on, steady. "I live in the building. It's just me."

And even though it's pointless to say it—*dangerous*, even—I need her to know.

"There is no one else."

No one but her.

Her fingers clench again, her chest rising and falling with uneven breaths.

"I... I need to say something." Her voice cracks.

"Okay." I step closer, pulse pounding. "Say it."

She smiles—small, sad—and I catch the faint shimmer of a tear in her eye before she blinks it back.

"That night in Vegas..." her voice wavers but she pushes through, "it was everything I imagined it would be. The way we walked and talked for hours, sharing truths without fear of being judged or rejected. It was magical. And it broke my heart when I couldn't have more. Couldn't carry it home with me."

She draws in a shaky breath. "But now that I've met Marlow, I get it. I understand why keeping your word to her is so important."

"Eslin—"

But she holds up a hand, cutting me off. "So I need you to stay hidden, Grant. Keep avoiding me. *Please.*"

She's begging. And fuck—*it's breaking her heart just as much as it's breaking mine.* Again.

I swallow hard, forcing down the knot lodged in my throat. "Okay."

But it nearly kills me to stop there.

I want to say more. Much more.

I want to ask her to take a walk with me—no expectations, no promises. No words needed.

Just to be near her. To breathe the same air for a little longer.

But then I hear footsteps and a familiar bark. Coach Jones rounds the corner with Rocky—the team's rambunctious pup—trotting at his side.

The sound pulls me back to earth, softens the ache in my chest just enough to breathe again.

I kneel down, letting Rocky barrel into me, tail wagging. I run a hand through his thick fur, pressing a kiss to his head. "Hey, Coach," I greet Jones, though my attention stays on Rocky. "Hey, *Coach Rocky*," I add with a playful growl, roughing up his ears.

Rocky's a former Navy SEAL dog who was retired early when they discovered he was too playful for that kind of work. Too friendly. My buddy from the unit called me, said he'd be perfect for a new life with us. I didn't hesitate. Brought him in for the guys here—and he's worked miracles for morale.

He's worked miracles for me, too.

When he's not with the players, he stays with me. My shadow. My calm.

"You ready to go home, buddy?" I ask softly, and Rocky barks his approval.

I rise, forcing my gaze back to Eslin. Forcing the words out with more control than I feel.

"Goodbye, Dr. Saunders."

She straightens, chin high even as her eyes shimmer again. "Goodbye, Mister."

CHAPTER TWELVE: 90'S, NOSTALGIA & MOSCOW MULES

Eslin

H is daughter.

I work with—*for*—Grant's daughter.

It's honestly one of the most hilarious and inconvenient things I've ever had to deal with. And keep in mind, I once had to share a bunkbed with my foster sister's pet lizard, so that's saying a lot.

Why does my love life insist on getting this complicated the moment I finally feel like I'm starting to get my footing? I've got the dream job. The dream apartment. My social calendar is slowly filling up with brunches and happy hours where I'm rubbing elbows with the rich Black folks my mama used to whisper about like they were royalty.

I should be coasting. Floating. Thriving.

Instead, I feel like I'm back in middle school trying not to say or do anything that might get me sent to the principal's office. Only now the "principal" is my boss's father. The man who, with one look, is able to pull me apart without touching me.

And what's worse? I care.

I've never been the woman who lost sleep over what someone thought of me. Not in school. Not in foster care. Not in my career. But somehow, all of a sudden, I want him to know he was right about me. About the woman he saw that night. The woman who captivated him for one perfect evening.

When we left things in Vegas, it felt romantic. This mysterious, suspended moment in time—two strangers who shared the kind of night you carry with you forever. It was everything I promised him it would be at the start of the evening.

Now that we're two people in the same city, breathing the same air, working in the same orbit, I keep catching myself wanting to preserve that mystery. To let him hold on to that version of me. The version he fell for. The one he said he was ready to upend his life for. Even though, seeing him now, seeing the choice he's made—I know those words weren't entirely true. They were beautiful in the moment. But like most beautiful things in Vegas, they were built for the night, not the daylight.

It's Friday, and usually I only schedule one appointment since I reserve the day to catch up on paperwork, reports, and general housekeeping for the team. But Luca needed an emergency session and I needed the distraction. Anything to keep my mind off of Grant Mills.

So, I opened up a spot.

One hour. One crisis.

One temporary escape from the man who still lives rent-free in my head.

"What's going on with you, Luca? You seem off."

His eyes dart around, won't settle, and his breathing's uneven. He looks like a spring ready to snap.

"I saw her."

"Saw who?"

"The girl!" he bursts out, voice sharp with frustration. "The one that's been messing with my head and throwing me off my game!"

I sit up a little straighter. "Luca, that's great! You said you couldn't find her. That you *had* to find her, right?"

"No. You don't get it. It couldn't have been her. I was hallucinating or something."

"Okay..." I say carefully, keeping my voice steady while trying to figure out where the hell he's going with this. "Luca? Where are you going with this?"

Luca's been seeing me ever since the emotional regulation issues started. He's always talked about *this woman* who's been messing with his head, but he's never quite said *how* or *what* exactly she's done. There's always this wall he won't let me past. And as much as I want to dig, I know forcing the pace would only betray the trust we've built.

Just as I'm mentally preparing my next question, my tablet lights up with a text—because of course, my phone syncs everything to the damn screen.

And I read it.

Marlow: *"Drinks still on for tonight? :)"*

"Shit!"

Luca jumps, eyebrows knitting together. "Coach Saunders?"

Did I say that out loud?

Shit.

"I—I'm sorry, Luca." I scramble, trying to recover. "I saw a message that startled me. I didn't mean to say that out loud. My bad. You were saying? About your feelings?"

But meanwhile, my brain has completely derailed because *how am I supposed to go have drinks with Marlow like nothing's happening?*

What am I supposed to say? *No, sorry! I don't want to sit across from you while daydreaming about sitting on your daddy's face... while calling him Daddy?*

Double. Shit.

Luca continues, his voice dropping like he's about to confess to murder. "You see, I feel like it's a sign. That I should take some time off the game and go find her. I can't stop thinking about her."

Finally, I've had enough. I lean forward, dropping the clinical calm and slipping straight into my best *big sister about to snatch you up* voice.

"Okay. Luca. Pause. Right now." I hold my hand up like a stop sign. "Can you please just start from the beginning and *tell me* what's going on? It's really hard to try to help you when you're feeding me details like I'm playing a damn game of Clue."

He lets out a breath like he's been waiting for me to snap. "I was wondering when you were going to ask."

"I'm beyond asking, Luca. I'm *insisting*."

He grins like this is all so amusing. "I married her."

I blink. "I'm sorry, *what?*"

I furrow my brow and sit back, trying to make sure my ears are still working. "One more time, please."

"I was in Vegas," he starts, "and some guy approached me to play on a modified version of that reality TV show *SightUnseen,* where—"

"The show where you sit in a pod for a week and get engaged afterward... sight unseen?"

"The very one."

My brain short-circuits. *Oh my God.* I actually saw that guy when I was in Vegas. Grant and I literally walked right past him.

"Okay, so you're telling me you signed up for this show, played it, and married someone?" My voice is calm but my blood pressure is sprinting for its life.

"Yeah." He says it sheepishly, and his damn British accent makes it almost impossible to stay mad.

"Luca! How have the press not gotten ahold of this information?"

"I used a fake name. And dressed like a pimp to disguise myself when we got married."

"You're lying."

"Not at all."

"I'm laughing, Luca, but this is the most insane thing I have ever heard in my life." I rub my temples, because my brain officially hurts. "Who else knows?"

"Just Coach, Will Huntley, Xavier Darcy, and Grant Mills. If I didn't tell them, I probably would've been benched by now. Or traded."

I frown. "And Marlow Mills? Does she know?"

He shakes his head. "I was advised not to tell Marlow just yet. Not until she gets her head around all the other scandals and we figure out a way out of this mess."

Great. More secrets.

I still can't believe what I'm hearing. I blink a few times, trying to gather my words and not sound as dumbfounded as he does flat-out stupid.

"So now, because you *think* you've seen her, you believe it's some kind of sign to take time off work and go find her?"

"I do, Coach." His voice is so sincere it almost hurts. "I just don't think I'm going to be right until I find her."

"Luca," I take a deep breath. "Could this also be a manifestation of your fears?"

He frowns, confused. "I'm not sure what you mean."

"Justice Trager's retiring sooner than later. His wife's expecting, and you're next in line for team captain. On top of that, there are talks of pulling you up for the World Cup to play with England. You step away now, Luca...you could risk *everything*."

He pauses. I watch him actually process it. "Shit. I guess you might be onto something."

I nod, folding my hands in my lap. "Maybe take a little time to really think about it before you make any decisions, okay? Evaluate your fears, your motivations...*and* your goals."

"Okay. I can do that." He nods like a student who's finally accepted the lesson.

"And besides," I add, raising a brow, "a marriage where you used your fake name isn't exactly valid, is it?"

He chuckles, standing to leave, and reaches out to shake my hand. "You should see this woman, Coach. One night and she ruined me for anyone else."

I know the feeling.

"Just don't let her ruin your career too, huh?" I say, trying to lighten the moment.

He flashes me a grin and heads out the door, leaving me sitting there alone—mentally spinning as I stare down at the blinking message on my tablet from Marlow.

Now I just have to figure out how the hell I'm going to get out of drinks with my boss while trying not to picture her father's hands on me every time she says his name.

Marlow bursts into my office right as I'm mentally scrambling for a believable excuse to cancel our drinks. The sad truth is I have absolutely nothing else to do tonight, but somehow *"I want to avoid spending time with you because I can't stop thinking about your father"* doesn't feel like a great option.

"There's somewhere I want to take you tonight, and I'm not taking no for an answer," she announces, full of pep and determination.

I hold up a finger, giving her my best *serious Black woman* stare. "I'm going to insist you tell me before we go. I don't just go places with white people without full disclosure."

She bursts out laughing. "Oh my goodness! Eslin, I will *never* get tired of you saying exactly what's on your mind."

I grin but level her with a look. "I'm joking, but I'm also serious! I do not know you like that!"

"That's exactly why I want us to get drinks," she says, still giggling. "So you can get to know me and find out that I would never surprise you with anything you've seen on *Dateline.*"

Dateline. Funny. I know your daddy watches that too. Joked about it the night we first met.

"Fine, but I'm still demanding you tell me where you're dragging me," I say, shutting down my computer, walking over to my wardrobe closet, and grabbing my purse.

"The Sanctuary," she beams.

I blink. "Come again? Church?"

"No!" She's laughing so hard now she's practically wheezing. "It's a lounge in the city! I heard it's 90's night!"

"You mean *Sanctuary,* no 'The.'"

"Yes! That's it. Have you been there?"

"I've heard about it, but no, not yet." I cross my arms, stepping back on my heel, studying her suspiciously. "Are you taking me there because I'm Black and that's the only Black establishment you know?"

She shrugs without a hint of shame. "Yes? But why does that matter if they also serve the best oxtail plates in town and play live music?"

The moment she decided to be completely honest about it being the only Black establishment she knew—and that she was taking me there because I'm Black—is when I decide to give her a chance.

At least she's self-aware. And honest.

It's not fair to keep her at arm's length just because of this crazy, tangled-up situation I've landed in. I'm a professional. I would never do anything to risk my job, and truth be told, I could use a friend.

Besides, anyone who can point me toward the best oxtail in town *has* to be good people.

"Touché, girl," I say laughing. "But let's be clear—outside of work? I'm *Blackity Black*. Work Eslin doesn't come out until Monday morning. Is that clear?"

She grins wide. "I don't know what that means, but I'm game!"

***

The live music is everything Marlow promised. Smooth vocals, a three-piece band—keyboard, drums, guitar—playing like they've been doing this together for decades. The kind of vibe that wraps around you like warm velvet, sinking into your skin and making you forget any problems waiting outside those doors.

Sanctuary is giving full *Love Jones* energy. Rich, intimate, and dripping in Black excellence from every corner of the lounge. The low lighting, the steady hum of laughter, the clink of glasses—it's like stepping into a space designed to celebrate us, by us.

I've got to give it to Marlow—she did good. Real good.

We're tucked off to the side, but I can still feel the pulse of the room—like the bass line is synced to my heartbeat. It's cozy, intimate, and exactly the kind of space my soul didn't know it needed tonight.

We're two cocktails in when Marlow spins toward me, her eyes dancing with curiosity and that tipsy glow that makes her just bold enough to start prying.

"So, tell me everything! Where you grew up? How many siblings you have? Do you have a boyfriend?" she fires off like an over-caffeinated FBI agent.

I take another sip of my drink, while Marlow waves down the server for her third cocktail. Oh, this girl is thirsty.

"There's really not much to tell. I grew up in New York City. I'm an only child. And I definitely do not have a boyfriend. In fact, I'm pretty sure God and Cupid have conspired to keep me single and celibate."

"Wow," she says, frowning like I just told her I lost my puppy.

"What?" I shoot back.

"You're pretty boring."

I grab a french fry and launch it at her. "Shut up! I had a weird upbringing, so I'm a weird person."

The foster care stuff can wait for another day. It's never a great icebreaker, and it damn sure doesn't pair well with 90's R&B and Moscow Mules.

The waiter drops off her next drink while I down my glass of water and request a refill.

I flip the conversation back to Marlow. "What about you? You dating anyone?"

I skip the other small talk because let's be real—I already know way too much about her from internet-stalking her father.

She laughs—but it's shaky. That kind of nervous, unsteady laugh that carries more weight than humor. And then, she full-on breaks. Tears. Full meltdown.

"Dating someone? How about married to a man named Declan that I met once and then ghosted because I had a wedding to get to but was so hungover that I forgot his last name, room number, and hotel he was staying at so I couldn't go find him? And now he's back in Italy probably sleeping with some hot girl named Francesca or something and I need a divorce?"

I take a long sip—scratch that, a gulp—of my Moscow Mule. "Okay...so, you're *not* dating anyone. Got it." I grin, trying to lighten the mood.

She sniffles and then laughs. "Oh God, do I have snot on my nose?"

"Yes."

We both laugh and she grabs a napkin, frantically wiping her face.

"I can't believe I just told you all that!"

You and me both.

Then my mind flashes back to Luca's confession earlier today.

"Don't tell me...The night we—" I pause, catching myself before I admit way too much. "You did that stupid *Sight Unseen* reality show thing?" *The same night I was trying to get in your daddy's pants!*

She gasps. "How did you know?"

"I've seen the guy in Vegas before. He tries to recruit people all the time."

She drops her head in her hands. "I can't believe I did that. My boyfriend cheated on me and then I got drunk and—"

"Yeah. Seems like you've been doing that a lot lately. Getting drunk."

She nods miserably. "Eslin, I'm the good girl. The one who does everything right. The one who never missed curfew. The girlfriend who sucks dick from the back!"

"Wait, what? You can do that?"

She nods vigorously, eyes wide and whispering like she's sharing a trade secret. "Hand to God. And the boys love it!"

At this point, I nearly spit out my drink. Lord. What have I gotten myself into?

Eslin is cool, and I've instantly related to her.

I laugh at her wild, unexpected confession. "You are something else."

"And completely not what you expected, huh?" she teases, flashing that mischievous smile.

I shake my head, still grinning. "Not at all! And girl, you's a *whole* married woman!" I yell just as the band transitions into a smooth, live rendition of *Poison* by Bell Biv DeVoe.

"OMG!" I squeal. "This is my song!"

"I love this song!" she shrieks, full-on white girl wasted but living her best life.

"Come on, Mrs. Mills! Let's go dance!" I say, pulling Marlow up as the beat drops, and we head to the dance floor.

And *that's* how I became friends with my boss.

And my crush's daughter.

We'll deal with this whole marriage bombshell later.

CHAPTER THIRTEEN: NUTMEG & KNOCKOUTS

Marlow

"We're at Biddy Mason Charter School today where the whole team is out in full force to help pass out backpacks and school supplies to the kids ahead of school starting. I'm here with one of the new team owners, Marlow Mills, who I'm told helped organize this event?"

I force my most polished smile. God, I hate these interviews. I knew public speaking would be part of this role, but dealing with the press is an entirely different beast—and let's just say I haven't exactly been the most graceful with the media lately.

"Yes, Rachel," I say, keeping my tone steady, pleasant. "Biddy Mason and the leadership team here have always had a special place in my heart. What they do for the community and the impact they have on these kids' lives...it was important to me that we helped shine a light on their work."

"That's beautiful. And I hear the Strikers have adopted Biddy Mason for the school year?"

"Yes!" I say, my voice perking up, proud of the program I've poured myself into. "I'm pleased to announce that every year, the Strikers will partner with a deserving school and offer activities like you see today—camps, mentorship programs, and motivational seminars from select players throughout the year.

"In order to qualify, schools must demonstrate a commitment to community service, fair treatment of all people, and academic excellence that includes the arts."

"That is wonderful," Rachel nods, smile tight. And then...here it comes. "Sounds like things are headed in the right direction. Especially after some of your recent embarrassments in the headlines."

I freeze for only half a second, but my face stays fixed in that perfectly polite smile.

Bitch.

"Yes, Rachel. Like anyone taking on a new role in any field, I've had a learning curve. But as you've noted, things are headed in the right direction."

Corinne Rutherford, the principal of the school, thankfully steps in at that moment, taking over to talk about the school's mission, and I take that as my cue to politely excuse myself before my professional mask cracks wide open.

Because if that woman had asked me one more passive-aggressive question about my so-called *mishaps,* I was fully prepared to shove that microphone up her nose.

I step away from the cameras just as my dad's car pulls up, and the second I see him step out, my grin grows, wide and pure, involuntary.

This is my first big event since officially stepping into my role with the team. My event. My idea. My project. And despite all the cameras, the reporters, and the unavoidable media attention that follows him everywhere, my dad insisted on being here. Just to support me.

That's the thing about us.

Growing up, just the two of us, I always understood why he couldn't be there for every little thing. I never resented him for working so much, for traveling, for grinding as hard as he did. I knew even then—if I made his life harder, if I added pressure—he might break. I accepted the times he couldn't show up and made sure he felt appreciated when he did.

And now that he's older and finally slowing down, he shows up. He's *here* more often than not.

The fact that he's giving up his old habits, trading in his playboy ways just to make sure I have every chance to succeed in this new chapter, that he chose me, it tells me everything I need to know. That his heart has always been right where it belongs...With me. For me.

I'm headed toward my dad, already picturing the way his face will light up when I finally make it over, when I'm intercepted.

"Ms. Mills. Shaun Kennedy from the *Cinnamon Grove Sun*. A moment, please?"

I pull my smile back into place. "Sure, Shaun. What can I do for you?"

He grins, a cocky, self-assured grin, and steps just a little too close—invading that polite bubble of space like he's testing the waters.

"I was hoping to ask you about the event today," he says smoothly, voice like he's rehearsed it in the mirror, "and then maybe ask you out for coffee."

I arch a brow, trying not to let the blush creeping up my cheeks betray me. "I see."

Shaun Kennedy. I know exactly who he is. The up-and-coming reporter who just made the jump from covering college sports to national leagues. I've seen him floating around events, always flashing that frat-boy charm—dark brown hair, sharp blue eyes, like someone who's been skating by on looks and charisma his whole life.

He's cute, though. I'll give him that.

But this is the first time he's approached me. For an interview or anything else.

"Well," I say, slipping into my most professional tone, keeping my composure tight. "Let's start with the first and see where we land, shall we?"

He clears his throat, presses a button on his recorder, and raises the mic. "Ms. Mills, looking lovely as ever today in your jeans and team jersey."

I shake my head, giving him a polite but controlled smile. "Thank you, Shaun."

"So, word has it Justice Trager is retiring sooner than later. Any insight on who Coach Jones is looking at for the next team captain? Sources say Chidubem is poised to take the lead."

"Well, you and your sources would need to check the facts with Coach Jones," I say, keeping my tone smooth and diplomatic. "I'm not here to influence decisions where I don't have expertise. Coach Jones will make the right choice and announce it when the time comes."

Media training for the win.

"I see." He lowers the mic slightly, eyes twinkling. "And about that dinner?"

"Are you still recording?"

"I am. I need your response on record so you can't weasel your way out of it later."

I gasp, hand over my chest. "I beg your pardon? I don't *weasel!*"

"Fine. So—dinner. You were saying?"

"I thought you said coffee?"

"The price just went up."

"The price?" I laugh.

He shrugs. "It's something my niece keeps saying to me whenever she wants something. I thought it might work here."

I shake my head, laughing. "It does not."

"Damn it. Coffee, then?"

As soon as I get my quickie divorce, Shaun.

But I keep that thought to myself. Instead, I turn and walk away, throwing a playful, "We'll see!" over my shoulder.

Eslin

The day is a glowing success, honestly.

I'm here to observe, to keep tabs on how the guys interact with the kids, the press, and—more importantly—each other. We've got a few players we anticipate might struggle with the media attention, or with the intensity of the crowds, but so far they're all handling it well. Not just well—*they're thriving.*

I scan the field and can't help but smile.

The Bridget "Biddy" Mason STEM Charter School—named after the formerly enslaved woman who became one of the most prominent businesswomen and philanthropists of her time—sits tucked in a small suburb of Atlanta called Cinnamon Grove.

Atlanta itself has become practically synonymous with wealth and luxury now—glittering high-rises, sprawling outdoor shopping centers, vegan cafés on every corner. But just beyond that polished veneer, just outside of Cinnamon

Grove—places where developers haven't rushed in with their bulldozers and their big plans, is the other part of the city, neighborhoods overlooked.

Places where thousands of children still grow up surrounded by poverty and limited opportunity.

That's why this school exists.

It was founded by a husband-and-wife team with a clear vision: to give these kids the tools they need to thrive, no matter their zip code. A STEM-focused curriculum, leadership programs, partnerships with businesses and community leaders—it's hope in brick and mortar. And today the Strikers are here to support that mission.

Out on the field, players are kicking around the ball with kids of all ages, laughter ringing through the air. On one side, a couple of the guys have set up chairs and—believe it or not—a small pop-up barber station. A few of the players are lining kids up for fresh fades and braids.

Near the entrance, more players are signing jerseys, autographing photos, taking selfies with wide-eyed little fans.

I have to hand it to Marlow, *she nailed this partnership.*

Everything about today feels intentional, warm, connected. No one's phoning it in. The team looks genuinely happy to be here, and the kids look like they're floating.

It's a good day.

In moments like this, it's easy to forget just how complicated things really are under the surface.

And wouldn't you know it—*complicated* just walked onto the field.

Grant Mills. One of Atlanta's most eligible bachelors, or so I've learned from some light internet stalking.

In the flesh.

He's barely made it five steps before he's surrounded by reporters, their cameras flashing, microphones shoved in his face—probably peppering him with questions about his "golden child" and her rapid rise within the club.

Marlow started this position with more than a few haters stacked against her. But I've watched her take the hits in stride. When she fumbles, she owns it.

When she's doubted, she keeps moving. She's earned every bit of the respect she's starting to command.

But Lord...*this damn daddy of hers?*

He's out here dressed in black slacks and a sharp black and red Strikers polo. Not as casual as the rest of us—definitely not slumming it with the players in jerseys and shorts. But casual enough for a man who probably clears twenty million a day.

Yes. I Googled that, too. Don't judge me.

Without thinking, I slip my phone out of my back pocket, flipping the camera to check my makeup. Pure instinct.

I've always been one of those women who can make a "dressed down" look ...look *good*. And today I'm rocking the hell out of it.

Even though I told Grant to stay hidden—hell, even though I told *myself* not to let my imagination wander where it shouldn't when it comes to him—here I am...wondering...*Does he like this look? On me?*

It was silly to think he could avoid me forever. That he'd stay hidden. So no. I'm not entirely surprised that he's here today. And if I'm being honest, I'm not entirely disappointed to see him. The man is fine.

Running into him the other day—finally confirming that the strange, nagging feeling was right, that it *was* him on the sidewalk—was the most incredible, most excruciating thing I've ever felt. The man who touched my heart so completely in just one night is so close and still completely out of reach.

I'd rehearsed what I'd say to him, if I ever saw him again.

Some ridiculous, foolishly hopeful part of me had spun out an entire fantasy. Words I'd say if I ever stood in front of him again. Words that might somehow convince him to give us a shot. To show him I'm not like most women my age. That life's carved a few extra layers into me. Seasoned me differently.

That I see him—*really* see him. Not the money. Not the headlines. Not the empire he's built with sheer grit and charm. I see *him*. The man beneath it all. The one who hides his soul behind swagger and seduction. The one who tells the truth when it matters most, because the idea of being a fraud terrifies him. The man I haven't stopped thinking about. The one I haven't been able to shake since the moment he first looked at me like I wasn't just someone passing through—but someone worth remembering.

I'd planned to tell him I don't need flash. I don't need the extras. I don't need to be entertained. I just wanted to try and see what a life would be like with just him. And see where it could go.

But the moment I found out about Marlow—that she was *his daughter*—everything changed.

Every hopeful idea. Every foolish plan died right there in Marlow's office.

Because I take my job seriously.

Because I respect her too much.

Suddenly, cheers erupt from the field, pulling me out of my thoughts. A fresh round of applause ripples through the crowd as another match kicks off—players mixing in with the kids, everyone grinning ear to ear.

Justice Trager, the current team captain—grizzled, grinning, and beloved—is out there too. He'll be retiring soon, but today, he's moving like a man ten years younger. He taps the ball upfield with easy control, passing it between two kids before flipping it back to one of the younger players.

The pace picks up—quick passes, shouts of encouragement—when one tiny player with pigtails and a determined gleam in her eye darts forward. In a blink, she slides the ball right between the legs of one of the players.

The kids on the sidelines lose their minds.

"*WHOAAAH NUTMEG!*" They shout in unison, little voices cracking with excitement, laughter and cheers bouncing across the field.

I smile, soaking it all in—actually feeling proud of this moment—just as something shifts in the air.

I turn and see Grant walking my way, wearing that smile—*that* damn smile—that instantly makes my panties feel like they've vanished into thin air.

I smile back.

And then—*lights out.*

Blinding impact. A *thud* that echoes in my skull. Pain blooms sharp and hot across the side of my head.

Someone gasps. Someone else yells.

I've been hit.

A soccer ball—launched hard and fast—straight to my damn head.

Great.

One minute I'm looking fly and unbothered—cool as hell in my dressed-down chic, looking unphased and unmoved by Grant *make me scream* Mills.

The next?

My head is nearly taken off by an eight-year-old with a lead foot.

What the hell are they feeding these kids?

Now, all the cameras are on me, and the guys from the team are rushing over, yelling, "Coach Saunders!"

A new nickname they've got everyone calling me.

And then Grant is there. On me before I can even blink.

My head is pounding so hard that if I close my eyes for more than a few seconds, I'm definitely going to pass out.

Fantastic. Really nailing that whole professional, put-together team therapist vibe right now.

Grant is at my side, steady hands on my shoulders, his voice low and firm.

"Eslin. You're hurt. Just sit still a second. You could have a concussion."

"I'm fine," I grit out, already trying to push myself up.

My head is spinning, the pounding in my skull only getting worse, but damned if I'm going to fall apart in front of him. In front of everyone.

"Eslin—"

"I said I'm fine!"

He doesn't move, doesn't let up. One brow arches in that maddening way that says he's not buying a word of it.

I manage to get to my feet, swaying slightly. My pride is screaming at me to walk it off. But as soon as I take a step, the ground tilts, my knees buckle, and I fall straight into Grant's arms.

Strong, steady, warm. His grip tightens around me instinctively. Our eyes lock, heat flashing between us, thick and sharp.

Too much. Way too much.

He's so pretty.

"Let me call an ambulance. Take you to the ER, get you checked out or something?" he says, voice edged with concern.

I hear Marlow from behind. "That's a good idea, Daddy."

Fuck me. *Daddy.*

She had to call him *Daddy* right now?

While he's cradling me in his arms, holding me like he's felt every bit of this ache I've been carrying? Like he's missed me just as much as I've missed him?

Perfect timing. Just perfect.

I jerk back, breath catching hard. I force my legs to move, steadying myself. "I've got it," I say quickly, breathless.

Without another word or glance, I turn and head for my car.

My driver, Sammy, is already there, back door open. I nearly sprint the last few steps and drop into the seat.

The door shuts, and finally, I catch sight of myself in the rearview mirror.

Grass tangled in my hair. My cute, chic ponytail of locs now crooked, lop-sided, with little sticks poking out at random angles.

Perfect. Just perfect.

Sammy glances back. "Are you okay?"

He clearly missed all the commotion and the goal that was scored on my head! I groan, leaning my head against the seat. "I'm fine. Just... get me home. Fast."

And if I'm lucky, maybe by the time we get there, I'll have figured out how the hell to erase the feel of Grant's arms from my skin.

CHAPTER FOURTEEN: HOUSE CALLS & HEARTBREAK

Grant

I hated letting her walk away so quickly.

Every instinct in me was screaming to stop her. To scoop her up, carry her somewhere private, and not let her out of my sight until I *knew* she was okay.

But making a scene would've been a mistake. It would've drawn Marlow's attention in an instant and the last thing I need is my daughter asking why I was so damn concerned. Why I felt this overwhelming need to look after Eslin so closely.

So I let her go.

But I'm still not convinced she's okay.

The stubborn tilt of her chin told me she'd brush it off, play it cool and pretend nothing was wrong. But the way she stumbled into me—how light she felt in my arms—told a very different story.

And even though I have no right to do this, even though I'm already crossing a line I swore I wouldn't, I pull out my phone and make the call.

Since Eslin left the school today, my mind's been in a loop—running through every worst-case scenario on repeat. I haven't been able to stop myself from wanting to go to her door, just to check on her. To see her. To know she's okay.

But without a reason, without an excuse, I'd look exactly like what she asked me not to be—intrusive. Crossing lines. Making this harder than it already is.

And this right here—what I'm feeling now—is exactly why I've spent so long keeping my distance from anything close to love. Why I've stayed guarded. Why I've been terrified to let anyone get this close again.

Because when I fall, I fall hard. I love hard. And I know myself—I'd worry too much, hold too tight.

I've already lost one love of my life.

Losing another? That would destroy me.

So I do what I know I can, from a professional position, even if that feels like a stretch. I call the team doctor.

"Dr. Shoup. Grant Mills here. We've got a team member who needs your assistance."

Dr. Shoup freezes for a beat when I tell him where he's going. My building. And we both know none of the players live here.

But to his credit, he doesn't ask. Still, I give him the rundown—what happened at the event, how Eslin hit her head, how she insisted she was fine but I wanted to be certain. And because he hasn't formally met Eslin yet, I add, "I'll meet you at her place. I don't want you to startle her."

I sound composed. Calm. Like I've got it all under control.

But the truth is, I'm nowhere close.

***

An hour later, I'm standing outside Eslin's apartment, Dr. Shoup a few steps behind me.

I check my watch, anxiety tightening in my chest.

Please don't be asleep. Please don't have a concussion and be doing the one thing doctors always warn against.

I draw in a breath, then knock.

Also, please have some decent clothes on because...a man can only take so much.

When she opens the door, there's already a frown waiting for me, like she knew exactly who it was before she even checked.

But what there isn't much of...is clothing.

She's standing there in a pair of those little boy shorts—the kind I used to absolutely *hate* seeing my daughter wear—and a simple tank top.

Only difference is...I like Eslin in those shorts.

I like her in them, a lot.

"What are you doing here?" She asks.

I hold out her phone. "You dropped this at the school."

She gasps, snatching the phone from my hand. "Oh my goodness, thank you! I emailed Marlow to see if anyone had seen it, and when she wrote back and said no, I thought I'd lost it for good!"

I'd grabbed it the second I saw it slip from her pocket. Tried to tell her. But she was so focused on getting away, on escaping the embarrassment, she didn't notice I was standing there holding it.

Her gaze flicks from the phone to the man standing beside me.

"This is Dr. Shoup," I say, keeping my tone even. "He's going to check you for a concussion."

Her mouth opens, ready to argue, but I cut her off.

"Once I know you'll be okay, I'll leave you alone."

And for both our sakes, I pray I can actually follow through on that promise.

After a beat, she steps aside and lets us in.

Her apartment is ten floors below mine, smaller, cozier—but still well-kept and inviting. The walls are painted a soft cream, with warm accents with throws, plants, framed prints. Nothing out of place.

It suits her.

I knew it would.

The low hum of the TV filters through the room—Scandal reruns—and I can't help but smile, picturing her squealing at the screen every time Olivia and Fitz steal a moment.

I feel closer to her somehow, just standing in this space. Like I've been given a glimpse into a part of her world I'd never dared to imagine.

But who am I kidding? I've imagined all of this.

I toured the space before she moved in, before she added her touches—before her scent lingered in the air, before the soft throw blankets and stacks of books made it hers. I made sure everything was perfect.

Moving to a new city, alone, as a single woman was hard enough. I didn't want her to worry about a damn thing when it came to finding a place to live or comfortable furniture. So I handled it. Quietly.

And for the two months she's lived here, I've imagined her in every inch of this space.

I've pictured her dancing in this living room, nothing but skin and that smile. I've imagined her curled up on the balcony with a book on lazy Saturday mornings, her bohemian locs spilling over her shoulders.

And I've spent more minutes—hell, *hours*—than I care to admit in the shower, imagining what it would be like to have my way with her right here, bent over that dining table that seats eight. I'd feast on her like I was eating for twelve.

Pull it together, Mills.

You can't afford to get hard while the pretty lady is being assessed for a head injury.

Dr. Shoup sets his bag down and walks her through the standard checks. Pupils. Eye movement. Balance. Reflexes. A few simple questions to test her memory and orientation.

Through it all, she sits up straight, answering calmly, even though I can see the weariness pulling at her.

Finally, he straightens, tucks his equipment away. "You're fine. No signs of a concussion. Just stay rested. No screens for a bit. No strenuous activity. Listen to your body."

She thanks him quietly.

I walk him to the door, shaking his hand. "Thanks for coming so quickly."

"Anything for Coach Saunders," he says, referring to the new miracle worker all the guys on the team have been bragging about. And I like that they call her that. Made her one of them.

Then, the doctor leaves.

When I turn back, Eslin is curled on the sofa, her legs tucked beneath her.

Without thinking, I reach for the throw blanket draped over the back of the couch and gently lay it across her feet.

She watches me for a long beat, eyes soft but sharp. Then she says, "You're terrified of losing the people you love, aren't you?"

I love that she can do that. Hate that she can do that. See me so easily.

She seems to realize the weight of her words and quickly corrects, "I mean, not that you...love me or anything. I wasn't saying that—"

I shake my head, a wry smile tugging at my mouth. "I know what you mean, Eslin. And yes, you're correct. When Marlow was sixteen, she made me sign a contract that I wouldn't make her leave the house in bubble wrap the way I always watched over her. I was...a little intense about her safety after her mother died."

Her expression softens. "How did she pass? If you don't mind me asking."

"Cervical cancer."

"I'm sorry."

"Thank you." I pause, letting out a breath. "I got the greatest gift of all from the short time we had together."

I reach down and tuck the blanket under Eslin's feet a little tighter.

"And I don't like how easily you see me when I've been able to hide from so many people for more than twenty years."

She smiles faintly, her eyes warm. "Occupational hazard."

There's a pause, her gaze steady. "But you don't have to worry about me. You don't have to fuss over me. I'm not going anywhere."

Hope stirs, unbidden, sharp. "Do you promise?"

She stills, looking straight into my eyes. "Promise what?"

"That you aren't going anywhere." My heart kicks up, the words tumbling out before I can stop them. "I don't know... maybe, once this all settles, once Marlow is fully acclimated to—"

I stop myself.

Because I already know how this sounds.

Like I'm asking her to wait.

Like I'm offering her a maybe when she deserves so much more than that.

"If you're asking me what I think you're asking me...to wait for you until you fully turn over your portion of the team to Marlow," her voice softens, but her tone is resolute, " the answer is no."

She sits up a bit and holds my gaze and my heart breaks just a little more before she even begins to speak. "Grant, I've spent my entire life waiting—to be picked, to be taken in, to be wanted. And what I've learned is, I have to choose me, *first*. Or I'll keep breaking my own heart...waiting.

"So while I admire what you're doing for your daughter and for yourself...I won't wait for you while I am reminded, every day, I wasn't worth choosing *first*."

I swallow hard, the air in the room suddenly too thick, too sharp to pull in. She's right.

She deserves more than that.

More than *me,* asking her to wait around like some afterthought. Like her worth could be measured in patience and sacrifice.

I'm ashamed. Ashamed those words even left my mouth. She deserves a man who'd choose her first. Every time. Without hesitation. Without conditions.

I force a breath, my voice rough with the truth of it. "You're right. And I'm sorry. Goodnight, Eslin."

I turn, each step toward the door sinking in deeper, the finality of it pressing heavier with every movement. A cold, suffocating fog settling over me.

Before I reach the door, I hear the rustle of the blanket and the soft shuffle of her getting up from the couch. Then she calls out to me—her voice quiet, but steady.

"Grant?"

I stop, turning back so fast I nearly stumble. Just hearing her say my name feels like a gut punch wrapped in silk.

"Yeah?"

"It was a great night, though, right?"

I smile, but it's tight, stretched over the ache in my chest. "Best fucking night of my life."

She starts playing with the hem of those shorts I love. "Shame it didn't end with a kiss, huh?"

"Biggest *regret* of my life."

She steps closer, slowly closing the space between us. My pulse kicks up like it's trying to outrun my good intentions.

"So," she whispers, just inches away now, tilting her head to meet my eyes. "Maybe we say goodbye. This time the right way."

"Couldn't agree more," I murmur.

Her hand rises, delicate fingers tracing the edge of my jaw, her palm warm against my skin. The second she touches me, the restraint I've been clinging to snaps like a frayed wire.

I dive in, capturing her mouth with mine—hungry, desperate, but reverent. I need to memorize her taste because I'm painfully aware our first kiss is also our last.

Her lips part softly beneath mine. She melts into me, hands fisting in my shirt, and for a moment, the world disappears. It's not rushed. It's not frantic. It's heartbreak disguised as passion—two people clinging to something they're both terrified to lose, even as they know they have to let it go.

For a second, I let my hands roam, unable to stop myself. I slide them down, cupping her behind, pulling her even closer. She's exquisite. Petite, soft and full in all the places that make my self-control fracture.

She moans into my mouth, and my erection pulses painfully as her fingers slide into my hair, tugging just enough to make me lose what little sanity I've been clinging to.

I kiss her like I'm trying to hold time still. Like if I kiss her deep enough, long enough, maybe we don't have to let go. Maybe goodbye doesn't have to come.

But it does.

When I finally pull back, breathless and desperate to stay, even as I know I can't, my forehead rests against hers.

"I've dreamed about doing that since you first sat next to me at that bar, Eslin Saunders."

Her breath hitches, voice low and shaky. "How dare you fucking kiss me like that, Mister? I was just starting to convince myself I could get over you."

She tries to make it sound light, but I can hear the weight under her words. Feel it in the way her hands won't let go just yet.

"I know the feeling," I whisper back.

Neither of us says anything else. We don't have to. The goodbye is already thick between us, sitting heavy in the air like a storm we're both too heartbroken to outrun.

"I left the team doctor's number there on the coffee table."

She looks back and smiles. "I didn't even notice. Thank you."

I bend down and press a kiss to her forehead. "I'm glad you're ok, Coach Saunders."

And then, with one last look, I turn and walk away—feeling like I've just left a piece of my soul behind.

And damn...can she kiss.

CHAPTER FIFTEEN: SALT & PEPPER WITH A SIDE OF SEXY LIPS

Eslin

I need to talk to someone.

Someone who won't judge me. Someone who can handle the full, chaotic download of my hot mess life without blinking. Max is buried in back-to-back meetings, and unfortunately, it's too early to head to the local bar and drown my feelings in tequila. So I head to the next best place.

"Happy Holidays! Welcome to *HollyDates!*"

I roll my eyes as I walk in. "It's not even Halloween yet, Holly."

She gasps like I've kicked a Christmas tree. "Excuse me, ma'am. It's post–Labor Day, which means we're *technically* on the on-ramp to the holiday season. So when I say 'Happy damn Holidays,' you say—what?"

"Geez, fine! Jolly police!"

"Good. Now let's try it again." She grins like she's deadly serious. "Happy Holidays!"

"Happy Holidays, Holly," I mutter, walking toward the coffee bar while rolling my eyes.

One thing I've come to learn about Holly since moving here is that she isn't just festive—she's full-blown, tinsel-drenched, peppermint-breathing *obsessed* with Christmas.

Sure, her coffee bar claims to celebrate *every* holiday—there's a plastic shamrock on the register for St. Patrick's Day and a tiny flag for the Fourth of July—but don't be fooled. The framed photos on the wall tell the truth. This woman lives for December.

People who've been regulars at Holly's for years rave about her December traditions. Every Friday night, she hosts *Home Alone* movie marathons, complete with free popcorn, themed lattes, and even a blow-up Michael Jordan-on-a-train display in the window—exactly like the one from the film. She throws *Love, Actually* dress-up parties too, where guests show up as their favorite characters and everyone cries together during the cue-card scene.

One person even told me about her *This Christmas* karaoke night, where Holly sets up a stage and insists everyone belt out Chris Brown's version of "This Christmas," along with the other holiday songs from the movie.

I won't be joining in for that one. I can't sing to save my life.

"Now that we've gotten our greetings and salutations out of the way, can we please get to the reason I'm here? I have *updates*," I say, my eyes wide.

Her eyes light up. "This sounds juicy and right up my alley for this time of morning!"

"Make it a double, girl," I say, dropping onto the barstool.

She hands me my drink in a glass mug, the steam curling between us, and leans over the counter with wide eyes and that trademark Holly intensity.

"Okay, girl. What's up?"

"He's here," I blurt out.

She drops her voice like we're about to discuss nuclear codes. "Who's here?"

"Grant. Remember the man from Vegas I told you about?"

Her eyes go wide. "The hot older guy you spent the magical night with? Salt and pepper hair with a side of sexy lips, voice like melted sin?"

"Damn, girl, you've got a good memory."

"You don't forget details like *that*," she says with a knowing nod. "But wait—you're saying it was *him* you saw on the sidewalk that day?"

I nod furiously. "Yes!"

"And he lives in the same building as you?"

I take a long sip of my latte, then let out a dramatic whine. "Uh huh!"

She claps her hands together. "So naturally, he's dicked you down all over his and your apartment and, what—you feel guilty for shitting where you sleep?"

Poetic, this one. "No," I say, blinking. "He's my boss's *father*."

Her jaw drops. "Oh, no!"

"Oh, yes."

"So, did you find out *before* or *after* you had sex?"

"We *did not* have sex!" I whisper-yell. "Did you hear what I just said? He's my boss's *father!* I can't cross that line!"

"Why not?" she shrugs. "I have. Not as hard as you might think."

"Not with my job. Not with the people I work with on a daily basis. That would be an HR nightmare wrapped in emotional devastation. And besides—he told his daughter he wouldn't date younger women. Remember? He's even *more* off-limits now."

Holly winces. "Wow, Eslin. That is... *excruciating.*" She reaches behind the counter and pulls out a piece of candy. "Want a candy cane?"

"No, I don't want a candy cane! I need a new job!"

"But I thought you loved your job?"

"I *do!* But I am having a hard time facing his daughter every day knowing I've had some very dirty, very *unprofessional* thoughts about her daddy!"

"And I'm guessing we can't tell her?" Holly asks, now sipping her own drink.

"Right. If anyone should tell her, it should be *him.* And something tells me if he wanted to do that, he would have already. So—"

"You're star-crossed lovers," she says with a dreamy sigh. "Destined to be together but the timing is all wrong."

"Are you always so freaking *jolly,* Holly?"

She shrugs with pride. "I've been told my sunny disposition could end wars."

"Girl, your fat ass and beautiful smile will do that all on their own," I say, before howling with laughter.

"That *has* been known to do some damage as well," she cackles, snapping her fingers in the air with one hand planted on her hip like she's about to bless the room.

Then she gets serious, leaning in again. "So. What are you going to do?"

"Keep avoiding him like I have been," I mutter, "and pray to God his daughter doesn't pick up on a damn thing."

She makes me another drink to go, sets it on the counter, and hands it to me like she's passing down sacred wisdom. "I think you should consider being honest. Life's too short to be without the one you love."

"It's not love," I snap. "It's forced proximity."

She holds her drink out with a warm grin. "Happy Holidays."

I roll my eyes and head for the door, still unsure how I'm actually going to avoid this walking complication in designer suits, but grateful I had someone to unload it all on.

"Happy Holidays, Holly."

CHAPTER SIXTEEN: PRIVATE JETS & PRESS JUNKETS

Declan

Georgia. Atlanta. *Hot-lanta*. Though I've been told more than once that nobody actually calls it that.

It's my first time in the southern part of the United States, and so far, my only real opinion is that it's just as damn hot as everywhere else I've been. Vegas included.

Only difference here is Atlanta can't make up its mind. One minute it's hot and sunny, the next it's hot and pouring rain. Like the air here is indecisive.

"Declan Agassi," a reporter calls out as I stand in front of the press backdrop. "How does it feel to be wearing a US jersey for the Atlanta Strikers?"

What a dumb question. How is it supposed to feel? The same as when I wore my Italian one.

It's my first official day as an Atlanta Striker—on loan—and apparently, someone thought it'd be a great idea to set up a press conference.

Without telling me. Or my manager.

Surprise.

Welcome to American football—*the other football*. Where the media circus seems to be part of the training regimen.

"It feels great," I say smoothly, pausing to glance at her name tag for the extra charm. "Rachel. Everyone has been really welcoming to me so far."

The only thing I hate more than press conferences... are *American* press conferences. I have to slow my words, round out my R's, soften my accent—just to make sure they understand me.

Every answer feels like I'm translating myself in real time. Like I have to be less *me* so they can follow along.

Another hand goes up. "The team captain says you're just the talent that could turn things around for the team. How does that make you feel?"

Like, no shit.

"It makes me believe I'm joining a team that sees my value, Shaun."

The cameras flash. The mics pick up every word. And I stay steady.

People always compliment me on how well I handle the media. How polished I sound. How pleasant I am to interview. But none of that comes naturally. It's discipline. Practiced control.

I've trained myself to never say the wrong thing. To behave like the cameras are always watching. To make friends with the people holding the pens, running the headlines.

Because I have to.

If I don't succeed—if I don't stay successful—my family won't survive. My father and my nonna back in Argentina, they're counting on me.

That's why the bonus the Strikers offered sweetened the deal and made my decision a little easier. I came here for my family.

How I managed to get married—and then somehow misplace a wife—in the short time I've been here in Cowboy Country? Well, that's an entirely different story.

I've done what I could with the limited American resources I have. Looked everywhere. But the night we got married, we slipped into the hotel through the back entrance—where cameras are conveniently turned off to keep paparazzi away. And when she left the next morning, my lovely mystery wife swiped my favorite hoodie, pulled it over her head, and walked out without ever showing her face to the cameras.

All I know is this: her name was *Maddy Mills.* Her best friend was getting married the next day.

That's it.

Though, the only Maddy Mills I managed to find died years ago.

My wife gave me a fake name. Great start to our happily ever after, honey.

After the press conference wraps, I head down to the field to meet the team at practice. But not before making one important stop—upstairs, at the executive offices.

I knock on the door three times. He told me he's rarely in the office, but made it a point to be here today for my arrival.

"Declan! Come in!" Xavier Darcy opens the door and pulls me into a hug like we've known each other for years. "How was your trip?" He asks, sounding like a real American cowboy with his accent.

"It was good, Mr. Darcy. Really good, thank you."

"Please," he waves his hand, "call me Xavier. Only my wife calls me Mr. Darcy."

Weird.

"Noted. Thanks, Xavier. The jet was a bit...over the top."

He laughs it off, as if flying across the world in private luxury is standard. "It's the team jet. It actually belonged to someone else. We bought it at a discount for the team."

I can't help but laugh. *A discount plane.* That's billionaire logic for you. "Well, it was a nice surprise. And an even better flight over."

Xavier didn't want me here at first. At twenty-five, he figured I was already too old for a transfer like this—at least by European standards. He thought I wouldn't be able to keep up with the pace of the league, wouldn't bring enough long-term value to justify the move.

In his mind, I was already closer to my peak than my potential.

But I surprised him.

I studied the team. Broke down the gaps, the weaknesses, the places I knew I could strengthen. I put together a full assessment and sent it to him and Coach Jones before negotiations even got serious.

And, of course, I sealed the deal with a little extra charm. Told them my father was a longtime fan of Coach Jones. And that my *nonna* thinks Xavier is "really cute."

That part was 100% true.

"I trust you got all of your fun out of your system that week in Vegas?" Xavier says, eyeing me with a half-smirk like he already knows too much.

Before my official move to Atlanta, Xavier let me borrow his personal jet and take a few of my buddies to Vegas. A full week in a penthouse. And one night I guess you could technically call a honeymoon—courtesy of Xavier Darcy.

Honestly? He's one of the kindest people I've met in this sport. Ruthless when it matters, but fair. Generous.

"Yes, sir. Plus, I'm sure Atlanta has plenty more for me to get into," I say lightly, forcing the words to sound casual.

Hoping I don't sound like a man starved.

A man who hasn't slept or eaten right since that night. Since *her*. Since the woman who flipped my life upside down and disappeared before I could even learn her real name.

Xavier laughs, but there's not much humor behind it. More like a warning wrapped in a smile.

"Well, not too much fun, okay? One of the reasons you ended up being good for this team was because you came with no baggage."

What about a—how do you Americans say it?—ball and chain?

"Right!" I nearly yell. "No baggage here, sir."

I stretch out my hand, giving him the most polished version of my 'model professional' grin. "Well, I've got to get to the field to meet the team. Coach will have my ass if I'm late on my first day."

"We can't have that." He claps me on the back. "Let's get drinks soon."

I nod. "You bet," I say, and I actually mean it. Because right now a forty-something-year-old man is about the closest thing I have to a friend here.

As I head toward the field to meet my new team, there's this strange pull sitting low in my chest.

But it isn't heavy.

It isn't uncomfortable.

If anything...it feels familiar. Strangely familiar.

Maybe it's the way the leaves are starting to shift on the trees, how the air smells like the start of something new but steady, like the seasons themselves are gearing up for another chance.

Even driving here earlier, walking these halls now—it all hums with this quiet rhythm I recognize but can't quite place.

It feels peaceful.

Settled.

Almost like home.

CHAPTER SEVENTEEN: COCOA & CONCUSSIONS

Marlow

Three months into my new role and, not to brag—but actually, yes, to brag—I am *killing* it.

At least in the areas that have been *graciously* designated for me to oversee: marketing and partnerships, team morale, and team relations—basically all the people-facing, vibe-controlling work that neither Will nor Xavier can be bothered to handle. They like their boardrooms, their spreadsheets, their closed-door negotiations. Meanwhile, I'm out here keeping this machine from falling apart at the seams. And frankly, I'm doing a damn good job of it.

The things men can accomplish when they put a woman in charge.

The team's on a roll, finally finding some rhythm after a rocky start. Playoff talks are getting louder. And according to the latest sales data, ticket sales are up.

The marketing side is also thriving. Tatum Black came on board as our new marketing director, and I've got to say, she's already moving like she owns the place. She's brought in a wave of new sponsorships, opened doors with diverse businesses, and is finding creative ways to connect us with a wider, younger, and much more engaged fanbase. The woman's a machine.

And, just like Xavier predicted, bringing in a team therapist was one of the smartest moves we made. Eslin Saunders has been nothing short of magic for this team. She's cracked through layers even *we* thought were impenetrable.

Take Matteo Santos, for example. Our quiet little wallflower who used to avoid cameras like they carried some contagious disease. The same guy who wouldn't say more than five words to anyone unless absolutely necessary? Now he's dating someone and letting us post a picture of him buying her flowers on social media. Is he leading team huddles yet? No. Is he suddenly the face of the franchise? Definitely not. But he's getting there. His confidence on the field has skyrocketed, and his steady growth has had this ripple effect throughout the locker room. Guys who once rolled their eyes at Coach Saunders, "the therapist," are now actively booking sessions with her.

Eslin and I have grown closer. Comfortable. There's a rhythm to our friendship I've never had with anyone I've worked with before. I've done the internships, held various roles in operations, sat through the awkward lunches and forced team-building. "Work friends" were always temporary. Shallow. Most of them only saw my last name, the money behind it, and made lazy jokes about how they'd never lift a finger if they were me or had my daddy's money. And almost instantly, a wall would go up.

I've never been the kind of girl who needed to be taken care of. Not by my dad. Not by some guy with a bank account and a blank check. Money has always been irrelevant to me. I wanted my own career, my own wins, my own damn name. I never wanted a shortcut. And it always rubbed me the wrong way when people acted like I should apologize for not using the silver spoon I was supposedly handed.

But Eslin is different.

She doesn't flinch at my last name, doesn't give a damn about who my father is. She doesn't chase my approval or play games. She's sharp, self-contained, and yeah—guarded. But not in a cold, detached way. In a way that tells you she's been through things, and survived them. She's the kind of woman who says little but sees everything. And somehow, she's become the one person in this whole place who feels real. Real enough that I actually want to know her. Not just work with her.

I spot Shaun Kennedy as I'm crossing the parking lot, headed toward the field.

"On the way to the owner's box?" he calls out, falling into step beside me.

It's our first home game this month and I'm buzzing with excitement. I haven't had a chance to meet our newest player yet, but everyone's been raving about how he's been dominating in practice. I can't wait to see him in action.

"Yes, actually," I say, smiling. "You headed to the press area?"

He grins, just a little shy, like he's trying not to look too eager. "Yes, but...I was also hoping to catch you. If I'm being honest."

"Oh, really?"

"Yes, actually. I was following up about that drink."

I lift a brow. "Coffee?"

"Whatever I can get."

"Some might say you're angling for an inside scoop, Mr. Kennedy."

He winks. "Only one way to find out."

"I don't have to find out anything at all. I'm not the one doing the inquiring, here. That's you."

He raises his hands in mock surrender. "Fine. I promise—no ulterior motives. I just want to get to know you a little better."

He steps a little closer, and I feel the warmth creep up my neck. That dangerous, flirty energy swirling between us.

"If I can take you on a coffee date, that would be a great start," he says, voice lower. "I'm not a coffee drinker so I'll take some hot cocoa."

I grin. "Maybe some banana nut cupcakes?"

"If that's what you'd like."

He grins and I can't help but notice his deep dimples and the way his blue eyes sparkle. "But please know, Ms. Marlow Mills," he continues flirtatiously, "I fully intend to charm you enough to graduate to dinner."

"Cute," I reply, playfully tugging on his press badge lanyard.

"Beautiful," he fires back without missing a beat.

I frown. "Huh?"

"Oh—I thought we were trading compliments. I figured I'm a little more than *cute*, but I'll take it."

I shake my head, laughing. "Whatever."

"So, is that a yes to coffee?"

"It's a maybe, Shaun. Things are complicated for me right now, so you're just gonna have to take a *maybe*."

His grin stretches wide, like he's just won something. "I'll take it."

Then he heads off toward the press area, leaving me standing there—pulse racing faster than it should, head spinning just enough to irritate me.

Get it together, Marlow.

I turn toward the entrance, where security is waiting to escort me inside, and I see Eslin waiting for me so we can head out together. I wave, getting ready to greet her, but before I take more than two steps, the loudspeaker booms across the stadium.

"Gooooooal!"

I glance up, just in time to catch the instant replay on the jumbotron. One of our players scores a clean, beautiful shot. The crowd erupts in cheers.

Then the camera pans to his face.

And my entire world tilts sideways.

The name flashes across the bottom of the screen like a cruel joke: Declan Agassi.

It's him.

The man I married in Vegas.

My husband.

The noise of the crowd dulls instantly, like someone pressed mute on the world. My breath catches in my chest, my vision narrowing.

I feel my heart pounding somewhere in my ears, the field blurring as everything starts to spin. The sun feels hotter. The air feels thinner.

"—Marlow? Hey! Are you okay?" I hear a voice, faint and distant.

Another voice—maybe Shaun's? They're closer now, worried. "Marlow? Marlow!"

I want to answer. I try. But my lips won't move.

The ground seems to rise up beneath me, and then—*everything goes back.*

CHAPTER EIGHTEEN: VEGAS & VOWS

Declan

That one night in Las Vegas.

Sasha, Anton and I...how do you say it? Our friendship goes way back. We're more like brothers. Since we were little boys kicking balls through the streets of Naples, eating gelato too fast, and getting yelled at by the neighbors for playing too close to the windows. Our fathers were best friends. Not just the kind who said hello at the café. They helped each other fix their roofs and fought like brothers over football teams and politics.

When my mother left us and disappeared out of nowhere, Sasha and Anton were the ones who stayed close. We didn't talk about it. I didn't want to. I just remember sitting on the curb while they passed me sunflower seeds and said nothing. Their fathers took mine to the bar and tried to drown the silence in cheap whiskey.

Without warning, one night, not long after my mother left, my father woke me and my older brother and told us to pack some clothes for a few nights away. Within hours, we were on a plane to Argentina. At first, we were told we were going to visit my nonna in a little town I barely remembered from childhood. But it wasn't long before me and Niko realized we would be there for much longer.

For good.

I was only eleven years old.

I was confused. Angry. Heartbroken, even. Italy was my home—my friends, my school, my life. And suddenly, it was gone.

But a week later, Sasha and Anton's families showed up at my nonna's door. They'd come to live in Argentina, too.

I still didn't understand why we left so suddenly, or why they had to come too—but none of us asked questions. We were kids. All that mattered was we were together. The world still felt upside down, but at least it wasn't lonely.

They're my brothers—my people. The ones I'd go to war for without thinking twice. I'd follow them into any battle, no matter how reckless their decisions might be. Even when their choices are questionable. Even when they drag me into the madness with them. Especially on nights like tonight.

"She's pretty," Sasha says, nodding toward the photo clipped to the paperwork we're all pretending to read.

"I noticed."

Like the overgrown children they are, my friends have been lingering around, restless, waiting for this so-called game to end. The dare that started as a joke, a laugh, something wild to mark the end of my "freedom," is somehow becoming the best night of my life.

We're watching from the edge of the room as Maddy finishes signing the last of the paperwork. Her brow furrows slightly as she reads each line, like she actually wants to understand what she's agreeing to. Most people don't bother to read anything these days. Especially not after that much tequila. But she's sharp. Sharp enough to scare me a little and that makes me like her more.

Sasha nudges me, whispering like an idiot. "She signs with her left hand. You know what they say about lefties..."

"Please don't finish that sentence," I mutter, but I don't look away from her.

Because while they're making jokes and acting like we're still in grade school, I'm standing here watching a woman I just met become something I didn't see coming.

Mine.

The producers made us sign all kinds of papers. One to confirm we were of sound mind—whatever that means. One to confirm we weren't being forced. And another that said we had to stay married for a full year if we wanted the prize. One million dollars.

I kept thinking about what my dad and Nonna could do with that kind of money. Fix the roof. Pay off the debts. Get Nonna her surgeries and my dad the quiet piece of land he's always wanted. Hell, maybe I'd even start something real for myself outside of football.

I knew this marriage contract was crazy. Everything leading up to this moment was crazy. But crazy has a name tonight. And apparently, her name is Maddy Mills.

Anton leans in, slinging an arm around my shoulder. "You don't seem too excited. If you don't want her—"

I grab his hand mid-sentence and squeeze. Hard enough to make him wince.

He yelps. "Okay! All yours. Got it."

Sasha chuckles. "Should we give you the talk about the boys and the bees?"

I roll my eyes. "It's *birds* and the bees, you idiot. And no—don't worry. I know exactly what I'm going to do to her. And exactly how I'll do it."

It's not that I'm not excited. I am. I just know better than to let it show. I'm focused—on the way she bites her lip while reading the paperwork like it's a contract to sell her soul. On how she rises onto her tiptoes to reach certain spots on the page, too short for the counter, and too stubborn to ask for help. She's a vision—messy, delicate, determined. And if I blink too long, this whole thing might be over before I can do a damn thing about it.

But if by some miracle—some wild, reckless twist of fate—I can convince her to give me the night, then I'll take the year. Gladly. That's the deal. That's the contract. But the contract doesn't say anything about how far I'll go to earn it.

I'll make her laugh. Make her sigh. Make her beg. I'll learn her body like a language and make her forget every man who ever thought they had a chance. By morning, she won't just be my wife on paper. She'll be mine—completely. No prenup, no fine print. Just...mine.

She turns and walks toward us, and the air leaves my lungs like she's knocked it out with nothing but a look. She left a lot out of the description of herself. Long, dark hair tumbling over her shoulders. Big brown eyes that could undo a man. Olive skin kissed by just enough sun.

My American girl.

My *Americana*.

"Are... are you ready? For this?" she asks, trying to sound confident, but her voice betrays her—just slightly.

I take her hand in mine, steady, firm. "You don't have to be nervous. There are no guns, Americana. You can say no and walk away anytime."

"I thought her name was Maddy or something?" Sasha mutters with a smirk.

"Shut up, Sasha," I snap, not taking my eyes off her.

"I'm not nervous," Maddy says, chin lifting. But her hand's trembling in mine. She still hasn't let go. "I'm just—"

"Nervous," I tease, giving her a smirk before bringing her hand to my mouth to kiss.

She bites back a grin. "Fine. A little nervous."

The producer who's been trailing us all evening walks over with a clipboard and a grin. "Are these your witnesses?"

"We didn't see anything," Sasha growls.

I sigh, rolling my eyes. "He means are you willing to stand up as witnesses to this shit show," I clarify, giving the producer a look that says *sorry for my idiot friends.*

Maddy leans in, close enough I catch a hint of tequila and something sweeter on her breath. But not before she lets out the softest, tiniest burp that makes me snort with laughter.

"Your friends are weird," she whispers, her voice husky and amused.

"So I've been told," I mutter back, and we follow the producer toward the chapel—if you can call it that.

My so-called groomsmen trail behind.

"I can't believe I'm doing this! This is so not like me," Maddy slurs, half-laughing, half-panicking as she stumbles slightly on the carpet.

"Oh yeah?" I glance at her, tightening my grip around her waist. I like that she's leaning on me. "What's making you do it? This...marrying me?"

She giggles. "Maybe it's the tequila. Maybe it's you."

She says it like she's guessing at the answer, like she might regret it later—or maybe never at all.

She doesn't really know. But I don't care.

Not when she's standing here.

Not when I've got her hand in mine.

Not when the next words out of my mouth might be *I do.*

I'm about to be Mr. Maddy Mills.

Or however you say it in America.

***

The ceremony lasted all of five minutes. Barely enough time to process what we'd just done. There were vows, ring-like things, and the kind of forced smile from the officiant that screamed *get out while you still have time.*

By the time the ink dried and the cheap bouquet hit the floor, Sasha and Anton were already halfway to the blackjack tables, high-fiving.

Finally alone, me and Maddy lock eyes for a second—long enough to feel everything we're both thinking but don't say out loud.

No hesitation. No words.

We just move—fast—through the hallway, toward the private suite Xavier let me borrow for the week. Her heels dangle from her fingers, and the hem of her black dress catches the light with every step like it's teasing me.

I think I know what comes next.

And she doesn't know it yet, but I've already made up my mind: If this is going to be a one-night story, I'm going to make it the kind that lives under her skin forever.

The kind that doesn't fade.

The kind neither of us will ever forget.

The elevator climbs, floor by floor, each ding hitting me harder than the last. My heart thuds heavier, like it's bracing for something it knows is coming but can't name.

Yes, it can. Maddy.

I glance down at her—the black dress hugging her curves like it was designed just for tonight. Just for this. It's technically our wedding night, even if tequila and a dare are the only witnesses that matter.

The tension between us isn't uncomfortable. It's electric. Like the split second before lightning strikes.

"A nickel for your thoughts, Americana?" I ask, breaking the silence.

We're passing the eighth floor. Twenty-two more to go.

She smiles. "It's a penny, actually. A penny for your thoughts is how the saying goes."

I reach into my pocket, pull a penny out, and with a grin, do the old magician's trick—pretending to pluck it from behind her ear.

"For your thoughts," I say, holding it out like it's worth everything. Like her thoughts are.

"I don't do things like this," she repeats.

"You've said that already," I reply, grinning. "Three times now, if we're keeping track."

She lets out a breath and looks up at me, eyes wide and honest. "Is it crazy that this doesn't feel crazy at all?"

Relief breaks through my chest. "I was hoping it wasn't just me."

She shakes her head. "It's not just you."

Floor thirteen.

"Maybe it's because we don't know each other," I offer.

"Maybe," she echoes, but there's a note of uncertainty in her voice, like even she's not sure that's the reason but she entertains it anyway.

I brush a strand of hair behind her ear. "So, tell me something about you."

She laughs, light and tipsy. "Why do people always ask that? Nobody walks around with an elevator pitch ready for that kind of question."

I furrow my brow. "Elevator pitch?"

She nods, a little unsteady. "Yeah. Your question's too vague." She squints at me. "What's your name again?"

I chuckle. "For the fourth time, Declan."

"Right." She draws it out like she's tasting it. "That's a pretty name. Declan. Sexy."

I shake my head, trying not to grin. "You were saying?"

"Hiccup! Right. 'Tell me something about you' is too broad." She blinks, trying to steady herself. "Ask me something specif... pacif..."

She's teetering. Drunk, but still cute as hell.

"Okay," I say. "Something specific. Tell me something no one else knows about you."

Her eyes widen like I've just dared her. "Oooooh. Good one."

The elevator dings—our floor.

"Go on," I urge as we step off. "I won't tell if you've murdered anyone before."

She bursts out laughing. Loud. Carefree. "No murders. I promise."

We round the corner, stop in front of the suite. It's sleek and massive—bigger than the house I grew up in with my dad and Nonna in Argentina.

She's still holding my hand, still in that ridiculously sexy black dress that tonight has transformed into a wedding gown. Her fingers are warm. Her grip hasn't loosened once.

And as I reach for the keycard, it hits me—I don't care how we got here. I just care that we are here. Now.

I swipe the key and open the door.

She pauses at the threshold, turning to me. "Aren't you supposed to carry me?"

I grin, stepping toward her. "What was I thinking?" I scoop her into my arms. "Come here, wife."

When I scoop her into my arms, her shoes hit the floor with a soft thud—but all I hear is the wild pounding in my chest. We lock eyes, and for a split second, everything slows. Craziest fucking thing in the world, and yet... it doesn't feel crazy at all.

"Kiss me, Americana. Kiss your husband."

And she does. Sweet and sinful, all in the same breath. Her lips taste like tequila and trouble. Like something I never knew I'd crave until just now.

CHAPTER NINETEEN: PERMISSION & PROMISES

Declan

That one night in Las Vegas.

I kick the door shut behind us and carry her across the threshold like we didn't just meet hours ago. Like this is something we've been building toward for years. Her fingers tangle in my hair, tugging, gripping, as she pants against my mouth and frantically licks and sucks my bottom lip like she's starving for me.

"This is really beautiful," she whispers, breath hitching.

I smirk into her mouth. "How can you tell? You haven't even opened your eyes yet."

She lets out a low laugh. "Maybe I wasn't talking about the suite."

That wrecks me. Whatever little patience I had left is gone.

"Does this fucking thing come off?" I growl, tugging at the lacy fabric hugging her curves.

She gasps. "Careful! This is a Crash Steele original!"

I toss her onto the bed, her laugh echoing like a dare. "We'll get you another one."

And with one swift pull, the delicate dress tears right down the middle. She gasps again—but this time, it's not about the dress.

It's about what comes next.

"*You're* beautiful," I choke out.

"Because I'm naked?"

"Because you're mine."

I lean down and kiss her, soft, slow, tender. Like I've waited my whole life to find this exact moment, with this exact woman. Maybe I have.

She reaches for the hem of my black t-shirt. *Only the best wedding attire for my American girl.* And I break the kiss just long enough to lift my arms and let her peel it over my head.

Her breath catches. "Wow."

I tilt my head, smirking. "What?"

"Tattoos," she murmurs, like she's just stumbled across a treasure map.

"You've never seen a man with so many tattoos?"

She shakes her head, her fingers moving, drawn to the ink on my chest like it's telling a story only she's meant to read. Her hands trace the designs sprawled across my chest, the words in Italian wrapped around ribs and muscle, inked memories of places, people, promises. Some of them broken. Some of them keeping me standing.

She doesn't ask what they mean. Not yet. She just touches, explores, and I let her. Because in this moment, she isn't just learning my body. She's reading parts of me most people never bother to ask about.

I hold my breath, silently begging her not to stop.

She doesn't.

Instead, she rises slowly, her lips brushing across my stomach. My fingers slide into her hair on instinct, anchoring me to the moment as her tongue trails a line down my torso.

She's undoing my jeans with practiced fingers, and suddenly I'm thrown—off balance, out of control. Like a kid fumbling his first time, desperate to make sure this isn't too much. That she's still with me.

The zipper eases down and I catch her wrist, stilling her. I tilt her chin so her eyes meet mine.

"Is this okay?" My voice is rough. "Do you want this?"

She smiles and it melts every goddamn nerve in my body. "I love how attentive you are. Making sure I'm okay," she murmurs, brushing her lips over my hip as she tugs at my pants.

I'm left in nothing but boxer briefs, my erection straining against the fabric. My beautiful bride eyes me like she's about to wreck me.

Then—Jesus—she runs her teeth over my dick through the cotton. Playful. Dangerous.

"For someone who wouldn't normally do things like this, you are excellent at teasing me. Toying with me."

She does it again, this time using her hand to squeeze where her teeth just were.

My hand fists tighter in her hair. "Fuck, Americana…Would you believe I imagined you…like this…the second I heard your voice?"

She looks up, eyes heavy, lips parted. "You hadn't even seen me."

"Some things," I say, brushing her cheek with my thumb, "you just feel."

She drags my briefs down and when I spring free, she gasps.

"Wow."

I grin. "You say that a lot."

She leans in, and my beautiful wife licks the moisture at the tip and my entire body shudders. I groan, jaw tight, and catch her before she can take more of me.

It kills me to stop her.

Every instinct is screaming to let go, to give in, to hand her everything—deep and raw, until there's not a breath, not a thought, not a single inch of space between the tip of my dick and the back of her throat.

But not yet.

I want more than her mouth.

I want *everything*.

I grip her arms and lift her effortlessly off the bed, her gasp caught between us as I crush my mouth to hers. I kiss her like a man who's been denied too long—hungry, hard, relentless.

"Not yet," I breathe against her lips, voice frayed with need. "Not like this."

I guide her toward the bathroom, every step strung tight with tension. The air between us crackles. Thick with want, heavy with everything unsaid. Her fingers curl around mine like she's fully aware and consenting of the fact that I'm about to ruin her—in the best possible way.

"Puts a whole new spin on the term *bridal shower*, huh?" she teases, her voice soft, eyes lit like embers.

I chuckle, already reaching for the faucet. Hot water spills from the tap, steam rising fast and curling around us like smoke. "I'm a filthy man," I mutter, casting her a wicked grin. "Allow me to clean up before I do very, very dirty things to you, wife."

She steps closer, skin bare and glowing in the warm light. "I've never showered with a man before," she says, almost like a confession. But there's nothing shy in her tone.

I open the glass door and hold it for her, letting my eyes drink in every inch. "Then I'm honored to be your first."

She walks past me, brushing against my chest. And just like that, we disappear into the steam—two strangers, one night, and no turning back.

She's taking me in now, fully, observing the ink that marks my body. "You don't like it? My art?"

She shakes her head. "I've just never seen anything like it." She kisses my chest, the highest she can reach. "It's beautiful."

The water spills over her shoulders, soaking her hair, tracing every curve like it's worshipping her the way I am.

She stands still, eyes locked on mine, lips parted, chest rising and falling with anticipation. I grab the showerhead and tilt it down, letting the stream drench her slowly—neck, collarbone, the swell of her breasts. She gasps as the water hits, her skin going slick, glowing.

"Look at you, Americana" I murmur, dragging the nozzle lower, watching the spray coat her stomach, her thighs. "You're pure fucking art when you're wet."

I set the showerhead back and drop to my knees without a word.

Her breath catches.

I press a kiss to her hipbone, then another, lower. My hands slide behind her thighs, anchoring her to me.

"Now," I glance up, voice gravelly. "Back to the question I asked you earlier."

She opens her mouth to speak, but I don't give her the chance. My tongue finds her clit—right where she's aching. Her head tips back, a sharp gasp tearing from her throat as her hands clutch my shoulders.

"Tell me," I growl between her thighs, between strokes and licks, slow, reverent laps of her wetness. "Something about you nobody else knows."

She moans, her fingers tangling in my hair, hips trembling under my grip. I drag my tongue over her again and she gasps like I've stolen every thought from her mind.

Her head drops back against the tile, breath shallow, voice barely a whisper. "I used to write myself love letters, pretending they were from someone who loved me."

I hum against her, savoring the confession, the way she's unraveling just for me.

"Say more," I murmur, mouth pressed to her heat. "And don't leave anything out."

"Fuck!" she cries, her voice echoing off the tile, hands clutching at my shoulders like she's not sure if she wants to pull me closer or push me away.

"We'll get to that, too," I smirk against her, then tighten my grip around the curve of her ass, pulling her closer as I dive back in—tongue relentless, merciless, devoted.

She's panting now, teetering on the edge.

"Tell me about the first time you got fucked," I rasp, voice rough and thick with lust, my mouth brushing over her with every word. "I want to hear it from your lips while mine are on you."

"My twenty-first—shit!" she gasps, hips jerking against my mouth.

"Mmm hmm," I hum into her, the vibration making her cry out again.

She claws at my shoulders, breath ragged. "How do you expect me to talk when your tongue is on me like this?"

"Shhh." I press a kiss to her inner thigh, then return to her center, slower now, drawing it out. "Just take your time, Americana. We've got all night."

And fuck, even that doesn't feel long enough.

"Again, with the nickname! Can you call me something else?" she says, breath catching, fingers tightening in my hair.

She's stalling.

I don't have time for stalling.

I don't have time for conversation.

I need to make her come.

I need to fuck my wife.

"Continue," I command, my grip tightening on her thighs as I drag her back to my mouth—where she belongs.

She swallows hard, her voice trembling as she tries to speak through the storm I'm building inside her. "My twenty-first birthday," she says. "It was rushed and painful and nothing spec—" Her voice shatters as I thrust my tongue deep inside her, fucking her with it, slow and unforgiving.

I explore every inch, tasting her, claiming her, pulling every truth from her body one gasp at a time.

"Declan," she breathes, my name breaking apart on her tongue like it's too much.

I glance up at her, locking eyes, holding her there with my hands, with my mouth, with everything I have.

She chokes out the rest. "It... it was nothing special."

I pause just long enough to meet her eyes. "Good. Then let me show you what *special* feels like."

She's unraveling in my mouth, slick and trembling, her body arching into me like it belongs here—exactly here. And it does. I kiss her thighs, her hips, her belly as I rise to my feet, her legs still shaking.

She looks up at me, eyes glazed and lips parted, her chest heaving. I reach out and brush the wet strands of hair from her face, then kiss her slow. Deep. She moans into my mouth, her taste still lingering on my tongue as I press her back against the tile.

"Are you ready for a *real* first time, Americana?"

She doesn't answer—just nods, eyes wide, lips swollen. That's all the permission I need.

"First," I say, as I lift her effortlessly, her legs wrapping around my waist. "You'll experience your first time being fucked in the shower," I whisper, as I slide into her in one smooth, aching thrust.

Her head falls back, a sharp cry echoing off the walls as I start to move—measured, deep strokes that pull a different kind of confession from her now. Pleasure. Raw and pure.

"Hold on tight, my beautiful *Americana*," I growl, gripping her hips from beneath to anchor us both. "It's been a while, and this first?" I growl as I thrust into her. Hard. "It's for me. It's mine too."

The water pours down over us, steam curling around our bodies as we move in rhythm. Her hands clutch at my back, nails digging in. I drive into her against the wall, savoring every second, every pulse of her body around me.

"You feel that?" I breathe into her neck, my lips brushing her damp skin as I drive deeper, her body trembling beneath mine.

"Feel my body chasing your pleasure while being filled up at the same time? Feel me delivering my entire soul to you through each thrust?"

She whimpers, clinging to me like she never wants to let go.

"That's what special feels like," I growl, voice rough, rhythm never faltering. "This... this is how a husband fucks his wife."

And then I give her everything—every inch, every ounce, every broken piece of me stitched back together in the heat of her body, the sound of her moans, the way she says my name like it's hers.

She comes with a cry, her body tightening around me, and I follow with a low groan, burying myself as deep as I can go.

But we're not done.

I carry my beautiful wife out of the shower, both of us soaked, dripping, breathless. She clings to me as I lay her on the bed, water still glistening on her skin like diamonds.

This time, I slow everything down.

No more urgency.

No more chasing release.

It's just her. Us.

She hiccups again—soft, shy, involuntary—and it's so fucking cute I almost lose my balance. My focus.

I think I love her already.

"You deserve everything special, Maddy Mills," I murmur, brushing a kiss to her shoulder.

Her face shifts for a split second—like my words hit a place she wasn't ready to open. But she hides it quickly. Pretends I didn't see it.

"Somehow I don't feel like I deserve this," she whispers, voice barely audible.

I don't let the words linger. I bend down and kiss them straight from her lips—slow and deep—taking her breath, her doubts.

"Don't talk about my wife that way, beautiful *Americana*," I say against her mouth.

She doesn't argue. Not really. Because even though she fights the nickname, I can feel her softening to it. Getting used to the way it sounds coming from my lips.

I kiss every inch of her like I'm writing her name in devotion with my mouth. She exhales, fingers tracing my jaw, eyes locked on mine as I slide back into her, slow and deep, fitting us together like a secret finally spoken out loud.

This isn't just sex.

This is a vow.

Claimed in sweat and moans and bare skin pressed together like truth.

"Never leave me," I choke out, and I don't give a damn that it sounds desperate.

Her eyes go wide. "What?"

I thrust into her—deeper this time, dragging a whimper from her throat as I push past the edge of what I can tell she's used to, where comfort meets stretch and surrender.

"You're mine," I whisper, then take her mouth again, kissing her like I own it.

She breaks my hold, breathing hard, and I pout—then punish her with another deep thrust that steals the air right out of her lungs.

"Ah! Shit!"

"Your lips are mine, too," I growl. "Give those back." I trace my tongue across her mouth. Possessive.

"So possessive, he is," she teases, her voice shaky but defiant.

"So talkative, she is," I fire back, smirking. "Maybe I should've let you stuff this dick in your mouth like you wanted."

She sticks out her tongue, mocking me, tempting me. And that's it. That settles it.

I fucking love my wife.

"I've got an exceptionally deep throat," she confesses, eyes dark, daring.

"And an incredibly tight pussy," I groan, thrusting again, loving the way she clenches around me like she's trying to keep me forever.

I love this.

The ease. The fire. The way we move like we've been doing this for years and will continue throughout eternity.

Who is this American girl?

And how the hell did she become my everything so fast?

We move like our bodies were made to sync like this. Her breath catches against my neck, fingers scraping down my back, our rhythm deepening with every roll of my hips.

"Promise me," I breathe, dipping my head to suck her nipple into my mouth, teasing it with my tongue until she gasps.

She brings one leg up around my waist, and I grab it, holding it there, burying myself even deeper inside her.

"What am I promising again?" she pants, teasing me with that damn edge that drives me wild.

"Never leave, *Americana*."

But she still doesn't answer.

Her silence flips a switch in me.

I slide out, flip her onto her stomach in one fluid motion, then thrust back into her from behind. Her back arches, her long dark hair spilling like silk across her shoulders.

"Shit!" she screams, voice cracking under the force of it.

"Funny," I growl, slapping her ass, the sound sharp, satisfying. "You've got no problem screaming everything *but* what I'm demanding of you, wife."

I reach for her hair, gather it in one fist, like I'm about to tie it up—but I don't. I wrap it tight around my hand, yank her head back gently but firmly, and fuck her harder, deeper.

I'm no longer making love to her.

Now, I'm fucking her with purpose, with ownership, with the full weight of the promise she still hasn't made.

Finally—the words.

I hear them, broken and breathless, as I grab the headboard, knuckles white, using it for leverage while I drive into her with no mercy. Hard. Deep. Unrelenting.

Breaking her in.

Breaking *us* wide open.

"I promise," she whimpers, voice trembling like her legs, like her will.

I lean down, bite her shoulder, then soothe it with my tongue—marking her and marveling at her all in one breath.

"Again, *Americana*," I growl against her skin. "Say it again."

"I promise...I won't go," she gasps, every word laced with desperation, surrender, truth.

"You'll stay?"

She's screaming now—louder with every thrust. From the stretch. From the burn. From the way I'm demanding more than just her body. I'm fucking the vow out of her, thrust by thrust.

Pleasure and pain crashing into each other as I wreck her with everything I am. And she gives it to me. All of it. Her body, her word, her fucking soul.

Mine.

CHAPTER TWENTY: FUGGITIVA & FLIGHT RISKS

Declan

The morning after that one night in Vegas.

The first thing I notice is the silence.

The second is the smell.

It hits me like a slap—sharp, sour, offensive. I crack one eye open and glance toward the window, light filtering in through heavy hotel curtains. Then I glance down.

Barf.

All over my lap.

"*Che schifo...*" I mutter in Italian, grimacing as I slowly shift upright. It's dried. Cold. And everywhere.

"Maddy!" I yell. Where the fuck is my wife?

No answer.

I reach for my phone on the nightstand, careful not to move too much and smear whatever this is my wife left behind. It's 11:03 a.m.

Not surprised I slept like the dead after the night we had. After what we did.

Hell, I barely remember crashing into bed. Just remember her body, her laugh, the way she agreed *this doesn't feel crazy at all.*

My wife.

I grin like an idiot for half a second.

Then frown.

Because the room is... quiet. Too quiet. Empty.

I glance to the bathroom—door open, lights off.

The floor is clean.

Her clothes are gone and, by the looks of it, my little *fuggitiva* took my sweater.

My wife is gone.

I look down at my lap again.

And all she left behind... is vomit.

"Fucking hell."

Happily ever after? More like happily never even got her number.

Chapter Twenty-One
PART TWO
Eslin

L et's get everyone caught up, shall we?

I'm currently living in the aftermath of a full-blown emotional natural disaster—epicenter: Las Vegas. Casualties: my grip on reality and everyone's relationship status.

My boss? Secretly married.

Our future team captain, Luca? Also secretly married.

And me? Secretly falling for a man I absolutely, definitively, *cannot* have—yet somehow find myself in dangerously close proximity to on a regular basis.

And the best part? No one knows about any of it.

Except me, of course.

I've officially become the keeper of everyone's secrets. A human vault of messy, high-stakes drama. And suddenly, what used to be a dream job is starting to feel more like a liability with benefits.

Meanwhile, my job as a therapist makes it a little easier to keep quiet about my feelings for Grant, too.

I'm trained to listen more than I speak. To hold space, not fill it. To stay neutral, no matter what storm is brewing under the surface. So I keep my face calm, my voice steady, and my feelings buried under layers of professionalism and practiced restraint.

It's ironic, really—helping everyone else make sense of their emotional chaos while quietly drowning in my own.

What I would give to drown in that man's bath water.

It makes no sense that Grant and I *can't* be friends. No matter how much we try to avoid each other—or how strategically unavailable I make myself to dodge any accidental run-ins—we somehow keep ending up in the same places. Circling the same conversations. Avoiding each other is becoming impossible.

And honestly, running into each other was even more inevitable. Especially since I'm Marlow's friend now. Sure, technically her employee too, but above all, *her* friend. Which means crossing paths with Grant was likely going to be part of the equation.

So instead of pretending he doesn't exist, or constantly looking for exits and rehearsing neutral smiles, I make a choice.

I decide to be Grant Mills' friend. *Just* his friend.

Because it makes sense.

Because I'm a professional.

Because I can handle it.

And maybe because I could really use a few good friends right now, too. Especially as the leaves turn and the holidays approach. I don't like being alone.

And since I respect Marlow too much to let this completely inappropriate, entirely inconvenient attraction to her father ruin the bond we're building, I make the only choice that feels halfway sane.

I decide to take them both. Marlow and Grant.

Just. Friends.

Nothing more. No mixed signals. No lingering looks. Just boundaries, maturity, and deep, controlled breathing when Grant Mills walks into a room.

I've got this.

Chapter Twenty-Two
CHAPTER TWENTY ONE: LIFE LINES & WHITE LIES
Grant

Present day

It's the first home match since the new player arrived, and for once, all three of us—me, Xavier, and Will—are in the same place at the same time like over-invested uncles. Normally, we'd split duties or tune in remotely, but ever since Marlow joined the front office, we've all been hovering closer. Protective. Proud. Quietly making sure she doesn't drown in the deep end.

She's good at what she does, but she's still new. Still figuring out how to hold her own in a world that demands twice as much from women and still gives them half the credit. And even though she'd probably smack me for saying this out loud, she somehow feels like all of our responsibility.

"Another drink?" Will asks, holding up the decanter like we're still twenty-five and immune to consequences.

"No," I say, shaking my head. "My doctor says I need to cut back."

"Guess the old man is finally changing his ways," Xavier chimes in.

I roll my eyes but don't bother correcting him. I've been seeing Dr. Shoup—getting my labs checked, cutting back on the bad habits, making sure this body doesn't betray me anytime soon. Not because I'm planning to run a marathon or reinvent myself. I just want to stick around. Be sharp. Be *present*.

For my daughter.

And maybe...for someone else, too.

Because I haven't actually given up hope. Not on her. Not on us.

"This old man will still kick your ass," I shoot back.

The room erupts—Will's drink nearly sloshes out of his glass, and Xavier's laughing so hard he's wheezing. We all know Xavier grew up on the mean streets of New Orleans and he'd have me face-down in a second. But the mental image of me trying is apparently comedy gold.

We're watching the game from Xavier's office because he's been so invested in Declan Agassi. I'll give it to him though, the kid was a solid move for the team. Strong foot, fast instincts. Exactly what we needed.

All the usual banter's flying—rookie stats, jersey sales, someone's hot take on midfield rotations—when I feel the buzz in my jacket pocket.

Everything stops when I see the text message flash across my screen.

Dr. Shoup: *Marlow collapsed. You need to come to her office now.*

The blood drains from my face.

Collapsed?

I'm already on my feet, heart thudding like war drums in my chest. Will notices instantly, his brow furrowing. "What happened?" he asks.

"I—I don't know. Marlow. She...Dr. Shoup says she collapsed."

My voice is hollow. Distant. But my feet are moving.

Will and Xavier don't ask any more questions. They just follow behind me as we rush down the hall.

They know what's likely going through my mind. The panic. Because I've been here before. Not this exact moment, not this stadium, but this feeling.

The fear. The helplessness. The disbelief that someone who was just laughing a moment ago could suddenly be not okay.

It's too familiar.

It happened once before. Years ago. The morning Maddy collapsed. The morning everything in me cracked open. The morning I found out I was losing my wife.

And now the memory claws its way back, sharp and vicious, like it never left. Like it's been hiding just beneath the surface, waiting for a moment like this to break me all over again.

My chest beats fast. My legs move faster.

"I'm sure she's fine," Xavier says, softly. But I can't breathe.

I need to see her. Need to know she's breathing, talking, upright—anything. God, Marlow. Please be okay.

When I get to Marlow's office, my heart nearly launches out of my chest.

Marlow's there—on the sofa in her office, surrounded by a few staff members. She's upright. Breathing. Talking.

She's okay.

"Munchkin," I blurt out before I can stop myself.

"Oh God," Marlow groans when she sees me. "I told them *not* to call you."

"You should know better than that," Will says with a shrug, like it's obvious. And it is. This staff knows damn well to think twice before keeping anything from me—especially when it involves *her*.

Xavier glances down at his phone, then starts casually inching toward the exit. "Well, looks like everything is under control," he announces, already halfway out the door. "I need to take this call from my wife."

"Thanks, X," I say, giving him a nod.

I drop to one knee beside Marlow on the sofa, heart racing even though she's upright and talking. "What happened, honey? Are you okay? Did someone hurt you?"

"A ball to the head, perhaps?" Will throws in, grinning, not missing a single beat.

He's still giving me a hard time after I stupidly told him about Eslin taking a soccer ball to the face during one of our community outreach events at Biddy Mason—and how I kissed her goodbye later that night.

Will hasn't let up, mostly because he genuinely believes I might've stumbled into something real. Something worth holding onto. I keep brushing him off, telling him he only thinks that way because he's deep in the fog of newlywed bliss—head over heels and drunk on domestic peace. But every time Eslin's name comes up and Will's nearby, he just gives me *that* look. The one that says he sees right through the excuses. The one that tells me I'm not fooling anyone.

He keeps pushing, insisting I should give Marlow the truth. That I should give her the *chance* to accept what's between Eslin and me. But he doesn't know my Low. He didn't see the flicker of disappointment in her eyes every time I entertained one of those too-young, too-eager women I used to date. He didn't catch the quiet, almost imperceptible relief on her face when she realized I'd stepped back from "the woman in Vegas"—for *her*. That I'd chosen her.

Marlow gives Dr. Shoup a pointed look. "See what you've done? Now he's all frantic."

Dr. Shoup just shrugs. "I have a daughter. I'd want to know, too."

Panic hasn't let go yet. "Want to know what?" I snap, stepping in fast, eyes locked on Marlow.

She sighs, brushing a strand of hair from her face like I'm being dramatic. "Nothing, Daddy. I'm fine."

"She got a little lightheaded," Dr. Shoup adds, rising to his feet with a grunt. "She should get some fluids. Lay down. Rest."

I step aside so he can gather his things, but I'm not taking my eyes off her.

"You sure she's okay, Doc?" I ask, my voice lower now.

"Perfectly fine," he says, and then he actually laughs, patting me on the back. "Women seem to keep collapsing or hitting their heads around you, eh, Mr. Mills?"

Fuck.

Nobody else knows I asked him to check on Eslin.

Nobody knows I was there. Kissing her.

I run a hand down my face, trying to keep it together. *Please, God. Don't let my daughter be the annoying, inquisitive thing she usually is?*

I force a smile. "I seem to have that effect on women."

"Wait. What does he mean, Daddy?" Marlow asks, narrowing her eyes at both of us.

This is when Will conveniently decides to announce his exit. "This seems like everything is going just great," he says on the way out.

Thanks, a lot.

I open my mouth, scrambling for a lifeline. "The day I took a soccer ball to the head," a voice cuts in, smooth and calm.

Eslin.

I didn't even see her standing there. I've been so locked in on Marlow—so consumed by her presence and the chaos swirling around it—that I missed just about everyone else in the room. But thank God *she's* here.

"Your father was nice enough to have Dr. Shoup check on me after the Nutmeg debacle," Eslin says smoothly, stepping forward with the kind of calm confidence that makes it seem like she's been waiting for the perfect moment to step in and save me.

Marlow nods slowly, her eyes flicking between us, suspicion softening just enough to let the tension break. That seems to settle it. For now.

I glance at Eslin. She's already looking at me.

I mouth, *Thank you.*

She doesn't respond. Just gives me that small, knowing curve of her lips that somehow manages to both rescue me and gut me at the same time.

I owe her.

And I'd do anything to repay that debt. Anything she'd let me.

Marlow gets up and stretches, heading toward the private bathroom off the corner of her office. "You people are so dramatic, I swear," she throws over her shoulder like nothing just happened.

I turn to Eslin the second the door shuts behind her. My voice low. "What happened? How did she collapse?"

She steps closer, and the moment her hand touches my chest—soft, steady, grounding—I forget how to breathe. The contact is small, but it feels like someone just lit a match in my bloodstream.

"I think you should talk to her," she says, professionally. *Too* professional. "I was heading out to the field when it happened. She passed out right in front of me. Scared the hell out of me, too. But she's okay. The doctor was clear."

I nod, even though my brain is working overtime just to stay focused on her words. I shouldn't. I really shouldn't. But I do it anyway—I cover her hand with mine, press my palm to hers, locking us together for just one second longer than appropriate.

"Don't get me wrong, Eslin," I murmur, my voice rough with everything I shouldn't be feeling, "I'm so fucking grateful you were here for her."

Here for me, I don't say.

I let out a tortured, humorless laugh. "But I hate that you're here right now."

Her brows pull together, lips parting slightly. "Why?"

I swallow hard. "Because—"

The door to Marlow's bathroom swings open and in an instant, the moment shatters.

Our hands fall apart like they were never joined. We both take a step back, sharp and instinctive, like kids caught in the middle of something we knew we shouldn't be doing.

Because that's exactly what it was.

And still, when she's near me, every line I've drawn starts to blur.

Every rule I've sworn to follow starts to feel like a dare.

Eslin doesn't look at me. Not right away. She shifts, adjusting the tank top strap on her shoulder like the weight of what just passed between us needs somewhere to go.

And all I can do is try to remember how to act normal. How to breathe through the insanity she stirs in me with just a touch. A look. A breath too close to mine.

I shift, turning my attention back to Marlow. "You sure you good, Munch?"

"I won't be if you keep calling me that!" she fires back, full of attitude and color again.

"Okay, okay," I say, hands in the air like I'm under arrest.

"Well, since you're fine, Low, I'll leave you for the rest of the game. See you tomorrow?"

"Thanks, Daddy. See you tomorrow. I'm making eggplant parmesan."

She perks up like a cartoon light bulb just flicked on above her head. "Oooh! *Eslin!* You should come! You keep saying you don't have any family or friends here. Join us for dinner!"

"Oh no!" Eslin and I blurt it out in unison, and if we weren't so caught off guard, we'd probably laugh at how perfectly synchronized it is.

"It's just that I'm sure Eslin has other plans," I add quickly, trying to steer the ship away from the iceberg.

Marlow tilts her head. "Daddy. I *just* said she doesn't have any family or friends here."

She turns to Eslin, who now looks like she's the one about to faint, or kill me. "Eslin. Come to dinner! It'll be fun. It's the beginning of October and Daddy and I like to put out all the Fall and Halloween decor."

Eslin tries her hardest to protest. "Marlow, I—"

"Come on! I *know* you're not doing anything!" Marlow insists.

I know I taught my kid to be persistent, but this is a little aggressive. Even if I am silently hoping she says yes.

Eslin glances at me, wide-eyed, looking for a parachute. I just shrug like an idiot. No way out of this one.

"Sure," she finally says. "Just a friendly dinner, right?" she asks, looking between me and Marlow.

"Just friends," I say, then correct myself. "A friendly dinner."

"Yay!" Marlow squeals. "Perfect!"

I smile, with my hands awkwardly in my pockets.

Perfect.

Friendly and perfect.

CHAPTER TWENTY TWO: GOD, THE UNIVERSE & BLACK BABY JESUS

Eslin

I should've known he'd come storming in.

It's the weekend. Prime territory for accidental run-ins and yet Marlow swore up and down her father never came to weekend matches, so I let my guard down.

I'm a stupid, stupid woman.

Because of course, God, the universe, and Black baby Jesus had other plans. Marlow collapses in the most dramatic way possible, and who shows up like a storm in pressed slacks and authority? Grant freaking Mills.

With his fine ass.

Looking like trouble dressed in country club perfection.

I'm not usually the girl who falls for the ones who look like they stepped off a yacht in the Bay, but *this man*? He wears a navy blue V-neck sweater layered over a crisp, checkered button-up like it's the uniform of a Greek god sent to ruin my common sense, my edges and esophagus.

"You are not gonna believe what happened," Marlow says, snapping me back to the present now that her father is safely out of earshot.

"Umm, you passed out and landed on hard concrete, Low. I just *might* believe you," I say.

Before she can respond, the office door swings open, and in blows a storm of kinky curls, curves, and pure energy.

"Girl! Someone said you were passed out on the curb outside! Are you okay?"

The woman practically glows with presence—big grey eyes, full lips, bold brows, and confidence that charges the air around her. She's the kind of woman people call "exotic" when they don't know what box to put her in. Long, kinky brown hair with honeyed highlights frames her face, and her skin's got that perfect sun-kissed glow that screams good genes and better lighting.

Her almond-shaped eyes flash with concern, but it's the curve-hugging jersey and the ridiculous ass underneath it that has me blinking twice.

Whoever she is, she's sexy and not forgettable.

Marlow waves her in like she's been waiting for her. "Eslin Saunders, I don't think you've met Tatum Black, our new marketing director."

Tatum spins toward me, her face lighting up. "Oh! Yes! Coach Saunders! I've been meaning to set up a meeting with you since I started!"

I blink, glancing between her and Marlow. "Oh really? Why?"

"Because! You're the miracle worker everyone's been raving about! I need to get your story out there—interviews, spotlights, all of it."

I wave her off. "Oh, that's not necessary. I'm not that special. Really not worth writing about."

"I'm fine, by the way," Marlow cuts in, her dry tone laced with exaggerated patience.

Tatum and I both turn to her and burst out laughing.

"Sorry! You were putting on makeup," Tatum says. "I figured that was a solid sign you were going to live."

Marlow rolls her eyes, but she's grinning. I look at her closely, wondering if she's going to pick up where she left off—before we had company. Because whatever she was about to say, it felt important.

Marlow gets up, crosses the room, and shuts her office door with a quiet *click*. When she sits back down on the sofa, her expression is all business, but the kind you gossip about over cocktails.

Tatum and I exchange a look. Something's coming.

I drop to the floor and cross my legs like it's story time in kindergarten, and Tatum follows suit. We look ridiculous. But, also ready for what's coming.

And judging by Marlow's face, this is going to be *juicy*.

"So... about that night in Vegas."

"Oh shit," I murmur, pressing my hands together under my chin and leaning in like she's about to recite scripture.

Marlow shoots me a look. Definitely not helping.

"Sorry," I whisper. Then louder, "Yes. I remember the night in Vegas."

I glance at Tatum, then back to Marlow. "Wait—does *she* know about that night? About the *husband*?"

Marlow shakes her head. "Nope. But I need input, and since you two are the closest thing I've got to a real friend circle right now, congratulations. You're now my stand-in bff's."

Tatum hops up, walks over to Marlow's little bar cart, and pours three glasses of whatever expensive amber magic she finds. She hands them out, then lifts her own with a grin.

"To stand-in BFFs," she says.

We clink. We sip.

And Marlow begins.

The Vegas story. The hot guy. The pods. The wedding. All of it.

And damn, it's even wilder the second time around.

I'm fanning myself like I'm the one who got married because it's sexier now, too.

"And you're seriously saying he's here?" Tatum half-yells, eyes wide with disbelief. "As in, *plays for the Strikers*?"

The coincidental run-ins and accidental marriages around this place must be studied. Like, by actual scientists. With charts. And lab coats. Because the level of romantic rendezvous happening here defies logic and basic human scheduling.

This all isn't just messy. It's practically a case study in what happens when you trap emotionally unstable adults in close quarters with too much sexual tension and not enough therapy.

It's basically an unscripted season of Grey's Anatomy.

"Yes! He's here!" Marlow groans, dragging her hands down her face. "And that's why I passed out today! The shock of it all!"

Tatum tilts her head, completely unsympathetic. "Babes. The *sex* of it all! I've seen the new midfielder. You're telling me you get to have guilt-free sex with *that* and you're upset? Help me understand the crisis here."

"The crisis," Marlow snaps, voice cracking just slightly, "is that this is the worst possible time for me to show up with a secret husband who just so happens to be our new player!"

"Yeah," Tatum nods. "The press would eat that up."

"Exactly!" Marlow hisses. "I've spent months rebuilding my name. People are finally starting to take me seriously. This will blow *everything*. My reputation, my credibility. My *dad* will lose his mind."

I raise a hand, stepping into the madness. "Okay, I hate to be the voice of reason here, but what exactly did you think was going to happen? You signed paperwork. There were *cameras*, right?"

"I used an alias," she says, defensive. "I figured if I found him first and got an annulment, it would all be handled before anything hit the media."

"Except now," Tatum cuts in, wagging her eyebrows, "your future ex-husband is here to *serve* you in more ways than one!"

That sends us spiraling into laughter again, Tatum's cackle setting the tone.

"Do not joke right now!" Marlow snaps, her tone frazzled. "What the hell am I supposed to do?"

I lean forward, a little more serious now. "That depends. Do you *actually* want to annul the marriage?"

She nods, fast and certain. "Yes! I have to focus. On the team, my reputation. *Everything else* but this man right now."

"Then go to him," I say. "Explain. Be honest. Tell him it was a drunken mistake in Vegas and that getting an annulment is best for both of you."

Her shoulders square like she's bracing for battle. She knocks back the last of her drink and slams the glass on the coffee table. "Fine. I'll do it. I'll go tell him I was intoxicated and not of sound mind when I married him—"

"And promised you wouldn't leave him?" I add, dryly.

"And licked the tip of his dick," Tatum throws in, completely deadpan.

"Okay!" Marlow screeches, throwing a cushion at her. "I get it! I made a *colossal* mistake and we have an entire *highlight reel* to prove it."

"At least you can blame it on Vegas," I offer.

"Right." She nods, pulling herself together.

She stands, slips on her shoes, checks her reflection in the mirror. Her shoulders roll back. Chin up. And then she's off. Marching out to ask her brand-new husband for a divorce.

CHAPTER TWENTY THREE: STRESS INK & SHORT CIRCUITS

Marlow

"I'm just going to get this over with and stick to my guns. Simple as that," I chant, over and over again.

Still, my hands are sweating as I walk the long hallway leading to the locker rooms. My heels click against the polished floors, echoing like warning bells in my ears. I'm doing this. I'm going to face him. The man I married.

The man I left without so much as a note.

The man whose kiss I can still feel like it's tattooed into my skin.

I round the corner, and there he is.

Declan Agassi.

He's in front of the press, smiling that lethal smile that's been haunting my dreams. He's charming the reporters, talking about the goal he just scored and how he's helping boost team morale. Like he belongs here.

I hang back in the shadows, keeping to the side as flashes go off and mics are thrust into his face. He says all the right things. He's magnetic. And mine.

No. Not mine.

Just technically. For now.

I'm about to turn around. Maybe I'll come back later. Or never.

But then the reporters disperse toward another teammate, and his eyes lock on mine like a heat-seeking missile. Like he felt me there before I had a chance to get away.

Everything in me jolts because I see *him* in an instant. Everything we began that night in Vegas.

"Maddy! How did you find me? What are you doing here?" he nearly yells. Then he runs toward me, across the room like no one else exists. His arms are around me before I can blink. "I thought I'd lost you for good."

I push him back, my palms flat against his chest, my heart pounding so hard I can hear it in my ears.

"What the fuck?" he says, stunned.

"Not here," I whisper. "Come with me."

I don't wait for him to respond. I grab his hand and drag him into the nearest supply closet, where balls and nets and adrenaline live.

The second the door closes, he's on me again. His lips crush mine and my entire body betrays me—melting into him, kissing him like I've missed him for years, not weeks. It's salacious. Addictive. Sexy.

It's heaven.

When we finally break apart, gasping, breathless, I feel the ground shift beneath my feet.

"Why the fuck did you leave me?" he growls. "Without so much as a fucking word or telephone number?"

He's beautiful. Angrier than I like seeing him, but still, god, *so* beautiful.

And then I notice them. "You got more tattoos?"

Before, they were mostly hidden, limited to just his chest and back. Now they've started creeping down his arms, curling around muscle and skin like temptation in black ink. And I'm trying really hard not to drool.

He shrugs, chest rising and falling with barely restrained tension. "I misplaced a wife."

I blink. "I don't see how the two correlate."

"I stress-ink."

"You what?"

"I get tattoos when I'm stressed. It's a thing. For me, anyway. And you left."

His hands grip my waist again. "As long as you're here, the need to ink goes away."

"Declan," I whisper.

"You remember my name now, I see."

He pulls me closer, and I feel every inch of him. His desire. His frustration. His determination to have me.

"I need to say this." I place my hands on his chest again, trying to push logic between us. "Las Vegas, what happened in Vegas, it was a mistake. We can't be married. I can't be your wife."

His face falls. "What the fuck are you talking about?" He lifts his left hand, points to a fresh tattoo on his ring finger. "We made vows."

My eyes widen. The date, June 12th, is permanently inked into his skin.

"Are you kidding me? Declan, it wasn't real. That night wasn't real. I have a real life and a real job and a real reputation that I've worked my ass off to build! *We* can't happen. Not right now."

He looks like I've hit him. But he stands tall. Proud. "Then when?"

"When, what?"

"You said not right now. So, I'm asking you when? When can we be together?"

I let out a sigh, saying the hard thing. "We need to have our lawyers speak. Figure out how to get this annulled."

He turns away and picks up a ball, throws it so hard it bounces off the wall with a loud bang. "Fucking hell, I will! You're my wife!"

I let out a sigh. Why am I suddenly emotional? "I'm some girl you married in Vegas! It happens all the time!" My voice cracks, a single tear falling. "Fucking Vegas, Declan!"

He stares at me. "It's Vegas? I don't know what that means. All I know is that Vegas is where my wife left me."

Of course he doesn't get it. No one's explained to him how Vegas and mistakes work.

"Covered in vomit, by the way!" He adds.

"Oh yeah. I'm really sorry about that. In my defense, I tried to wake you. You were dead to the world."

He steps closer again, and I swear, my body starts vibrating from the memory of him. I vividly remember what it felt like to have him under me. Over me. Inside me.

I can't do this.

"The prize money, Maddy."

I freeze when I become painfully aware that I also never told him my real name.

"What?"

"There's a million dollars on the line. If we stay married for a year."

"I remember," I say carefully, "but Declan, you're a professional athlete. Surely you don't need—"

"Don't pretend to know what I need."

"I'm sorry, I—"

"Just say you will? Say you'll stay married, even in secret, so we can get the money."

"I'm sorry. No. It's too risky. If the press finds out—"

"About your mistake, you mean?" he finishes, voice cold now.

He's hurt. But too proud to beg.

"Fine," he says through gritted teeth. "Can I have your phone number, at least? So I can put you in touch with my lawyers?"

I nod. He hands me his phone. I type in my number and email address, hit save.

"It's under Marlow. Marlow Mills."

He lets out a humorless laugh. "Fucking hell. I didn't even know your real name."

"I'm sorry, Declan. Really sorry."

"We're not done, Americana."

But I turn towards the door and don't look back.

I just walk away, shutting the door behind me, leaving him in the dark.

Now to go air-dry my panties. Because apparently, he has more tattoos, and *sweet hell*, I had no idea ink could short-circuit my entire nervous system the way it just did.

CHAPTER TWENTY FOUR: MOTHERS & MEMORIES

Declan

Americans and their relentless need to talk—about everything, all the time, for absolutely no reason. It's maddening. Pointless. A national obsession with feelings and over-explaining.

And yet, here I am.

Sitting in the over-decorated office of Dr. Saunders—Coach Saunders—because Coach Jones said if I didn't, I'd be benched. No therapy, no game time. That was the deal. And with cameras already catching me unraveling, the club's PR team apparently thinks a few deep breaths and a talk about my feelings will fix me.

Good luck.

It's been two weeks since I found out who Marlow really is and where she's been this whole time. And while I spent the better part of three months tearing through every lead, chasing the ghost of the woman who disappeared on me, convincing myself the way she left had to be some kind of drunken mistake, she was busy figuring out how to erase me from her life.

Because I wasn't the memory. I was the regret. The mistake.

"Declan," Coach Saunders begins, folding her hands in her lap like she's about to gently deliver a harsh blow. "I remember how excited the team was when we found out you were joining. You were bold, sharp, great with the press. A clean slate. No drama, no attitude. And unlike some of our other players, I was told you came with no baggage."

Her voice is calm, but there's an edge of curiosity beneath it. Not judgment, just confusion she's trying to wrap words around.

"No history of behavioral issues. No tension with the media. So help me understand..." she leans in slightly, eyes steady. "What's going on?"

I lean back in the chair, arms crossed, jaw tight. Every part of me wants to shut down, stay silent, ride this out until the hour's up. But something in her voice, measured, professional, not loaded with pity or judgment, cracks through the wall just enough.

So I speak.

"I was seven," I say, slowly. "My brother was twelve. Our mother left. No fight, no warning. Just... gone. One day she was tucking me in, and the next, nothing."

The words feel foreign coming out of my mouth. I've never said them out loud. Not like this.

Sasha and Anton never pushed. In all the years we've known each other, they gave me space, not questions. And my brother Niko, he shut down completely. After she left, he turned to stone. Unshakeable. Unreachable.

So talking about our mother became the thing we all silently agreed to avoid. It wasn't a rule, just a shared instinct. A wound we learned to walk around. History we preferred to leave buried.

But I've never been in this situation before. Never felt this off-balance.

So maybe it's time I try something different. Maybe it's time I talk.

"I'm sorry that happened to you," Coach Saunders says softly.

I nod, eyes down, fingers tugging at the hem of my shirt. Why the hell am I nervous?

"We were still trying to make sense of it. Her leaving. *How* she left. No goodbye."

I pause, jaw clenched against the memory.

"My father came into our rooms in the middle of the night, told us to pack. We moved to Argentina the next day. New language. New life. Same hole in my chest."

I pause, staring at a point on the floor, but I'm not seeing it. I'm back there—in that room, confused and scared, clutching a backpack and watching my brother try to be brave for both of us.

"My nonna helped raise us. My dad did what he could. He worked, he tried. But the message stuck: women leave. They love you, and then they leave."

I glance up. Her pen is still, her gaze frozen.

"I've kept women at arm's length my whole life. I don't trust easily. And then this night in Vegas happened."

I let out a dry laugh. It's sharp and humorless.

"I don't know why, but I trusted her. And she turned around and proved me right—and left me soaking in my own regret, and in her actual vomit, for good measure."

Coach Saunders chokes. "I'm sorry, who did what again?"

"Fucking Maddy. Marlow! My *wife!*" I snap, throwing my hands in the air.

Her eyes go wide, but she recovers quickly, smoothing her expression into something neutral.

"I see," she says, clearing her throat. "And Maddy is..."

"I married her in Las Vegas. She said she'd stay. Said she wasn't going to leave me like my mother did."

"She said those exact words?"

"Not word-for-word, but close enough," I mutter. "Now she's demanding a divorce and call me petty, doc, but I don't want to let her have it."

Coach raises an eyebrow. "So what, you're stalling?"

I shrug, damn near proud of it. "Let's just say I've made it *complicated*. I 'accidentally' gave my lawyer the wrong spelling of her name on the first draft."

She shakes her head, but I don't miss the faint flicker of a smile tugging at her lips.

"Well," I add, "*she* gave *me* the wrong name when we got married. So technically, that one's on her."

"Sure. Let's go with that," she says, clearly humoring me. "What else have you done to drag out what should be a pretty quick procedure?"

"I sent her all the divorce papers in Italian and made her have them translated."

She lets out a sigh, fighting a laugh. "Why, Declan?"

"Because I'm not done with her, doc," I say, matter-of-fact. "And if she wants out, she's gonna have to *work* for it."

She starts scribbling something in her notes, probably labeling me emotionally unstable, unhinged, or whatever the clinical term is for *irreparably broken hearted with a petty streak,* but I keep going.

Because if I stop now, I'll have to admit what all this really is.

Grief.

Love.

And the absolute refusal to let her become just another person who left.

"Then I had my lawyer add clauses that didn't make sense. Like custody of a dog we never had; Nutmeg. I may have spent two full days in litigation arguing over visitation hours. That one was my personal favorite."

Coach Saunders puts the pen down and just stares at me.

I stare right back.

Unapologetic.

Still not signing those papers.

She's blinking slowly like she's trying to process whether I'm serious or simply clinically unwell.

"Declan," she says carefully, "you have me at a loss."

"Thank you," I reply, leaning back like I've just won something. "Means a lot."

She shakes her head. "Yeah, that wasn't a compliment. Have you tried talking to... Maddy?"

"Marlow," I correct sharply.

"Right, sorry," she says. "But have you? *Really* tried talking to her?"

"Have I tried?" I scoff. "Of course I've tried. I've called, texted, emailed. I sent flowers to her office. Even a singing stripper gram with a man who looked like me, wearing my jersey."

"You did *what?*" she nearly yells, leaning forward like she misheard.

"It was the only way I finally got her attention."

"And what did she do?"

"She threw a soccer ball at my head. But at least she reacted." I pause. "Still wants the divorce, though."

"Go figure."

I run a hand down my face, the frustration eating me alive. "I don't know what else to do, doc. Is it crazy that I love her? That my breathing hasn't been right since the morning I woke up and she was gone?"

She doesn't answer right away. Just watches me with something almost soft. Understanding?

"It's not crazy at all, Declan," she says finally. "But for a marriage to work, both people have to want it. And it doesn't seem like she does. Maybe it's time you let her go. Maybe it's time you find someone who wants the same thing you do."

I snap.

"What the *fuck* don't you get, Coach Saunders?" I shoot to my feet, fists clenched at my sides. "There *is* no one else! You keep asking why I'm off my game, why I've suddenly got ink crawling up my neck like I'm unraveling—it's *because of her!* I don't want to be like this. I don't want to feel out of control. But for the fucking life of me, I can't figure out why I'm not right without her."

I pause, chest heaving. "So no, I reject your nice, neat little suggestion. I *found* her. And I'm not ready to let her go."

I turn, ready to storm out, rage burning hot in my throat. But the next thing she says lands heavy, even though it's the calmest thing she's said to me.

"Then maybe," she says, "it's time you show her what she's missing without you, too."

Maybe it is.

CHAPTER TWENTY FIVE: SWEATER WEATHER & SOCCER DADDY

Eslin

I 'm doing this. I am actually doing this. Enacting my friendship mode with Grant. Being a grown-up about our boundaries. Proving it can be done by accepting his invitation to join him and his daughter for a friendly, no-big-deal dinner.

But first, I need a pep-talk.

"Happy Holidays! Welcome to HollyDates!"

"Happy Holidays, Holly, girl!"

Yes, I say it now without giving her a hard time. At least it's October.

She's even transformed the place for the time of year. HollyDates in the fall is what I imagine heaven looks like for women who hoard throw pillows and pumpkin-scented candles. The whole café looks like it was personally blessed by the Autumn Fairy.

There are copper lanterns lining the entryway and mums in every shade of burnt orange and burgundy crowding the window boxes. The usual pastel color scheme has been temporarily replaced with deep maroons, mustard golds, and forest greens. And there are pumpkins everywhere. *So many pumpkins.*

A fake leaf garland frames the coffee bar, with twinkle lights tucked between the branches, and the chalkboard menu has been redone with curly handwriting that says things like *Cinnamon Sugar Bliss* and *Sweater Weather Latte.*

It's obnoxiously cozy. Sickeningly charming. And entirely on-brand for Holly.

"Hey Eslin! Funny seeing you here on a Sunday morning!"

"I know, but lots happening and I needed to chat. Do you have a minute?"

I'm not usually the type to spill my deepest secrets with girlfriends. I never passed notes in class about the boy I was secretly obsessed with. Never saw the point in dissecting every glance or overanalyzing a crush when you didn't even know if he'd remember your name a week later.

But lately, my brain's been uncooperative, to say the least. Unpredictable. Loud.

And when that happens, apparently, I do what normal women do.

I gab.

I gush.

I dish.

"Sure, honey! What's going on?"

"First," I say, sliding onto my usual stool, "can I try a sweet potato scone and a nutmeg latte, please?"

"Coming right up!" Holly grins, darting behind the counter like she's been waiting all week for this drama drop.

"So, I decided to try being friends with—"

She gasps mid-steam, eyes wide. "*Soccer Daddy?*"

I laugh. "Is that what we're calling him now?"

"That's what *I* call him," she says with a shrug. And honestly, I think I might start calling him that, too.

"Yes," I sigh. "I've decided to try being friends with *Soccer Daddy*. And I'm joining him and Marlow for dinner tonight."

She hands me my warm scone with the kind of care reserved for holy offerings. "I mean, I *get* it. Being his friend makes sense. But what made you decide to actually go over there for dinner? You think you can handle that?"

"I *can* handle it," I say, lifting my chin. "I just don't know how to *act* around him without Marlow picking up on the tension."

"Masturbate," she says with a straight face, without missing a beat.

"...What?"

"Masturbate," she repeats, like she's giving me medical advice. "It's the only way to make sure there's no tension when you're around him. You gotta get it out of your system."

"Okay, first of all—I've tried that. And if *you're* calling him Soccer Daddy, then *you* know why that doesn't work. The man is sex on a platter with a billion-dollar pension."

"Right. My bad," she says. "So then maybe cancel dinner. Because if the tension's as bad as you're claiming, you're gonna end up being the dessert."

I shake my head. "Wow. So helpful. I'm *so* glad I came to talk to you."

She plants a hand on her hip. "Look, I'm not the friend who gives a gentle pep talk your delusional ass isn't ready for. I see the way your eyes dart and your breathing shifts when you talk about him. You do *not* belong in close quarters with a man *that* tempting."

"You underestimate my ability to resist temptation," I say, trying—and failing—to sound convincing.

She arches a brow. "Then why are you here? Asking me how to handle it?"

I lower my head in mock shame. "Because I'm afraid I'll crawl under the dining room table and take his dick into my mouth when Marlow isn't looking!"

"Exactly, pumpkin." She says.

She doesn't have to be all smug about it.

I sigh, defeated. "Okay. So what do I do?"

She leans in with the seriousness of someone giving state secrets. "You're gonna go to dinner. You're gonna smile, say polite things, and focus on Marlow, your *friend*."

I nod. "I can do that."

"And when dinner's over," she levels me with a stare that could stop traffic, "you *do not* stay for coffee. Or wine. Or a casual chat about your dreams. You hear me?"

"Why not? Wouldn't that be rude?"

"Under normal circumstances? Yes. But you, sweetheart, have a full-blown inferno in your vagina, and you do *not* need the social lubricant."

I snort-laugh. "Got it. No social lubricant."

"And then you go home. You light a candle, take a breath, and masturbate *again*. Because you will *definitely* need it."

"You're right," I sigh. "And damn, these scones are amazing."

"You're welcome," she says smugly.

I take my drink to go, and head home. Off to scrub my walls and distract myself from the inevitable storm that is dinner with Grant Mills.

***

Grant's place is just a few floors above mine, but it may as well be another world.

Where mine has a lived-in chic and warm feel, Grant's penthouse is sleek and modern—like everything in it was chosen by someone who understands restraint as an art form. Floor-to-ceiling windows frame the city like a painting. The furniture is all clean lines and rich textures, each piece probably worth more than my monthly rent in New York.

There's a grand piano in the corner, untouched but impressive, and a glass bar cart stocked with liquor that looks too expensive to drink. It's quiet up here in a way that feels intentional, like the world can't touch him this high up.

I've imagined this place before. Pictured him here—walking out of the shower, towel slung low, wet hair curling against his neck, those impossible blue eyes catching the light just right. I've imagined him cooking dinner for his daughter, setting plates on that long, polished table with casual, capable hands.

And I'd be lying if I said I haven't imagined nights exactly like this one. The three of us. Eating dinner. Talking about our days. A little crazy, a little tender. Almost like a family.

The kitchen smells like garlic and simmering tomato sauce—rich, heady, nostalgic. One of my foster mothers used to cook like this. She could've easily been a chef. I remember being little during the holidays, breathing in these same scents, letting them wrap around me like something close to safety. The herbs and seasonings cling to your clothes, announce themselves to the whole block like a proud secret.

I stir the pot carefully, making sure nothing sticks, while Marlow slices eggplant beside me.

"My dad always says I should've been an Italian chef," she grins.

"You're definitely halfway there," I say, flicking a basil leaf at her.

She laughs, swats at me playfully, and goes back to slicing eggplant like she actually was trained for it.

It's easy between me and Marlow now. Comfortable in a way that feels earned. She's let her guard down more in the past few weeks than I imagine she has with anyone in years. And somehow, I've done the same. Not on purpose. Definitely not by design. But that's the thing about real friendship—it sneaks up on you when you're not looking.

If her father didn't live rent-free in every corner of my mind, I might even be able to enjoy it more.

But also, I hate how many secrets sit between us. Professionally, I know confidentiality is part of the job. I'm bound to it. I remind myself that every day. But it doesn't make it feel any less heavy. Because I'm not just holding space for clients anymore—I'm holding actual secrets. About me. About her father. Even about her husband and the buried grief he's only just started to unpack in therapy.

And some days, I wonder: if Marlow knew all of it—everything I've kept from her—would she still call me friend?

She's in storytelling mode, and I'm letting her go off.

"My dad and I have always been close. Like, really close. He was my whole world for a long time," she says, her voice softening, just enough to show the shift. "Especially after my mom died. He never let me feel it too hard."

She doesn't get misty. Doesn't crumble or pause for dramatic effect. She just says it plainly, like it's a fact she's lived with so long it's settled in her bones.

"He hasn't been with anyone since. Not really. He's had dates, sure. Girls here and there. But nothing that meant something. It's like he's waiting. Or protecting something. Or maybe himself."

"Maybe he's just not the settling-down type," I offer, too lightly and my chest immediately closes, tightening around the words.

"No, that's the thing," she says, pouring us both wine. "Lately, he's been different. Talking about slowing down. Wanting something real. Something more. I've even started trying to fix him up on dates."

She takes a sip of wine. I take a gulp, the conversation suddenly too close for comfort.

"There was one girl, though," she says, her voice dropping. "Vegas," she says, looking around.

And I choke.

Wine shoots down the wrong pipe and I'm coughing into my elbow like a complete moron. Real smooth, Eslin.

"Jesus, are you okay?" Marlow asks, eyes wide as she grabs a napkin and reaches toward me.

I wave her off between coughs. "Fine. Totally fine. Just—wrong hole. I mean pipe!"

Because pipe doesn't make me think about penises at all, either.

Trying to steer the conversation away from the trapdoor opening beneath me, I manage, "Must've been some girl."

My voice sounds almost normal. My heart, however, is doing sprints.

"Yeah, sounds like it." Marlow shrugs. "He doesn't say much about her. But whatever it was, something about her stuck with him."

No kidding.

I set my glass down, pulse still hammering beneath my skin, and force my brain to pivot before my face gives me away.

"So. About Declan, currently known as husband," I joke, glancing around to make sure Grant's still out of earshot.

He is.

Marlow freezes. Then she exhales, long and worn out.

"Yeah. That."

I lean against the counter, elbow propped, eyes on her. "You don't have to go there if you don't want to."

"No, it's fine. It's just *complicated*. He's sexy as hell, obviously. Accent for days. More tattoos than should be legal. But he's also intense. And something in me...no, everything in me...is screaming I don't need that kind of intensity in my life right now."

"And how are things going with the divorce?"

I ask it casually, like a good friend would—like I haven't already heard every messy, melodramatic detail in weekly therapy sessions with her soon-to-be ex. Marlow hasn't had the time to vent, and I've kept my mouth shut like I'm supposed to. But still, I'm dying to know if her side of the story sounds anything like his.

She lets out a dry laugh. "Impossible. He's pulling the most ridiculous stunts. My lawyers are bleeding me dry over paperwork that should've taken a week, tops. But Declan's acting like I burned down his entire world."

"His feelings are hurt," I say quietly, without thinking.

She blinks, takes another long sip of her wine. "I don't get it. We knew each other for twenty-four hours."

"Sometimes," I say, eyes glued to the bottom of my glass, "that's all it takes."

The room stills for half a second before Marlow tilts her head. "Sounds like you know something about that?"

And right on cue, I hear his voice from behind us.

"Know something about what?" Grant asks, stepping into view with his wine glass and that maddening calm of his.

"Oh, nothing," Marlow says too quickly, her voice a little too bright.

"We were just talking about adapting to things we didn't think we could handle," I say smoothly, keeping my eyes on Grant like it's a game of chicken I've already decided to lose.

He picks up the wine bottle, and as he pours, his gaze doesn't waver. Not once. It's dark and unreadable, but I feel every unspoken word behind it like heat licking up my spine.

Damn you, Holly. She was right.

"I see," he says.

My stomach tightens. I should feel called out. Exposed. Maybe even embarrassed. But all I feel is the unbearable tension strung between us, pulled taut and humming.

Marlow keeps stirring her sauce, blissfully unaware she's playing third wheel in a scene that's about three seconds from combusting.

"Thanks for agreeing to dinner tonight," Grant says finally, setting the bottle down. "It's been a long time since Marlow's let someone invade our time."

That lands heavier than I expect. It nudges something inside me—soft and a little raw.

"Guess that makes me a friend of the family," I reply, hoping my voice doesn't give anything away.

His jaw ticks. His blue eyes go a shade darker.

"Friends, huh?"

The word sounds like a threat on his tongue.

I lift my glass and meet his stare. "To becoming friends when we didn't think it was possible."

Marlow turns just in time, grabbing her glass with a flourish. "I always knew it was possible for us to be friends, Eslin. Apparently all it took was a damn good plate of oxtails!"

We clink glasses, the sound light and casual—completely at odds with the tension wrapped around my chest.

"Don't forget to make eye contact," Marlow says with a grin.

"Not to worry," Grant murmurs, his eyes finally leaving mine just long enough to clink glasses with her.

But not before he burns me alive with one last look.

Dearly beloved,
We are gathered here to mourn my panties.
They have drowned.

***

Dinner is awkward, but the conversation flows well enough. Like we all agreed—silently and without eye contact—to just act normal. Grant asks me the kind of questions you'd expect on a first date. Hobbies. Favorite books. What kind of music I like. As if he didn't already hear the answers when we walked all night under the Vegas lights.

I pretend it's the first time I'm saying them. Smile just right. Keep my tone breezy. Like none of it means anything.

"Dinner is spectacular, Marlow. I've never had eggplant parmesan before," I say, setting down my fork.

"Thanks so much! It's one of my favorite dishes to make," she beams.

I shake my head. "She's a boss and she cooks. Who raised you, woman?"

Grant clears his throat, raising his hand. "Guilty."

I blush and sip my wine. "You should be proud."

He looks at Marlow like the sun set and rose with her. "Every day."

Marlow groans, dramatic. "Okay, enough of that! Who wants dessert?"

"I'll take some!" I say quickly.

"Daddy made his famous peach cobbler!" she announces proudly, running off to the kitchen.

"Daddy?" I glance at Grant, eyebrows raised, and we both lose it—snickering at the accidental nickname. But I don't miss the way he bites his bottom lip when I say it. Like he's thinking about things we definitely shouldn't be thinking about with his daughter in the next room.

"I mean, you? You made peach cobbler?" I ask, trying to steer my brain back to safer grounds.

He nods, very proud of himself. "From scratch."

I laugh. "I don't believe it. How did *you* learn to make peach cobbler?"

He raises a brow. "Why are you asking like that?" He leans in, "is it because I'm white?"

I gasp then laugh. "It is absolutely because you're white! Now spill! Who taught you to make peach cobbler from scratch?"

He laughs, then shrugs. "When you're a single dad, you'd be surprised how many women offer to cook for you, take over your life. I had nannies to help with the heavier lifting, but I figured I'd get more out of learning some of the other things myself. Cooking. Doing Low's hair. Stuff that actually matters."

"I see," I say, biting back a reaction that's equal parts impressed and aroused.

It's not fair. Nothing about this is fair.

Marlow proudly brings in a still-warm pan of peach cobbler and a tub of whipped topping, but halfway to the table, she pauses. Her face goes a little gray.

"Marlow? You okay?" I ask.

"Yeah, honey. You don't look so good," Grant says, standing.

And then it happens.

A sound. A very small, but very undeniable sound.

She freezes. One hand over her mouth, the other over her stomach. "Oh God."

Grant's eyes go wide. "Honey?"

I lean in, placing a hand on her shoulder. "You wanna lie down?"

Another fart. This one slightly more confident.

"Umm. Uhh. I'll be back," she says, and darts down the hallway.

The second she's out of sight, it's like the dam breaks.

We both burst into laughter. Full-bodied, can't-breathe, wipe-your-eyes kind of laughter.

It only takes a few more seconds before the laughter fades into silence—and the realization settles in like smoke.

We've been left alone.

Grant

Denim has never made my dick hard.

Until tonight.

This woman walked into my home like seduction wrapped in soft blue fabric, and suddenly I'm ruined. This dress. A barely-there, button-down jean dress that clings to her like it was sewn onto her skin. Every curve, every sway of her hips, it's all there, unapologetically on display.

Why does she have to be so damn beautiful?

It's torture. The kind you feel in your teeth, in your fists, in your zipper.

It's wrecking me. Having her here, sitting across from me like we haven't already crossed so many lines that shouldn't be crossed. Like we haven't both tasted something real—something passionate enough to ruin us for anything less. And now we're expected to pretend? To smile, make small talk, act like we're nothing more than polite dinner guests over eggplant parmesan and peach cobbler?

But what was I supposed to do? Tell Marlow, Eslin couldn't come over because I'm afraid of what might happen if we're left alone? That her laugh gets under my skin? That her voice rewires my entire brain? That I can't stop replaying that night in Vegas—wishing I'd stopped holding back, pushed her up against the wall, and fucked her senseless right there, right then, until the moment she whispered, *I do*?

Of course not. I couldn't say that.

It's all so maddening. The way she laughs too loud at my daughter's jokes. The way her lips linger on the rim of her wine glass. The way her eyes keep flicking to me like she's trying not to look.

The laugh we just shared still lingers in the air. It feels like foreplay. Everything with her does.

"Let me get the table cleaned up while we wait for Low," Eslin says suddenly. And I know the exact second she decides to throw herself into cleaning.

When silence starts to press too heavy between us, when we both realize Marlow's absence leaves no buffer to our need.

She starts stacking dishes like it's a timed competition, avoiding my eyes like they're dangerous. Which, fair. They are.

"I'll help," I offer.

She shakes her head, fast. "No, I've got it. Marlow made this great meal. You made dessert. It's the least I can do."

She's already halfway to the kitchen before I can say anything else. But I follow her. I can't help it. Watching her move, nervous and flustered, doing everything she can not to acknowledge the static between us, feels like a challenge. I lean against the doorframe as she puts the dishes in the sink, rinses, stacks, rinses again. She's all tight shoulders and forced focus.

Then it happens.

She turns too fast, her heel catching on the edge of the rug. I see the moment her balance slips, but I don't reach her in time.

The crash of glass shatters through the kitchen.

Women really do keep falling around me.

"Uggh!" she mutters, crouching down.

"I've got it," I say, already grabbing the broom and dustpan from the corner. "Just stay back."

But she's on her knees with a towel before I can stop her, blotting up the red wine bleeding across the marble. Her movements are rushed, like if she just scrubs hard enough, she can erase the last five minutes. Erase me.

The wine comes up easy. The tension does not.

She walks over to toss the towels in the trash, and that's when I see it.

"Eslin."

She pauses. Turns.

"You're bleeding."

She looks down at her hand, then back up at me, her eyes wide.

I rush to her and pull her to the sink, turning the cold water on full blast.

"Here. Run your hand under it," I say, voice low but firm. She nods, obeying without a word, and I hate how good that feels.

I leave her there and head to the laundry room, grabbing the first aid kit like muscle memory. Gauze, antiseptic, bandages—my hands move on their own, but my brain is chaos. Tight. Loud. Screaming things I've tried for weeks to silence.

And this is where everything snaps.

This is where unbearable becomes *fuck it.*

Fuck the rules. Fuck the boundaries. Fuck pretending I don't want her with every breath I take.

I return to the kitchen and set the supplies on the counter beside her. She looks up, confused and beautiful and flushed from the adrenaline.

"Eslin," I say, voice sharp with everything I've been holding back, "I'm going to bandage you up. And then you need to leave."

Her brows pull together. "What? I don't understand."

"I thought I could do this," I say, trying to keep my hands steady. "I thought I could be near you. Be friends. Keep it clean. But this is—"

"Too close," she finishes softly, not even pretending it's a question. She knows.

She takes a step back, like her body understands the danger before her brain can catch up. "But you promised," she breathes. "You promised you'd be on your best behavior."

I shake my head, slow and sure. "That was a one-night-only special for you in Las Vegas, Eslin Saunders. I probably should have made that clear. You really shouldn't be here. Probably shouldn't have said yes to dinner."

I take a step forward. She takes another back. Fuck, I love this dance—her breath hitching, her eyes wide, her body betraying every word she's trying to hold on to.

"You can't walk into my house, wearing that dress, and expect me to sit across from you like I'm made of stone. Like I don't want to tear it off with my teeth and have you right here, bent over this counter."

Her eyes go wide, but she doesn't run.

"Grant," she breathes out. "My job. Marlow," she says, the words rushing out like she's trying to remind herself, to anchor herself to a vow.

"I know," I say, steady now. "I respect you. You know I do."

I take one last step closer. Close enough to feel her breath ghost across my mouth. "Which is why I've told you to leave. Because in about twenty seconds, it's not going to feel like I respect you at all."

"I think I understand," she breathes. "But for clarity's sake, what does disrespect from Grant Mills feel like?"

I reach for her hand, still slick from the water, and hold it steady. The cut between her thumb and forefinger is shallow but bleeding. Just enough to make her flinch. Just enough to make me lose my mind.

I bring her hand to my mouth. And I taste her.

I suck. Then lick. Then suck again—slow, deliberate, like I'm trying to identify the ingredients in the flavor of her skin. Apples. Cinnamon. Vanilla. Danger.

This is desire—pure and undiluted. This is every silent thought, every sleepless night, every boundary unraveling between us. It's too much. It's everything. And still, I make myself let go.

"Oh, the fucking disrespect I could rain down on your body, Eslin." My voice drops, rough and edged with restraint. "But I can't give that part of me to you. It's too dangerous. I wouldn't know how to stop."

I step closer, just enough for her to feel it—what I'm holding back.

"I'd never let you come up for air."

"Air," she breathes. "So overrated."

I smile. "Who needs the stuff, right?"

She shakes her head, holding my gaze. "Not us."

Fuck. My heart.

With that, I bandage her hand with the kind of care that makes my chest ache. Then I look at her—one last time—and give her the only mercy I have left.

"Leave, Eslin. I'm begging you."

She opens her mouth, searching for a word but nothing comes out. Finally, she clears her throat.

"Okay," she whispers. "I...I think I need to go check on my cat."

I blink. "You have a cat?"

Her lips curve into a sly smile. "The kind that curiosity kills."

I smirk. "And licks and sucks, apparently."

She lets out a breathy, nervous laugh.

I take a step back, forcing distance. It's the only kind of control I've got left.

Eslin gathers her things quickly, eyes down, pulse thrumming. And then, she walks away.

And I let her. I have to.

"Hey Eslin?"

"Yeah?"

"I'd still like to try being your friend."

She nods as she walks out of the door. "Okay, Mr. Mills. Let's be friends."

When Marlow finally comes out of the bathroom, looking pale but apologetic, asking where Eslin went, I don't miss a beat.

"She had to go feed her cat."

CHAPTER TWENTY SIX: NET, BALLS & NIPPLES

Declan

The ball kisses the pitch like it's been waiting just for me.

I drop my shoulder the second it touches my boot, shielding it from the guy on my back. He's taller, broader—too confident. I use that. Let him overcommit just a bit, then flick the ball inside my left and pivot hard.

Gone.

He lunges. Too late.

I hear their right-back barking orders, but the moment's already mine. I don't need to look to know I've got a runner peeling wide—Matteo, always dependable, dragging defenders with him like a net pulling open the ocean.

I fake the switch, let the ball roll a breath longer, then slide it into Kai's feet instead—short, sharp, like we're swapping secrets. He doesn't even blink. Knows what I want before I say it. One-touch return.

Ball's coming back.

Space's closing.

But I see it—just a sliver between center-backs. That's all I need.

I explode through the gap like it owes me something, dragging my cleats across the grass as if I'm carving a signature.

Their keeper sees me. Charges.

But I've already made the decision.

Inside of the boot. Calm. Low. Left corner.

The net ripples like it's sighing for me.

I stumble—just for a second—because even when I clear my mind, Marlow slips in like smoke under a locked door.

So I do what Coach Saunders told me:

Breathe in.

Visualize.

Focus.

Net.

Ball.

Nipples. Shit!

Net.

Ball.

Now.

I also say a silent prayer that my wife is watching.

Then it happens. That half-second of nothing—pure silence before the sound rushes in.

The crowd erupts.

I jog back down the pitch, chest rising, lungs burning, but my mind?

Clear.

Every pass. Every step. Every fucking second of that play felt like breathing again.

"Goooooal!" echoes through the stadium, followed by a wave of laughter and chanting—"Fragilé! Fragilé!"

Some joker on the team told a reporter my last name was straight out of the movie *A Christmas Story*.

"Must be Italian," the headline read. So now whenever I score, Fragilé is what they chant.

Idiots.

I wanted a cool American Nickname.

But I don't care. Not right now.

Because in this moment, no one's asking me to move on.

No one's telling me to let her go.

I'm not being haunted or gutted or fucking left behind.

I'm being celebrated by people who actually want me.

The game ended in a draw. More than I could've asked for, considering how off I've been, but I try not to let it get to me.

I showed up. I scored. I breathed.

"Declan," a reporter calls from the sidelines, Shaun Kennedy, a leech with a press badge. "You seemed to struggle a bit on the field today. What happened?"

I clench my jaw. Smile like I don't want to throw the mic across the field.

"I scored a goal. Does that look like I was struggling to you?"

Coach Jones steps in, running interference before I say something that'll end up splashed across every sports headline from here to Madrid.

"I think what Declan is saying," he begins, tone careful, diplomatic, "is that we all have rough days. But even on his rough day, he was still able to perform."

I let the words hang in the air, jaw clenched, resisting the urge to fire back at the smug press line. He's not wrong—I've been off for weeks. First touch like a brick, passes mistimed, like my body forgot how to follow my instincts. Today is the second match in a row where I looked like a shadow of myself the moment I crossed the white line.

I've stopped with the stunts with Marlow. The petty games. Tried to be a grown man about it and show her I want her heart. But she's locked me out completely. Won't respond to texts. Won't pick up my calls. Forces everything through the lawyers like I'm some pest she's trying to be rid of.

And I'm tired.

If I hadn't signed a contract, I'd have packed up and flown back to Italy weeks ago. But I'm also competitive to my core, and giving up has never been my thing.

You heard the coach—even when I'm bleeding out, I still perform.

Maybe it's the ache of missing her. Maybe it's the high of hearing my name shouted by a crowd that still believes in me. But right now, I make a decision. The next time I see Marlow, I'm going to remind her exactly why she said yes to me.

Why she couldn't stop whispering that it felt right.

And why she was never supposed to leave.

Right after I get rid of this fucking reporter, that is.

"Right," the reporter nods, smelling blood. "So again, Declan, what's going on with you out there that you have to perform through such *hard* times?"

Fucking hell, Shaun. The guy's a bloodhound for cracks in the armor. And today, I happen to be bleeding.

Shaun Kennedy has been on my ass since the day I joined the Strikers. Always digging, always needling, throwing out loaded questions like he's got some personal vendetta I can't quite figure out. He circles like he's waiting for the perfect moment to pounce.

"Is it all suddenly too much pressure for you?" he asks.

My gaze snaps to him, jaw tight, the heat in my chest flaring. "No, Shaun."

My voice is low. Controlled, but he has no idea that it's moments before something breaks.

He doesn't flinch. Just presses on, that smirk of his practically begging for a headline. "So, perhaps you're homesick, then? Missing family?"

He thinks he's clever. Thinks he's circling in for the kill.

I turn slowly, locking eyes with the camera, letting the silence stretch, letting the tension coil tighter with every second. The world around me blurs. It's just me and the lens now. Just me and her, wherever she is.

I take a breath. "Yes, Shaun. That's it. Missing my family."

His eyebrows lift, surprised he's gotten something out of me. "Back in Italy, you mean? Your family or your teammates?"

But I don't look at him.

I don't look at anything but the camera when I say, deliberate and steady, "I'm missing my wife."

Let her hear it. Let her see it. Let her feel it in her bones.

I'm not moving on. I'm not forgetting.

And this—me off my game, pissed off at the world, lost in a storm of ink and anger—this is what happens when you leave a man who was never going to let you go.

So she can run. Pretend like Vegas never happened. Pretend like we didn't burn the world down that night and call it love.

But I remember. And I won't be right—this team won't be right—until my wife comes back to me.

CHAPTER TWENTY SEVEN: PUMPKIN SPICE & PARTY PLANS

Marlow

The office smells like cinnamon. Again. Tatum insists it's a "seasonal vibe," which really means she dumped half a bottle of pumpkin spice essential oil into the diffuser on my desk.

"I'm telling you, this Halloween party is going to be everything," Tatum says, spinning in one of my office chairs. "Black lace, feathers, red lighting—very grown. Exceptionally sexy."

"Well, let's just make sure it's not 'budget prom,'" I mutter, flipping through our guest list. "Don't forget about signage, press, RSVPs—"

"Handled." Tatum waves her hand like a queen. "All of it. Trust me, I've got this."

"I'm trying to set my dad up with someone for it," I add casually, scribbling a note in the margin of my planner.

Eslin's head snaps up so fast I hear her neck pop. "Oh really? How does he feel about that?"

Her voice hits a little too high, like a cracked violin string.

"He says he's open to it," I say, shrugging. "He hasn't actually gone out with anyone yet, but I figure this could be a good, low-pressure way to meet someone."

"I'm sure he'll come around when he's ready," Eslin says, sipping from her water bottle. She seems tense.

"And if he hasn't gone on a date or gotten a girlfriend by the Thanksgiving Fall Formal we're hosting with the local high school, I have the perfect plan," I say, leaning back with a grin.

"Oh?" Eslin says.

I nod. "Mmm hmm. We're auctioning off some of the players and franchise staff for charity dates at the Fall Formal and guess who I'm throwing into the pool?"

Eslin takes a sip—then promptly chokes on it.

Tatum jumps. "Girl, are you okay?"

Eslin coughs, waving a hand. "Yeah—water went down the wrong pipe."

I tilt my head at her. "You sure?"

"Totally. Just—surprised. How...how does your dad feel about being thrown into the auction pool?"

"He doesn't know yet."

Eslin nods way too fast. "Cool. Cool, cool. Just curious."

We turn our attention back to the game just as a roar echoes through the stadium outside. The sound of thousands screaming "Gooooooal!" pierces through the office windows.

Tatum raises an eyebrow. "Fragilé did it again."

I groan. "That ridiculous nickname."

Eslin leans in. "How has it been with him?"

I glance between them. "As well as can be expected. We have our final meeting with the lawyers tomorrow. We sign everything, making this marriage like it never happened."

"Wow," Tatum breathes. "How does that make you feel? That it's going to be over?"

I chuckle, more to myself than them. "I might actually miss his crazy pranks. But other than that, this needs to be done before the press gets a hold of the story. It's gone on long enough."

"I hear you," Eslin says softly.

I sit up straighter because this cannot turn into my pre-divorce pity party. "Enough about me. Who are you taking to the party, Eslin?"

She waves me off. "I thought the point of going to one of those things was to meet a masked man who will sweep you off your feet!"

"Well, considering you probably know the medical history of half the masked men who will be in attendance, I think it's safer to just bring a date. Besides, Coach Jones has been sniffing around lately."

Eslin's eyes widen. "Really? Him? No way."

"Oh yes, honey," Tatum adds. "He's always looking at you like he wants to love you in a special way, you hear me?"

Eslin laughs. "I'm certain I don't know what you two are talking about. Besides, I don't think I can date him."

"Why not?" Tatum frowns. "He's not a patient, right?"

"No. Nothing like that."

"Then what?" I press.

But Eslin just goes quiet. Her mouth opens, then closes. "You know what? Never mind. I'm sure I'm trippin'. I might actually give Coach Jones a chance."

"I, for one, definitely think you should," Tatum says. "Before I have my arms and legs all over that man like a damn octopus!"

"Eww!" I laugh. "That just sounds excessive."

Suddenly, the room is filled with the chime of two phones buzzing on the glass coffee table.

Tatum grabs hers first. "Girl..." she says, her eyes glued to the screen.

Eslin picks hers up. Her eyes go wide. "Girl," she echoes.

"What? What is it?" I ask, standing.

They both look up at me like I've just stepped into an ambush.

"Turn on the TV," Eslin says, eyes serious.

I rush to my desk, grab the remote, and hit the power button. The screen flickers to life, and a live sports feed fills the room. A reporter holds a mic up to Declan, still in his jersey, sweaty and breathless from the match.

He looks into the camera, unblinking.

"I'm missing my wife."

My glass of water slips from my hand, shattering on the tile. I barely register it.

All the blood drains from my face.

"Is he serious right now? Are you fucking kidding me?!"

Tatum gasps.

Eslin stares at the screen like it might start bleeding.

And me?

I feel everything inside me shatter just as fast as that glass.

Declan

Did I just blow up my life?

Maybe.

Did I just drag Marlow into the blast radius with me?

Also... maybe.

But in the moment, I didn't care. I meant every word.

She needed to know. She needs to feel the wreckage she left in her wake. The sleepless nights, the fire in my chest that won't burn out, the way her silence echoes louder than any crowd I've ever played for. I didn't just say it for the cameras. I said it for her. Because I'm done pretending I'm okay.

And before I can talk myself out of it, I'm storming through the corridors of the front office like a man who hasn't slept in days. Because I haven't. I'm running on caffeine, adrenaline, and the hope that if I look her in the eye, I'll finally get through.

I need to see my wife.

Not the boss. Not the executive.

My wife.

And God help anyone who tries to stop me.

And then I see her.

She's sitting with two other women and I'm thirty seconds from screaming at them to leave.

Except I see that one is Coach Saunders so I keep my cool.

For a moment.

Then it hits me—Coach Saunders must've known the whole damn time. That the Marlow I kept ranting about in therapy was *this* Marlow. My wife. And I've got to hand it to her. She played it cool.

But now... now I've got a new problem.

I'm going to have to break it to Marlow that her trusted confidante also knows what she sounds like when she comes.

I gave Coach Saunders a very detailed play by play of our wedding night.

The other woman in the room notices me standing there then clears her throat. "Umm. Low?"

Meanwhile, my wife is yelling at the top of her lungs.

"I cannot believe that fucker! Did he say my name? How long before people start digging into who Declan Fucking Agassi's wife is? That arrogant fucking—"

"Honey," I interrupt. "I'm home!"

I like seeing my wife all fired up. It means she still cares.

I happen to like that a lot.

She's standing behind her desk, eyes locked on the TV, looking like every mistake I've ever made—and the only one I'd make again in a heartbeat.

She turns slowly, her gaze meeting mine like a blade.

"You!" she yells, voice cutting through the air just before she snatches a stapler and hurls it at my head. "You selfish, entitled *asshole*! Why the hell would you do that?!"

I duck, the stapler bouncing harmlessly off the floor. I pick it up and examine it casually. "Good to know," I say calmly. "You can't aim for shit."

"I swear to God, Declan. I will end you."

"Ladies," I say calmly, never looking away from my wife. "Unless you want to experience the unholy and indecent way I'm about to fuck my wife, I'd suggest you leave."

The blonde with the curls blinks, then mutters, "Yeah, that sounds like our cue."

Shoes click. The door creaks open. And then I'm alone with a woman who still wears my name and looks two seconds away from hurling something else heavy at my head.

Her eyes blaze, panic flaring under the fury. "Declan," she breathes. "What the hell is wrong with you? This could've been over. Tomorrow. We could've walked away clean."

I hear her. I just don't care.

I slam the office door behind me. The sound cracks through the air like a gunshot.

I cross the room without slowing. One long stride, then another, until her bravado falters and she instinctively steps back.

Too late.

There's no escape now.

And that's exactly how I want it.

"Declan—"

I hear voices coming from around the corner so I slam my other hand down on the frosted glass button on her desk. The windows fog instantly, erasing the world outside. We're alone. Sealed in.

She yanks her arm back, eyes flashing. "Are you insane? People saw you come in here."

"Oh no," I mock, voice low and dark. "Someone might see me kissing my wife. Imagine the scandal. Wonder what they'd say if they heard the dirty things the sweet Americana moaned with her legs locked around my face."

Her eyes flare, but she shoves at my chest. "What is wrong with you?" she hisses.

"You broke your fucking promise," I snap.

"Again with that? Declan, this isn't—"

I cup her cheek with one hand, cutting her off before she can say something I'll never forgive.

My tongue teases the seam of her mouth, and her hands come up, pressing against my chest. It's reflex—pure instinct—and that's what gets to me. Because it means she still wants me.

My wife still burns for me.

She breaks our kiss. Tries to brush past me. I block her. She spins away again, and this time I let her go—watching as she storms across the room into the small bathroom tucked into the corner of her office.

I follow. I don't knock.

She's standing by the sink, gripping its edge like it's the only thing keeping her upright. Her back is to me. That doesn't stop me.

I grab her hips and pull her back against me. She gasps, but doesn't move.

"You broke your fucking promise," I breathe against her neck.

"Declan, don't start—"

I don't touch her. Not yet.

Instead, I reach around her and turn on the faucet. Warm water. Soap. My hands move purposefully.

The ritual I began with my wife—cleanliness before sin—on our wedding night. I want to still honor that.

She watches me in the mirror. I watch her right back. Her eyes burn. Her jaw's tight. She's seething—and beautiful in that furious, trembling way that comes before she breaks.

"What do you think this will accomplish?" she snaps.

I don't answer. She always talks more when she's nervous.

When she wants me.

My hand slides around her waist, past the band of those soft, sinfully thin leggings she always wears that torture me. She tries to spin out of my hold, but I press her against the counter, body to body, so close it's war.

Her eyes roll to the back of her head and she nearly moans in pleasure but she stops herself.

She's still fighting.

"What's that, *la signora* Agassi? Or do you like it when I call you my Americana, instead?"

"Fuck you," she spits, voice cracking.

I smile, dark and unrepentant. "*La signora* Agassi, it is."

"You're insane."

"And you're my remedy," I growl, my tongue brushing her ear. "The sickness, the cure, the entire fucking reason I breathe. Come back to me, Americana."

"Declan—"

"I'm going to make you come now, my beautiful wife. That okay for you?"

Her silence is permission. Permission born from need so deep, it chokes out words. So I don't stop. I continue sliding my hand down the front of her leggings into her panties. I am eager for what I will find.

My wife is wet for me. Waiting.

"You can't be serious!" She hisses.

"Shhhh," I whisper as I slide a finger inside her. "This will be so much more enjoyable if you just give in to me."

My fingers work slow, relentless circles over her center, until her hips are moving with mine, her breath falling apart in shaky little bursts.

"Look at yourself," I murmur. "This is what you run from. What you pretend you don't want."

"Fuck you," she breathes again.

"So pushy with the demands," I tease. "I promise, I'm trying, Americana. But if you're still cursing at one finger..." My hand moves deeper. Slower. Rougher. "Maybe you need two."

"Shit," she gasps, hips jerking as I work her. Filling her, breaking her, giving her exactly what she won't ask for but needs like air.

She shatters then. Her body bowing, her mouth parting in a soundless cry. Her knuckles go white on the porcelain. Her thighs tremble.

I don't stop until she's done. Until the last twitch, the last moan, the last broken breath.

When I finally pull my hand free, she jerks away like I burned her.

Her eyes meet mine in the mirror, glassy with aftershock. But then something shifts. I see it click—the change from sated to shame.

She spins, shoving me with both hands as she leaves the bathroom.

I follow her.

"This isn't me," she spits. "You make me someone I don't recognize."

"Maybe it *is* you," I growl. "Maybe you just don't recognize her outside of me!"

"Exactly," she snaps. "And that's why I need this divorce from you. This isn't the *me* I need to be."

I step back like she slapped me. "Stop fucking saying that."

"Declan—"

"I said stop!" My fists curl at my sides. My jaw locks. I turn away from her before I say something I'll regret.

Before I can say anything more, there is knock on her door.

"Good afternoon!" The woman says and she looks vaguely familiar.

She's wearing royal blue glasses, blonde hair with blue streaks and overalls. Like a five year old.

"Oh! Yay! Both of you are here!" She says excitedly.

Shit. Who is this woman? Did someone find out about me and Marlow already? What did I do?

"I'm Chelsea Raymond with *SightUnseen*, here to do your follow-up interview for the show!"

Chapter Twenty-Nine

CHAPTER TWENTY EIGHT: FOLLOW-UPS & FAKING IT

Marlow

I'm having a hard time forming actual words. My brain knows the English language—I use it daily—but right now, all I can manage is, "I'm sorry. A what, now?"

Chelsea barrels into my office like she lives here. Hair bouncing. Clipboard in hand. Zero awareness that she's walked into a war zone.

"Your follow-up!" she chirps, as if this is a normal day. "Now that you and Declan are past the thirty-day back-out period, the contract automatically renews, and you're officially part of our finale episode!"

I glance at the spot on the floor where I last threw my stapler and curse the fact that it's out of reach. If Declan had just signed the damn divorce papers when I asked, we wouldn't be in this mess. I wouldn't still be legally bound to this charming, infuriating jackass with cheekbones that should be illegal.

Declan clears his throat beside me. "Forgive me and my *wife*, Chelsea—"

"Stop calling me that," I hiss, but he ignores me.

"We weren't expecting you. Can you remind us what this follow-up interview involves?"

"Absolutely!" Chelsea beams. "So, when you got married and signed all those fun little documents in Vegas, you agreed to either file for annulment within thirty days, letting the show know, or commit to a full year of marriage. Surprise! That milestone passed and I am so excited to tell your story! And how cute is it that you ended up working together?"

"Ha! Cute," I say, entirely too loudly. "And what happens if we back out now?"

"I'm glad you asked. People try that all the time." She continues with a fake but deadly smile on her face, "But since you did sign a contract, we'd sue you for breach, then we'd run lots of unflattering reports on TMZ about you. It all gets very ugly." She pauses before she adds, "Ugly for you, of course. Not us. We wouldn't break our word to you!"

I blink. Once. Twice. Declan, that smug bastard, just leans back on his heel like this is amusing.

Chelsea continues, undeterred. "But, since you're *not* backing out, this first meeting is just a check-in. No cameras, no pressure. But the next one? That'll be recorded. We'll need some fresh footage for our 'Where Are They Now?' segment before the finale airs."

"I'm sorry, Chelsea." My laugh escapes somewhere between nervous and unhinged as I try to keep a lid on the rage bubbling just beneath my skin. "I just thought we'd get a warning bell or something. A call. Maybe a smoke signal that said, 'Time's almost up before you're tied to this lunatic for the rest of your life?'"

Declan strolls up behind me and slaps me on the ass. "Where would be the fun in that, how do you say in American? Buttercup?"

He knew. That smug, manipulative bastard knew about the clause the whole time. That's why he dragged his feet. Why he played all those ridiculous games. None of it was random. This was his plan from the beginning.

Back me into a corner. Leave me no clean way out. Force my hand until going through with this ridiculous charade became the only option I had left—even if it meant risking my reputation, my position, my entire damn career.

I step down on his foot with full intent. He drops like a sack of flour, pretending he's tying his shoe.

"Fuck!" I hear him hiss.

"So, funny story, Chelsea," I say through clenched teeth as she eyes us like we're two feral cats. "Tomorrow, Declan and I were actually going to—"

"Move in together!" he cuts in brightly, bouncing back up like nothing happened. "If we'd known you were coming, we would've had you bring cameras for the big move-in."

"What?!" I yell. "No. He's—"

"My wife is simply being cautious," he says smoothly, placing a hand over mine like this is some kind of press conference and not a hostage situation. "We haven't revealed our nuptials to the team yet. You know how it is—her father being who he is, her being who she is. The optics. They're...complicated."

Chelsea nods thoughtfully. "I see. Totally understandable."

"So naturally," Declan continues, as if he's not making this up as he goes, "Any TV or media coverage of us must be held off until..."

He looks at me, waiting for a save.

"After Christmas. New Year," I blurt out, because at this point, my body is no longer responding to my brain. It's running purely on survival instinct.

"Completely fine!" Chelsea agrees, beaming.

I look at Declan like he just negotiated my ransom.

"These won't air until the Spring so we can make sure your interviews are later in the schedule."

"So kind of you," Declan says warmly.

"I'm sorry. Would you excuse us for a moment? I need to have a word with my...Declan."

I grab Declan by the arm and yank him into the bathroom, shutting the door behind us.

"What are you doing? What the hell is wrong with you?" I whisper-shout.

He just shrugs, infuriatingly calm. "Saving your ass. You're welcome, by the way."

"Saving my ass? How is this saving anything?"

"You heard her! If we backed out now, the network would air everything. You'd get sued. Do I need to spell it out? Your dad, the team—it would all blow up. You want that mess just to prove a point?"

I grit my teeth. Damn it. He's not wrong. I hate that he's not wrong.

"Fine," I hiss. "So we're doing this."

"We're doing this, Americana."

"Don't say it like that. Don't look so smug. You're still the enemy."

This *absolute* asshole takes the hand he just had inside me and brings it to his mouth like he's tasting wine.

He licks. Sucks. Moans like I'm the best thing he's ever put on his tongue.

"And God," he murmurs, eyes locked on mine, "do I love crossing enemy lines."

"You lunatic."

"For you," he simply says.

Then he washes and dries his hands and reaches for mine, maddeningly warm and sure.

"Come on, *la signora* Agassi," he says. "Let's go play happy couple."

When we step out of the bathroom, Chelsea's already made herself at home, casually inspecting the office like she's on a tour. She pauses by a shelf, scans the walls, and cocks her head.

"Funny," she says with a little grin, "no pictures of you two anywhere."

I keep my tone light but firm. "Chelsea, we've been over this. We're keeping things quiet—for now."

She snaps her fingers like she's just remembered. "Ah, right! Where is my head these days?" She pats her stomach with a proud smile. "Pregnancy brain."

"I see," I reply, smiling despite myself. There's something charming about how eager she is to share the news, like we're all part of some big secret together.

She flips to a fresh page on her notepad. "So, tell me—how's married life? Any surprises since the wedding?"

I let out a dry laugh. "Well, aside from the minor detail that my husband turned out to be the team's new midfielder and now I have to manage him while trying to earn the respect of a staff, who still thinks I got here by nepotism? Or were you hoping for something a little more romantic?"

Chelsea just hums and scribbles notes, completely unfazed.

Okay. Maybe that came out a little harsh.

"I think what my wife left out," Declan cuts in smoothly, flashing that diplomatic smile. "Is how I've made it my mission to make her life easier, even from a distance."

Chelsea lifts her brows, intrigued, and of course, he leans into it like he's reading straight from a romance novel.

"She has a demanding job, so I've been sending over her favorite pastries on mornings I know she has long meetings. Flowers on her desk every Friday. And not just roses, I actually pay attention. Lilies, gardenias, once even wild sunflowers because she mentioned them in passing. I take notes," he says proudly.

At least the asshole is a good liar.

I blink, caught somewhere between baffled and furious that he's spinning fiction this well. Chelsea looks seconds away from swooning.

"She refuses to let me do her laundry," he adds with a chuckle, "but I've been stocking her fridge. I leave little notes on the oat milk and eggs. And yes," he says, slipping his hand around my waist with that same infuriating charm, "that's why we've decided to move in together. It's just... easier to take care of her properly that way."

Chelsea melts. I want to combust.

"Oh," she says, pressing a hand to her heart. "You two are just—wow. I *love* love."

Declan squeezes my hip. "So do I," he says.

"You'd better sleep with one eye open," I whisper under my breath.

When the interview ends and Chelsea's heels finally click out of range, Declan turns to me.

"And you're moving in with me."

I blink. "Okay, first of all—we're going to have to actually *discuss* that. And second, why the hell would you just assume I'd move in with you?"

"Because your father lives in your building. And he can't be anywhere near the sounds I'm going to pull out of you."

He presses a soft kiss to my cheek. I am completely speechless with that comment and my traitorous body immediately reminds me of the feelings those sounds bring.

"Can't wait to welcome you home, wife."

Chapter Thirty

CHAPTER TWENTY NINE: STAND-INS & SWORN SECRETS

Marlow

I'm not proud of it, but as Declan leaves my office, completely unaware that I'm seconds from starring in the most creative episode of the true crime show, *Wives with Knives*, I pull a childish face behind his back and mumble under my breath, "Can't wait to welcome you home, wife," in a teasing, whiny voice.

Then, I send the DEFCON-1 emergency group text.

Me: *Stand-ins! Assemble! My office. Now.*

Eslin is the first to respond.

Stand-in BFFs: *We were waiting in Tatum's office anyway. Be there in two.*

I follow up with a more urgent request.

Me: *Bring the tequila Tatum keeps hidden in her cabinet.*

Tatum doesn't miss a beat.

Stand-in BFFs: *Oh, she's summoning the good stuff? This is serious. On the way, babes.*

I don't know what I'd do without Eslin and Tatum right now. I went from being the girl everyone invited to be a bridesmaid because I came with my daddy's yacht and a flawless toast, to having two real friends who know all my darkest secrets. Mostly because marrying a stranger in Vegas tops the list of wildest things I've ever done.

College sophomore year not included.

Since Tatum joined the team, I've noticed Eslin relax more around both of us. Maybe it's because Tatum's biracial, and Eslin doesn't feel like my token friend anymore. With Tatum in the mix, she sees I'm not collecting friendships like accessories—I just need people I can be real with. Women I can vent to, cry with, and maybe drink too much tequila around when my life inevitably blows up.

Two minutes later—right on cue—my stand-ins file into my office like a well-trained crisis response team. Tatum makes a beeline for the bar cart, already pulling down glasses. I snatch the tequila bottle from her hand and take a long, unapologetic swig.

"Oh! Okay then," she says, carefully lowering herself onto the couch like she knows this is going to be good.

Eslin settles in beside her, eyes sharp with curiosity. "So, I'm guessing your little chat with your husband didn't go well?"

"Nuh uh," Tatum cuts in. "That man said he was about to do *unholy* things to you. Did he at least follow through?"

I groan and flop dramatically into my chair. "So, here's what happened—"

"That's Black girl code for, *what had happened was*," Eslin mutters, and we all burst out laughing, the tension breaking just enough for me to breathe again.

Once we settle down, I take another sip and nod toward Eslin. "To answer your question, no. The talk didn't go well."

"But did he do the unholy things?" Tatum presses, wiggling her eyebrows like this is a rom-com and I'm the lead in denial.

"God, no. Well...sort of?"

Eslin extends her shot glass toward me with authority. "Pour. Then speak. Slowly."

I refill hers, hand the bottle to Tatum, and then I spill everything. Every filthy, inappropriate detail—from the kiss, to the threat of being sued by a TV network, all the way down to the way he licked his fingers like he was savoring me.

When I finish, there's a moment of stunned silence.

"So, you're staying married now?" Tatum finally says, blinking like I just told her I joined a cult.

I bury my face in my hands. "Ugh. Yes. For now, I guess? Or at least until I can figure a different way out of this."

"Why?! I thought you were signing the papers tomorrow!" Eslin says, half laughing, half horrified.

I lift my head and mutter, "So did I. But apparently, I was too drunk to remember the fine print from that night—get the marriage annulled within a certain grace period or you agree to participate in the finale episode. Try to call it off after the fact and you get sued."

"Are you sure you can't talk to your dad or any of his friends to help get you out of this? You're surrounded by billionaires, for Christ's sake!"

"No!" I blurt out, more panicked than I mean to sound. "They can't know. Don't you get it? I promised all of them I could handle this job without drama. Without bringing any personal mess to the team. And now I'm married to Declan after a drunken night in Vegas. That *is* the mess. I just need to fix it before they find out."

"Oh damn, girl, that's awful!" Eslin winces.

Tatum lifts a finger. "Umm...awful for who? Did you *see* the way that man's eyes burn for her?" she says, turning to Eslin before shifting her gaze to me. "Girl, he is going to *rearrange* your entire reproductive system and you better let him."

"Ew! Tatum!" I groan. "That's not the point of any of this."

"Says who?" she counters, deadpan.

"Me! The person trying not to destroy both our reputations while cohabiting and not screwing up his shot at a million dollars."

Eslin leans forward, confused. "Wait—why living together?"

"Because the show does *random* check-ins and Declan, in all his genius, announced we'd be moving in together so they could start filming from there."

Tatum clasps her hands together like she's just been gifted a rom-com plot. "I love this for you. Call me delusional, but what if all of this is happening for a reason?"

I snatch the bottle of tequila and take another swig straight from the neck. "And what would that reason be?"

Eslin reaches over, softening her voice. "Maybe to show you something you've never let yourself have before. And maybe you could be something for him, too."

I narrow my eyes. "*Too*? Did he say something?"

She freezes for a beat—professionalism kicking in—but doesn't take the bait.

"I'm just saying, maybe this isn't a total mistake," she shrugs.

I scoff. "Right. He did it on purpose for a million dollars."

"It's not nothing," Eslin says gently. "Especially considering where he comes from."

That makes me pause. "And how exactly do you know where he comes from?"

Her head snaps toward me. "First of all, that's literally Google-level intel. Second and third—how the hell have you *not* looked up the man you accidentally married?"

"Because I was too busy *not* getting attached. I didn't want to know anything that would make me like him—or worse—want him!"

"Well," Tatum says with a wicked grin, "sounds like that plan is going *great*. There's no way you're resisting that man once you move in."

I stand tall, arms crossed. "I absolutely can. You clearly don't know who you're dealing with. I am the queen of stubborn. *Headstrong* is my love language."

Tatum cackles. "Yeah, and I have a strong feeling you're about to redefine the word *headstrong* within forty-eight hours."

"Wanna bet?" I challenge, chin high.

"Oh, I'll take a piece of that," Eslin jumps in. "I got a hundred on Marlow losing the battle, *and the panties*, before day two."

"Count me in," Tatum adds, raising her glass.

I glare, then burp like a lady. "Game. On."

Declan

I love Sunday mornings. The birds are chirping, coffee's brewing, and the steady rhythm of movers hauling boxes echoes down the hall. Not just any boxes—my wife's things. Into my house. I paid the movers extra to make sure they came early, early enough that her father wouldn't notice, and used the service entrance so no one else in the building could catch on. Every precaution, every penny, worth it. Because today, finally, my wife is coming home.

I'm on my third cup of espresso, standing at the edge of the kitchen counter as they carry Marlow's designer luggage through the front door. I've even commissioned one of the guest bedrooms to be converted into a full walk-in closet. Not because she asked, but because I've seen her off-duty wardrobe. The heels, the tailored suits, the polished accessories. She looks like she just stepped off a runway in Milan half the time. And I've dated enough high-fashion women to know they don't travel light.

If this is going to work—this illusion, this stunt, this beautiful disaster—we're going to need a truce. And that starts with making room for my wife. I don't want her feeling like a guest or an accessory to my life—even if this whole thing has to stay secret. Even if she'd rather be anywhere else.

Her SUV pulls into the driveway like a warning shot. I don't move. Just sip my espresso and listen to the quiet parts of the morning slip away.

She steps out, and the cup nearly slips from my grip.

She's wearing one of those damn workout sets she always wears and this one might be the death of me. Cream-colored, soft and barely there, the fabric clings like it's in love with her. The pants are sheer on the sides, hugging every curve like they were custom-inked onto her body. The matching jacket is cropped and open just enough to expose a sliver of skin and cleavage.

I grip the counter instead of the cup.

Dio mi aiuti.

I live in Cinnamon Hills, an exclusive gated community tucked inside Cinnamon Grove—a neighborhood where every home looks like it belongs on the cover of a luxury architecture magazine. Clean white exteriors, glass-paneled facades, minimalist landscaping, sharp lines, and matte black finishes. The kind of place where electric vehicles charge quietly in the driveway and you're more likely to run into a pro athlete or tech founder than a neighbor walking their dog.

When I first moved here, I got lucky and ended up renting a house from Damond Battles, an NBA star who'd just been traded to Phoenix. He was supposed to be gone already, but I arrived in Atlanta earlier than expected and we overlapped. I had to stay in the house while he packed up to leave for his new home. I figured it'd be awkward, two strangers passing in the halls. But instead, we hit it off. He introduced me to a few of his teammates, helped me settle in, even gave me the inside tips on the best gyms and lowkey restaurants in town where fans wouldn't bother me.

When I mentioned I wanted to turn one of the guest rooms into a walk-in closet for my wife, Damond laughed so hard he nearly dropped his protein shake, then immediately demanded the full story. Once I gave him the abridged version (minus all the emotional landmines), he shook his head, grinned, and said, "You're already fucked, man." Then he sent over the best contractor in the city, told me to spare no expense, and made sure the job got done right.

Now even members of the NBA are invested in my marriage's success.

She's gorgeous, my wife. And if she weren't so damn stylish, I'm convinced she'd be in full mourning attire with head-to-toe black and dramatic sunglasses, like she's arrived for a funeral. Most likely mine.

"Welcome home, my love," I say with a slow smirk, leaning against the doorframe like I've been waiting for this moment all morning.

Maybe my whole life.

She doesn't even blink. Just breezes right past me with two duffle bags slung over her shoulder like weapons.

"Where am I sleeping?"

"No hello kiss?" I toss back, trying to keep it light.

She stops long enough to fix me with a sharp glare. Jesus. It felt like it was straight from the playbook of my Nonna—deadly, silent and absolutely final.

"Fine. No kiss," I mutter under my breath. "Follow me."

I sigh and push off the doorframe, letting the smug grin drop as I lead her through the house. The floors are polished concrete, sleek and cool under our feet, the high ceilings giving the space a museum or gallery-like quiet. Sunlight pours in through floor-to-ceiling windows, bouncing off white walls and beautiful art pieces Marlow doesn't even glance at.

We turn a corner and head down the private hallway toward the guest wing. "This will be your room," I say, opening a set of double doors.

The space is massive. Modern. Elegant. A king-sized platform bed with a low-profile headboard, layered in crisp white linens and soft charcoal throws. Clean-lined nightstands with built-in wireless charging. A minimalist glass desk sits beneath a wall-mounted smart screen. On the far side, sleek black doors open to a walk-in closet—unfinished, waiting for her touch—and a spa-like en suite bathroom with slate tiles, a soaking tub, and rainfall shower.

"You can change anything you want," I say, stepping aside to let her walk in. "Paint, furniture, layout—whatever makes you feel more at home."

She drops the duffles with a thud. Doesn't even look around. "I won't be here long enough to redecorate."

I nod slowly. "Still trying to figure out your escape plan?"

"Absolutely," she mutters, brushing past me again, this time toward the closet. "This isn't my home. It's just another mess I have to clean up."

Her fire doesn't scare me. She thinks it's a shield, that all this edge and attitude will keep me at arm's length. But all it does is draw me in closer. I'm a heat-seeking missile, and she's both the target and the trigger—my detonator, my ruin.

"Well, Americana," I say, my voice low, smooth. "I was hoping to begin our *mess* amicably. Perhaps by sharing dinner tonight?"

"I can't," she says, too fast.

I frown. "Don't tell me you have a date on our first night living together."

"It's a standing dinner. With my father. Every Sunday."

The sting hits deeper than I expect. I used to cook Sunday dinners with Nonna and Niko while my father worked late shifts. I didn't realize how much I missed the ritual of it until just now when I was told I couldn't even be in the room.

"I see. And since we're a secret—"

"Right. You understand, don't you?" she says, but there's no question in it.

Before I can answer, she steps forward, crowding into my space, forcing me backward until I'm just outside her door. She doesn't slam it, just closes it gently, but with finality.

"It's fine," I say sweetly. "I'll make dessert."

CHAPTER THIRTY: STICKS & STANDOFFS

Eslin

F all has to be one of my favorite times of the year. The smells, the colors, even the strange beauty of things dying away. Fall reminds you everything has a purpose, a place, and, maybe most importantly, an ending.

It's a beautiful Sunday morning in Cinnamon Grove and it was begging me to slow down and breathe it in. When I was younger, my old foster mother, Ms. Judy, would've had my butt in church by now, sitting in the second pew, wearing something stiff and respectable. But today, I'm in leggings, sipping on a nutmeg latte from HollyDates, walking through quiet streets that feel like peace.

I'm just leaving the café, adjusting the strap on my top, when I spot him.

"Rocky!" I call out, crouching to greet the team's beloved pup, who wags his whole body in response. I rub behind his ears, laughing when he tries to climb into my lap.

When I finally stand, I find myself staring into other familiar eyes. Blue ones. Beautiful ass blue ones.

"Hey there, *old friend,*" I say, still smiling as I look up at him.

"Hey, *old friend,*" Grant replies, his voice rich and easy. "Just leaving the gym?" He gestures at my workout set, the matching olive green top and leggings I almost didn't wear because they felt too sexy.

"Yeah. Then grabbed a drink from Holly," I say, lifting my latte.

We stand there, smiling nervously. The tension is thick, humming just beneath the casual energy we're pretending to have. Neither of us moves. And I want to say something—ask him how he's been, maybe suggest we sit down at

Holly's and split a scone like normal people with normal pasts. But he beats me to it, stealing whatever words were just forming on my tongue.

"Hey, Eslin?"

"Yeah?" I answer too quickly. Too eagerly.

He hesitates just a second, then, "Care to take a walk with me and Rocky?"

I nod, the word "sure" barely out of my mouth before we fall into step, heading toward the dog park.

Like friends.

At the crosswalk, we stop under the blinking red light. The quiet stretches, and it suddenly feels like the moment is about to crack open.

"So, are you going to the team Halloween party?" I ask, watching the light instead of his face.

He shrugs. "Marlow's trying to force me. Been trying to fix me up with someone."

I cringe.

Grant and I have kept a respectful distance. We've shared rooms, meetings, team events where we are always measured, always professional. I've managed to dodge Sunday dinners at his place with Marlow more times than I can count, always having something come up last minute. Grant and I simply agreed being *that* close again was a terrible idea. So we avoided it at all costs.

But I'd be lying if I said it didn't twist something in my gut every time she casually mentions wanting to set him up with some eager socialite or freshly divorced soccer mom. The tight, nauseous feeling becoming a regular visitor every time she shows me a new dating profile on Caché Elite.

So I know I'm playing with fire even asking about his love life. But what else are friends supposed to talk about? The weather? The news? The way his sweatpants leave nothing to the imagination and have me clinging to the last threads of my sanity?

"Marlow set you up with anyone interesting so far?"

His pause says everything.

"You mean anyone that reminds me of you? Anyone that comes close to you? No, Eslin."

I close my eyes for a second, trying to steady the thrum in my chest. Then I sigh and lie to myself.

"You have to stop that, Grant."

He feigns ignorance. "What?"

"You know what you're doing," I say, cutting my eyes at him.

He lets out a sigh. "Fine. I'll try," he says with a grin, and we both know he's lying.

Just like he probably knows I don't want him to stop.

"To answer your question, no," he continues. "I haven't met anyone interesting."

"But you have gone out with women?"

He glances down at me. "Now, you're going to have to stop doing *that*."

"Doing what?"

"Acting like you'll maim or murder any woman I so much as smile at."

I laugh, too loud. "No! I'm just making light conversation with a friend."

"Right. Just friends." He nods slowly, knowingly. "Well, then yes, friend. I've gone out with a few women. At Marlow's request." It felt like he *needed* to add that part.

"Have you gone out with anyone more than once?"

He sighs again, deeper this time. "You really want to do this?"

I raise my hand like I'm in a support group for victims of self-inflicted heartbreak. "Emotional cutter. Party of one."

A pause.

"Fine. One. That's it. We went out twice but never hung out again."

Something like hope dares to flicker in my chest. "Why not?"

"Because she apparently forgot she was in love with someone else. A woman."

I stop walking and look up at him. "Come again?"

"At the end of our second date, which was fine, just nothing that would likely ever happen again, her former roommate showed up on her doorstep."

"Oh my god. Like... during the goodnight kiss?"

"Just before," he says. "And the woman tells her she's been in love with her for five years and couldn't watch her fall for someone other than her. The person who knows her so well, she memorized her sleep rhythm."

I stare. "She said that? Her sleep rhythm?"

"Yep. Said I hadn't memorized her breathing patterns well enough to be worthy of her woman's love."

"Wow."

"Right?"

"Creepy. But... kinda sweet?"

"Okay, thank you. I thought I was the only one who thought that was a little creepy."

I love that he's a little like me.

We both laugh, real and full this time, the tension easing just enough.

We keep walking, just a few yards from the dog park now.

"What about you?"

"What about me?" I ask, like I don't already know what he's digging for.

He laughs under his breath. "Are you going to the team's Halloween party?"

"I am, actually. Got the perfect costume and everything."

He wipes a hand down the back of his neck. "You should be proud of me," he says, voice dipping into something dark and rough.

"Oh yeah? Why's that?"

"Because about thirty wildly inappropriate things just crossed my mind, and I didn't say a single one."

I grin. "Good boy. Do you want—"

"See..." He says it like a warning.

"Sorry," I add quickly, biting back a laugh.

He smirks. "So, tell me, Eslin Saunders. Will you carry a red rose that night? So I'll know who you are?"

I should lie. Brush it off or change the subject. But I've never been good at softening the blow. So I just say it.

"I'm actually going with Jones." I clear my throat. "Coach Jones."

He stops. Dead in his tracks. And poor Rocky gives him a look like he is not having it, pulling hard toward the dog park in view.

"Eslin. Him?"

His voice is strained. Half heartbreak, half disbelief. There's a thread of something else too. Possessive. Like he can't quite believe I'd offer even a sliver of myself to someone who isn't him.

And I hate it.

Hate the way it coils in my chest. Hate that it matters. Hate that after all this time *he* still matters.

I shrug, trying to look casual. "Why not him?"

"Don't get me wrong. Darren's a solid guy. Respectable. Steady. But he can't be *the* guy."

My stomach tightens, because if he wanted to stop me from going out with Coach Jones, all he'd have to do is say the word. "What are you trying to say?"

He hesitates. Looks at me, then away. "He just...Not him."

We keep walking. Mostly because Rocky's about to dislocate his shoulder if we don't. But also because if we stand still too long, I might do something reckless.

Like agree with him.

Like fold and finally say I'll wait for him.

We reach the dog park, and he crouches to unclip Rocky's leash. The dog bolts forward, tail wagging like he hasn't seen his friends in months.

"He's been socialized pretty well for a dog who grew up with a SEAL team," I say.

We both watch Rocky blend into a tangle of dogs, running and sniffing and playing like he's never known anything else.

"Yeah," he says, brushing his hands off as he stands. "He gets along great with the others at doggy daycare. And he seems really happy."

There's a beat of quiet before he speaks again.

"I'm sorry." His voice is soft and careful. "I don't have the right to ask about your dating life. And definitely not to weigh in on *who* you date."

I glance at him, then away. "It's fine. I nearly drowned on my own saliva when Marlow told me she was fixing you up with people," I confess, with a dry laugh I don't really mean.

He smirks, eyes on the dogs. "Coach Jones has definitely made me want to file for some internal personnel changes."

"Good thing we're professional and know how to exercise restraint, right?"

"Barely," he mutters, under his breath.

"But I think this friendship thing we've been trying has been working out okay, don't you?"

He turns to look at me, eyes sharp with meaning. "Only because I haven't had you over for dinner again, yet."

His voice is intentional and laced with *everything* that sentence could possibly mean.

I clear my throat, suddenly hyper-aware of the coffee in my hand. I take a sip, desperate for the distraction—anything to mask the fire that just shot down my spine.

Because now my brain is busy imagining that dinner. And not the kind with candles and silverware. The kind that ends with him eating me on his dining table. Or his kitchen island. Or whatever damn surface is closest.

I'm not picky.

"Sometimes I just want to let my intrusive thoughts win," I say, watching the happy dogs run wild around the park, owners clueless and content.

Grant clears his throat. "What kind of intrusive thoughts are we talking about here? Because if it involves us finding the nearest hotel room, I promise—I won't judge you."

I laugh. "Not that. I mean, sometimes I just want to be *that* person. Yell the 'T' word in a place like this and let chaos unfold."

He leans in, lowering his voice. "You mean...'treat'?"

"Yes!" I say, trying not to burst into laughter. "One loud 'treat!' and it's total mayhem."

"That's pure villain behavior," he says, grinning now.

"Oh, come on. You're telling me you've never wanted to pick the asshole option?"

He snorts. "Please. I've made a career out of picking the asshole option. I dismantle companies and sell them for parts."

"So you're not just an asshole—you're the king of assholes."

"Guess that makes me royalty," he says, snatching my coffee and taking a sip like he owns it.

"Hey! That's mine!"

"And it's terrible," he says, grimacing.

"You stole it. How are you complaining about something you *stole*?"

He shrugs. "Maybe I just wanted to taste you again."

My heart skips. Heat climbs up my neck, and I look away before I do something stupid. Like suggest we head to his place. Or mine.

Rocky, and the Atlanta Strikers' bad boy ways rubbing off on him, charges across the park and interrupts a game of fetch between a golden retriever and his flannel-wrapped owner. He snatches the stick mid-air and takes off in the opposite direction, tail high, full gallop.

"Rocky! No!" Grant yells.

We both crack up, watching mischief unfold in real time.

"That dog's a menace," I say through my laughter.

"He's misunderstood," Grant replies, grinning. "A little like his handler."

I glance over, still smiling, then let the question escape before I can second-guess it. "What was your wife like?"

His face changes. Not closed off, but thoughtful. And then, somehow, soft.

"She was fire," he says simply. "Italian. From Milan. Hated waiting. Loved being in control. Spoke with her hands. Cursed like a sailor but baked like someone's nonna. Beautiful. Loud. Fiercely loyal. And she never let me off the hook for anything."

I nod, trying to swallow the lump in my throat. Because without even saying it, I can hear what he's really telling me. *She was just like Marlow.*

I'm actually enjoying getting to know more about Maddy when the first complaint rolls in.

"Hey! Control your dog!" a woman in a matching vest-and-dog set barks across the lawn.

"Rocky! Drop it!" Grant calls, but Rocky doesn't even glance back. He's prancing now, showing off his stolen stick like a trophy.

Another man joins in. "Get your mutt back on his leash before I call the authorities! This is an off-leash park and your dog is clearly not trained to handle this kind of interaction!"

"Hey! Watch who you're calling a mutt!" Grant yells.

"Excuse me," I say, loud enough for half the park to hear, "but if your dog's that emotionally unstable over a stupid stick, maybe *he* should be playing with the little doggies!"

The man starts arguing back, the woman's huffing, and now we're being surrounded by grumbling dog owners glaring at Rocky like he's the anti-Christ with four paws.

"I can't believe this," Grant mutters. "You people have got to lighten up!" He says, louder.

"You need to get your dog trained and keep a muzzle on your lady or don't come to this park!"

Grant's fists ball at his sides and I think I see multiple veins pop out the side of his neck. "Muzzle? You want me to pick you up so you can come say that to my face, little man?"

I look to Grant, eyes wide and full of mischief. "Do you want me to do the asshole thing?"

Grant doesn't hesitate. He nods. "Do it. Do the asshole thing."

I spin toward the angry circle and raise my voice like a battle cry.

"WHO WANTS A TREAT?!"

Chaos erupts.

Every dog within fifty feet loses their damn minds—tails wagging, leashes jerking, some full-on sprinting toward me, dragging owners behind them. It's a stampede of fur and fury and confused joy.

"Leash him!" I shout, and Grant clips Rocky's leash just in time.

As we make our escape—grinning like criminals—I take a final sip of my now-cold coffee and say, "God, I love fall."

CHAPTER THIRTY ONE: BISCOTTI & BOUNDARIES

Marlow

D inner at Daddy's was exactly what I expected—same old stories, same pinot noir, same half-hearted jabs about how I work too much and how he *definitely* dates too little. I let it play out for as long as I could, then faked another bout of citrus-induced nausea to cut the evening short.

Still, I didn't leave empty-handed. I packed up a plate of the seared ahi tuna and mango ceviche and told myself I was just grabbing leftovers like always. But the truth is, it was for Declan. And thankfully, Daddy didn't press.

We live on opposite sides of the building so he also misses the fact that I don't go home. Not to my home at least.

Marlow's got a man.

The drive back to Declan's feels different.

It doesn't feel like everything is on fire and I'm a decision away from detonation, *different.* More like the kind of different that creeps in slowly and it's practically intoxicating because it feels a little *too* good.

The sky's an inky, late-night blue, the streets are quiet, and there's this maddening hum of contentment settling in my chest like it belongs there.

And it should piss me off.

Because I'm supposed to be spiraling. I should be anxious, furious, and halfway to drafting an exit strategy in my head.

But instead, I feel calm. Steady. Like something inside me exhaled for the first time in a while.

And for a second, that calm—this *different*—doesn't feel like a threat. It feels like something I've been needing all along and never even realized how much.

Until the inevitable gut-punch reminder slams into me.

This kind of different? *This* brand of forbidden, secret-marriage, emotionally reckless different can burn everything I've worked for to the ground. Not just my life—but the lives of people I care about.

And that's the thing about *different*—it rarely shows up with flashing lights or sirens. Sometimes, it sneaks in soft, wrapped in a slow smile, barefoot in a kitchen, and waiting to undo you with something warm and sweet and utterly inviting.

Because the second I step through the front door and close it behind me, that's exactly what hits me.

A wave of buttery warmth wraps around me, thick with sugar and something citrusy, like orange zest and vanilla had a baby and baked it in heaven. It's not store-bought. It's not from a box. It's rich and real and homemade. There's honey in it. Almonds, too. Maybe even a little bit of magic dusted in powdered sugar.

And in an instant I know exactly where *different* is hiding tonight.

Declan is standing at the counter, shirtless, his forearms dusted in flour, focused with the same intensity I've seen him bring to the field. A tray of golden cannoli shells cools beside him, while another batch bakes in the oven—judging by the smell alone, they're nearly done.

The counter is a perfect storm of pastry prep: a bowl of ricotta filling piped with care, strips of orange peel on the cutting board, and a snowdrift of powdered sugar waiting on a plate.

"You've got to be kidding me," I say, stepping into the kitchen.

He glances up, flashing a too-proud grin. "Welcome home, wife. I told you I'd make dessert tonight."

"Right," I mutter, eyes trailing down the line of his body, "I just assumed you were joking. And would be wearing more clothes?"

He grins, pleased with himself. "Do you like it?"

"Yes. I love cannoli," I admit, stepping closer. "I've been wanting to learn how to make it for years."

I can see the flicker of disappointment in his eyes when I sidestep the real bait in his question. He wanted a reaction. A blush. A flirty comeback. Maybe even a confession about how good he looks half-dressed and dusted in flour.

But I won't give him that.

He rounds the kitchen island, stepping in close—too close—and reaches up above my head. I realize there's a sleek rack of hanging kitchen tools just overhead, but the way he moves feels more like a hunter closing in.

"I can teach you," he says.

A breath of air rushes out. "Uh. Sure. Sure, I'd love that. Where'd you learn?" I fan my shirt slightly. Is it hot in here? Of course it is. The oven's on.

"My nonna," he says, the word rolling off his tongue like silk and smoke.

"Your grandmother?" I clarify, even though I already know.

He nods. "Yes."

"She raised you?"

"Her and my father."

"In Italy?"

Something about the way he says it—his posture, the faint, faraway gleam in his eye—makes me suddenly want to know everything about him.

"Some in Italy. The rest in Argentina."

"Why two different countries?" I ask before I can stop myself. My dad always said I was too nosy when I was younger.

He smiles, lazy. "That's for another day, Americana. We don't need to unpack family history on our first night together."

My hand flies to my chest like it might shield me from his heat. "We're not... it's not our first night together."

His smirk deepens. "Oh, trust me. I remember."

"That's not what I meant," I snap. "We're not together. Not like that. I'm just staying here. Sleeping here."

His eyes narrow. "Will you be fucking here, too?"

"Excuse me?" I gasp, shocked and flushed. "I would never bring a man here."

His gaze turns murderous. "Not if you don't want someone's blood on my hands, you won't." Something in his gaze tells me he means it. "I meant," he says, tone flat and possessive, "will you be fucking *me*, wife?"

It doesn't sound like a question.

"No, Declan. That part of this *marriage* stays in Vegas."

His gaze drops to my chest. "Your nipples say otherwise."

I stiffen. "My body's response to you is nothing more than that... a response," I lie, because I'm one breath away from climbing onto this kitchen island and inviting him to ruin me. But I have a bet to win. A sliver of pride to protect. And I'm not ready to hand either over to this man—especially not like that.

I like it better in the shower.

"Suit yourself," he says, backing off with maddening ease. "But I'm on the other side of the house in the master bedroom, if you change your mind."

"I won't." I snap the words too fast, too firm—like a defiant teenager stomping her foot.

But then he steps forward, and I instinctively step back until the edge of the coffee bar presses into my spine. He's holding a cannoli now, casual in his hands.

"I guess," he murmurs, lifting the pastry. "I'll just have to survive off the memory of one unforgettable night in Las Vegas... with my wife."

"Exactly," I say, my voice shaky. Unconvincing.

He raises the cannoli, brushing it lightly across my bottom lip. "Open for me, Americana."

"What?" My voice catches. "Wha—huh?"

"Open," he says again, lower this time. "So you can taste."

I part my lips, and he slides a bite in. The second the flavors hit my tongue—citrus, creamy ricotta, the perfect crunch of the shell—I moan, eyes fluttering closed against my better judgment.

When I open them again, he's closer. Too close. His head dips and I barely register the brush of his mouth before he licks powdered sugar off my bottom lip.

"Mmm," he hums. "Delicious."

"Declan, bet—" I stammer, catching myself. "I mean, you better stop."

Because I have a bet to win.

Because I can't let myself fall for the one person who could unravel everything I've worked for.

And because you're not my husband.

You're just the mistake I'm trying not to repeat.

Even if my body keeps forgetting that.

There's an elegant round table in the corner of the kitchen with two bamboo chairs. But it's what's *on* the table that stops me cold.

"Are those my bras and panties? Folded?"

Declan glances at the stack, then back at me. "I washed them."

"You washed my panties. And bras." My voice comes out strangled.

Since I'd be splitting time between two places, I'd ordered an extra set of unmentionables to be delivered here. I assumed his staff would drop them in my room. Wrong.

"You're supposed to wash new underwear before wearing it," he says, as if that explains everything.

"I *know* that, dick face. What I don't understand is why *you* took it upon yourself to do it for me!"

"You're welcome."

I exhale slowly, collecting myself before I commit homicide against the beautiful man that is my husband.

"We need rules. Boundaries, Declan," I stammer, the words scraping their way out of my throat. It's the only defense I have left. If I say it out loud, maybe my brain will finally catch up and remember he's the hazard I keep forgetting to run from.

His eyes narrow, and I hate how even that looks good on him. "What kind of boundaries? For what?"

I sidestep quickly, putting the kitchen island between us like it's a barricade that could actually hold.

There's a half-drunk glass of wine on the counter—I know it's his, but I grab it anyway and finish it in one long pull. Desperate for something to still me.

He tilts his head, that maddeningly calm expression back on his face, and moves toward me again. It's like the concept of space between us is optional for him. And he always chooses option-*closer.*

"You mean boundaries like what's mine is yours, and what's yours is mine?" he says, gesturing at his now empty glass. That Italian accent curling around every word like a dare.

"No," I snap, sharper this time. But who am I kidding? Even *I* can hear the tremor beneath my voice. "I mean real boundaries, Declan. No sex. No flirting or innuendos. No crossing lines we can't uncross."

"If that's what you prefer," he says with a grin. *"I'd prefer not to have a tsunami of sex flood my panties when you're near."*

I keep that to myself, though I'm certain he can already feel it in the air. The way he moves tells me he's reading me. Sensing me.

"And when the cameras do show up? For the check-ins?" He asks, closing the gap even more. "You want us to act like strangers then?"

I blink. "We can...perform."

"So, kissing?"

I nod. "Fine."

"What about touching?" he asks, and it's not innocent. "How much?"

"Holding hands. That's it."

He smiles, and it's sexy. I mean, infuriating. "And how do we know it'll look real if we don't practice?"

"Declan—"

But he silences me the way he always does—like restraint has never been in his vocabulary. His mouth crushes mine, and there's no slow build, no prelude. Just fire. Just him. His tongue claiming space like he's leaving something behind, like this kiss is a transaction and I'm now in debt.

This man kisses in Italian.

And if memory serves me right, he fucks in Italian too.

And I think I miss him.

He pulls back just enough to touch his forehead to mine, breath ragged. *"Perché mi combatti così, Americana?"*

My voice is barely a whisper. "What does that mean?"

He exhales, like I've wounded him. "Why do you fight me so, Americana? Why do you fight this," he pants, pointing between us. "When your body's begging for it? For me?"

And as he stares into my eyes, quiet, steady, like he already knows how this ends, I can barely remember the reason why myself. Why I'm fighting this. Why I thought rules would protect me from him. From us. From this pull I can't explain.

This obsession. This growing addiction that is becoming my husband.

CHAPTER THIRTY TWO: DRESS-UP & DEFIANCE

Marlow

Growing up, no matter how many board meetings were on the calendar or how many last-minute flights he had to catch, my dad always showed up for fall. Hayrides, pumpkin patches, haunted houses that were one electrical spark away from a lawsuit—he was there. Every time.

Halloween was my mom's favorite season, and after she passed, he made it his personal mission to make it mine too. He carved pumpkins like a surgeon, made the best damn cider you've ever tasted, and once sewed an entire unicorn costume by hand because I saw one in a catalog and casually mentioned I liked it. Sure, he was likely over-compensating for missing so much throughout the rest of the year. And the costume was hideous. But he was also just *that* dad whenever he had the opportunity to be. The one who did too much, in the best possible way.

So yeah, dressing up for Halloween has always been kind of my thing. I never missed a chance to go full fantasy—fairy wings, pirate boots, glitter in places it had no business being. It was the one night a year where reality didn't matter. I could be anything, anyone. But this year hits different. This year I wanted to be different.

I didn't want to be cute. Didn't want to be whimsical or clever. I wanted to be *hot*. Unapologetically, skin-tight, jaw-droppingly hot. Just one moment to feel like I still own my own body, my own choices, my own damn narrative without feeling like I'm performing for the cameras. To remind myself that I can still walk into a room and set it on fire, just because I feel like it.

Because work is becoming the thing Daddy warned me about—*a definition more than a destiny*—and Declan's got me twisted up in ways I hate admitting. The way his tattoos snake down his arms and across his chest like a treasure map straight to my pleasure. The way he watches me—quiet, steady, always reading the room and adjusting without ever asking for credit. He takes care of me when I'm not looking. Even when he's not sure I'll stay. And that right there is what scares me.

I can't tell if he's trying to win my heart or if he's just trying to *win*. Like there's a game clock ticking in his head and he's betting on how long it'll take before I cave. Or maybe he really just wants the money. And because I don't know which it is—because I've never been in anything that felt this confusing—I do what I do best. I push. I keep him at arm's length. I make it hard. And it's getting to him.

It's getting to me, too. But I'm doing my best to ignore it.

Coincidentally, it's also the day I'm scheduled to be at his house, and I decided to get ready for the party here. Declan is brooding. The TV is on, lights dim, one arm slung over the back of the couch while old match footage flickers on screen. Shirtless, tattoos on full display, muscles flexed in all the wrong ways. He's a walking distraction, and I'm dangerously close to throwing away my dignity just to climb into his lap. If he wasn't everything I know I shouldn't want.

My maddeningly irresistible husband is getting harder to ignore with every breath I take near him.

I pause in the hallway, adjusting the neckline of my costume. It's black leather, skin tight, strategically scandalous and everything I desired to accomplish tonight with this ensemble.

I watch my husband for a beat. "Aren't you going to the party?" I ask, even though I probably should know. But I've been toggling between this house and my apartment like a product of divorce with joint custody, so we haven't exactly had a heart-to-heart about our Halloween plans.

He doesn't look away from the tv. "Not going."

Okay. The brooding fútbol player was cute for a minute but now he's starting to piss me off.

It's been his thing ever since I told him I'm not going to play pretend with him just because the paperwork says wife. This marriage isn't fate. It's a mistake. But he still looks at me like I mean more. Like one emotional night in Vegas somehow turned us into something real. It didn't.

This isn't a love story. It's a glitch. A drunk detour neither of us planned for. One day we'll both look back and laugh at how reckless it was. How easy it is to mistake comfort for connection when you're too inebriated to tell the difference.

But seriously, why does he have to be so pretty? Unfairly pretty. This man's face turns logic into noise. Sharp jaw, those ridiculous lips, and a body that looks like it was designed to ruin lives. One glance and everything I've planned—every carefully built reason to stay away—starts to fall apart.

Instead of having a real conversation like a grown adult, he's been sulking. Acting like I broke his heart. He's covered in new tattoos I never saw coming and he's always playing broody Italian music that is beginning to grate on my nerves.

I asked Eslin if the constant tattooing was a real emotional coping mechanism or just Declan being extra. She gave me her therapist voice and said, "It's not our job to police how someone chooses to process pain."

Great. But I'm the one dodging landmines while he turns himself into a moody mural. How many tattoos does one man need before he figures out how to say, *I want you* without bleeding it into his skin?

"It's a mandatory team event," I remind him. The same team that has been growing increasingly concerned about his *inking* habit.

"I don't celebrate Halloween. I thought this was the land of inclusivity or whatever. My body. My choice."

I scoff. "It's the land of legally binding contracts, you dick. And attending team functions is part of yours."

And this. Our other norm. Fighting. We can't be within ten feet of each other for more than ten minutes without it spiraling into round seventeen of the same damn argument. Me calling him out for not doing what he's contractually obligated to do for the Strikers, and him firing right back that I'm not exactly holding up *my* end of a certain contract either.

He doesn't just want me living here full-time. He wants the *other* marriage stuff. The touching. The kissing. The kind of earth-shattering and unholy lovemaking that feels too honest to fake. Intimacy that turns lines into dust and makes me forget I ever drew them.

Everything I felt in Vegas. Everything I swore would stay there.

The second I let Declan in, it's not just my self-respect I'm gambling—it's the fragile grip I have on who I am without someone to anchor me. I know what it feels like to love something so fiercely, so completely, only to have it ripped away before I could understand what life looked like without it. That kind of loss rewires you. And maybe it's something I should be unpacking in therapy, but the truth is, I can't risk loving something else that could disappear. Not when I'm still haunted by the one person who did.

Still, here we are. Trapped in this push-pull purgatory, stuck trading jabs in a game where no one wins and both of us leave pissed off and unsatisfied. I can feel it happening in this moment. The tension building, the silence thickening, that sharp little tilt of his jaw he gets right before he calls me out for keeping him at arm's length. We're circling the same argument again, about to fall into it like muscle memory.

I don't know if it's the pressure from work or just being too close to him for too long, but I can't tell what I want more—proving I'm right, or giving in to how badly he wants me. Lately, the need to win feels less important than the way he looks at me, like losing to him wouldn't really be losing at all.

I don't need this right now. I can't want him.

I storm into the kitchen, heels clicking across the tile like gunshots. The fridge door flings open with more drama than necessary, because I'm annoyed and hot and slightly hormonally unhinged. My hand skims the shelves, and when I don't see that familiar row of silver cans staring back at me, I nearly lose it.

"And where the hell are my diet sodas?" I yell, head halfway in the fridge like I'm expecting them to magically appear.

"They're gone," Declan says coolly from behind me.

I freeze. "Excuse me?"

"I threw them out." He says it like it's a line item on a grocery list and not a full-blown declaration of war. "They're trash. Artificial sweeteners, zero nutrients, and they make you crash. I replaced them with organic juices. Natural energy. Pineapple-ginger, beetroot, the good stuff."

I turn slowly, stare at him like he's lost his Italian mind. "You threw away *my* diet sodas."

I don't consider myself to have an addictive personality. I'm type-A, structured to a fault. Control is how I survive. But when it comes to my diet sodas? The ones I've been drinking since I was sixteen? Control, couth and all decorum goes out the window. I will end a fucking life.

I keep them everywhere I know I'll be—my apartment, my car, my office, my dad's house—strategically stashed like survival gear. It's one of the only non-negotiables I gave his house staff which was to always keep them stocked. But this fucker, my husband, he didn't just cross the line. He bulldozed it, torched the remains, and dared me to say something.

He nods. Shrugs. "You'll thank me eventually when you've got more energy than you know what to do with. Maybe more energy for your husband."

I don't speak. I reach into the fridge, grab the first thing I see—a lone tomato—and hurl it straight at his arrogant head. It hits him in the collarbone, bursts like a popped pimple.

"I see you still haven't improved your aim."

"What the hell is *wrong* with you?"

He wipes the splatter off his chest, unimpressed. "If you wanted to lick food off of me, Americana, I prefer chocolate syrup. Whipped cream, maybe?"

"You're unbelievable."

"And you're underdressed."

My eyes narrow into razor slits as I slam the fridge shut. "What are you talking about?"

He lets out a tortured breath, stepping further into the kitchen. Still shirtless. Still with tomato residue on his chest. "Where the hell do you think you're going dressed like that, wife?"

I fold my arms. "It's Halloween. It's a costume."

He glares. "Marlow."

"What?"

"That's not a costume, it's an invitation."

I take a step forward. "And what exactly am I inviting, husband?"

He steps forward, too. "If you're leaving the house dressed like that, the only thing you're inviting is trouble."

He takes me in some more. "You'd think you were inviting your husband to turn a house into a home inside your tight, wet—"

I cut him off with a sarcastic laugh. "Oh, get over yourself. You think I get dressed for *men*?"

"I think you get dressed to be seen."

"By you?"

"By the looks of it right now, *everyone*."

I breathe out a humorless laugh. "So now you're the morality police?"

"No. I'm the man who married you, remember?" His voice sharpens. "The one who *knows* how it feels to have you pressed up against him and doesn't want to share even a goddamn *glimpse* of that with anyone else. You can call it fake all you want but I can assure you, my bullets are not."

We're close now. Inches. Our breath tangled and hot between us.

"You don't get to play the possessive husband, Declan."

"Why? Because you're still pretending this doesn't mean anything?"

"Because it doesn't. It *can't* mean anything. And because I'm not your fucking property!"

He grins. And it's not playful. It's sharp. Unyielding. "What's mine is yours, right?"

"What?"

"You're not my property," he confirms, stepping in, "but if we're married, half of this sorry excuse for a costume is. No need to wait for the divorce. I'll take my half now."

His hand moves quick, intentionally, and catches the edge of my neckline. His eyes lock on mine.

"Don't you dare—"

He licks his lip.

I don't even know when he grabbed it, but suddenly there's a knife in his hand, slicing clean through the neckline of my black bodysuit. The leather gives with a soft tear, splitting right at the collar.

Riiip.

My breath halts. The front falls open, peeling away to expose the exact strip of skin that's been testing his restraint since he laid eyes on me. "Declan!" I gasp.

He leans in. "Find a new costume or you're not going anywhere."

My heart hammers in my chest. His hand hovers at my side, not touching, just close enough to set me on fire.

"You're out of your damn mind," I whisper.

"Maybe." He breathes. Nearly panting. "But I'm also crazy for my wife. And I'm not letting you walk out of here looking like every man's fantasy."

His gaze drops to my lips and then my cleavage. "This," he whispers seductively, "is all mine."

I should slap him. Hell, I should twist his testicles until he begs for mercy. But I don't. I just stand there—bare, breathless, and shaking. The space between us hums with everything I've tried to ignore and everything he's been begging for.

We don't move.

We don't touch.

We just *burn.*

His eyes are lasered on mine, like he sees every piece of me I've tried to hide. Every inhibition. Every ache. Every lie I told myself about not needing him. Wanting him.

And still, he waits.

I've kept my distance. Built walls. Weaponized silence. But none of it holds now. Not when I'm standing in front of him stripped of everything but truth—and it's screaming inside me.

He doesn't beg anymore. Not with words.

His stillness *is* the plea.

Come back.

Come home.

Be *mine.*

We're standing on the edge of a cliff, and there's no turning around. Not after this.

We are too close.

Too far gone.

And I'm about to fall.

I think I'm ready to.

"Why do you fight me so, Americana?"

It's a question he's asked before—dozens of times, in different ways, with different tones. And I've always had an answer. Sharp, practiced, armored.

But this time, with him taking up all the air, all the logic, all the space in my chest, I've got nothing. No words. No retort. Just silence and a heartbeat that won't slow down.

He's finally done waiting for an answer. He's done waiting for me to decide to fall. To stop fighting.

His hand slides to my neck, firm but gentle, steadying me. And then he kisses me—soft, unhurried. Tracing the shape of my mouth with his tongue like he's grateful just to breathe the same air.

I moan into him and I try to pull back because, what the fuck? I'm crazy, right?

Declan pulls me closer.

My once sexy costume now falls to pieces as he begins gingerly removing what he's just cut to shreds.

"Declan—"

"I love the way you say my name. Say it again."

"Declan, we—"

"Shhh," he murmurs, unclasping my bra from the front with a practiced flick. "Let's just see what happens when you stop fighting. Do you remember what that felt like? Not fighting me?"

His head dips, his mouth closing over my breast, tongue swirling over my nipple, teeth grazing just enough to make me whimper. Every flick is calculated, every bite a punishment and a reward.

"Hmmm, *Señora Agassi*," he whispers against my skin, the name vibrating through me.

"Declan, we need—"

"To give in, *mia moglie bella*."

I'm in nothing but a thong now, and that disappears with one sweep of his hand.

I'm bare to him. Open.

He touches me, and there's no hiding it—I'm soaked for him. Aching. Every stolen glance, every night I ended with my hand between my thighs, trying to silence the memory of him, is now crashing down on me.

Running down my thighs and towards him.

My husband.

He kisses me, tongue hungry and demanding, while his fingers stroke my clit in tight, devastating circles. I gasp into his mouth, hips rising to meet his touch.

"You've needed this," he growls. "Admit it."

And I do. Because for some reason I can't lie to him.

"Yes," I pant. "Fuck, yes."

He slides a finger inside me and groans, deep like he's found something he lost.

"Just like I remember. Just like my wife."

He stills, gaze pinned to mine, unblinking. Not just looking. He's searching.

"Has anyone touched you like this since our wedding night?"

Wedding night. The way he says it.

"No," I whisper. And it's the truth. I've been haunted by that night ever since I slipped out of his bed and tried to pretend I didn't belong there. Beside him.

Declan drags his fingers out of me and I crave them but he swiftly lifts me like I weigh nothing. His hands are strong but shaking just a little. I can tell he's barely holding himself together.

I wrap my arms around his neck, feel the rigid heat of him pressed against my stomach. He's hard—God, he's hard—and I swear I feel it pulse when our bodies align. That hunger I've been running from is not just mine. It's his too. Relentless and untamed.

He carries me across the kitchen, his mouth dragging hot kisses along my jaw, my neck, my shoulder. And then he lays me down—right on the cold marble of the kitchen island.

The irony isn't lost on me.

This island has seen every version of our war. Arguments. Standoffs. Silence. And now?

Now it'll see surrender.

His hands glide down my body like he owns it. And maybe he does.

"Spread your legs for me," he commands, voice thick with hunger.

I obey without hesitation. There's no fight left in me. Only need. Raw and blistering.

He steps closer, eyes dropping to where I've opened for him, and he lets out a low, filthy groan. His tongue drags slowly across his bottom lip like he's savoring the thought of me on his tongue.

Like he's starving.

"Fuck," he mutters. "Look at you."

The heat in his gaze is unbearable. Adoration. Possession. *Craving.*

And when he sinks to his knees, hands gliding up my thighs with a reverence that feels like a warning, I know I'm about to be ruined, again.

Just like he did on our wedding night—when he made me forget my own name.

This time, though, it's different. I'm sober, yes. Fully compliant. But there's something heavier in the air. A finality. Like this isn't just about lust anymore. It's about claiming. About taking back what never should've been ripped from him.

He grips my hips, dragging me to the edge of the island, and hooks one of my thighs over his shoulder. His palms skim down the backs of my legs, squeezing, owning, before sliding them apart, baring me completely.

His mouth is so close I can feel his breath against me—warm, teasing, full of intent.

But he doesn't dive in. Not yet.

Instead, he presses a kiss to the inside of my knee. Soft. Reverent.

Then another, a little higher. And another.

Each kiss is a torment. His stubble brushes the sensitive skin of my inner thigh as he makes his slow ascent, taking his sweet, merciless time. I squirm, my hands gripping the marble, my breath hitching with every inch he climbs.

He nuzzles into me, tongue flicking out to trace the crease where thigh meets core. My hips jerk, and he chuckles low, devilish.

"So impatient," he murmurs, lips brushing my skin.

Then *finally* he presses a kiss directly to my center. And my body answers him like it never forgot who my husband was.

Even after only one time.

He starts slow, his tongue parting me gently, lazily licking through my folds. Exploring. Teasing. Drawing circles around my clit but never quite touching it, driving me mad. My hips roll involuntarily, chasing more contact, but he just pins me down harder, groaning into me.

"Fuck, you taste like heaven," he growls. "Like mine."

Then he goes deeper.

His mouth wraps around my clit, and he sucks—firm and slow—before flicking his tongue in quick, maddening strokes.

My back arches. I cry out. His grip tightens around my thighs, holding me steady as he eats me like he's starving, like it's the first time and maybe the last.

I'm nearly seeing into another dimension, body strung so tight I could snap, when it hits me—He's not just trying to make me come. He's trying to make me *stay*.

To anchor me with pleasure so deep, so consuming, that I forget how to walk away. *Or walk*, if memory serves me correctly.

He slides two fingers inside me, stretching me just right. His tongue keeps working above, relentless and precise—circling, flicking, sucking with devastating rhythm. Curling. Stroking. *Filling.*

My thighs tremble. My breath shatters. I clutch the edge of the island so strong I feel like I could break it.

And all the while, he devours me like he's got something to prove.

Because maybe he does.

"Declan! God!" I gasp, already teetering on the edge, every nerve in my body stretched thin.

"Don't call me your God," he rasps, his voice ragged with restraint. "Not when *I'm* the one on my knees for *you*, wife."

He presses his mouth harder against me, groaning as his tongue works me over. The sound rumbles through me, a growl that vibrates straight to my center, setting everything inside me ablaze.

"Come for me, *Señora*," he commands. "Right here. Right now."

And with his tongue lapping, his fingers thrusting, his name on my lips—I do.

My hands claw at the edge of the counter, hips bucking as I fuck his mouth. "Declan—oh my God—"

He holds me down, not letting me move. Not letting me get away from it. From him.

The orgasm hits before I can brace for it. It slams through me like a freight train, dragging his name out of me in a cry that would shame a woman with less pride.

But I have no pride left. Not when it comes to him.

He rises, eyes dark and wild, pulling open his belt with one swift jerk. His dick springs free—thick, proud, flushed—and I feel my core clench in pure anticipation.

"On your stomach," he says.

I hesitate.

"Now, *Señora Agassi*."

And I turn, just like that. Like I never stopped being his.

CHAPTER THIRTY THREE: HOT, BOTHERED & BITCHY

Eslin

I can't believe I let them talk me into this. Me, a grown-ass woman, dressed up for a Halloween party like I don't have real bills and a reputation to maintain. But here I am—Poetic Justice braids swinging, high-waisted jeans hugging all the right places, black crop top just shy of modest, and yes, I'm even chewing gum like Janet. With Bixa Beauty's Nude Margaret Monroe Lip Whip on my lips, I know I look good.

The Supper Club is even more stunning than the whispers promised. I've heard stories of what goes down here, who slips in and out under the radar, what kind of secrets live between the shadows of velvet curtains, low-lit lounges and private suites. But I've never dared to step foot inside. Not because I couldn't, but because I wasn't sure I could walk out the same.

There's something about this place. The sharp scent of money and musk. The way the light cuts across crystal glassware. The way the walls seem to hum with the kind of indulgence I've spent most of my life convincing myself I didn't need.

But tonight the air feels different. Electric. Like something's about to happen—something I didn't see coming. The kind of night that doesn't ask for permission. That doesn't wait for you to feel ready. The kind that pulls you in before you can remind yourself to stay away.

It's the same hum I felt that night in Vegas with Grant. The night we didn't sleep together, but still he somehow managed to ruin every other man for me without even touching me like that.

And still, for some reason, instead of turning and walking out, I step in. All the way.

"Girl, you are *killing* that Janet Jackson look!" Tatum calls out as she struts over, two drinks in hand. She passes one to me with a wink.

"Thank you! I see you went full Foxy Brown tonight?" I say, eyeing her up and down in her leather and gold.

"Original Pam Grier, baby," she grins. "She's my spirit animal."

I laugh. "Why am I not even a little bit surprised?"

We take a beat to take it all in—the crowd, the music, the vibe. "You really did an amazing job with this," I say, glancing around at the luxurious Halloween setup. "But what made you choose *this* place?"

Tatum smirks. "One of the owners owed me a favor, and I figured, why not go big? What other team is throwing a party like this? It's sexy, it's bold—"

"It's *so* you," I cut in, and we both crack up because even though we haven't known each other long, I've got her number. Wild, creative, always down to stir the pot.

She takes a sip of her drink, eyes scanning the room. "You seen Marlow yet?"

"Not yet," I say, rolling my eyes. "Last I heard, she and Declan were fighting again over a costume or something."

Tatum huffs. "Oh, the newlyweds are fighting again. Shocker."

"Right," I say with a smile, keeping my tone light. "Even if the whole thing isn't real, I think Declan's just tired of keeping their relationship a secret."

It's more than that. A lot more than that from what Declan has revealed in our sessions. But the fact that he's tired of being a secret is the only thing I *can* say since Marlow gave us that much herself. But even that little sliver of truth feels like walking a tightrope. I'm carrying too much—truths that aren't mine to share, feelings I've buried so deep I can't tell where they end and the lies begin.

Tatum nods slowly, swirling the drink in her hand. "Yeah," she says thoughtfully. "I think Declan really believes that if they stop hiding—if they go public—Marlow might finally drop the armor and let something real happen. Because as long as she has to keep it a secret, she'll never let herself feel it."

She doesn't know it, but Tatum is absolutely right.

I shake my head, exhaling a breath as I scan the crowd. "Honestly, I'm shocked one of them hasn't committed murder yet."

"Or mounted the other in one of the supply closets at work," Tatum says with a wicked grin.

I lift my drink in mock salute. "Right? Forget murder—I can't believe sex hasn't happened. We're both down a hundred bucks and for what? So she can stay hot, bothered and bitchy?"

Tatum leans in, dropping her voice. "You don't think she's lying, do you? About not sleeping with him?"

"Please," I scoff. "Marlow's way too wound up to be getting dicked down on the regular."

"Touché," Tatum laughs.

I tilt my head, narrowing my eyes at her. "And where's your date tonight?"

She grins and waves a perfectly manicured hand like she's brushing off a speck of dust. "Oh, honey. I am not a 'bring sand to the beach' type of girl. I like to see what's on the buffet before I commit to an entrée, if you know what I mean."

I snort, nearly choking on my drink. "Oh, I know what your nasty self means."

One thing I learned about Tatum right away? She doesn't do filters. She speaks her mind, owns her space, and lets her freak flag fly without a second thought. Her Black and Asian roots give her a kind of boldness that's rare—fearless but intentional, sharp but deeply rooted. Especially for a Black woman in a world that keeps asking us to shrink.

She's the head of marketing for a major sports organization, walks into boardrooms like she owns them, and doesn't waste her time with boys who play games. That kind of confidence is magnetic. It makes me respect her—and if I'm being honest, maybe even want to be her—just a little.

Tatum and I are nearly doubled over in laughter when it happens again.

That shift. The one that always gives him away before he even speaks.

The air tightens. My skin prickles just before...

"Good evening, ladies."

Grant fucking Mills.

"Good evening, Mr. Mills!" Tatum sings. "We were just talking about your daughter!"

"Good evening, Mr. Mills," I echo, softly. More careful, more controlled.

He gives a polite nod. "Please, call me Grant."

Tatum is still the one talking—but Grant isn't looking at her. His eyes are on me. Only me. And the rest of the room might as well disappear.

I see it hit him when he notices the costume. His gaze lingers, slowly taking it all in before his voice drops just above a whisper. "I loved that movie."

I make an effort to chew my gum. "Me too," I say, something soft and unsteady in my tone. "I used to watch *Poetic Justice* every day after school. Might've even started in middle school," I add, the words slipping out before I can filter them.

Grant reaches up and takes the end of one of my braids between his fingers. His thumb brushes it—gentle, like it might break.

"The outfit doesn't do you justice," he murmurs. "But I like it on you all the same."

His voice curls around me like smoke. I feel Tatum shift beside me, and just like that, Grant snaps back into himself—realizing we're not alone. Realizing we're in public.

"I...well, I'd better find my colleagues," he says, already retreating, voice clipped and casual, like he didn't just touch me like a secret.

Tatum grabs my arm like she's holding onto a live wire. "O. M. G."

I whip my head toward her. "What?"

"I *saw* the way that man just looked at you!"

I make a beeline for the bar, hoping distance will calm the thrum under my skin. "I'm sure I don't know what you mean."

Tatum chases me. "You are a damn lie, Eslin Saunders. That man wants you. Like, wants you, *bad.*"

Just as we reach the bar, she plants both hands on my shoulders and spins me to face her. "Do *you* have a thing for him too? Oh. My. God. Your best friend's dad. Eslin, does Marlow know? Does—"

I slap my hand over her mouth. "Yes, he has a thing for me. Yes, I maybe *kind of* have a thing for him too, but it started *before* I knew who he was. *Before* he knew who I was."

Tatum yanks my hand down. "Wait—what *started?* You slept with him?"

"No! And would you keep your voice down?"

I glance over my shoulder, paranoid someone's eavesdropping. Then I lean in and tell her everything—about Las Vegas, the man I kissed, the secret I buried, and the very real problem named Grant Mills.

"And, no, Marlow absolutely does not know."

"Girl! How are you even dealing with all that? I'd be going crazy holding all that in!"

Finally, someone close I can actually talk to.

My job demands I carry the weight of everyone else's problems, tuck away their secrets, their shame, their fears. But no one ever thinks to ask where I'm supposed to put mine. And since I rarely have time to hand over a copay and sit across from someone with a framed degree on the wall, I don't get much of a release valve.

Max is in Canada, buried in her own cocktail of chaos and bliss. And as happy as I am for her, it's been harder than I thought—keeping all of this in, swallowing it whole.

Especially with Marlow.

She and I are getting closer every day. She's becoming a real friend. Someone I trust. Someone I'd never want to hurt. Which makes all of this *impossible*.

So I let my guard down with Tatum. Just a little. Just enough. Because maybe, if I say it out loud—if I share this out loud—she can help me figure out how the hell I stop myself from falling for the one man who's completely off-limits.

My best friend's father.

I look up at Tatum, and for some inexplicable reason, a tear threatens to escape. I blink it back with a sharp breath and a forced smile. "How am I dealing with it?" I let out a dry, humorless laugh. "Hennessy. Neat, please?" I say to the bartender without looking away.

"Oh shit!" Tatum says, impressed by the drink order.

"I'm dealing with it by journaling, crying, avoiding—"

"Masturbating?" she throws in, soft and deadpan. It makes me laugh despite myself.

"Yes, actually. Lots and lots of that."

Her expression shifts. Still light, but layered with concern. "But seriously, E... so that's it? You two are just calling it, friends? And you're okay with that?"

I take a slow sip of the drink that just arrived, letting the burn chase down the ache in my chest. "Yeah. What else can we do? He's made this noble, infuriating commitment to Marlow. And I'm not about to betray my job—or her. I have ethics. Standards. I'm not going to set fire to everything just because my body and my heart are on different pages."

Tatum watches me for a beat, like she's weighing her words. "I don't know, girl...maybe you're overthinking it. Maybe talk to Marlow. See if there's room for this to *not* be impossible. You never know what life's lining up for you two down the line."

"I hope she's talking about me and you."

I freeze, heart stuttering, and turn to find Coach Jones standing there, grinning like he's been waiting for his cue.

"Oh! Darren!" I say, startled. "I didn't hear you come up." *Sneaky bastard.*

And part of me wants to ask—*how much did you hear?*

He gestures toward the drink in my hand. "I was about to ask if I could buy you a drink but, looks like you've already gotten started."

I take another sip. Nervous as all hell. "Yeah. I..."

"I forced her to have a celebratory drink with me. I just landed a big celebrity guest for our Fall Masquerade Ball!"

Coach Jones smiles. "Well, congratulations indeed. You really have been doing some great work. This party included. All the buzz around town was in no small part to you, I imagine?"

"Guilty as charged!" Tatum says with a wink and I pass her a silent thank you for the save. "Well, I am going to go and survey the buffet," she says and I laugh, knowing that she's talking about the men and not the food.

"Ok girl. We'll catch up later?"

"For sure." She leans in and gives me the bougie girl kiss, one on each cheek, before sauntering off.

Coach Jones turns to me. "You look cute, Ms. Jackson," he says and I blush. "Thank you," I say.

Coach Jones is unfairly sexy—tall, dark, and carved like an athlete who never quite left the game. His skin is a rich espresso tone that somehow manages to glow, and his smile? Blinding. Teeth so white you'd swear they've never met red wine or coffee a day in their life.

Born and raised in South Africa, he became a household name on the international soccer circuit, known for his explosive speed and tactical brilliance. Twenty years later, he's traded his cleats for a clipboard and now stands as the head coach for the Strikers.

And while he's managed to rack up some respectable and impressive wins, the truth is he's still finding his footing. Maybe it's because he looks like he could still suit up and take the field—young enough to be mistaken for a player, confident enough to prank like one. Coach Jones isn't just charming. He's disarming, too. And that makes him all the more interesting to me..

But he also might be exactly what I need right now—a distraction with a six-figure jawline and enough swagger to make me forget the minefield I'm tiptoeing through.

He's safe in the way a man who flirts for sport can be. Low stakes. No history. And best of all, not my best friend's father.

I take in his costume. "I'm digging your look, too. Run DMC fan, huh?"

Coach Jones grins, tugging playfully at the chunky gold chain around his neck. He's wearing a classic black Adidas track suit with the white stripes, crisp white sneakers, and a tilted bucket hat that makes the whole ensemble pop. It's a perfect homage to the iconic rap group, and it suits him well.

"I honestly didn't have a costume," he admits, glancing down like he's just noticed it himself. "The guys said I couldn't show up without one, so Luca raided his closet and made this happen."

I laugh, the tension between us slipping a little. "Well, Luca did good. You look like a real American rap star."

He chuckles along with me, and the sound is warm, easy. "Thanks for agreeing to hang with me tonight," he says, rubbing the back of his neck. "I wasn't sure if you'd say yes, considering your, uh, proximity to my players. And the fact we work together."

I lift my glass and take a slow sip. "As long as we take things slow. No assumptions, no expectations about what this is or where it's going, it's fine. I'm fine to hang."

He nods. "Making your boundaries known up front—I respect that."

Rockwell's *Somebody's Watching Me* starts blasting from the speakers, and before I can process the shift, he leans forward with a grin. "Care to dance, Coach Saunders?"

I place my drink down on a high boy table and slip my hand into his. "Sure, Coach Jones."

As we hit the dance floor, the team erupts into cheers and whistles, egging us on like overgrown kids. He spins me once and I laugh—full-bodied and unfiltered.

"So," he calls over the music, "what other rules does Coach Saunders have about dating her?"

I shoot him a warning look. "What makes you think I have rules?"

"Because you *definitely* have rules. Am I wrong?"

Not sure how he managed to clock me as someone with dating rules, but I'll give him credit for being so observant. Most people don't notice that about me, not right away.

Growing up the way I did—always the new kid, always the temporary one—I learned the hard way not to get too comfortable. I used to get attached fast. To the people, the homes, the smell of certain kitchens. I'd fall in love with the idea of being part of something permanent before I even knew if I was wanted there.

And when I wasn't chosen or when the foster mother found out she was pregnant and suddenly didn't want the extra weight of a teenager, or when a family decided I was "too old to mold," I got sent away. Again.

So yeah, I built rules. Not just for others, but for me. Rules like: don't get attached to someone who doesn't make it safe to do so. Don't say I love you first. Don't hope for more than what's been offered.

They're survival rules. And they've served me well.

But I don't say any of that out loud. It's not first-date material. Hell, it's barely third-date material. So I smile, keep the edge off my voice, and leave all the messy, haunted parts where they belong. Hidden. Contained. Mine.

"Okay, fine!" I laugh. "I *definitely* have rules."

"See! I knew it! Let's hear them."

"I don't kiss on the first date. I don't believe in definitions when it comes to relationships. I believe in checking in consistently to make sure both people are still in it. That we both still want the same things."

"I see," he says, impressed.

"And I don't think sex defines a relationship. Intimacy does."

Those words fly out before I can stop them. Unpolished. Me. And I don't usually open up like this—especially not to someone who technically qualifies as a colleague. But maybe I needed to say it aloud. Maybe I needed to feel like someone was listening. Or maybe I just hoped it would be too much and he'd decide this wasn't worth it.

But he doesn't flinch. Doesn't falter.

And that scares me a little.

Everything slows. The music, the crowd, the lights—muted like they're underwater.

Except my pulse.

Coco Jones starts singing *Here We Go,* and the second the lyrics drift through the speakers, I feel it in my chest.

Like the universe implanted a cruel reminder of what I'm trying to forget.

I look up and there he is.

Grant.

Standing just off the edge of the dance floor, a lowball glass in his hand, untouched. His eyes locked on me. On us.

He's not angry. Not scowling. But tortured.

His jaw clenched. His brow tight. His grip on the glass so rigid I'm surprised it hasn't shattered.

Darren's hand tightens at the small of my back and I feel it. That sharp, unmistakable burn. That low ache that starts in my gut and spreads like wildfire through my ribs. It's instant. Intimate. Unforgiving.

My body's still dancing with Darren Jones, but my soul's already been ripped from the moment and placed in Grant's hands.

The lyrics hit again. *Soon as I finally meet someone that I like...Here we go.*

It's a cruel echo.

Because I do like Jones. I really do. But the second Grant came into view, the second his eyes touched me, it didn't matter anymore.

My breath goes shallow. My steps falter. I try to ground myself, focus on the man holding me, moving with me. But my heart's off rhythm, matching only one frequency in the room.

His.

The moment the music fades, so does the little bit of calm I was clinging to.

Coach Jones and I step off the dance floor, and before I can fully catch my breath, Tatum slides up beside me like she's rescuing a cat from a burning building.

"The banquet area's ready, and dinner service is about to start," she says, low. Then she leans in closer, eyes apologetic. "And I'm sorry in advance for the seating arrangement."

My stomach tightens. "What does that mean?"

Before she can answer, Darren steps in, still smiling from our dance. "Everything okay?"

I glance toward the edge of the dance floor, instinctively searching for Grant—but he's gone. Like a ghost that only I could see. A haunting I'm not sure I'm ready to give up.

"No. I mean...yeah." I force a smile. "Just...ready to eat?"

"Starving," Darren says, and the three of us make our way toward the banquet area.

I can't help it. I keep looking. Scanning every corner, every dimly lit lounge space. No Grant.

The banquet setup is modern opulence. Long velvet-draped tables stretched across the room, framed by sleek leather dining chairs. Low lighting glows from gold-trimmed sconces. Instead of traditional round tables, there are lounge-style groupings—black leather sofas and marble cocktail tables mixed in with dining spots. It's like the high-end Supper Club met a luxury sports lounge, and they had a perfect, moody baby.

We make it to our assigned table, and that's when I see it.

Two name cards. My name nestled between *Grant Mills* on one side, and *Coach Darren Jones* on the other.

My entire body goes still.

Tatum winces as she slides into a seat across from me. "I told you I was sorry," she whispers.

Darren holds out my chair like the gentleman he is, and I sit. Slowly. Dreading the burn I know is coming the moment Grant walks up and claims the seat on my other side.

He doesn't make me wait long. I feel him first. That quiet gravity pulling at my skin.

And then he's there. Sitting beside me.

Close enough to feel. Close enough to touch.

CHAPTER THIRTY FOUR: PRIVATE SUITES & PUBLIC SECRETS

Grant

I'm not a jealous man.

At least, I didn't think I was.

I was married to a woman who looked like she was carved from Roman marble. Maddy was graceful, poised, and impossible to ignore. Men stared. Whispered. Bought her drinks right in front of me. But I never blinked. Never doubted her loyalty to me.

But apparently, two decades and one stolen taste of Eslin Saunders is all it takes to turn me into a murderous maniac.

Because right now, the way Darren Jones has his hands on her waist makes me want to put my fist through a wall. Or his face. Either works.

And the worst part about all of this is she's smiling.

Not politely. Not professionally.

Smiling like she's free. Happy. Like she forgot I exist.

It's fair. I'm not hers. She's not mine.

But try telling that to the fire clawing at my chest, to the sharp tension in my jaw, and to the heat pulsing in my hands like they're looking for something to break.

I can't watch them slow dance a second longer.

I turn and walk. Calm on the outside, storming on the inside.

Straight to my private suite upstairs—same one I've kept for years. The one with the same ghost of my old life tucked into every corner.

How poetic. That they chose *this place* for the party.

The Supper Club—my stomping ground, my kingdom.

The scene of a thousand late nights, whispered deals, all-night flings, and earth-shaking power plays.

But ever since Eslin Saunders crash-landed into my life, this place has all lost its shine. The women, the drinks, the power—it all feels muted without her.

If she's not here, I don't want to be either.

But tonight, she *is*. She's here.

I take a few minutes in my suite to get myself together before heading back down to the banquet. I need to look composed by the time Marlow arrives—like I'm not on the verge of imploding over her best friend. Like I'm not unraveling every time I see Eslin laugh at someone else's joke. Especially his.

I keep telling myself she's better off with someone like Darren Jones. But every time I repeat that narrative in my head, I start fantasizing about running the man over with my truck, dumping the body off the side of my boat, and pulling a full-on *Dexter*.

I push the thought down and head into the banquet room. And that's when I see it—see *her*. Sitting at our table. Positioned like a temptation straight out of scripture.

Right between me and Darren.

Let's see who leaves the strongest impression by the time this night is over.

Let's see who she remembers when the lights come up.

Let's see who Eslin Saunders won't be able to forget.

I take my seat and settle in calmly. Like I'm sneaking up to my prey.

"So, Coach Jones," I say, lifting my glass. "How are you enjoying yourself tonight?"

Eslin turns her head sharply, eyes cutting to me. "Don't," she mutters under her breath.

But I don't even blink. My eyes stay on him. I didn't ask her.

"Fantastic, actually," he begins, smiling and clueless to the tension crackling around the table. "Got the hottest date here, Miss Poetic Justice herself, and the vibe's incredible."

I nod once and lift the glass to my lips, letting the bourbon burn a slow trail down my throat.

It feels like fire.

"You've got that right," I say evenly. "You definitely brought the hottest date here tonight."

"Grant. Please," Eslin whispers through clenched teeth, her hand suddenly landing on my thigh beneath the table.

It's a warning. A quiet plea.

All it does is flip a switch.

"I see you went with the minimalist costume," Darren says to me, his tone light, but nosy.

I don't do costumes. But Marlow insisted it would help her image if I showed up "on theme" and supportive. So, I threw on a tux and a black masquerade mask and called it a compromise.

"Yes. Minimalist," I say, dryly. "Let's call it that."

He chuckles, still trying to *connect*, I guess. "So what are you supposed to be?"

Holy hell. This guy. I meet his gaze, calm but sharp. "I'm a secret, Darren. Call me a secret."

I almost miss it but I hear Tatum from across the table whisper, "Oh shit."

Eslin clears her throat beside me—a subtle warning.

I'm starting to enjoy feeling her squirm.

Two points for me. Zero for Coach Candy Ass.

Servers float through the room in sleek black-on-black uniforms, setting plates with the kind of reverence usually reserved for royalty. Low conversation buzzes around us, silver clinks against porcelain, and soft music hums beneath it all. But none of that matters. Not with her hand resting where it shouldn't be.

I don't think, just act. I take her hand and move it higher. Straight to where I'm already hard for her.

She gasps. Doesn't pull away. In fact, she squeezes. And I look Darren Jones dead in the eye.

"I always had a thing for Janet Jackson growing up. You?"

He chuckles, oblivious. "Big time. Posters all over my dorm at boarding school. She was *everything.*"

The first course arrives—seared scallops atop truffle risotto, saffron cream drizzled like artwork. The table reacts with impressed murmurs.

Eslin tries to pull her hand away, but I don't let her. Not right away. I hold it. Hold her gaze. Daring her to look away first.

"You are going to get me in trouble," she whispers through a tight smile.

"You are going to drive me to murder," I mutter back.

"I'm on a date, Grant. What do you expect me to do?"

She jumps suddenly, breaking contact.

"Did you just kick me?" she snaps across the table.

"Sorry!" Tatum chimes in, wide-eyed and innocent. "Girl, my foot fell asleep!"

We finish our first course and next, miniature heirloom beet salads arrive, each leaf and smear of goat cheese arranged like edible art come out.

Coach Jones has been charming all night. Gracious, attentive, and flirtatious in a way that would usually make a woman feel like the center of the universe. And Eslin plays along. She smiles at his jokes, leans in when he speaks, and matches his banter with that dry wit she's mastered so well.

But it's all surface. At least to me. The polished smile, the polite nods—none of it hides the truth. I see it in the way her jaw's a little too tight, how her shoulders haven't relaxed once all night. The way her eyes keep flicking to mine like she's tracking landmines with every breath.

She hasn't touched me again since she pulled her hand back. And she's slowly edged her body away from Darren with each passing minute, barely angling toward him when he speaks.

But none of that matters. Not when the air between us still crackles—still hums like her fingers never left the hard length of me beneath the table. Like some invisible current is still flowing between us, daring one of us to make the next move.

I don't care who she came with. I don't care that Darren Jones has his hand on her chair or that he's acting like the perfect gentleman on this little date. I want her. I want her hands on me. Her eyes on me. Her loyalty wrapped around me like an oath. And every time she smiles at him or laughs a little too loud, it spikes something hot in my bones.

Fuck. Right. Not mine. But hell if I'll sit back and watch her become his.

"So, Grant," Coach Jones says, his tone as breezy as his grip on reality. "What are you going to do once you officially hand the reins over to Marlow?" He chuckles like it's all a joke. "Usually, a man like you's got a yacht and swooping up some hot young thing. Or a few, if what the tabloids say about you are true!"

Eslin chokes like the words sucker-punched her straight in the throat.

"You okay?" Darren asks, patting her back with a little too much familiarity.

"Yes!" she manages. "Wrong pipe."

He hands her water. "Drink this." She drinks. She listens. And I hate how she listens to him while fighting me at every turn.

"Thanks," she says, soft and grateful.

I set my glass down. Hard. "To answer your question," I say, not bothering to soften the edge in my voice, "I haven't quite decided what comes next. I still have several companies to manage, and I don't plan on slowing down anytime soon."

I lift my drink again, stare straight at Eslin as I add, "As for the hot young thing? Let's just say, I've never had any trouble *stealing* those up."

She clears her throat. "He said swooping."

I hold her gaze. "And I said stealing."

"Ouch!" Eslin yelps, snapping her head toward Tatum. "Girl, seriously?"

Tatum shrugs, wide-eyed and innocent. "This damn foot just keeps fallin' asleep! Must be these heels I'm wearing." She waves it off like it's nothing. "Anyway! Have you seen Marlow?"

"No!" Eslin hisses through gritted teeth. "Maybe you should go *call* her!"

"She texted earlier," I cut in. "Said she's running behind. Something about a wardrobe malfunction."

Eslin and Tatum exchange a look. One of those wordless conversations women seem to master. I catch the hesitation in it but decide not to ask.

Darren leans in, his hand resting casually on the back of Eslin's chair. "I'm gonna grab a drink. Want anything?"

She looks up at him "No, thank you. I'll be here when you get back."

"I'll have a Macallan, if you're taking orders," I chime in.

"*Asshole,*" Eslin scoffs but only I catch it.

He nods, grinning. "Sure thing, Mills." Then he strolls off, just as Bruno Mars and Cardi B's "Finesse" drops through the speakers.

Tatum perks up like she's been hit with electricity. "Oh, hell yes. My jam!" She jumps to her feet, hips already swaying. "You've gotta honor the '90s when the groove hits this hard!"

She drags a few others with her to the dance floor, laughter trailing behind. The table shifts, the energy thins—and then, it's only us. Me and Eslin.

The music pulses. Lights flicker like heat lightning across her skin. Everyone else is spinning, lost to the beat. But we sit, still and charged, like something unspoken is winding too tight between us.

She doesn't look at me at first. Her eyes stay fixed on the crowd.

"Grant, you have to stop."

My jaw clenches. "You expect me to sit here and watch him touch you like that? Like he has the right?"

She turns, finally meeting my gaze. "You don't get to act like this unless you *want* someone to discover your feelings!"

"*My* feelings? So it's just me?" I lean in, my voice dropping. "Tell me I'm imagining it. Tell me I'm the only one losing my damn mind."

She doesn't answer.

"Eslin. Tell me it's just me."

"I can't think when you're this close."

"Good," I murmur. "Because I haven't been able to think straight since the second you walked back into my life."

My hand slips under the table—reckless. I've always been good with both hands, but it's my left that moves now, slow and precise. I find the zipper of her jeans, tug it down inch by inch, my knuckles brushing her skin.

She doesn't stop me.

Her breath catches, sharp, shaky, like she's been holding it since the moment Darren walked away.

I find the edge of her panties and slide them aside, baring her heat to the cool air and the weight of my touch.

"Grant—"

"Shh." My fingertips brush the edge of her wetness, slick and warm. "Don't lie to me. Not when your body's already told the truth."

She shifts, barely, but it's enough. Enough for me to slide two fingers between her folds and feel how ready she is. How far gone we both are.

My eyes lock on hers. "You still want to pretend this is one-sided?"

Her lips part. No words. Just her pulse pounding against my wrist, her thighs trembling under the table, and the quiet, desperate truth of her not pushing me away.

"I never said it was one-sided—" Her voice breaks, a gasp strangled in her throat. "Shit. Grant."

"I have no right to you, Eslin," I say, my fingers moving between soft, slow circles over her clit and then sliding deep inside her, knuckle-deep. "I know that. I know I shouldn't ask. But I'm going to ask anyway. Demand it."

Her hips jerk against my hand. The bass of Usher's *Good Kisser* vibrates through the floor, and I match its rhythm—stroking her, teasing her, claiming her with every thrust of my fingers.

"Ask me," she pants. "Fucking say it."

"He doesn't touch you like this," I growl. "He doesn't make you sound like this."

"Are you insane?"

I push my fingers deeper. "Very. Now promise me—"

Her breath catches on a moan, her head bowing, hands gripping the edge of the table like it's the only thing keeping her from screaming.

"I'm coming—"

"He can't give you this, Eslin." I drive deeper, adding pressure, another finger. "Say it. Promise me."

"Shit!"

Three fingers now.

"Shit!"

"Wrong answer."

Across the room, I see Darren walking back toward us, two drinks in hand and none the wiser.

"Grant, he's—" Her voice is frantic, flushed with panic...and pleasure.

"Promise me."

"You're fucking crazy!"

"And my fingers are still inside you. Do you want him to hear you moaning my name while you come?"

She clamps her lips shut, eyes wide—then she shatters around my fingers.

"Fucking hell—I promise! I promise!"

"Promise what?" I murmur, not letting up.

"Shit!" she gasps. "I promise he can't touch me like this."

I press deeper, slower now, drawing every last tremor from her.

"No one but me?"

"Grant—" She begs.

"The clock's ticking, baby."

Not wanting to really give us away, I withdraw my fingers just as Darren strolls up, completely oblivious. He sets the drinks down with a laugh.

"You two looked like you were in a pretty heated debate."

Eslin shifts in her seat, eyes down, cheeks flushed. She's trying to breathe like she didn't just fall apart under the table.

But then I hear it—a whisper, faint and fractured. *"Nobody but you."*

I grin then whisper, "Good fucking girl."

I look up and make eye contact with Darren, I swirl my glass, then dip the same two fingers I just pulled from Eslin into the Macallan.

I bring my gaze to Eslin, stir once, slow and deliberate, before bringing them to my mouth.

She watches, frozen.

I suck them clean.

"Eslin and I were just placing a little bet on the next match."

CHAPTER THIRTY FIVE: BANQUETS & BLUSHES

Eslin

I can't believe he just did that.

Worse—I can't believe what I let him do.

Every rational bone in my body was screaming *no*, and still, I sat there and took it. *Let* him. Let his hands wander like they belonged there, like *I* belonged to him. And I'd be lying if I said I didn't want more.

I am a stupid woman.

Weak-willed.

A common whoremonger!

Uggh!

Grant Mills is off-limits in every imaginable way. My best friend's father. A man nearly twice my age. A man with the kind of control that makes smart women forget their rules.

And yet here I am. Still craving the touch I should've pushed away. Still aching like I'm starving and he's the only thing that's ever fed me.

It's like he's built this secret garden around us—quiet, dark, and full of fruit I have no business touching. But the more I taste, the harder it is to stop going back for more.

We're at the part of the evening where the party is winding down. The lights are low, the crowd thinning. Tatum's off to the side finishing up interviews with the press that showed up uninvited. Marlow still hasn't made an appearance, and part of me wonders if that was by design—like Grant and I were given one more moment we shouldn't have had.

And even though he slipped out a half hour ago, I keep glancing around the room like I'll find him in a dark corner, watching me. Like a ghost. My secret.

"Ready to go?" Coach Jones asks, his tone casual, unaware of the turmoil brewing beneath my skin.

I nod, smoothing my hands down the front of my jeans and grabbing my jacket. "Yeah. Let's get out of here."

We walk in silence toward the exit, his hand gently guiding me through the remaining crowd. But just before we step out into the cool night air, he leans in "Uh... Eslin? Your zipper's down."

I freeze, eyes wide. And suddenly I remember exactly why. My skin heats with a fresh wave of embarrassment, and I turn away, fumbling to fix myself as fast as humanly possible.

He chuckles. "Hell of a party, huh?"

I don't even respond. I just laugh it off, nod once, and step into the night, praying the cool air will sober my thoughts—and that my body forgets the man I'll never be allowed to want.

"Hell of a party, indeed!"

"You really do look cute, tonight."

"Thanks," I manage.

"You are different than I expected. Outside of work."

"Oh yeah? How'd you think I would be?"

We pass a group of ladies in sexy costumes and clearly over the legal limit of alcohol.

He gestures towards one of the women in a skimpy angel costume. "Most women are excited to get dressed up and sexy for Halloween, but you wear the most covered up version of Janet Jackson anyone has ever seen for a costume."

I shrug. "I've never been the kind of woman who has to flaunt it to feel it. Sexy isn't about how much you show—it's an attitude. A presence. Either you carry it, or you don't."

He lets out a sharp breath and I can tell he's impressed by my bravado on the subject.

I had a foster mother named Karen who used to be a prostitute, but she turned her life around long before I ever showed up at her door. She was tough, honest, and unapologetically herself. And she used to tell me the realest things. Things no caseworker or guidance counselor ever dared to say.

"There's more to being a woman than what's between your legs," she'd say. "Don't let television or some fool with a smooth mouth convince you otherwise. Sex appeal doesn't come from skin. It comes from self-respect. That's where the real power is."

For the two years I lived with her, Karen was less like a mother and more like the big sister I never had. And I think, looking back, I learned more about being a woman in that small apartment with her than I have anywhere else since. About sensuality. About strength. About owning my presence without apology.

The sidewalk is a blur of color and chaos—tiny witches and pint-sized superheroes darting between stoops, plastic pumpkins swinging from sugar-sticky fingers. Parents trail behind in hoodies and costume accessories of their own, coffee cups in one hand, phones in the other. There's laughter, someone blasting "Thriller" from a speaker on their porch, and the warm glow of jack-o'-lanterns flickering in every direction.

It's the kind of neighborhood scene I used to dream about. One I never quite belonged to. One I was always passing through.

Coach nudges his head toward the crowd. "You think you want a family some day?"

I let out an uncomfortable laugh. Most men don't like my answer to this question. "Who me? No." And I leave it at that, because no is a complete sentence. But because it's Darren Jones, he doesn't let it sit there.

"Bad childhood?"

I look at him. "Why would you assume that?"

"Because most women who don't want kids usually want to cut off the possibility of something happening to a child they love, like what happened to them."

He says it so matter of factly like he read a page straight from the book of *me*.

"Something like that." I let out a sigh and decide to share a bit of myself with him. "I grew up in foster care and saw how many children went unnoticed, unwanted and unloved. And I always said that if I ever decided to have children, I'd pick one of them. A child that hates every birthday because it means they are one more year closer to aging out of a system that only chooses infants. Babies that can be molded."

"Wow," he says, and it's not for show. It's the kind of "wow" that carries weight. He grabs my hand and gives it a firm squeeze. "I love learning about you, Eslin Saunders."

"Thank you for not taking pity on me," I say quietly.

"Thank you for not hiding your truth with me. I respect that."

We round the corner and the sound hits first—laughter, music, the unmistakable thump of bass spilling into the streets. Holly's is lit up like a scene from a movie. Streamers hang from the awning, fog machines cloud the sidewalk, and people in everything from cheap wigs to couture-level costumes flow in and out of Holly's like it's the hottest spot in town. Holly turns her place into party central for every major holiday, and Halloween is practically her Super Bowl.

Tatum is in the middle of a small crowd, sipping something pink and commanding attention like she was born to do it. I catch a glimpse of Marlow with Declan at the far end of the patio, surrounded by a few other Strikers players, drinks in hand, all laughing like they're in on a secret. I want to charge over and ask her where the hell she's been and why she didn't come to the team party, but I know better than to start something in front of everyone. I'll text her later.

"Looks like Holly's hosting the after party," Darren observes, nodding toward the crowd.

"Want to stop in?" I ask, suddenly not in a rush to head home and risk wandering up to Grant's penthouse and offering myself to him.

"Sure. But before we do—" His voice dips, slower now. Serious. And I can already feel the shift coming.

"Yes?"

"There are a lot of people from work over there. And you know how the guys can be."

I let out a short laugh. "Don't I know it."

"So, if you want this between us to just be a one-time thing, or if you'd rather keep it friendly, I'm okay with that. I just—look, I don't want to be the guy catching heat from the team for falling into something that's not even real."

Is he really trying to define this after one date?

"Darren," I say evenly. "We are friends. What we are beyond that is undecided. I don't know you well enough yet to say what this is or what it could be. So if you're asking me to spare your pride by keeping this quiet around the guys, fine. We'll keep things professional until we figure it out."

He nods, like it's not exactly what he wanted to hear but it settles something inside him. But I still see something else—the hesitation in his eyes, the flicker of disappointment that settles behind his easy smile. It's the moment he realizes I'm not the type to fall in line just because the vibe is good for one night. I'm not a quick claim. Not some box to check off.

I don't care how long I grew up wanting to be desired, I won't settle.

I'm nothing to be taken off the market. Not without a damn good reason. And if there's ever a time for Coach Jones to learn that, it's now.

Also, our boss had his fingers inside me not more than an hour ago and I'm still trying to process my explosive orgasm.

"Well then, Eslin Saunders," Darren says, flashing that polished smile and perfect white teeth. "I'd love to be your friend."

His tone is light, but there's something in his eyes that doesn't match. A quiet challenge. Maybe even a warning.

I smile back. "Good. Let's start there."

CHAPTER THIRTY SIX: PB + NIGHTCAPS

Eslin

Holly's smells like roasted espresso, sugar, and the faint tang of sass that follows its owner everywhere. I'm nursing a holiday coffee on a Sunday morning before a workout, watching the steam curl up like it's trying to hypnotize me into *not* thinking about my crazy life.

It's been a few weeks since Halloween, and I've gone on two more dates with Coach Jones. He's...*nice.* Cultured. Easy in a way most of the American men I've dated aren't. No games. No second-guessing. Honest. Intentional. Almost as intentional as Grant is about making it painfully clear he hates that I'm dating him.

Grant's been keeping tabs on me through Marlow, somehow finding out when my dates are, then *coincidentally* showing up on the sidewalk with Rocky every single time I'm about to leave. Like he can't help but plant himself in my path, reminding me exactly who he is and where he stands, even though he knows he can't have me.

What he doesn't realize is, he doesn't have to do a damn thing to stay in my orbit. He's been living there since the night we met.

"So, tell me all the things. All the drama." Holly skips any pretense of small talk and jumps straight into what she's become for me—a caffeine-dealing counselor, keeper of my secrets, and occasional bad influence.

I groan. "Everything is a mess. I hate my life."

She leans in, eyes sparkling. "Tell me more."

"Me and Marlow are getting closer—like little-sister close. Her father is practically stalking me now that he knows I'm dating the soccer coach, and did I tell you about Halloween when he—"

Holly throws up a hand. "Stop. Please don't make me relive that story. I masturbated for a week after you told me the first time."

"Noted," I say with a smirk. "It was the sexiest, dirtiest thing I've ever experienced. And that's the problem. I'm not this dirty woman who hides things from the people she cares about. I am not the therapist teetering on the edge of breaking client privilege because it's all just *too much.*"

She cuts me off mid-rant. "Here. Taste this."

She's trying a new seasonal coffee flavor and I perk up because I love being her taste-test dummy. "What is it?"

Her smile could light a tree. "I'm thinking of calling it Holly's PJs or P.O.J."

I take a sip. "What does it stand for?"

"Peanut butter on Java. Oat milk whipped topping made with peanuts from local Black farmers."

"I love it. Sweet, creamy, right amount of nut."

"That's what she said," Holly deadpans, and we both crack up.

We've bonded over *that's what he said/she said* jokes almost as much as coffee.

I squint at her cup. "But wouldn't it be PBJ?"

She glares. "Heiffer! Did I say peanut butter and *jelly*?"

"No, ma'am."

"Thank you. Now you're gonna tell all your rich friends to come get a taste of my new drink, right?"

"Yes, Holly. I'll make sure everyone gets a taste of your crazy invention–P.O J."

"Thank you. Now, back to you."

I groan. "I know. What should I do?"

"Listen, while I *did* take nine hours of life coaching classes for my life coaching certification, I think you're gonna need someone a little more qualified than me. This," she gestures to me like I'm a walking case file. "Everything you're dealing with, is heavy, mama. You need to talk to someone. Someone more able to handle this than your local neighborhood coffee lady."

I laugh, then exhale, the sound more like acknowledgement than amusement. She's right.

One of the first things you learn as a therapist is that you *will* need your own therapist. A safe place to unburden yourself. In all my years of practice, I've never actually had that. Never thought I needed it.

Most of my work has been coaching spoiled executives and counseling people whose biggest obstacle was getting out of their own way. But this job? Being the team's therapist and performance coach? It's an entirely different beast.

Beautiful boys pretending to be men, each carrying enough baggage to sink a ship, burying it all in the game until the whistle blows and they're left with nothing but the weight of it again. It's heartbreaking.

And to add insult to my already fragile professional ethics, I've gone and fallen in love with my best friend's fine-ass father.

"You're right," I admit, my voice softer now. "I do need to talk to someone."

I squint, lowering my head a little in mock shame. "So...it's *really* a bad idea if I go over to his house for Sunday dinner with him and Marlow tonight, huh?"

Holly looks at me like I just spit P.O.J. straight in her F.A.C.E. "Bitch, what have we been talking about this whole time? That man is too fine for you to be in the same *zip code* without supervision! Why would you walk straight into the line of fire like that? Marlow is your friend. Grant is off-limits. Your vagina is one bad choice away from turning into a four-alarm blaze. I beg you—do not go to that man's house!"

I sigh. "Too late. I'm making the cornbread."

***

In the name of avoiding temptation—and by temptation, I mean Grant Mills in all his fine-ass, broad-shouldered, salt and pepper glory—I choose an outfit that practically screams *safe*. A black jogging suit and black-and-white sneakers. No heels. No cleavage. No risk.

I was told to dress down tonight, and when I warned Marlow that "dress down" for me usually means Timberlands or sneakers, she just shrugged and said I could come however I felt comfortable.

I love her for that. I love that every time I crack open the lid on my weird, shadowy self, she doesn't look away. Doesn't judge. She just meets me where I'm at and stays there.

By the time I'm seated at their massive dining table, the house smells like hot oil and lemon. Marlow is mid-story, animated, explaining how the fish we're eating was caught earlier this morning.

"On Dad's boat," she says, proud and glowing. "We battered and fried it as soon as we got back."

I glance at him. Grant grabs a piece of the cornbread I made, forearms flexing, completely unaware—or pretending to be—of the ache he triggers in me.

I remember in Vegas when he told me he and Maddy used to spend whole weekends out there on his boat. Sun. Water. Silence. Her beside him with a book. The memory presses against my ribs.

I keep my tone light. "Do you get out to the boat often these days?"

He lifts his water, measuring his words. "I'd like to, but..." A beat. "It's not the same without Maddy, and it's never as fun when it's just me. So, I like to ensure I have good company with me."

He smiles over at Marlow. Today's company.

Do I want to know if he's had *other* company on that boat? Other women? Yes. Do I want to risk ruining my friendship with Marlow to find out? Maybe. But instead, I wait. It's not time.

"So, Eslin," Marlow jumps in, redirecting. "How are things with Jones? He seems so smitten with you every time I ask him about you!"

I catch the way Grant swallows.

"Yes, Eslin," he adds, smoothly. "How are things with Jones?"

Bastard.

I smile sweetly. "Great. Thanks. Anymore cornbread anyone?"

"I'm fine thanks. It was really good, by the way!" Eslin beams. Clueless.

My attempts to change the subject are useless.

"Oh, come on! Don't be shy," Grant teases from the far end, and I shoot him a murderous glare. "Is coach Darren Jones everything you ever dreamed of in a man?"

If he weren't at the other end of this gigantic table, I'd knee him in the nuts.

"He is nice, respectful, kind—"

"Sounds delightful," Grant mutters under his breath.

"Good in bed?" Marlow waggles her eyebrows.

And I see Grant's wine slosh over the rim. Meanwhile, as Marlow keeps firing questions at me, not paying any attention to her filthy father, he's dragging his tongue along the side of the glass, licking the wine that spilled.

Deliberate. Slow. Dirty.

"Can we change the subject, please?" I snap, heat crawling up my neck.

"So that's a no? No good in bed?" Marlow presses.

"It's a 'let's not talk about things like this in front of your father!'" I hiss.

Because I don't want him knowing Darren and I haven't even kissed. I don't want him sensing I'll barely let another man touch me unless he can make me feel even a fraction of what Grant makes me feel just by *looking* at me. I don't want him knowing that, even though I swore I wouldn't wait for him, some pathetic, stubborn part of me is doing exactly that.

She leans back, hands up in surrender. "You're right. We'll save it for tomorrow's happy hour with the Stand-Ins."

"Great idea."

Grant just sits there with that look—smug-ass, fine-ass, bastard.

"What about you, Low?" Grant turns to Marlow. "You seeing anyone?"

Payback, bitch.

"Yeah, Low," I add, grinning. "Anyone getting your attention these days? Any players trying to push up on you?"

Grant snaps. Protective. "I'd better not hear about any players trying anything. We've talked about this, Low. These men are trouble and—"

"I can't afford trouble right now," Marlow says, finishing her dad's sentence.

I take a sip of my wine. "Right. Definitely can't afford anything remotely close to trouble. Or tattoos or—"

She glares at me, pretend coughing, while flashing me a middle finger.

I stick out my tongue.

"Like I've said before, I am not focused on dating right now," she says carefully.

"Oh yeah? What are you focused on?" I prod.

"*Bitch*," she mouths, eyes wide.

"*Yo daddy*," I mouth back.

"I am focused on my job. My responsibilities that keep mounting by the day." She looks to her dad, sweet as pie.

"Speaking of which, since I'm taking over most of your responsibilities, I'm glad to see *you* finally accepted a date invitation from Malina Matthews later tonight!"

This time I spill *my* drink. And it's not subtle or sexy. It's on my black hoodie.

Grant grins. Obviously enjoying this.

I narrow my eyes. "A date. Tonight. With Malina Matthews?" I try for casual, but the edge in my voice could slice through the cornbread.

He leans back, clearly savoring the moment. "What about her?"

"Oh, I don't know. How about *how* you two got together?" I twirl my fork, like it's no big deal. Like I'm not already annoyed at the thought of her perfect little billionaire life brushing up against his.

Marlow answers for him. "I was at a team function, and she asked about Daddy. Said she's always thought he was handsome and I offered to hook them up."

Traitor.

"How nice of you! Thoughtful." I say with a fake smile.

Malina Matthews. Billionaire heiress of Matthews Media. Perfect long, blonde hair, perfect wardrobe, perfect damn name. Honestly, it would never work. This family already has way too many people whose names start with M. It would be confusing on Christmas cards.

"Just...lovely," I say, forcing a smile so tight it could crack a molar.

"It's just a drink," Grant says, and there's a flicker in his tone. Like he's trying to reassure me, maybe even himself. "I can't keep saying no to Marlow every time she sets me up. She'll think I'm holding out for someone special."

His gaze catches mine, intentional. "Someone specific," he adds.

"And we can't have that," I say—only to him, my voice low enough that it doesn't carry.

For a moment, neither of us moves. The air between us feels heavier than it should, dense with all the things we keep shoving into the shadows in the name of oaths, honor, and respect. We're locked there, caught, like breaking eye contact might shatter whatever fragile control we have left. And I can see it—clear as day—want and restraint warring in him, just as they are in me.

If we don't look away, if we don't break this, Marlow will notice. She'll *know*.

So I force my body to move, my chair scraping lightly against the floor. "Before you go," I say, pushing the tension back down where it belongs, "let me make everyone a nightcap. My treat."

Grant leans back, one brow lifting in that slow, assessing way that makes my pulse skip. "One drink," he says, the corner of his mouth curving. "What could it hurt?"

I flash a sweet, innocent smile. "Of course. Just one."

While I'm in the kitchen mixing drinks, Grant disappears down the hall to change. I line up three glasses, adding a splash of whiskey here, a drizzle of honey there—just enough to make them look innocent.

Grant's drink gets a little *extra* attention. A generous pour of magnesium powder, stirred until it vanishes without a trace. One of my foster mothers used to keep some with her at all times and I never understood why. Now, I send up a silent thank you to the heavens for her wisdom because I keep magnesium capsules on me everywhere I go.

By the time I return to the living room with the tray of drinks balanced on my hands, he's back.

And damn.

Black slacks. Black turtleneck. The kind of outfit that makes him look like every woman's ideal book boyfriend and every man's benchmark. He's clean-shaven, hair perfectly in place, smelling faintly of cedar and something darker. He looks dreamy. Dangerous. And like someone who has no business taking Malina Matthews anywhere.

I set the drinks down on the coffee table, sliding his glass toward him with a smile so warm it could be framed as hospitality. "Here you go."

He takes it without question, fingers brushing mine. I keep my expression pleasant, sipping my own drink to disguise the flicker of satisfaction curling my lips.

Because tonight, no matter how flawless Malina Matthews looks in whatever couture cocktail dress she's probably poured herself into, she won't be getting much of Grant Mills' company.

Not when I've made sure he won't survive the first drink without an urgent, very inconvenient trip to the bathroom.

CHAPTER THIRTY SEVEN: DATE NIGHTS & DETOURS

Grant

Malina Matthews is even more polished in person than she was in my memory, which is saying something. Perfect posture, perfect manicure, and a smile that could probably sell bottled water to a drowning man.

For most men in my world, looking for arm candy that will never disappoint, she's *perfect*. We've crossed paths more than a few times over the years through industry fundraisers, charity galas, events where everyone knows everyone's business before the dessert course. And this woman always had an audience surrounding her.

Malina runs a sprawling media empire, a portfolio of specialty magazines that somehow manages to cater to wildly different audiences—cooking, solo travel, tech. She's built a reputation for spotting market gaps before anyone else even realizes they exist.

Once, years back, she'd asked for my advice on a company she was looking to acquire. I spent a late afternoon combing through their financial data with her, pointing out what wasn't on the surface—where they were bleeding money, why their numbers didn't match their story, and how she could leverage that weakness in a sale. She took my suggestions, closed the deal, and sent me a thank-you bottle of twenty-year-old Scotch.

Outside of that, I've never really thought of her as anything more than a polished, strategic acquaintance. One I happened to respect for her brains as much as her beauty.

Which is why, when Marlow mentioned her as a potential date, I was intrigued. Not sold. Just curious. I couldn't help but wonder what exactly my daughter was playing at. Sure, on paper Malina and I looked compatible. Both successful, connected, seasoned enough to know what we want. But the truth is, we couldn't be more different.

Malina is all sleek lines and calculated charm. A woman who thrives in boardrooms, on red carpets, and in glossy magazine spreads. Me? These days I'm more drawn to wild, fun, carefree energy that makes you forget the time and your better judgment. Even if that side of them only comes out when no one's looking.

I take another look at Malina. Really look. I can admire her. Respect her. Even enjoy her company. But no matter how much I like the *idea* of her, she could never be the reason I haven't dated anyone else in months.

She could never be Eslin.

We're barely into our first drink when it happens.

A low, traitorous rumble in my stomach.

Malina reaches across the table, her manicured hand resting lightly on mine while I pretend to study the menu. "I'm really glad you agreed to come out tonight. Our secretaries were getting sick of trying to coordinate our schedules."

I grin, though sweat is beading at my hairline. "Ha! Yeah. Sorry it's taken so long. Just busy," I manage. Because at this moment, I'm actually too busy focusing on the small war breaking out in my gut to come up with anything clever.

I shift in my seat, praying she didn't hear that ominous gurgle over the low hum of the restaurant.

The waitress appears just as Malina changes the subject to the one topic she's clearly most passionate about—herself.

"Can I get you two started with some appetizers?"

"Uh, no—" I start, but Malina steamrolls right over me.

"Actually, I'm a bit famished."

Well, shit. Please don't let her order something that takes longer than five minutes to hit the table. I'm not sure how much time my digestive system has left on the clock.

"I'll have the duck nachos, please," she says, smiling as she hands the menu over.

"Coming right up!" the waitress chirps before heading off.

Malina is full of conversation this evening. "I simply can't believe they expected us to pay full price after the CEO was caught with his hand down his assistant's pants, plummeting their stock prices!"

She's talking about her latest media acquisition, her words crisp and precise. I nod along like I'm actually processing any of it, but then—another rumble. Louder this time.

Jesus.

If that noise had come from the table instead of me, I'd be reaching for the salt to sprinkle on it.

I take another sip of water, trying to drown the problem before it becomes one. Bad idea. My gut twists like it's wringing out a towel.

"Are you alright?" she asks, tilting her head.

"Fine," I manage, smiling in a way that feels... unstable. Not charming, not suave—more like a man who just heard the Jaws theme playing in his intestines. "Just...uh...excuse me."

I stand up slowly, trying to maintain dignity, but my pace to the bathroom says *four-alarm emergency*. It's the kind of walk you do when you're not sure if running will make things better or much, much worse.

Once inside, I make it into the stall just in time to avoid becoming a headline on one of Malina's own gossip sites. The next few minutes are...well, let's just say they're not fit for polite conversation. Not fit for impolite conversation either, honestly.

I text my assistant from the bathroom: *Tell Malina I had a work emergency. Apologize. Tell her I'll call later.*

By the time I finally step out, the table where Malina had been sitting is empty. She's gone and I'm genuinely grateful. Not just because she didn't see me at my most vulnerable. But because, after only a few minutes of conversation, I already knew she'd never light my fire.

She's beautiful, sure. 'Engineered in a lab,' beautiful. But even with all that effortless beauty, there's nothing in her that sparks anything in me. If anything, the disaster in my stomach feels like divine intervention.

***

I make it home an hour later, ten pounds lighter, ten times angrier, and wondering if my digestive system will ever trust me again. I'm barely through the lobby when Eslin steps out of the building gym, hair pulled back, cheeks flushed from a workout, looking irritatingly pleased with herself. And sexy as hell.

"How was your date this evening?" she asks, smirking.

I stop. Stare. Narrow my eyes, mentally rewinding the night like a crime scene investigator. The last person to see my stomach alive and thriving was Eslin, standing in the living room with that innocent smile she uses when she's about to be anything but.

The thought hits me. No—she wouldn't. Especially if she doesn't want me. Especially if she's still dating that pompous ass with the perfect white teeth, Coach Jones.

"What," I say slowly, my voice flat with suspicion, "did you put in my drink?"

She blinks at me, all faux innocence. "Why, Grant, whatever do you mean?"

My stomach growls in answer.

I glare harder. "Eslin, why would you do that?"

She doesn't answer. She just turns on her heel toward the elevator. The elevator that doesn't even go to my floor, but I follow her anyway, my pulse hammering.

"Eslin!" I whisper-yell through gritted teeth, trying not to sound like the old man chasing the pretty young thing through the lobby. "Eslin, answer me!"

"I don't know what you're talking about, Grant!"

The doors slide open and three people shuffle out before we step inside. The second the doors close, it's just us—too much air and not enough space.

I back her against the wall, my shadow swallowing hers. She stares up at me. She's still glistening from her workout but the heat in her eyes isn't from the gym.

"I've sat and watched you parade Darren Jones in front of me—"

"You have *not* sat and watched! You made sure, every single time I went out with him, that I had you on my mind."

"But still...I let you go, Eslin."

Her chin tilts in defiance. "Let me? As in permission?"

"No. As in your freedom, Es. I'm trying to give you that freedom. And you have to give me the same."

The elevator dings for her floor, but I haven't been this close to her in days and I'm not ready to let this moment die.

My hand finds her waist. My eyes drag over her—how the black sports bra and pants cling to every curve, the way her chest still rises and falls like she's been running from something she can't shake.

Maybe me.

"This is me," she whispers, her head angling towards the elevator doors.

I pull her closer until my need is pressed against her, making it impossible for her not to feel exactly what she does to me every fucking time she's near.

"Does he touch you? Have you let him touch you?"

Her breath hitches. "Why?"

"You *know* why."

"Grant—"

"Does he make you want to forget me? Forget my touch?"

Her answer is barely a whisper, shaky and raw. "No."

It's not enough. I need it spelled out, carved into the air between us. "No, what? No, he doesn't touch you...or no, he doesn't make you want to forget me?"

Her gaze flickers down, then rises again, locking with mine. Those big, dark eyes—equal parts defiance and surrender—shake me like they always do. "All of it. No to all of it, Grant."

She swallows, her voice softer now. "I promised."

And that word...*promised*...lands in my chest like a match in dry grass. That night at the Halloween party immediately rushing to mind.

My hands find her neck, my forehead pressing to hers.

"I'm sorry for this."

She closes her eyes. "Sorry for what?"

"All of it," I whisper.

The elevator dings again. The doors open and close. But neither of us moves.

"I'm sorry for making you make that promise. For touching you like I owned you. For touching you like once would be enough. For making myself believe I could be near you and be fine."

A tear escapes down her cheek and I kiss it, then lick it.

"Eslin? If you want me to do better at letting you go, say it now. I'll go into hiding again. I'll stay away. I'll disappear if that's what it takes for you not to get distracted by me."

She opens her eyes, holding mine. "And what does *not* doing better look like?"

I move before I think, pulling her mouth to mine like I've been drowning and she's air.

Her taste is heat and ache and punishment all at once. My tongue finds hers, and it's not a kiss—it's a yield. Succumb.

My chest aches with the force of it, and I swear a sound almost breaks free from me when she pulls away to look at her phone.

I didn't even feel it vibrate but I catch the shift in her expression as she looks back up at me. "It's Marlow. She needs me."

Shit.

She presses the button to open the door. I force myself to step back.

Step aside.

"Grant, I'm sorry for tonight."

Her voice is soft, shaky.

"I don't even know what's gotten into me. That's the thing when it comes to you—I don't know who I am right now. I don't know what I need from you. I honestly don't. I'm a mess of confusion and secrets, and every time I'm near you, I get reckless. Careless."

My chest tightens, because she's not wrong—I've seen it in her eyes, the way she comes apart the second we're close. And still, hearing her say it out loud feels like a blow.

Her gaze flicks to mine then, sharp and vulnerable all at once. "So while every single part of me is screaming for you to come closer...to stay close...I think I need you to...*try harder.*"

One tear escapes before she can stop it.

"Please."

I nod once, tight, and let the elevator close between us.

And then she's gone again. Just as my stomach lets out a murderous rumble.

CHAPTER THIRTY EIGHT: CAMERAS & CHEMISTRY

Marlow

Declan and I have been...becoming *acquainted*. He's gone all in on taking care of me—cooking, forcing me to sleep, stocking the house and office with actual vegetables—and I've stopped pretending I'm not falling for my fake husband.

It's just after 10 p.m. on Sunday when my phone lights up with an unknown number. Probably a player or someone in the front office.

"Marlow Mills?" I answer.

"Marlow! Chelsea Raymond with SightUnseen. So glad I caught you before it was too late."

My heart kicks. "Chelsea! Hi! What are you doing calling? I mean, how are you?"

She giggles. "I keep odd hours, so I forget normal people stop taking calls by now. But I wanted to see if you'd be up for a visit from the crew tomorrow?"

"Um... tomorrow? So soon?"

"They're called pop-up visits for a reason!"

"Right," I say, stalling, twisting the hem of my sweatshirt between my fingers. "I just need to make sure Declan will be in town—he is a traveling athlete and all."

"Good idea! I mean, sure, we could just meet with you, but it would be great to see your chemistry in person! I've seen the tapes from your time in the pods and, let's just say, you two are the couple we are all rooting for!"

I blink, preparing to full on lose my shit. "There's...footage? From the pods? Has any of it aired?"

Chelsea lets out an airy laugh. "Oh, honey. You really didn't read anything you signed, did you?"

I thought I did. I thought I combed through every clause, every NDA, every stack of papers they shoved in front of us. But maybe I was too distracted. Too drunk. Too busy trying to convince myself that getting legally married to a man I'd only known through a wall wasn't the dumbest idea of my life.

"There were cameras everywhere except your honeymoon suite," Chelsea continues brightly. "And no, to answer your other question, none of your sessions have aired or been teased yet. Declan made sure of that when he called in last week."

I freeze. "Declan called? Last week?"

"Yes. He didn't tell you? He said you were stressed at work and he wanted to make sure that none of the footage got leaked that would make your life more difficult."

I press the phone harder to my ear, trying to process. Declan called them? On his own? To protect me?

My chest squeezes. Damn it. He takes care of me even when I don't realize it. Even when I don't ask. Even when I don't deserve it. I really am falling for this man.

"How about I check in tomorrow morning to see if Declan will be around?" Chelsea's voice cuts back in, snapping me out of my spiraling. "I'm really not supposed to give you this much heads-up, but like I said, it would be great to see you two together. Authentic. Unscripted."

I swallow. *Authentic. Unscripted.* Exactly what I've tried to avoid being with him—and exactly what I can't stop myself from becoming the moment he's near. Around Declan, every guard I've built slips, every mask falls away. With him, I am nothing but myself. Unmasked. Unfiltered. Authentic and unscripted.

"Sure, Chelsea," I manage. "Check back tomorrow morning."

We hang up, and I immediately call Declan. He's out with a few teammates. Boys' night and I hate to bother him, but we need to strategize.

Two rings. No answer.

I call again. No answer.

Fine. He's the one who set up location sharing on our phones. I tap the map.

And freeze.

The Supper Club.

"Are you kidding me?! You're at a fucking sex club?" I yell at no one.

I fire off a group text.

Me: Stand-Ins! Treat as urgent! Assemble! Meet me at The Supper Club!

Tatum replies in two seconds.

Tatum: Sounds all kinds of kinky. Count me in.

Eslin takes a beat.

Eslin: I don't know what we're in for, but I could use whatever you've got in mind.

I call my driver, pacing the sidewalk while I wait, anger buzzing beneath my skin like static. By the time the car door shuts behind me, I'm practically vibrating.

The whole ride over, I chew myself out in circles. For letting him charm me with that lazy grin and those damned tattoos. For letting my guard down because of his tenderness I didn't see coming. Because of the way he says *wife* like it means something. Like *I* mean something.

Clearly, I don't.

Because I'm sitting in the backseat of a black SUV, heading straight to *The Supper Club*. The Supper. Fucking. Club. A place that screams indulgence, secrecy, *public sin*. If he's in there, of all places, it's not just betrayal—it's humiliating. It's Declan telling the world what I didn't want to admit to myself: I let him in far enough to hurt me.

Good thing no one really knows about us. Because if the world knew—if there was even a chance that the world could see me heading to a sex club to hunt down my cheating *husband*—it would certainly end us for real. It feels like it's ending us now.

Each block the driver carries me closer, each second I sit stewing in the backseat, I can feel something unraveling inside me. Whatever fragile, dangerous thread had been tying me to Declan—his tenderness, his persistence, the illusion of safety he gave me—it's snapping one coil at a time.

And the worst part? It's not just anger burning through me. It's disappointment. It's heartbreak.

Because I thought he was different.

My nails dig crescents into my palms as I replay every soft look, every breakfast he cooked, every night he insisted I get rest, every time he reached for my hand like it was his right. I let myself believe he was different. *My husband.* Ha.

By the time we pull up to the curb, I'm a storm in sneakers, ready to explode.

And there they are—Eslin and Tatum—waiting for me on the curb like two avenging angels. Both in lethal black dresses, heels sharp enough to end a man, their faces carved with curiosity and the promise of danger.

I explain, my voice tight with rage. "My *husband's* phone is pinging inside. Which means *he's* inside. Which means *I'm* about to go cut a bitch!"

"I'm really loving this bad bitch side of you! Who knew you had a little violent streak?" Tatum teases.

Eslin raises a single finger, professor-mode activated, before letting her gaze sweep down over her and Tatum's outfits. "Um. Okay. So, love the energy. And you know we got your back and all, but I feel like maybe...just maybe...you should have warned us about what we were doing beforehand. Because clearly—" she gestures to her plunging neckline, "—we are dressed for the wrong occasion. And I usually carry vaseline for things like this."

I raise a brow. "Vaseline?"

Before I can respond, Tatum mutters, "Clearly, you have no idea who you're dealing with," and spins on her heel like an action hero mid-scene.

"Where the hell are you going?" I call after her.

"BRB!" she shouts over her shoulder, sprinting toward the valet stand like she's about to tackle someone and steal their car. The poor valet boys scatter, not sure if they should stop her or just get out of her way.

Two minutes later, she reappears smirking, clutching a massive black duffel bag like it's Santa's sack of vengeance. She drops it at our feet with a dramatic *thud.*

I frown. "What's this?"

She huffs like it's obvious. "Thankfully, I always travel prepared for either a workout or a beat down. The attire is the same either way."

"I'm sorry?" I blink.

"There are workout outfits in here that me and Eslin can change into. Extra shoes and everything. Once we're inside, we'll use the facilities, put our sexy clothes in a locker, and then go yank some slut off your husband's dick."

Eslin and I trade a look. Then shrug in unison.

"Sounds like a plan to me," I say.

Chapter Forty

CHAPTER THIRTY NINE: SUPPER CLUBS & SHOWDOWNS

Marlow

The Supper Club is high-end, members only, and the kind of discreet that costs an annual salary. Since my father has been a card-carrying member since I was a teenager, I'm able to get in on his name whenever I want.

The main floor looks like a designer lounge—sleek bar with crystal decanters, a velvet-roped VIP, a low stage for performances (music during the week, other types on weekends), and beautiful staff weaving through with trays of complimentary drinks. If you didn't know better, you'd think you'd wandered into a very expensive hotel bar.

Five minutes later, Tatum and Eslin exit the locker corridor in black leggings, sports bras, and sneakers—hair up, earrings off, ready to square up. I was already dressed for a fight so now we look coordinated.

"Should we ask someone if they've seen him?" Tatum asks, her voice a little too eager.

I shake my head. "No. I prefer the element of surprise."

We pile into the elevator, the air between us thick with adrenaline and simmering anger. My pulse drums in my ears, but what steadies me—what fuels me—is the presence of my Stand-Ins at my side. No hesitation. No questions. Just loyalty. They're ready to go to war for me on little more than my word and a phone ping.

My phone glows in my hand, Declan's little blue dot pulsing like a beacon. I can feel my pulse syncing with every ding. Second floor. Third. Fourth. Each chime might as well be the strike of a war drum.

The doors glide open and for a second I forget how to breathe.

The fourth floor doesn't look like the den of debauchery I had conjured in my head at all. This place looks like money. Quiet, understated, luxury hotel money. Muted cream carpet underfoot, gilded numbers glowing softly on each door, lighting low, designed to soothe or seduce. The scent of something expensive lingers in the air, faint sandalwood layered with the sweetness of champagne.

Some suites are shut tight, giving nothing away. Others have smoked-glass windows with half-drawn curtains, offering quick flashes of silhouettes and shadows moving inside. A pair of red heels abandoned outside one door, a man's jacket draped neatly over a brass handle at another. Every detail feels like proof of what I came here dreading.

My husband is here with another woman. And I'm going to murder is manhood with a machete.

The bass from the main floor has faded to a dull hum, replaced by this heavy silence that feels too knowing, too polished. Like the walls themselves are in on the secrets being kept here.

My phone buzzes, hard and insistent in my palm. I glance down and the dot pulses again—looks like he's right next door.

"Bastard," I whisper, the word ripping out of me before I can stop it.

We gather outside the door, whisper-arguing strategy.

"Bang on it like the angry wife and yank that hoe off your man," Tatum votes.

"Or, Eslin interjects calmly, "play it cool. Get proof, then decide your response."

Then she leans in and places a hand on my shoulder. "How are you feeling?" she asks me, gently.

"I don't need therapy shit right now, Es. I need to punch something."

"Okay, Mayweather. Calm down," she mutters. "I'm asking because if you're hurt, don't let that decide your reaction. You could say or do something you don't mean. You honestly don't know what he's doing here."

"It's a sex club," I deadpan. "There are only a *few* things other than sex he'd be doing here."

"Exactly," Tatum says, cracking her knuckles.

I decide I've had it. Enough waiting. Enough overthinking. Enough wondering what fresh humiliation is waiting for me behind this door.

"You know what? Fuck it."

My fist connects with the wood in a furious rhythm. Each pound louder than the last. "Declan! Bring your lying, sleazy, cheating ass out here right now!" My voice ricochets down the corridor, sharp enough to draw curious glances from the cracked-open door across the hall.

"Old, tattooed, fine ass!" Tatum suddenly hollers beside me like a hype-woman with no filter. Or good comebacks.

Both me and Eslin whip our heads toward her, jaws slack.

Tatum blinks, hands on her hips. "What? Sorry. I've never been good at trash talk. That was the first thing that came to mind."

Eslin groans and drags a hand down her face. "Lord, help us."

Before I can snap back, the lock clicks. The door creaks open.

I brace myself for a half-dressed woman stumbling out. For Declan's guilty face. For a scene that'll ruin me.

But what greets me instead?

Not moans. Not naked limbs.

But a freaking study hall.

Books stacked like mini skyscrapers. Flashcards scattered across every surface. Whiteboards filled with equations and sticky notes like confetti explosions. And right in the center, Matteo, and Luca— looking up at me like I've just interrupted Sunday school.

"What are you doing here?" Declan demands, eyes flashing from me to my backup squad.

"What am I—what are you doing here?" I snap.

Matteo lifts a flash card slowly. "Uh... derivatives?"

Declan scrubs a hand over his jaw. "We're helping Matteo prep for his college entrance exams."

I blink hard, my brain trying to catch up with what my eyes are showing me. "At. A. Sex. Club." I enunciate each word like I'm sounding them out for a toddler, because apparently that's what this situation calls for.

Declan's jaw tightens, like he's bracing for a punch.

Luca, bless his idiot heart, pipes up with a shrug. "I'm a member and—"

I snap my glare to him so fast he nearly swallows his own tongue. "Not helping."

Matteo, cheeks flushed and a stack of neon note cards clutched to his chest like they're state secrets, blurts, "I don't want anyone to know I'm studying for the exams."

Tatum bites back a laugh, failing spectacularly. "Honestly? Kind of genius. If I had a math tutor in here, no one would ever interrupt."

Eslin side-eyes her. "Girl, please. You can barely focus in a Starbucks. You would get nothing done here."

"He's embarrassed, Marlow. No one in his family has ever been to college and he didn't want to say anything in case he fails."

I drag my hands down my face, exhaling a long groan. "So, let me get this straight. I stormed into The Supper Club—" I jab a finger at Declan, then point at Matteo and Luca—"ready to murder somebody because my *husband's* phone was pinging here, only to find out you three degenerates have turned a luxury sex den into an SAT prep class?"

The word hangs there like a fire alarm I can't silence.

Luca's eyes go wide, his jaw practically unhinging. Matteo actually drops his note cards, the neon stack fanning across the carpet in slow motion.

"Husband?" they echo, voices overlapping in one horrified gasp.

The room tilts. My stomach lurches.

Oh. Shit.

I wasn't supposed to say that. No one outside of my friends and Declan was supposed to know that.

Heat rushes to my cheeks. My mouth opens, then closes, then opens again, scrambling for some clever spin. "I—uh—I meant—"

But nothing comes.

Declan's arms fold across his chest. He doesn't say a word, which somehow makes it worse. He's just standing there, watching me scramble.

"Oh my God," Matteo whispers, eyes flicking between me and Declan. "You guys are *married*?"

My hands start flailing, trying to shove the words back into the air. "I mean—it's—it's not like that, okay? It's—complicated."

"Complicated?" Luca repeats, his grin spreading. "Complicated how, boss?"

My pulse slams against my throat. The walls feel too close, the sticky notes mocking me with words like *integrity* and *equation*. All I can think about is if this gets out, if the team hears, if the press hears.

I glance at Declan, silently begging him to step in, to rescue me from the mess I just spilled all over the carpet. But his mouth just curls, infuriatingly calm and I can tell he enjoys watching me sweat.

Fucking bastard.

Before I can dig the hole any deeper, Eslin slides in like the seasoned therapist she is, eyes darting between Luca and Declan.

"Luca?" she says smoothly, though her teeth are clenched like she's holding back a scream. "You and Declan have a lot more in common than you might think."

Luca's brow furrows. So does Declans. Confusion written all over their faces.

"I don't understand." Luca says.

Eslin's smile sharpens, still strained. "I can't break privilege. But...think about that thing you told me a few weeks ago. And the thing I talked you out of doing because of a certain...incident? In a certain city of *sin*?"

Luca's mouth parts. His head tilts. You can practically see the gears grinding behind his eyes before the lightbulb clicks on. His gaze snaps to Declan, wide and scandalized.

"No way. No freaking way!"

"Luca—" I start, desperate, but it's too late.

"You got married on *SightUnseen* in Vegas?!" he blurts, pointing at Declan.

Declan doesn't even flinch. Doesn't deny it. He just leans against the door frame, arms still folded.

"So, let me get this straight," Matteo says slowly. "You two are *married*—from some reality TV show—and didn't tell anyone?"

Declan angles his head toward me, smirk tugging at his lips. "She wouldn't let me. My wife seems to think being tied to me would ruin her reputation."

I scoff, heat rushing to my cheeks. "Not now, Declan."

He shrugs.

Luca suddenly throws his hands up. "At least you *know* who you married." He pauses, squinting as if the thought itself is exhausting. "The only reason you haven't heard about *my* wife is because I don't exactly remember her name."

That breaks us all. Even me, despite myself. Giggles burst out, laughter spilling across the room until my ribs ache.

"Marlow here gave me a fake name when we got married."

"No way!" Luca says again and another round of laughter begins.

I sober quicker than the rest, cutting in before anyone can forget what's at stake. "Alright, funny as this is, I need to know this stays in this room. At least about me and Declan."

"At least until I remember my bloody bride's name," Luca adds, which earns him another round of chuckles.

Matteo looks around, his expression torn between wide-eyed awe and boyish mischief. "So you want me to keep quiet, huh? What, you want me to swear over a blood oath or something?"

Declan leans forward then, grin sharp but his tone suddenly heavier, carrying that quiet authority that makes grown men twice his size straighten up. "No blood oath needed. Just know if you say anything, I'll make sure you won't make it to study hall for a month."

The threat hangs there. Dark. Serious.

And damn it all—scary yet sexy.

I look over at Declan, the fire in me cooling as I take in the sight of note cards and sticky notes plastered across the walls. My chest tightens, not with anger anymore, but with something closer to shame for assuming the worst.

I married a good man and I almost didn't recognize it.

"So, studying. That's all you were doing? No slutty skanks hanging all over your penis?"

Declan doesn't snap back or bristle. He just pulls me in, grounding me instantly, and presses a steady kiss against my mouth. My shoulders sag with relief as he pulls back just enough to whisper, "No slutty skanks, Señora Agassi."

His grin is soft, satisfied, and then he kisses the tip of my nose, soothing every jagged edge of my doubt.

Eslin throws up her hands. "So we're standing here all greased up and ready to fight for *nothing*?"

Declan glances past me to my girls, still in their backup fight gear, then back at me. "Greased up?"

I shake my head, this time with a breathy laugh instead of rage. "Don't even ask."

"Noted," he says. "Did you bring the town car or the SUV?" he asks.

"The SUV brought me. Why?"

He kisses me again, slower this time, and when he leans back, his grin is easier, lighter. "Well, wife, I kind of like you being jealous. Showing up with your own little hit squad, ready to tear this place apart just because you thought some woman was near me."

His eyes soften, even as his voice dips rough. "Where I come from, that wins a man's heart before anything else."

My smile tilts, small but real. "Murder?"

"You'd kill for me." His thumb brushes over my jaw, his eyes never leaving mine. "I'd die for you. We fit, Americana."

He's right.

This man pulls things out of me I didn't even know I was capable of feeling. Fire and fury I can't always control. Rage, sharp enough to make me storm a sex club with my ride-or-die girls in tow. Jealousy that burns hotter than anything I've ever known, all because the idea of losing him makes my chest ache. He makes me crazy, reckless, ready to commit actual felonies—and somehow he does it while being the sweetest, most tender man I've ever let near my heart.

I don't recognize this version of myself, but standing here in his arms, I don't hate her either. Because the truth is, I *would* kill for him. Just as easily as I know he'd bleed for me.

We're fire and gasoline. Dangerous. Addictive. Impossible to put out.

We fit.

Behind me, Tatum groans. "Aww! How *sweet*," she drawls sarcastically. "Now that the lovebirds are back together, Eslin and I will be going back downstairs to change into our hoe attire and let some rich men order us expensive drinks."

Declan just smirks, not looking away from me. "That's fine," he says easily.

"Because I'm taking my wife home." Then he leans down, lips brushing the shell of my ear, voice a promise meant only for me. "And I plan to feast on her all night long. She's the only supper club I'll ever care to be a member of."

Chapter Forty-One
CHAPTER FORTY: HEADLIGHTS & HEAT
Declan

The second the door shuts, I've got Marlow's face in my hands. I don't even wait for the driver to pull away—I drag her mouth to mine like I've been holding my breath all night.

Her lips part under mine and we're a mess immediately—tongues colliding, tasting, taking. She's warm, sweet, intoxicating, and I can't get close enough.

My wife.

The thought hits me harder than the kiss. The way she stormed into that club tonight proved it—she's finally stopped fighting what's been burning between us since the moment we met. From the second I heard men try to win her in those pods, I knew. I claimed her instantly. She's mine. And since that day, I've never wanted anything so completely.

I fist her ponytail, tugging until her head tilts back, her neck bared just for me. The sight makes me salivate. I sink my teeth into her skin, hard enough to make her jolt, and the sound she lets out nearly undoes me. I soothe the sting with my tongue, dragging a slow, wet line from her collarbone all the way to her ear.

She moans and it sparks through me, sharp and electric.

Her hands slide under my jacket, clutching at me like she's staking her own claim. Every tug, every scratch of her nails through the fabric is proof—she wants me just as fiercely.

I kiss her harder, sucking at her bottom lip, swallowing the little sound she makes. The driver is a ghost, the city nothing but a blur. All I see is her, all I feel is her heat, her fight, her surrender—finally, fully, mine.

She laughs against my mouth, but it turns into a gasp when I fist my hand in her hair again, tilting her head so I can kiss her deeper. My other hand stays locked on her cheek, thumb brushing the soft line of her jaw as if it'll brand me with the memory later.

She claws at me—my jacket, my shoulders, anything she can anchor herself to—dragging me in until her body is pinned against the window. The glass fogs, the driver shifts uncomfortably, but I couldn't care less. The world can burn outside this car for all I care. Right now, there's only her.

Her taste floods my mouth, sweet and sensual. The small, needy sounds she makes when I take her bottom lip between my teeth take me apart in ways I'll never admit. She writhes beneath me, restless and desperate, and Christ—so am I.

Her mouth is wild, perfect. She's a fucking storm—and I want to drown in it.

Her hand slips lower, bold, teasing, pressing against the ache that's been torturing me since the second she stormed into my life. My wife. And I've never wanted anyone, anything, more than I want her.

The quiet click of the partition breaks through as the driver gives us some privacy. And then we're alone. No audience. No restraint.

She knows it too. I see it in the flicker of her eyes before she shifts, sinking down, her gaze locked on mine as she kneels at my feet.

"Marlow," I breathe, voice tight. "My love, you don't have to. I can wait until we get home—"

Her hands work my zipper as if I haven't said a word. "What if I can't...wait?" She asks, and silences me with a single lick, her tongue tasting me, teasing me, claiming me.

"Fuck." The word rips from my chest, raw and reverent, because she's taken the last of my control with one slow sweep of her tongue.

"I'm sorry," she whispers against me before dragging her mouth the length of my shaft, deliberate and slow, like she's savoring her favorite sin.

"For what?" My voice is a growl, my grip tightening in her hair, but I can't think of a single reason this woman should ever apologize.

"For assuming the worst of you," she says, tilting her head just so, before she swallows me whole—deep, perfect, her throat tightening around me until my vision blurs.

"Good fucking girl," I groan, the words pulled from the center of me as I fist her ponytail, guiding her mouth over me again and again.

The windows are fogged, the air thick with heat, and the backseat pulses with the filthy, unrestrained sounds of my wife taking me deeper. It's all so beautiful—her gasps, her sucks, her chokes as she strains for air—breaking me apart with every inch that she takes me deeper.

And heavens me, my wife is apologizing in the only way she knows how...with devotion on her lips and the most devastatingly sensual surrender I've ever witnessed.

Each movement of her mouth is a confession, each gasp a vow. She's unraveling me, until there's nothing left but need and the violent thrum of desire coursing through my veins.

"Look at me," I rasp, and when her eyes lift—dark, glistening, locked on mine—it's over. I'm done. Ruined. I'll always be ruined for her. My wife. My salvation. Mrs. *fucking* Agassi.

She doesn't falter. Doesn't stop sucking. Doesn't stop taking me deeper, like her only purpose in this world is to bring me to my knees.

"I want to see what my wife's face looks like when I empty myself down her throat."

She nods, giving me permission, giving me everything. Approval. Access. Her devotion, written in the silent shimmer of her gaze.

I cradle her face in my palms, the only softness I have left to give, before I surrender to the hunger that's been clawing at me all night. I thrust into her mouth, hard, desperate, relentless, until my release tears through me and I spill every last piece of myself down her throat.

And as she swallows me—every drop, every ragged moan—I realize this is what forgiveness feels like. This is what it feels like to absolve the only woman who has ever had the power to destroy me.

For her, I'll forgive anything.

CHAPTER FORTY ONE: POPCORN & THE POPE

Eslin

G rowing up the way I did—bounced from one house to another, suitcase never fully unpacked—Thanksgiving was never more than a date on the calendar. Another day to get through. Another reminder that family dinners and warm traditions belonged to other people, not me. Plus, I knew enough about America to understand that pilgrims and Indians weren't clinking glasses in a cheerful union that day. It wasn't some storybook holiday to celebrate—it was blood and survival dressed up with turkey and pie. So, I never saw the point in pretending. No handmade traditions. No "what are you thankful for" circles around the table. Thanksgiving, for me, was just another Thursday.

That is, until I met Maxine Palmer—hopeless romantic and holiday enthusiast. Max is the kind of woman who has a Pinterest board for every season. Since the day we became friends in college, Max has refused to let me sit out a single holiday. Halloween? She shoved me into a Cleopatra costume and dragged me to three different frat houses. Juneteenth? She insisted sparklers were "non-negotiable." And one Christmas, when I moved into my very first apartment, Max flew to New York, took me to a tree lot to pick out the cheapest, cutest pine she could find, and helped me decorate my very first tree.

For the first time in my life, someone gave me traditions. She gave me belonging. I hadn't felt like I had a family until Max came barreling into my world, planting herself firmly in my heart, and making me her sister in everything but blood.

So while I'm genuinely excited about the Thanksgiving gala Tatum has planned for the team, her over-the-top soirées regarded as nothing but legendary, I'm mostly counting down the days until I get to wrap my arms around Max again when she comes for Thanksgiving. And this time, she's bringing her new man, Eli. I can't wait to meet him. I've never met a Black lumberjack.

It's Friday night and I'm just about to start the marathon of taking down my braids so I can wash and prep for the stylist Marlow's bringing in for the gala tomorrow when my phone rings.

Coach Jones.

I roll my eyes at the name on the screen even though he's done nothing wrong. "Hey, Coach!" I answer brightly, tucking my phone between my ear and shoulder while I pop a fresh bowl of popcorn, grab a bottle of wine, and cue up *Scandal* from season one. Again.

Olivia Pope is my emotional support bitch.

"I wish you would call me Darren," he says, his tone half a whine, half a chuckle. "No woman I have ever dated has called me Coach the way you do."

Dated.

The word makes me shiver, and not in a good way. I still haven't told Coach Jones—Darren—that this isn't going anywhere. That this little situationship expired long before it began. He never stood a chance.

I don't like stringing men along, but every time I think about breaking it off, I freeze. It's easier to delay because there are moments when I think I really could be into him. But those moments never last.

"So, what have you got going on tonight?" he asks, his South African accent rolling out warm and bubbly.

I perk up, but not at him—at the thought of my actual plans. "Just taking down my hair, washing it, watching old episodes of *Scandal*." It doesn't escape me that I sound more excited about Shonda Rhimes reruns than about this man on the other end of the line.

He laughs. "Ah, the old ritual of Black women taking their hair down. You want some company? I can help—I've done it plenty of times for my mom and sisters."

My heart stops. Company? In my apartment? With my hair half out and looking like a baby porcupine? Oh, no.

"That's sweet," I start carefully, trying to find the polite exit ramp, "but I prefer to take my hair down by myself. I'm paranoid about someone cutting too high on the braid and snipping my hair."

"I get it," he says quickly, no offense taken.

"Will I see you tomorrow at the gala?"

I told him I'd be too busy working the room with Tatum to bring a plus one, and he bought it. A small part of me doesn't want Grant to see me with him and I hate how guilty it makes me feel—Darren's nice. Like... *too* nice.

"Yeah, I'll be there. That's why I'm taking my hair down. Marlow's got a stylist coming to get us all glammed up."

"Nice!" he says, cheerful as ever. "Well, I won't keep you. I just wanted to say hello. And, hey, save a dance for me tomorrow, will you?"

I know...I'm the villain in this man's story.

"Thanks, Coach...Darren. I'll see you tomorrow."

I hang up, stare at the phone for a long beat, and sigh. Time to end this before he wastes his tenderness on a woman whose heart is already tangled up in someone else.

Just as the microwave goes off, signaling that my popcorn is ready, all the power in my apartment goes out.

It's pitch black. My heart lurches, a hot rush of panic flooding my chest. I fumble for my phone, swiping up the flashlight. The beam is small, weak, but it's enough to cut through the darkness.

I sweep it around the apartment, looking for...something. A fuse box? A switch? Do apartments like this even have one? I don't know. I've lived here a while and never bothered to find out. I call Marlow, hoping she might know, but it goes straight to voicemail. She's probably at Declan's, tangled up in tattoos and trouble.

The beam of my flashlight shakes as I make my way to the door. I pull it open, glance down the hall. Every single light is on. The hum of electricity is steady. So it's just me. Just my apartment.

Perfect.

I don't want to do it. I shouldn't do it. But I do it anyway. My thumb hovers over his name for less than a second before I press call.

He answers on the first ring. "Is everything ok?" His voice is rough, alert, and that makes me believe he'd come running no matter the reason.

Relief softens me. "Yes. No. My lights are out in my apartment. Can you come over to help me find the fuse box before I call an electrician?"

"Be right there."

The line clicks dead, and my pulse jumps.

A few minutes later, there's a knock at my door. And that's when I realize I've already started taking out my braids. Which means my hair is half-done, sticking out in uneven tufts, looking like a damn brillo pad. Grant Mills is about to see me at my most... unvarnished. With a damn nappy head.

But when I open the door, he doesn't even blink. Doesn't mention my hair. Just strides in with a flashlight like he owns the place, heads straight for the closet in my bedroom, flips a couple of switches and—voila. The lights blaze back on.

"Oh my goodness, you are a life saver!" I exhale, clutching my chest. "I thought I was going to have to take my hair down in the dark!"

His brow furrows. "Take your hair down? Like... your braids out?"

I giggle, suddenly shy. "Yes."

His gaze lingers, curious. "I've always wondered how you got those in. And how you take them out."

That's when he notices. The popcorn on the counter. The wine bottle, already open. His eyes flick back to me. Tentative. Almost shy.

"Are you preparing for a night of *Scandal* reruns?"

I blink. "How did you guess?"

"The wine and popcorn gave it away. I may have watched an episode here and there," he confesses.

I grin. "Here and there, huh?"

He shrugs. Then he hesitates, his mouth tips like he's asking something bigger than the words suggest. "You, maybe, want some company?"

"Yes." My answer falls out so fast it startles me. But the truth is, while I didn't want Darren Jones to see me all nappy-headed and vulnerable, I don't mind if it's Grant. I don't mind him seeing me.

Why do I keep putting myself in danger like this? Why do I lose all sense the second his shadow crosses my line of sight? Every time he's near, it's like my body is wired to move toward him, no matter how much my mind screams to turn away. Why can't I stop? Why can't I stop chasing the fire I know will burn me alive? Why can't I stop running straight into him—like he's not the very thing I should be running from?

I've always read about the *fuck it* moments in romance novels—the precise second when someone decides to throw reason out the window, silence every voice of logic, and step into the thing they know they shouldn't want but can't stop craving. The point of no return. And standing here, with him so close I can feel the air shift around us, his presence pressing in on every nerve, I know I'm teetering on that edge. One breath away. One heartbeat away. Almost there. Almost more than halfway to *fuck it*.

We settle onto the couch, popcorn bowl between us, scissors, plastic bag, and rat-tail comb laid out like tools for a quiet ritual. I cue up *Scandal*, and soon Olivia Pope's white coats and reckless entanglements fill the room.

Somewhere between seasons one and two, I hand Grant a braid and show him how to work it loose. His big hands fumble at first, too cautious, tugging like I'm made of glass. I laugh, guiding his fingers until he finds a rhythm. Slowly, we fall into sync—him unweaving, me dropping braids into the bag at my feet, the simple intimacy of it weaving something else entirely between us.

Hours pass like minutes. We've burned through nearly two seasons, our commentary sharp and ridiculous—laughing at Fitz, rolling our eyes at Cyrus, agreeing that nobody but Kerry Washington could ever be Olivia Pope.

By the time we reach season two, episode nineteen, it's late. Huck is muttering *"752"* over and over on the screen, my scalp is tender from hours of unwinding, and Grant is concentrating harder than I've ever seen him. Tongue caught between his teeth. Brows furrowed like this is brain surgery and not just hair.

And then it happens.

Snip.

The sound slices through the room.

I freeze. Slowly, I turn, suspicion already crawling up my spine. "What was that?"

Grant flinches like a kid caught with his hand in the cookie jar. "What was what?" he says too fast.

My eyes narrow. "Grant."

He tucks his hand behind his back, still holding something, still gripping the scissors. "Nothing. Totally fine. Everything's... intact."

"Grant." My voice sharpens.

He gives me a sheepish grin, then—God help me—tries to blow the severed braid behind the couch cushion like it's incriminating evidence.

I catch a glimpse of the braid and notice the length. It's too long.

My jaw drops. "Did you just—?"

But it's too late. The answer to my unfinished question hangs in the air, undeniable. A thick braid in his guilty hand. Way too much hair clinging to it.

"Oh my *God.*" Panic floods me, my hand flying to the back of my head. "What did you do?!"

His face crumples. "Okay, okay—I might have... clipped a little too close. But you moved!"

"I did *not* move!" I groan, clutching the missing piece of me like it's a body at a wake. "You cut my actual hair, Grant! Not the braid—the *hair!*"

He stammers, horrified. "Shit. Shit. Es, I'm sorry. I was—I got distracted by Huck, and the whole 752 thing, and—"

"You think?!" I collapse against the couch, eyes squeezing shut. "What the hell is my stylist going to do with this?!"

Onscreen, Huck whispers *"752"* again, rocking back and forth in place.

I throw my arm over my face, start rocking back and forth myself and mutter, "Yeah, Huck. Same!"

Grant's voice is careful, almost tiptoeing. "So... I feel like maybe I should go and let you deal with this."

I pin him with a glare sharp enough to kill a lesser man. "Give me my scissors, hand me my wine glass, and get out."

His brows lift. "I just said I'd leave—"

"Don't *correct me* in my own damn house!" My voice cracks with embarrassment. "I know what I said!"

For half a second, his mouth twitches—like he's fighting a laugh—but I'm too wound up to care.

"Eslin, I'm really sorry," he rushes. "If there's anything I can do—find you a different stylist, buy you the fanciest wig, whatever you need—just—"

"Get. Out!" I snap, each word its own bullet.

He raises both hands in surrender and backs toward the door. "Okay, okay—I'm going."

The moment it shuts behind him, the fight drains out of me. My chest caves. Tears spill.

Not because of the hair—though the hair is a real problem. No, I cry because tonight I caught a glimpse of what it could be like to just...relax. To let myself be. To be seen in all my unguarded ridiculousness—my head half-undone, braids in a bag at my feet, my hair sticking in every possible direction—and not be met with disgust.

Grant saw all of that.

He saw me.

And the ache in my chest—I can't decide if it's humiliation... or relief.

Relief that someone saw me stripped of polish and pretense—messy, awkward, undone—and didn't flinch. Didn't mock. Didn't bolt for the door until I made him leave. Relief that for once, I didn't have to hide the parts of myself I usually keep locked away. He saw every imperfect strand, every sharp edge, every uncurated piece—and he stayed.

He didn't send me back.

Didn't make me feel like too much.

If anything, the only one who couldn't bear the sight of me in this moment...was me.

CHAPTER FORTY TWO: SECRETS & SOFAS

Eslin

I sit down on the soft leather couch, already nervous before she even opens her mouth. The space is cozy but intentional—warm lamps, abstract art, a small fountain trickling in the corner like it's supposed to trick me into feeling calm. It doesn't. Not when my chest is this tight.

This was the only appointment she had available, so despite the scarf tied over my head and the fact that I look like the second coming of a crackhead, I still show up. Of all days, it has to be today—the day of the masquerade ball—when my bald spot is begging for divine intervention and a stylist's miracle. Thankfully, her office isn't too far from my building.

Dr. Mikari, as her profile said everyone calls her, greets me with the kind of calm that makes me want to unravel right there. And when she leans forward with that classic therapist question—*what brings you here?*—I don't just answer. I spill.

"Here's the thing, Dr. Mikari," I blurt, words tripping over each other. "I am new in town, with a new job, and I've met these wonderful people who have become like family, but I'm also keeping *a lot* of secrets from them. Including my best friend. And my boss. Because if I tell her I have very real feelings for her father, it could ruin everything! But I'm also keeping a secret *about her* from her father and—"

She lifts a hand, calm but firm. "How about you take a breath?"

I clamp my mouth shut, embarrassed, and grab the glass of water she gave me when I first arrived. One long sip, a shaky exhale. "I'm sorry," I mutter, pressing the glass to my knee. "I think I've just been waiting for the opportunity to—"

"Unburden yourself?" she offers, one brow arched.

I'm not discriminatory about who I let guide me from a therapist's perspective. Help is help. But there's something about sitting across from someone who looks like you, who may have walked through similar fires—or at the very least has the empathy to understand them—that hits differently. It settles into you in a way that feels less clinical and more... safe. Comforting in a way I didn't know I needed.

"Yes." I nod furiously, my locs bouncing. "Yes, exactly."

Her smile is small, patient. "Alright then. Let's start from the beginning."

So I do. Vegas. The secret marriages. The mess of emotions that followed. Every tangled piece of it, pouring out in fits and stutters until the words are gone and I'm left slumped against the cushions, raw but lighter somehow.

"I understand how challenging it is to carry around so many secrets, especially when you're in such close proximity to the very people you're trying to shield from the truth. For whatever reason. But I also think you might be selling your community short."

My brows knit. "What do you mean?"

Dr. Mikari clears her throat, her tone measured. "From the way you've described these people—Marlow in particular—I don't think she would react as viscerally as you're assuming."

I let out a humorless laugh. "Not according to her father. And she's part Italian. The girl's got spunk, and I'm not entirely sure I can take her."

That earns a smile from Dr. Mikari, even a small laugh before she schools her face again. "Be that as it may, her father sees things through the lens of a parent. Friends—true friends—get through to us differently. And it sounds like you know that."

I nod slowly. "Sure. But...I've never had *this* before. Any of it."

She tilts her head. "I'm not sure I understand."

I grip the glass of water tighter, the words heavy in my throat. "I've never had a friend like her. And I've also never had feelings for a man like him. For *any* man. So even though a part of me wants to run straight to Grant and just...give

him all of me, consequences be damned—I can't risk losing what I've built with
Marlow."

"Because it feels like a family," she finishes softly.

My throat tightens. "As crazy as it sounds, yes."

"It doesn't sound crazy at all." Dr. Mikari leans forward, her eyes steady on
mine. "But one thing about family—they fight, they break, they bend. And they
make up. Love doesn't let them stay away too long."

I nod a silent agreement.

By the time we wrap up, I'm gripping that empty glass like it's glued to
my hand. "I've never needed my *own* therapist before," I admit softly, "but
now...with all of this, with these feelings I can't seem to fight...I hope I can count
on you."

Dr. Mikari's eyes soften, and she gives me the kind of nod that feels like
permission. "Of course. And lucky for you, I have a slot open for new patients."

Before I leave her office, I pause with my hand on the doorframe and turn
back to her.

"I'm seeing Grant at a ball for work tonight," I admit, my voice softer, almost
guilty. "And I know myself well enough to know what will happen if I'm around
him. Every time we're close, my ability to resist him just vanishes more and more
each time."

Dr. Mikari tilts her head. "Is there a question in there somewhere?"

I exhale, shoulders slumping. "How do I resist him, Dr. Mikari?"

She folds her hands in her lap, her tone measured but edged with something
knowing. "I think the better question is...how long do you really believe you'll
be able to? How long can you both keep walking this line before it consumes
you?"

***

The mirror's gold trim is gaudy, but it does the job. I swipe another line of
liner under my eye, blot my lipstick, and give my reflection a once-over. Perfectly

polished. Mask in place. No one in this ballroom would guess that just last night, I was crying on my couch over a bald spot and the man who gave it to me.

Thankfully, the bald spot was more like a speck and the hairstylist did her best work, adding a few hair pieces to mask spots. And I look good. I just can't wait to put my braids back in, it's become part of my brand, my identity and I have grown to hate being without them.

The bathroom door swings open and laughter spills in—high, tinkling, reeking of champagne and entitlement. I keep my head down, fixing the strap of my gown, until someone's words cut sharper than any blade.

"Honestly, I don't care who else bids. The silver fox is mine."

Silver fox. My stomach plummets.

Grant.

I turn my head just enough to catch the reflection in the mirror. Malina Matthews, draped in crimson silk, her mask sharp as her smile. She's leaning toward two other women, voice low but not low enough.

"I've been trying to bag him for months," she continues, twirling a diamond earring like she's plotting world domination.

"Finally, Marlow decides to play cupid and *bam*. An auction. His daughter is practically delivering him to me on a silver platter." She laughs, throaty and triumphant. "And once I've paid my price, I'll throw *myself* on a platter for him later. He's mine. It's only a matter of time now."

My pulse hammers. I grip the counter to ground myself because the room feels like it tilts sideways. I want to whirl on her, spit fire in her face, tell her she doesn't know him the way I do—doesn't know how he takes his whiskey or the way his eyes crinkle when he's actually laughing, doesn't know that his walls are high because he still mourns the love of his life.

But my tongue stays locked in my mouth.

Because I can't have him either.

And if I can't, then why should it matter if she tries?

The very thought slices me in half—hurt and fury tangled so tight I can't tell them apart.

I glance again, really *look* at her. Malina. Gorgeous, successful, a little cut-throat. And damn it, on paper, she makes sense for him. She's in Grant's world. She could slide right in without breaking stride.

And Marlow clearly wants this. She's invested. She's orchestrating it. Her father being happy with a woman like Malina is something she can get behind.

I'm the complication. The secret. The mess.

I press a tissue to my lips and swallow hard, my reflection blurred in the mirror.

If he's meant to be with someone...maybe it should be her.

Then I look at her again.

Nah. Fuck her.

Grant

Since I wore a black masquerade mask for Halloween, I decided to wear a gold one for this ridiculous ball Marlow insists I participate in. I stopped at the tie though. I've worn suits and ties for the better part of thirty years and I've come to enjoy life without them. Without the stuffiness.

So this black suit, white button-up, and my gold mask ensemble will have to do. It's enough to serve the purpose of the night. Enough to stay hidden from the right people. But also enough for her to notice me.

Just in case.

When I got home last night, I couldn't sit still. I paced my living room like a caged animal, replaying every second of the evening in her apartment. The laughter, the wine, the way she leaned into me when Olivia and Fitz ended up in an *inevitable* situation. It felt like we'd done it a hundred times before. Being in her space felt like redemption. Like coming home.

Of all the ways I'd imagined being with her behind closed doors, in her apartment, I'd run through the possibilities more times than I could count. I pictured her curled against me, maybe even drifting off to sleep there—soft, unguarded, mine for just a moment. But never—not in my worst imaginings—did I think it would end with me standing there like an idiot, scissors in hand, and a chunk of her hair lying on the floor.

I've tried everything from texts full of apologies, even a peace offering of croissants from Holly's delivered to her before her stylist arrived, still warm from the oven. Her response? A single middle finger emoji. Nothing else.

For a moment, I'd thought I'd broken through. That she'd actually wanted me there, in her space, in her life. And I was ready—ready to dive headfirst, no hesitation. Now all I can do is sit here, replaying the sound of scissors through her braids, and pray she doesn't break into my penthouse in the middle of the night to pour acid in my shampoo.

The gala is already in full swing by the time I arrive. A blur of sequins and champagne flutes, violins humming somewhere behind the chatter. I've been to more events like this than I can count, and they've all blurred into one long evening of handshakes and polite laughter. The only difference tonight is her.

I spot her instantly. Doesn't matter that the ballroom is overflowing with sequins, feathers, and gowns made to blind a man. My eyes don't wander. They land on her, like they always do.

Eslin.

Silver mask catching the light, lips painted the color of forbidden fruit, hair styled so perfectly you'd never guess what happened last night. She looks like she belongs here—regal, untouchable. And yet, all I can see is the girl from her couch.

The one laughing at Olivia Pope's drama with a bowl of popcorn in her lap. The one who trusted me enough to let me close, to let me see her unpolished, unguarded. The one who didn't need a mask or a gown to be the most stunning woman in the room.

And no matter how flawless she looks tonight, I can't unsee that girl—the one with hair scattered everywhere and light in her eyes. The one who makes even disaster look beautiful.

I should keep my distance. God knows I've told myself that enough. But every time I see her, that resolve lasts about as long as it takes for her to glance my way

And she does. Right now.

Even across the ballroom, I feel it when her eyes land on me. The pause. The inhale. Like something inside her skips and sputters before finding its rhythm again. And I know—because it happens to me too.

So I lift my glass, a silent toast across the crowd, like it means nothing. Like she's just anyone.

But I know she isn't.

And worse—so does she.

"Daddy! Perfect timing! You're almost up!"

"Perfect timing for what, and what exactly will I be up for?"

Marlow beams at me. "Remember I told you about the auction? We're auctioning off key players and members of the front office for dates to raise money for charity."

I vaguely remember something about that. But if memory serves, that was the same night Eslin decided to test her skills as a back-alley chemist and slipped me a magnesium cocktail strong enough to take down a horse. So if I've blocked out parts of that conversation, it's with good reason.

"The auction," I repeat slowly, taking a sip of my drink like it might help me survive whatever fresh hell my daughter has signed me up for. "Yes."

"You're lucky I love you," I add.

"Yes, I am." She grins. Then she grabs my arm, tugging me toward the front of the ballroom where a curtain conceals the chaos backstage. "Now come on! Let's go pimp my dad."

I sigh, because only Marlow could make human trafficking sound like charity.

***

The ballroom hums with anticipation as the velvet curtain parts, and Luca Chidubem strides onto the stage. Even in a black suit and gold mask, this kid radiates swagger—the kind that makes the women in the audience sit a little taller, lean a little closer, fan themselves with their programs.

The announcer, a wiry man with a booming voice and the speed of a New York auctioneer, claps a hand on Luca's shoulder. "Ladies and gentlemen, feast your eyes on tonight's next prize! Six-foot-five of prime athletic power, a smile that melts ice, and commanding field presence you've all seen on the highlight reels—give it up for Luca Chidubem!"

The crowd roars. Luca throws a playful wink and waves like he's already won MVP.

"All right, let's start the bidding nice and easy. One thousand dollars for a private dinner with Mr. Chidubem. Do I hear one thousand?"

Hands shoot up instantly.

"One thousand—yes, thank you, front table. Do I hear fifteen hundred?"

Another hand. Then another.

"Fifteen hundred—yes, thank you, back row in the sequins. Two thousand now, who'll give me two?"

A brunette in the second row raises her hand. The announcer points like a man possessed.

"Two thousand to the lady in sapphire! Do I hear twenty-five hundred?"

The bids come faster, the numbers climbing like they're nothing but pocket change. Luca lifts his arms and flexes just enough to send another ripple of laughter and cheers through the room.

"Five thousand! Yes, thank you, ma'am in the gold shawl. Five thousand on the table, do I hear six?"

"Six thousand!" another woman calls.

"Six! Do I hear seven?"

The room is alive now, women shouting numbers, laughter bubbling, the announcer's voice ricocheting through it all.

"Seven thousand! Yes! Eight, do I have eight?"

"Eight!"

"Nine?"

A pause. A hush, almost.

Then, from the back of the room, clear and calm, "Ten thousand."

The crowd gasps. Heads turn, trying to see who dared throw down that kind of money.

The spotlight swivels, landing on her. A woman in a flowing crimson dress, mask of red and black lace that hides every inch of her expression except the tilt of her mouth. Cool. Confident. Unmoved by the attention.

The announcer milks it, slapping his hand against the podium. "Ten thousand! Ten thousand to the lady in red! Going once—going twice—"

He draws it out, but no one dares to top her.

"—and SOLD!" He slams the gavel down with theatrical flair. "To the woman in the red dress and the mysterious red-and-black mask!"

The crowd erupts in applause, Luca bowing deeply, grinning from ear to ear as though he's just been drafted all over again. The woman in red doesn't so much as flinch. She simply raises her champagne glass, as though she's been planning to win him all along.

When Luca strides off stage, blowing kisses and bowing like he's just scored the winning goal, the room is still buzzing from that ten-thousand-dollar finale. The announcer is practically giddy, the women in the audience starry-eyed, champagne flutes clinking in approval.

I should be relaxed. I should be used to this—eyes on me, the spectacle, the attention that's followed me my whole adult life.

But I'm not.

Because I know who else is in this room.

"Up next, ladies and gentlemen," the announcer crows, "A true legend. Father to one of the fiercest women I've ever met, a man whose presence commands every room and instantly claims hearts—Mr. Grant Mills!"

Applause erupts, echoing off the ballroom's high ceilings. I paste on a smile. The one I've worn for decades. The easy grin, the confident swagger. The old Grant.

I step into the lights, give a small wave, the grin never slipping. I look like I'm enjoying this, but inside, I feel tight. Restless. Because somewhere out there in the sea of glitter and velvet, Eslin Saunders is watching. And the last thing I want is for her to think this is who I am. That I'm still just a man parading himself for random women.

Then I catch Marlow at the edge of the stage. She's clapping, radiant, her eyes shining with pride. My girl asked me to do this, and I'll be damned if I won't give her a show. So I push the nerves down, raise my arms a little higher, and wink at the crowd.

"All right, let's start the bidding at one thousand for Mr. Mills," the announcer calls, voice slick and quick.

Hands shoot up immediately.

"One thousand—yes, thank you. Fifteen hundred? Two? Twenty-five hundred?"

The numbers climb faster than I expect. Three thousand. Five. Seven. Ten.

I arch a brow, laugh lightly, leaning against the podium as though this is all a game. And then it changes.

The energy sharpens.

Two women are locked in a duel. Their hands shoot up before the announcer can finish, voices slicing through the air.

"Fifteen thousand!"

"Seventeen!"

"Nineteen!"

And then I see her.

Malina Matthews.

Even under the red and black mask, I know that profile, the stubborn set of her jaw. She doesn't just bid—she attacks. Like winning me is the prize she came here for.

But why? After the disaster of that night—me bolting for the bathroom mid-date, leaving her to sip wine alone—I figured she'd never want to lay eyes on me again. Yet here she is, dropping money like it's nothing. Malina knows what she wants. And clearly, she still wants me.

"Twenty-four thousand!"

"Twenty-five!" Malina snaps, her voice like a dagger.

The room gasps, then bursts into applause before the announcer can even bring down the gavel.

"Sold! Twenty-five thousand dollars to the blonde-haired lady in the red dress and mask!"

The crowd roars, clapping and cheering. I stand there, shocked, my smile feeling stiff at the edges.

Marlow beams, clapping furiously, her pride filling every inch of the space.

And then—movement. A flicker of silver.

Eslin.

Her mask gleaming, her lips painted that impossible wine-red, her whole presence like gravity itself. But then—she turns. She bolts. Disappearing into the crowd so fast it knocks the air from me.

The applause doesn't matter. The money doesn't matter. Even Marlow's pride doesn't soften the tight ache in my chest.

The very thing I didn't want to happen, just did.

It's all fun and games—charity, spectacle, the kind of event meant to dazzle. I get that, and I'm sure she gets it too. But I saw her face before she turned away. Saw the flash in her eyes when Malina threw down that final bid.

Eslin knows Malina does want me and she'll stop at nothing to take me. She's not being shy about that.

But the thought of Eslin believing—if only for a second—that she'd have to compete with that? With *her*? It twists something in me I can't live with.

So I don't think. I don't weigh appearances or consequences or what this will look like on the gala floor. I just move. I follow her.

CHAPTER FORTY THREE: RED DRESSES & RECKONINGS

Grant

The gala is a blur behind me—the applause, the cheers, the weight of twenty-five thousand dollars for a date I don't give a damn about. None of it matters. Not with Eslin disappearing the way she did. Not with the look on her face when Malina's bid won.

I find her in the dim silence of an unused ballroom where the chairs are stacked and silver trays wait for tomorrow's event. The lights are low, shadows stretching long across the floor, but I can hear her before I see her. Quiet, ragged cries that rip me open.

"Go away, Grant."

Her voice cracks, but it still slices straight through me.

"How did you know it was me?"

"I can always tell it's you," she whispers, not turning. "I can always feel you."

Then why do you keep running from me? The words stay stuck in my throat, pounding at my ribs, demanding to be free.

Instead, I move closer, my steps quiet across the carpet until I'm behind her. She's braced against a table, shoulders trembling, her back to me like she can't bear to face me.

"You saw the look in Marlow's eyes," she finally says, voice breaking. "She wants you happy. She wants you with Malina."

I reach out, unable to stop myself, and let my hand rest on her shoulder. Just that little bit of contact, grounding us both. Connecting us.

"And I want you," I say, my voice rough with everything I've held back for too damn long. "Fuck, Eslin. How many times do we have to do this dance?"

She turns, slow, like the weight of it might crush her. Her eyes are wet, her cheeks flushed. "I don't know," she breathes. "And I have no right to say this. No right to demand this, but Grant—"

A single tear slips free, sliding down her face. "Not her."

My chest caves at the sound of it. "What are you asking me, Es? What are you saying?"

She shakes her head, fiercely this time, like she's already bracing for the war she just started. "She can't have you. If you got to make that demand of me with Jones, then I get to make this demand of you when it comes to her. Not Malina."

I reach for her mask, peel it away, and then do the same with mine until there's nothing left between us. No disguises. No barriers. Just her and me, bare in every way that matters right now.

"Say it, Eslin," I growl, my hands tight at her jaw. "Say it to me now so we can stop playing these fucking games."

Her breath trembles against my mouth then I hear a faint whisper escape her when she says, "Fuck it. I'll wait for you. I'll wait for Marlow to get on her feet and then we can tell her. Everything."

I kiss her, soft but claiming, a brand she can't shake. "Say it again."

She shakes her head. "I'll wait for you."

I tug her lower lip between my teeth, just enough to make her gasp. "One more time. Tell me. Promise me."

Her eyes lock on mine, fierce through her tears. "I'll wait for you, Grant."

That's all it takes. The words imprint themselves into me. A vow. A tether. The only thing I've been needing, starving for, since the moment she crashed into my life.

I cup her face in both palms, my thumbs brushing dampness away. I kiss her tear first, tasting the salt of her hurt.

Then her mouth. Soft, like she might break if I'm not careful.

Her arms slide beneath my coat, curling tight around me. I feel her nails drag down my back through my shirt, sharp and possessive. It's not pain—it's a claim.

And something in me breaks wide open.

I lift her, her gasp hot against my throat, and carry her deeper into the shadows where no one will dare interrupt. Where I can finally—finally—take what I've been starving for.

"Grant—what if—"

"Months, Eslin. Months I've been waiting for permission to taste you like this." My voice is rough, cracking with restraint I've lost all hold of. "I'm not waiting another second."

Each step I take, I hike her dress higher, until her thighs bare themselves to me and she hooks her legs around my waist.

And then I feel it. The slip of lace. A damn thong.

My groan shakes the walls.

"Does anyone touch you like this?" My hand slides between us, finding her already wet, slick and desperate.

"Never. No one but you," she whispers, voice breaking just as my fingers part her heat.

I reach a stack of chairs shoved against the wall and set her on top, her body aligning with me at the perfect height. I drag her closer until she has no choice but to open for me.

"Spread your legs, Eslin." It's a growl, a command. This beautiful woman obeys.

"Such a pretty pussy," I rasp, drinking in the sight of her glistening for me.

She lets out a shaky laugh. "Are you going to stare at it all night?"

"I'd love to," I murmur, lowering myself, hunger sharp in every word. "But I'm a starving man, Eslin Saunders. And I was always taught never to play with my food."

"Especially while it's still warm," she teases, breathless.

I don't give her a chance to say another word.

I grip her thighs, drag her to the edge, and bury my mouth in her soaked center.

Her cry shatters the silence. She locks her legs around my neck, threading her fingers through my hair, rocking against me like I exist only for this—only for her.

And I do.

Her legs clamp around me tighter, her hips rocking into my mouth like she's desperate to fuse herself to me. I let her lead, let her grind, let her ride my tongue as if she's in control—until I decide she's not.

I pin her hips down, flatten my tongue against her, and lap up every drop, every cry, every tremor that runs through her body. She's gasping, half-pleading, half-cursing my name, and it only fuels me more.

"Grant—oh fuck—" Her voice cracks, her thighs trembling.

I slide two fingers inside her as I suck her clit hard, curling into that spot I know will undo her. She bows forward, grabbing the back of the chair for balance, and then it happens—her body arches, her cry tears through the dark, and she shatters against my mouth.

I don't let up until she slumps, panting, her legs falling open, spent.

But I'm not done. Not even close.

I rise, capturing her mouth in a deep kiss, letting her taste everything that's been building between us. Without breaking away, I lift her off the stack of chairs and turn her toward the table piled high with catering trays. She steadies herself against the edge, still breathless, her dress hitched up around her hips.

"Grant—" she starts, breathless, but I'm already behind her, already dragging my zipper down.

"Bend over," I growl, untamed, dripping with everything I've held back from this woman.

She obeys without a flicker of hesitation, folding forward over the table, her back arching in a way that almost undoes me on the spot. The sight of her offering herself to me like that burns itself into me.

I lean down, teeth grazing her shoulder before biting, then soothing the mark with my tongue. My hands find her breasts, molding them, her peaked nipples telling me she's nowhere near finished with me, either.

My grip slides down to her hips, holding her steady as I push into her with one deep, unrelenting thrust. The air shatters with the sound of my curse—raw, jagged—because nothing has ever felt like this. Nothing but her.

She gasps, her fingers clawing at the table as I slam into her again—harder, deeper.

"Fuck, Eslin," I grit out, leaning over her, pressing her down as I move inside her with relentless need. My breath is hot against her ear. "I want to be gentle. I swear I'll make love to you later—slow, soft, like you're lying on a bed of roses. I'll give you that. But right now?" My thrusts grow sharper, rougher. "Right now this is mine. This is for every month I couldn't touch you. Every night I spent awake, knowing you were with that fucking wanker. Knowing you belong to me."

"Shit! Grant!" she cries out, her body shaking beneath me.

"I want to be gentle, baby." I drag my teeth along her neck, groaning as her body tightens around me. "But you feel too good. Too fucking good."

She pushes back against me, meeting every thrust, her whimpers mixing with my groans, the sound of us filling the empty ballroom.

"You're mine," I growl into her ear, pounding into her, sweat beading at my temple. "Say it."

Her voice cracks on a moan, broken but certain all at once. "Yours, Grant. I'm yours."

The words gut me and I swear they lodge somewhere deeper than bone. For the first time in months, the war inside me goes quiet. No questions. No doubts. Just her.

And hearing that—here, now, in this dark room that smells like wine and wax and everything we shouldn't be—I believe her.

I still, burying myself deep as I can go, and let go. Emptying everything I've held back, pouring every ounce of rage, longing, and love I've carried into her. Giving all of me to this beautifully forbidden woman who undoes me without even trying.

I don't know how we got here. I don't know how this will end, or what storms are waiting for us on the other side of this night. But I do know one thing with a clarity that cuts through every doubt—I love this woman.

As she straightens, her arm curling around my neck, pulling me close like she's afraid to let go, I make a silent vow. To protect her. To protect *this*. To guard whatever fragile, furious, beautiful thing we've built with everything I have left to give.

She's mine now.

She's home.

Chapter Forty-Five
PART THREE
Marlow

BREAKING NEWS – By Shaun Kennedy

The Atlanta Strikers are no strangers to headlines, but this week, the whispers around the team are louder—and far stranger—than usual.

Multiple sources have confirmed rumors of a **secret marriage** involving a key member of the Strikers' roster and a woman deeply connected to the club. The pair are said to have wed in Las Vegas months ago under unusual circumstances, but the union has been hidden from the public—and even, reportedly, from teammates. Who exactly tied the knot remains officially unconfirmed, but if true, the revelation could shake the foundations of the team.

Meanwhile, the Strikers' **Thanksgiving Gala**—planned as a night of charity and celebration—was overshadowed by scandal. Several attendees reported that two individuals disappeared from the ballroom, only to be discovered later in what's being described as a *very intimate encounter.* The identities of those involved are being kept quiet for now, but speculation is rampant, especially after several guests noticed familiar faces missing during the night's peak.

Adding to the drama, **Grant Mills,** the club's enigmatic figure and longtime "Silver Fox," shocked even insiders by commanding the **highest auction bid of the evening—$25,000—for a single date.** The woman behind the winning mask? Believed to be someone from his past, determined to claim him once and for all. Were these the two guests heard in an intimate encounter?

And as if the off-field secrets weren't enough, the Strikers are unraveling on the pitch as well. Reports confirm a violent intra-squad altercation during practice between teammates **Luca Chidubem and Croix London.** The clash turned so physical both men were fined, and while the club insists it has "handled" the matter internally, no real explanation has been offered.

What raises eyebrows is how such a brawl could erupt under the watch of **Marlow Mills,** who only recently stepped into a leadership role with the Strikers. For someone expected to steady the ship, the optics aren't great—first secret marriages and scandals at the Thanksgiving Gala, now teammates literally beating each other up on her field. If this is Marlow proving she can handle herself at the helm, many are left wondering: what happens when she really loses control?

A secret marriage. A tryst behind the gala's locked doors. And teammates turning on each other in the middle of training.

Right now, the Atlanta Strikers seem less like a soccer club and more like the city's most dangerous soap opera—and the truth behind these mysteries is anyone's guess.

Stay tuned. The biggest plays of the season might not be happening on the field.

—Shaun Kennedy, *Sports Insider Daily, Cinnamon Grove Sun*

CHAPTER FORTY FOUR: NUTMEGS & NEWS BRIEFS

Eslin

The emergency Stand-In meeting Marlow calls feels less like a strategy session and more like a courtroom. We're huddled in her office—me, Tatum, and Marlow pacing like she's preparing to prosecute the entire world.

The news brief is everywhere. Secret marriages, Thanksgiving Gala scandals, and the cherry on top—whispers are circulating that someone saw Grant sneak off. Someone heard his name being whispered...yelled.

Someone.

Surprisingly, the potential leak of her secret marriage was the least of Marlow's worries. In her mind, it could just as easily be her or even Luca that the press had stumbled onto so she decided not to worry about it until she absolutely had to. What consumed her now, what had her pacing and snapping at anyone in reach, was the question of who exactly had her father been screwing at the gala?

I am a mess of nerves. Because not only did someone hear us, they took it and handed it over to the press like it was currency. The very first time I let myself go with Grant, the first time I gave in completely, and it's splashed across the city like some sordid secret.

And worse, I have to sit here, stone-faced, while Marlow rages about it. While she talks about her father like he's the reckless one, the embarrassing one, the liability we can't control. I have to nod, to look just as shocked, as though I don't already know exactly who was calling his name.

As if it wasn't me.

"Malina swore it wasn't her," Marlow snaps. "So who was it? Who the hell would be reckless enough to sneak off during a gala we were *hosting*?"

I keep my face still, keep my mouth shut, though the words are burning inside me.

It was me.

Tatum, ever the wildcard, twirls her pen. "People lie. Malina could've been playing coy, keeping her conquest a mystery. Everyone said she was willing to do whatever it takes to snag your father."

"Then why," Marlow counters, "would she lie about being the one caught fucking my father! Screaming his name for all the world to hear! My father's." She lets the word *father* fall like an accusation.

She stops pacing, finally leaning against her desk, and sighs. "I can't control him. I can't control what he does any more than I can control the damn weather. But if he doesn't get his shit together, this team is going to be eaten alive by the press. And me right along with it."

Her anger is sharp, but underneath it I hear the ache. The disappointment. And it only twists the knife in me deeper. Because if she knew I was keeping this secret from her—if she ever found out from someone other than me—I wouldn't just lose her trust. I'd lose her.

Tatum raises a hand, mercifully cutting through the tension. "Did anyone ever figure out what Luca and Croix were fighting about?"

I flash her a silent *thank you* with my eyes. I can't stand talking about Grant and his supposed recklessness any longer.

Clearing my throat, I force myself back to business. "Coach Jones said it has something to do with a girl, but I haven't pressed them yet. I've got a session with both of them tomorrow—Huntley and Xavier's orders."

Tatum leans back, wide-eyed. "Uh oh! Big bosses calling the shots?" she teases, but her lightness falls flat when Marlow slams her pen down.

"Yes. Because clearly, I can't do this job!"

I cross the room towards her. She's sitting on the edge of her desk, too wound up to use the chair. "Sweetie. You are amazing at this job. If a man had these kinds of setbacks, they'd call it a learning curve. You? You're a badass. You're doing something nobody thought you could."

"And you look damn good doing it!" Tatum chimes in with a wink.

Marlow exhales, her shoulders sagging before she straightens again. "You're right. I *am* a badass. I *am* doing a damn good job." Her eyes darken. "It's my father who's fucking everything up."

"Exactly!" Tatum blurts out, but my head snaps toward her, pleading silently for her to stop piling on. Every word feels like another strike against him—against us.

"Thanks ladies. I really needed this."

Tatum joins us at the desk anyway, looping her arms around both of us until we're caught in an awkward girl group hug. I've never really had one before, but in spite of everything, it makes something in my chest loosen, just for a second.

But then I glance up. And there he is—filling the doorway.

My heart leaps. My lips betray me, curving into a smile before I can stop it. Correction—a *beam*. And panic flickers through me because I have to smooth it away, fast, before anyone notices. Before anyone realizes that my first instinct at the sight of Grant Mills is something far too close to desire.

I clear my throat, realizing he's probably here to smooth things over with his daughter. Not to see me.

"Uh, Low? Grant...Your dad's here," I say and we break the hold we have on each other.

Grant steps into the office, tentative. "Can I speak to you, munchkin?"

"Don't call me that! Especially not at work where I am still trying to earn respect while cleaning up your messes!"

Tatum and I both wince. "We'll just go," I say, not even bothering to put on my shoes that always end up on the floor in Marlow's office because the carpet is so plush.

I grab my shoes, my purse and my pride and scurry out the door.

***

Thirty minutes later, a knock lands on my office door.

It's him.

"Hi," he says softly.

"Hi."

An immediate smile tugs at my lips but his face doesn't match mine. His shoulders are heavy, his eyes shadowed.

"How is she? How's Marlow?" I ask carefully.

"Pissed," he admits. "And I feel like a damn fool, Es. I'm so sorry for dragging you into the middle of this. I should've waited. I should've controlled myself. I should've—"

I rise, stopping his spiral with a gentle hand pressed to his lips. "It wasn't just you. It was both of us. We both crossed that line. But I do appreciate you being willing to carry the weight of it." My chest tightens. "I just don't think it can last this way."

He shakes his head once, certain. "It won't."

"So we'll tell her," I say, eyes locked on his.

He nods. "When?"

I let out a sigh. "Working on that. But soon. Okay?"

He nods again. "Okay. Soon."

Then his eyes soften, the fight in him quieting as they trace over my face. He exhales like it costs him something to say it. "What?" I ask.

He leans down, pressing his forehead against mine, his voice barely above a whisper. "You sure are pretty, Dr. Eslin Saunders. I wish I could kiss you."

A quick glance toward the open doorway makes my pulse jump. No one's coming. I rise onto my toes and press a fleeting kiss to his cheek.

His grin breaks through, crooked and irresistible. "What are we, in study hall?"

I smirk, lowering my voice to match his. "It's a prelude, Mr. Mills. Come see me tonight."

And because I know his daughter's secret, I know she won't be home to catch him sneaking into my place.

"Are you doing the team's Thanksgiving dinner?" he asks.

Since so many of our players don't have family nearby for the holiday, we decided to host a dinner here for anyone in the league who might otherwise spend it alone.

"I am. My friend Max is coming down, and she's going to help me make all the pies."

He smiles, and despite the salt and pepper streaking his hair, his grin is still boyish. Almost child-like. "I'm looking forward to it. To sharing a holiday with you."

I shake my head, baffled by this new softness in me, and hear myself say, "It will be our first Thanksgiving together."

His brows lift, teasing, but his voice dips lower. "Why, Eslin Saunders, do you plan to keep me around for a while?"

I smirk, covering nerves with bravado. "We'll see."

I say goodbye to Grant, excited about the promise of tonight. But just as soon as I turn to close my office door, my phone buzzes. A message from Marlow.

Marlow: *Sunday dinner. After Thanksgiving. Daddy's place. We're decorating the Christmas tree. Be my buffer between me and my dad?*

I stare at the text, my chest tightening. Family dinners. Traditions. Marlow tugging me even closer into her circle when I'm holding a secret that could blow it all apart.

I type back one word, my fingers shaking as I hit send.

Me: *I'll be there.*

CHAPTER FORTY FIVE: SWEET POTATOES & SNEAKY LINKS

Eslin

It's the Wednesday before Thanksgiving, and while the offices are shut down, the Strikers' staff has been working around the clock to transform the banquet hall into something that feels like home. With so many of the players far from their families, I told Tatum I wanted the space to feel like walking into a living room—warmth instead of polish. And my girl definitely delivered. Baby pictures taped to the walls, framed family portraits propped on side tables, old quilts thrown over the backs of couches. Not sterile. Not professional. Just...home.

Max arrives today, and since she despises peeling potatoes, I'm determined to have them done and ready to boil before she shows up. I'm in my kitchen, at my apartment, standing barefoot at the counter in nothing but one of Grant's crisp white button-ups, working through the sweet potatoes for the pies I promised to bring.

The bowl on the counter is already half full, the peeler gliding through the skins in smooth curls. It should feel ordinary, almost domestic. But nothing about being wrapped up in this man feels simple.

I don't even hear him approach—just feel him. His chest pressing against my back, his hands sliding around my waist, pulling me flush against him.

"Grant," I warn, trying to keep my voice sharp even as my breath gives me completely away. "I'm not going to get anything done if you keep messing with me."

"I don't care," he murmurs, and his breath fans across my neck like fire.

I glance down just in time to see his fingers at the buttons of his own shirt—my shirt now—slipping them free one by one. By the time it's fully open, his hands are sliding around me, cupping my breasts.

"Grant..."

"Shhh," he hushes against my ear, one hand drifting lower, teasing until he finds that spot that makes my knees go weak. His fingers circle my clit, pressing, commanding. "I know I haven't been the most gentle."

I gasp, clinging to the counter. "Understatement of the decade," I manage, but the words fall apart on a moan.

It's been like this with him since the gala. We've made love in my apartment, in his penthouse, once nearly in the locker room before we came to our senses. And yet no matter how many times he takes me, he always finds a new way to unravel me. A new way to make it feel different. Better.

I guess experience really is the best teacher and it has certainly taught him well.

In one sudden, effortless motion, he scoops me up and carries me down the hall. My arms fly around his shoulders, breath caught in my throat. But instead of the bedroom, he stops halfway, pinning me against the wall. One arm holds me in place, steady and strong, while the other fumbles at his zipper with desperate need.

It's reckless. It's wild. It's us.

His mouth claims mine, kissing me senseless as he holds me there, my body caged by his strength and undone by his hunger. Still, before he gives me more of the pleasure he's been pouring into me all week, his eyes soften, searching mine like he needs me to hear this.

"You know what I'm most grateful for today, Eslin?" His voice is low, reverent.

I can barely breathe. "What's that?"

"That day you sat next to me in Vegas. Because I almost talked myself out of talking to you."

I feel him at my entrance, hot and ready, pulsing like he hasn't already been inside me over and over the night before.

"What changed your mind?" I whisper, smiling.

He kisses me again, and this one tastes like love. "Your eyes."

Another kiss, deeper, as he pushes into me, and I wince against the sweet ache of soreness.

"Your smile."

His grip tightens, his hands sliding down to hold my thighs, parting me, lifting me, making me his all over again.

"Your heart."

His movements start slow, a rhythm that feels like worship. "I'm sorry I can't get enough of you, Es. I'm sorry you've made a ravenous monster out of me. But I love being inside you."

My arms cling tighter around his neck as he glides me up and down, filling me until I forget everything else.

Potatoes be damned.

I bury my face in his shoulder, biting down against the tide of pleasure as it rips through me. But even as my body trembles around him, a single tear slips free. Then another.

Because I love this man. At least, I think I do.

And that truth aches almost as much as the release. Because I can't tell him. I can't shout it out or whisper it against his skin. I can't let the secret of us breathe in the open air, not when it could shatter everything else around us.

So I cry quietly against him—half from joy, half from fear—hating that I can feel this much for someone I can never fully claim.

Because Grant Mills is amazing. He is wonderful. And he is mine in every way that counts. He feels like home.

By the time we're both spent, my body a trembling mess against his, I can barely stand upright. He kisses me once more before dragging me into the shower, turning the water hot.

For a few minutes, it's heaven—his hands soapy, slick, sliding everywhere. But when he presses his grin against my neck and mutters something about *going again*, I all but shove him away.

"Threaten me with another erection, Mills, and you'll have to tell my friend Max why she is stuck peeling sweet potatoes!"

He laughs, low and wicked, as I rinse off in record time and dart out, leaving him under the spray.

"Now, let me try peeling potatoes again before I get interrupted by my insatiable sneaky link," I mutter to no one, tugging on a pair of leggings for armor as I return to the kitchen.

Clearly, my body is not safe with this man if I'm not wearing pants.

The potato peels curl into a pile at my feet, the bowl on the counter slowly filling with bright orange flesh. My hands keep moving, but my mind drifts, ears tuned to the faint rush of water still coming from down the hall. How everything about this feels so *good*.

And while it should feel ordinary. Simple. Nothing about him—about us—is simple.

I'm halfway through another sweet potato when the doorbell rings.

I freeze, staring at the door as if it's going to tell me who is behind it. Then, wiping my hands on a towel, I force a smile onto my face and open it.

Maxine Palmer stands there, all glowing skin and unapologetic energy. She's shed the sharp edges of her city armor for something softer—an oversized sweater, worn-in boots, the kind of outfit you wear when someone makes you want to stay a while.

The second our eyes meet, it's instinct. We squeal, rush into each other's arms, and jump up and down like we're twenty again. It's loud, ridiculous, and everything you'd expect when someone reconnects with a missing piece of themselves. And that's what Max is to me—home wrapped in a person.

Beside her is Eli. And when she says his name, her voice does that thing—bright and sharp with pride, soft with affection. "Eslin, this is Eli. Eli, meet my best friend, Eslin Saunders."

Eli is *big*. Tall, muscular, dark chocolate brown, long hair. Beautiful. I genuinely did not know lumberjacks came in Black but here he stands.

Eli extends a hand, warm, steady. "I've heard so much about you."

"Likewise," I say, and I mean it. He looks like every story Max has whispered down the phone finally found its shape.

I shake Eli's hand, firm and polite, then drag Max into another hug—because one just isn't enough. It's been ages, but the second she's in my arms, it feels like we're those two college kids again.

At the start of summer, Max and I had plans to road-trip to Canada for a romance conference. But luck—or maybe fate—had other ideas. I got sick and couldn't make it. Max, being Max, refused to cancel. She went on her own and wound up stranded in a ditch on the wrong side of the border with no friendly faces in sight. Lucky for her, Eli showed up. And seeing him now—and more importantly, seeing the way he looks at her—I finally understand why she never came back.

As I'm showing Max and Eli to the guest room, timing betrays me again.

Grant appears. Damp hair pushed back, skin still flushed from the shower, dressed in a gray jogging suit that somehow makes him look both relaxed and devastating. He stops when he sees us, eyes flicking briefly to me before settling politely on Max and Eli.

"Company," he says, voice low but even.

Max raises a brow, lips curving into something smug. "Well, well. Looks like I'm not the only one with surprises."

I freeze, not sure how to handle this. Max has been so wrapped up in Eli that I haven't exactly unloaded any of this onto her. Tatum and Holly have been the ones keeping me upright through the chaos. And now Dr. Mikari.

"So, uh, Max. This is Grant Mills. Grant, this is my best friend Max—and her boyfriend—"

"Fiancé," Max corrects with a grin that nearly splits her face. My jaw drops, and before I can stop myself, I'm squealing, hugging her all over again.

When we finally come up for air, Grant extends his hand to Eli, then to Max, polite as ever. Max, of course, ignores it and pulls him in for a hug.

This part feels normal. The part where you introduce your boyfriend to your best friend, and they actually seem to get along. Where life feels easy, seamless.

Grant doesn't linger, apparently he's got cooking to do of his own. But he also doesn't shy away from leaning down and kissing me goodbye—right in front of them. "I'll see you tomorrow?"

The smile that spreads across my face is impossible to fight. "See you tomorrow, Mister."

The door clicks shut behind him, and I turn back to Max, still reeling from everything at once. She just levels me with a look, lips twitching into a wicked grin.

"Okay, bitch. I need details. I'll even peel the potatoes."

Chapter Forty-Eight

CHAPTER FORTY SIX: TURKEY & TOUCHLINES

Marlow

I t's Thanksgiving, and the arena doesn't look anything like an arena anymore. The banquet hall has been stripped bare of its usual formality and transformed into something that feels like a giant living room in a log cabin. Warm golden lights strung across the ceiling. Long tables lined in mismatched linens, covered in steaming bowls of collards, mac and cheese, turkey, cornbread stuffing, candied yams.

Family photos hang on the walls, baby pictures of players mixed with shots of them on the field, so it feels like we're in somebody's home.

Caterers wear jeans and flannels instead of uniforms, blending in like aunts and uncles at a family reunion. Players sit shoulder to shoulder, playing spades and dominoes at the corners of tables, passing plates down with easy familiarity. It feels loud, messy, chaotic. It feels like family.

Declan came early to avoid suspicion, like he always does, and I love how easily he moves through the crowd, how his quiet charisma seems to disarm everyone in his path. Even with the tattoos winding up his arms and that brooding edge he sometimes carries, people feel at ease around him—*I* feel at ease around him. Where others see ink and shadows, I see the man who steadies me when the world feels like it's waiting for me to stumble. And somehow, just by being here, he makes it easier for me to breathe.

The press is circling me like vultures, feeding the rumor mill about who's secretly married and who's hiding what. They want me to slip up, to confess. To give them something to prove I'm failing at holding this team—and myself—together. Add that to the fact that we lost our last match, and suddenly, every glance feels like a judgment. Every headline feels like a knife.

I've been wound so tight I've dropped five pounds without trying, my nerves chewing away at me while Declan urges me to just tell the truth so no one has a secret to hold over me anymore. And I want to. But fear is stubborn, and mine has teeth.

I remember how long I waited to tell Daddy about Jeremy. How I clung to him longer than I should have, convincing myself that time would make him real, that all his red flags would somehow soften into Christmas lights if I just waited long enough. But deep down, I always knew Jeremy wasn't it for me. He never stirred that part of me that wanted to give my whole heart, the way Daddy once told me the right man would. So it feels almost poetic—cruel, but fitting—that just when I was finally ready to push past every screaming instinct to cut Jeremy loose, to finally let Daddy into that part of my life, Jeremy went and knocked up another girl.

Declan isn't Jeremy. He couldn't be further from him. Where Jeremy was selfish, Declan is steady. Where Jeremy crumbled, Declan stands solid. He's everything I never saw my father be with a woman. He's... him. And yet here I am, holding on to this secret like it's my salvation, when maybe it's nothing more than a chain tightening around my own neck.

Because as I watch him now—sitting cross-legged on the floor, surrounded by the players' kids, letting one of the admin's little girls tug at his curls and twist them into uneven ponytails—something inside me aches. He doesn't care about how it looks. He doesn't care about pride, or appearances, or whether people think he's too serious to sit there and giggle with children. He just...is.

And maybe that's what scares me the most—that I've been molded by years of watching my father, a man who plays hard but dodges love even harder, and I've mistaken that as the blueprint. That Declan couldn't possibly be different. That marriage, love, men, would always mean keeping part of myself locked away for safety. Because I was never sure what love was supposed to feel like, only that it never seemed real enough to surrender to completely.

But Declan isn't my father. He isn't Jeremy. And right now, the only person standing in the way of my happiness is me.

"Boss lady is here!" Eslin chirps, grabbing a couple of the ice bags from my arms before they cut into my fingers.

I grin at her hair, light catching in the braids. "I see you couldn't wait to get those braids back in!"

She flips one over her shoulder like she's on a runway. "Girl, you know I can't stand combing my hair every day. Soon as that gala was over, I called the Africans and told them to take me *STAT*."

I frown. "The Africans?"

She laughs, shaking her head. "Sorry—it's what I call the African hair salons. They've perfected this assembly-line technique where multiple stylists braid your hair at the same time. I was in and out of the chair in two hours flat."

My eyes widen. "That's *impressive*."

She shrugs, a smirk tugging at her lips. "The Africans usually are."

We both laugh, the sound bubbling between us as we weave through the kitchen with our bags of ice.

"I swear, Eslin Saunders," I say, shaking my head. "I learn something new from you every day. Usually some cultural gem I've always wondered about but never had the nerve to ask."

It's true. Having her in my life feels like a gift—her stories, her quirks, even the ache in her past. She carries the hard things like they're blessings, and being around her makes me grateful for the reminder that you can.

We set the ice down by the drink station, caterers streaming in and out behind us. Eslin leans against the counter, eyes glinting with mischief. "Sooo," she sings, "how are things at home, Mrs. Dodging-the-spill-of-her-secret-marriage?"

I groan, burying my face in my hands. "Don't remind me! Things are fine at home. More than fine. And Declan doesn't understand why I won't just let the secret out. But..." I lower my voice. "I don't know how to tell him I'm waiting for some magical sign. Something to prove he won't hurt me. That he won't turn out like—like so many men do."

I stop short of saying *like my father.* For some reason, I still give him grace because of the love he so obviously still carries for my mother, the thing that's kept him closed off to the possibility of anything new.

Even with the bustle around us, Eslin wraps me in a hug, tight and grounding. She pulls back and searches my face, her eyes sharp but soft.

"Let me ask you this," she says. "When you picture the man worth your whole heart—the man you promised yourself you'd wait for—what does he *feel* like? Not what he looks like, not what reporters will see. What does he feel like for you?"

The answer shoots out. "Safe."

She nods. "Good. What else?"

"Understanding."

Her smile deepens. "That's two. Keep going."

I smile, because in naming it, I finally hear the truth out loud. Declan unlocks a version of me I didn't even know was there. A woman unburdened. A woman untethered. "Free."

Eslin's grin is knowing, like she's already pieced it all together. "Anything else?"

My throat tightens, a tear threatening at the corner of my eye as the truth settles over me. "That man feels like Declan."

Her voice softens, but her words hit hard. "So...you 'bout done waiting for the perfect sign? 'Cause, honey, sounds like you already got the perfect man."

I hug her again, grateful for the way she can cut through my chaos and hand me clarity without even trying. And I don't miss her words. The way she asked if I was "'bout done" echoed something my father once told me about my mom—that she used to ask him the same thing when he was circling around the truth he already knew. Or when she was tired of waiting for him to get done fishing on his boat.

But there's something about that, about the way Eslin said it, asked the same question my mom used to, that feels like more than advice. It feels familiar.

When we return to the banquet hall, it's already buzzing—players, coaches, front office staff, all the familiar faces gathered in clusters of laughter and chatter.

I drift toward the fireplace where my dad sits with Xavier Darcy and Will Huntley, the three of them hunched together like they're about to take over the world.

"Is there a management meeting someone forgot to tell me about?" I tease, forcing lightness into my voice because I'm still a little angry at my father. No, disappointed.

"Never," Xavier says smoothly, a grin forming. "We know your daddy couldn't be trusted to take anything seriously right now, so we would never exclude you." His tone is playful, but the glance he shoots my father carries weight—he's clearly hinting at the scandal still simmering in the press.

Will, however, doesn't bother with jokes. His voice is sharp, slicing right through the hum of the room. "Un-fucking-believable, this guy. You had six months and you couldn't even keep it in your pants for—"

"Will," Xavier cuts in, warning in his Southern drawl. "Cut him some slack. You know this was different."

I frown, my stomach tightening. "Different how? What's he talking about, Daddy?"

For the briefest second, I catch it—the shift in my father's posture, the way his jaw flexes, the sharp, desperate glance he sends Xavier. Begging him to shut up.

He stands, leaning down to kiss my forehead like he used to when I was a kid. "I'll tell you later, Munchkin. I promise," he murmurs, then escapes before I can press further.

Weird. Very weird.

Eslin

Justice is mid-sentence when I walk up, Autika perched beside him, glowing and very pregnant.

I offer her a smile. "Glad to see you two are doing well—settling into retirement life, almost."

Autika rubs her belly, smiling. "Almost is right. But he's refusing to retire completely. Decided we're staying here in Atlanta after the season."

Justice smirks, but beneath it, I catch the stubborn pride set deep in his jaw. "I just can't see myself walking away from the Strikers. Not yet. Doesn't matter if retirement's staring me in the face—I've only been with this team a short time compared to others, but it's mine. Always will be."

Autika nudges him. "Especially since Luca doesn't seem to be stepping into your role the way everyone thought. After that fight with Croix."

Justice shakes his head. "He's throwing away an opportunity to play on the world stage for a woman. Shame."

Autika rests her hand on his. "Well, babe, you know love will make a man burn the whole world for the woman he loves."

Justice slips Autika a side-eye. "Or make a woman *kidnap* the man she loves?"

My eyebrows shoot up. "Excuse me?"

Autika gasps, swatting his shoulder with a sharp slap. "Justice Trager! Really? You just *had* to go there?" She groans, turning to me with an apologetic smile. "Ignore him. He loves bringing up old stuff. I said I was sorry a long time ago!"

I blink, caught between laughter and confusion, my mouth opening and closing before I decide to stay quiet. I'd heard whispers—some wild story about Autika kidnapping this man and practically forcing him to propose—but I always brushed it off as locker-room gossip that got twisted over time. But now, seeing the way they're both grinning through it...maybe it wasn't just a rumor after all.

I school my face into something neutral, willing the conversation to shift away from Luca and Croix. Anything I could add here would be breaking privilege, and that line isn't mine to cross. I've already told Luca in private what I believe to be true—that any woman worth her salt wouldn't let him torch his career or his friendship with Croix. Justice seems to share the same conviction, and I cling to the hope that with his steady hand and leadership, the boys will eventually come to their senses.

Before the silence can stretch too long, Max appears in a whirl, tugging Rocky by the leash. "Hey, Eslin! Can you please help with this dog? He keeps eyeing the ham and I'm not sure I can hold him back!"

Rocky, the menace. Weeks of obedience training, and he's still the same rambunctious tornado. No wonder the Navy couldn't keep him.

"Let me see if Grant can get him," I mutter, scanning the room. But Grant is nowhere in sight.

"Coach Jones!" I call instead, spotting him across the way. Maybe he can distract Rocky before the dog wipes out the buffet.

Max mutters under her breath, "One day that man is going to get tired of being Grant's replacement."

I snap my eyes to her. "Would you stop it! That is not what he is or was—it was just bad timing."

"I'll say." She smirks.

Coach Jones approaches, smiling, utterly clueless as I try to hold Rocky back from lunging toward the food.

Max leans in with another whisper. "Maybe just let him down sooner rather than later? He doesn't seem to know your heart is already entangled with someone else."

I ignore her jab, paste on a polite smile. "Coach Jones, this is Max. Max, this is Coach Jones."

He nods, easy, greeting Max with a friendly handshake. "Good seeing you today, Coach Saunders."

"And you, Coach Jones."

Max mutters under her breath again, "How does this man not know you're not into him? You sound like you're buttering toast."

He looks at me. "Got any plans for tomorrow? I hear Black Friday's something I shouldn't miss around here."

I shake my head. "Actually, I plan to spend the day in bed watching reruns of old Christmas movies. Personal holiday tradition."

He grins. "Care for some company?"

I sigh. "Um... let me think about it?"

Max fake-coughs. "Chicken!"

Before I can roll my eyes, some kids toss a ball across the banquet hall, and Rocky takes off like a rocket, dragging his leash.

"Rocky!" I yell, but it's useless. He's already bowling kids over in his quest to play.

Coach Jones laughs. "Well, let me know what you think. I've got some movie favorites I'd love to share." He jogs after Rocky.

I nod. "Sure thing."

When he's gone, I turn to Max. "It's complicated, okay?"

She smirks, wicked. "And complicated is headed your way right now."

I follow her gaze and see Grant. My chest warms before he even opens his mouth.

"Happy Thanksgiving, Es. You sure are pretty."

The grin I give him is so wide, even Justice and Autika notice. "Happy Thanksgiving yourself, Mister."

"Can I talk to you for a moment?" He asks.

Relief floods me—anything to get away from this tangle of conversations.

I glance at Max. "Why don't you go climb that lumberjack over there?"

She winks. "Oh, don't worry, I will."

Grant leads me down the hallway toward the bathrooms, pressing his forehead against mine once we're out of sight. His voice is rough. "I can't stand not being able to touch you."

"I know," I whisper back. "But you should really back up before someone sees you."

"I know. But I tend to get reckless when I'm forced to pretend I'm not into a beautiful woman."

"You think I'm beautiful?"

His smile is boyish, unguarded. "You know you're gorgeous. *Fine, fine,* as I've heard Luca say about his mysterious woman."

Before I can scold him, his hand slides to the back of my neck, pulling me into a deep, lingering kiss. I melt against him.

Then, with that familiar mischievous glint, he tugs me into the men's room.

"Ah!" I yelp, half-laughing, half-scandalized.

And while Grant swears it'll only be a few minutes, the "few" turns into fifteen—fifteen long, breathless minutes where he wrings me out against the wall and promises he'll finish what he started later.

When we finally step back into the hallway, cheeks flushed, hearts still racing, Grant can't resist grabbing a full handful of my ass. I yelp again, spinning to smack his chest before stealing another quick kiss.

But that was reckless.

Because the second I turn around, Darren Jones is there. A few feet away. Frozen. His eyes bounce from my lips to Grant's hand still hovering near me, to my flushed face. Stunned.

"Coach. Darren," I start, voice trembling, but the words fall apart. What could I even say?

"Jesus, Eslin." His voice is sharp, wounded. "I knew you were holding back from me, but I thought it was something from your fucked-up childhood—"

Grant's voice cuts in with a growl, dangerous. "I'd be very careful about the next words out of your mouth, Jones."

Darren's gaze flicks to Grant, and then back to me. His jaw tightens before he huffs out a humorless laugh and shakes his head.

"Yeah," he mutters, bitter. "Sure thing. Boss." Then he turns and walks away.

I whip back to Grant, panic flooding through me. "What the fuck are we going to do?"

He looks at me, just as rattled, though his expression hardens with resolve.

"We have to tell Marlow."

CHAPTER FORTY SEVEN: COMFORT FOOD & CONSEQUENCES

Declan

I've had more turkey than a man should reasonably consume in one sitting, an obscene portion of something glorious called candied yams, and just enough sweet tea to drown a horse. Add to that the growing headache from the army of ponytails Gladys' daughter, Julia, has knotted into my hair, and I'm not exactly at my sharpest. And yet, I'd still rather endure this than answer Xavier Darcy's wife, who's spent the better part of the afternoon asking if I'm connected to the Agassi Crime Syndicate in Italy. For the record, I was always told to never answer that question—and for my own safety, and my wife's, I'm avoiding eye contact with the short-haired woman at all costs.

Nevertheless, my first American Thanksgiving isn't nearly as grim as I imagined. In fact, it's...good. Warm. Loud and a little hectic, full of laughter, food, and family in a way I hadn't realized I missed. And yes, a part of me wishes I could take Marlow home to meet my father and my nonna. But I don't mind that, for now, the days begin and end with just her.

I don't mind that she's my family now.

Maybe it's the way she's finally letting me take care of her. Maybe it's the way she trusts me with her secrets, piece by fragile piece. Or maybe it has everything to do with how our mornings usually start—with my wife firmly planted on my face. Whatever it is, something about this wild, unexpected marriage, about the way we've stitched ourselves together, feels like magic. Like it was always meant to be. And that, without question, is something I can give thanks for again and again.

Speaking of Señora Agassi, I seem to have lost track of her. She's been working the room and it's been torture keeping my eyes off of her. Call it separation anxiety, but I like having eyes on my wife. Knowing where she is and that she's safe.

I weave through the banquet hall, first finding Tatum with a drink in hand. "Have you seen Marlow?"

Tatum shrugs. "She went that way, I think."

That way leads me toward the kitchens, where I catch Coach Saunders—of all people—slipping out of the men's room wearing an apron. Yes, it's unsanitary, but she also moves too quickly, her smile genuine but too practiced, like she's covering something up. Wonder what I've just missed?

"Everything okay, Coach Saunders?" I ask, brows raised.

She lifts her chin. "Cooking emergency."

"In the men's room?"

"Exactly!" She says, shaking her head as she walks away. As if she's actually just answered my question.

I keep moving, following the quiet hum of voices until I reach the entrance hallway. That's when I see her. The woman I married and the prick who can't seem to take a hint.

But she's not just talking—she's *fighting*. Her voice is sharp, laced with all the fire of her bloodline, and standing opposite her is none other than Shaun Kennedy, the bastard with ink on his hands and too much interest in other people's lives.

She's tearing into him, the perfect Italian wife in full flight, every gesture sharp enough to cut glass. And it's killing me not to step in, not to tear him limb from limb for looking at her like that. But I promised her I wouldn't do anything to expose us. Not until she was ready.

Then I see it.

His hand. Reaching for hers, a cocky smirk carved into his face like he's toying with her, like he's *flirting*.

Something inside me bristles, tightens. My vision narrows.

And then I remember he's also the reporter who printed the gossip in the first place. He's the one leaking the rumors that have half this city speculating about my wife. About *our* secret.

How? Who's been talking? Not my friends. Not the few teammates who overheard that night at the Supper Club—they're too loyal, too smart to risk my wrath. No, this stinks of Kennedy digging where his nose doesn't belong.

And that won't do.

I step closer, just in time to hear Marlow hiss, "I will end you."

Shaun chuckles, tilting his head. "You and what army?"

That's my cue.

"Careful what you wish for, Kennedy," I growl, my voice low and sharp enough to make him stiffen.

Both their heads whip toward me, startled. Marlow's eyes flare wide for just a moment—then soften with something else entirely. Relief.

And Kennedy? He pales.

Good.

"This has nothing to do with you, Agassi." Kennedy tilts his head, smirking. "Or perhaps it does? So many secrets swarming around this team." His arrogance drips, every word sharpened to wound.

Marlow's eyes flash. "What the hell do you know?"

Kennedy takes his time, savoring the moment. "Enough. Enough to own the both of you if I wanted. I've got tapes—your wedding, your little surprise pop-up visit for the show. All of it."

Her voice cracks with fury. "How did you even get those tapes?"

Shaun just shrugs. "You've got forty-eight hours to make a choice. You give me the exclusive—your story, team insider information, everything—stories no other reporter has access to. Or I leak the footage to the wolves."

He only grins. And then he turns, strolling away like he hasn't just put a target on his back.

Marlow trembles beside me, her hand balled into a fist. I slip mine into my pocket, already pulling out my phone.

"Declan—who are you possibly calling right now?" she demands, her voice tight with panic.

"My brother," I answer, my thumb already dialing. "If Kennedy has that kind of access, then he's connected in ways a normal reporter shouldn't be. And Niko..." My jaw tightens. "Niko will find out how. And he'll know exactly what to do."

Chapter Fifty
CHAPTER FORTY EIGHT: LEFTOVERS & STOLEN KISSES
Eslin

I t's Sunday dinner after Thanksgiving, and Grant's house smells like leftovers and cinnamon from all the pumpkin and sweet potato pie laying around. Declan and Matteo both came tonight—Marlow made up the excuse that they were still homesick, so she didn't have to leave Declan at home. And Grant didn't even blink. He made it clear that he never minds extra people at the table so the extra company actually made him happy. And if he noticed that Marlow and Declan happened to arrive at the exact same time, he didn't say a word.

The men are in the media room, shouting at the screen as a European football match blares in the background. The sound drifts into the kitchen where Marlow and I stand side by side, hands busy with dishes but voices low.

"We agreed, for now." Marlow says, her voice sharp with determination. "We'll give Kennedy his damn exclusive, but only to buy time. Declan's brother will figure out exactly what he's into. Then we'll cut him off at the knees."

I frown, wiping my hands on a towel. "Declan's brother? What does he have to do with anything?"

"And can he help get rid of Coach Jones before he says anything about what he saw at Thanksgiving?"

I shake my head at my damn self. I've been watching entirely too much Scandal.

Marlow exhales. "Your guess is as good as mine. But apparently, he's...connected." Her voice dips lower, cautious. "When I pressed Declan on what that meant, all he said was I have a lot to learn about my in-laws. About his family."

Her next words are as pointed as the look she gives me. "Either way, Niko will get answers. We're just waiting."

"It all sounds so *espionagey*," I say in a whisper.

"Is that even a word?"

I shrug. "Who cares. It fits!"

I have so many more questions about her mysterious husband, but before I can press her, Matteo drifts into the kitchen, hands shoved deep into his pockets, a nervous smile tugging at his lips. "Coach Saunders, did you hear the news?"

I shake my head. "No, I did not!"

He glances over his shoulder toward the living room, then lowers his voice like he's afraid the walls might tattle on him. "I got into college. I'm the first one in my family to go, and..." His grin widens, pride breaking through. "I'm going to be a teacher."

I can't help it—I drop the dish towel, throw my arms around him, and squeeze him tight. "Congratulations, Teo! I'm so proud of you. And I know your family will be too. Have you told them yet?"

He shakes his head, his eyes soft with excitement. "Not yet. I'm waiting until Christmas Eve. Gonna tell them as a gift."

I hug him again, my heart swelling at the shy kid who once barely spoke to me now standing tall with his dreams in his hands. "Congratulations again, papa."

He grins sheepishly. "Hey, I told you—only family calls me that."

I put my hands on my hips, giving him the kind of look that dares him to argue. "And what are we?"

He laughs, shoulders loosening. "Alright, you're right. The Strikers are a family."

Matteo heads back into the media room and Marlow isn't far behind him. My smile widens when Grant comes through the door.

"You look real good in my kitchen, Eslin Saunders," Grant says, his voice always sounding like he's tasting the words before letting them go.

"Stay away from me, Grant Mills," I shoot back.

"Why?" His mouth curves into that devastating grin as he inches closer. "Because you know the next thing out of my mouth will be that you *taste* even better in my kitchen?"

I laugh, the sound spilling out before I can stop it—bright, helpless, like he's pulled it straight from my chest. These days, I always laugh with him. And now that he's mine, I don't just laugh—I glow.

"That's exactly why. And also how we ended up in trouble!" I jab, smirking at him. "Have you spoken with Jones?"

He frowns. "Why would I be the one to speak with him? That's your situationship."

I snatch up the dish towel and swat him across the chest. "Don't start! He's your employee!"

Grant leans against the counter, maddeningly calm. "And what exactly am I supposed to do, Es? Intimidate him into silence? Pretty sure that's illegal."

"I don't know. But I'm pretty sure my murder is gonna be illegal too, and that's exactly what'll happen if Marlow hears this from anyone but us... me!"

"Breathe," he says softly, tilting his head as if the weight of my panic doesn't scare him at all. "Take a breath for me, hmm? It's going to be fine."

And damn him. He knows how to settle the storm raging inside me, even if he's the one still stirring up the hurricane in my panties.

He leans in, feigning interest in the bottle of wine beside me, but at the last second dips down, brushing his lips against my cheek in a kiss so quick and soft it steals my breath.

"Would you stop it?" I hiss, smacking his chest even as my skin warms where his mouth just was. "You're gonna get us caught!"

"Speaking of which," he murmurs, his lips grazing the shell of my ear, sending a shiver straight down my spine, "when do you think we should tell her?"

"I don't know!" My voice comes out sharp, hushed, as I swat at him again. "Every time we try to figure out the best approach, I end up pinned to a wall or a countertop by your penis!"

Grant throws his head back and laughs—loud, unapologetic, and it fills a room. "You say the craziest things," he manages between chuckles, his eyes shining with mischief.

"And you're just plain crazy," I counter, but there's no bite in it. Only fondness.

Only love.

"For you, Eslin Saunders? Guilty as charged." His grin softens, his hand slipping down my arm until his fingers curl around mine. "But... just for a little longer, can we keep this? Ours. Just ours. Without the questions. Without the speculations. The press has moved on, the story's dead. We can wait another week or two."

I study him, the boyish smile, the warmth in his eyes, and even though the turmoil still twists inside me, I nod. "Alright. Another week. *Maybe* two." I relent.

"Good." His voice dips lower, almost secretive. "Because I want to take you away. Next weekend. To the lake house Will, Xavier, and I own. Just us. No hiding, no interruptions. Just you and me for a few days where we can be out in the open."

The thought of it makes my heart trip. I lean closer, whispering, "I can't wait." Then, quick as a thief, I steal a kiss from his lips before we step into the living room. Me holding the tray of class cups and Grant bringing the bowl of eggnog.

The scent of pine greets us immediately. In the corner stands the most beautiful live Christmas tree I've ever seen, delivered and waiting just for this. Branches reach high, wide, their needles fresh and green. Boxes of ornaments litter the floor, and everyone is encouraged to either hang something meaningful or make their own at the craft table set up by the house staff.

There are tiny soccer balls painted silver and gold, delicate glass boots with little cleats. For Matteo, ornaments painted in bright reds and greens with Mexican embroidery patterns; for Declan, miniature gondolas, hand-painted Italian flags, and one lopsided Santa riding a Vespa. Laughter fills the air as the tree slowly comes to life.

Declan slips a hand low and grabs Marlow on the butt, making her squeak and nearly drop the ornament in her hand.

"You okay, munchkin?" Grant asks, watching her curiously.

Marlow waves him off, cheeks flaming. "Fine! Totally fine."

"You sure?" I tease. "You seem really jumpy!"

Marlow shoots me a murderous glare.

I laugh, but my stomach still twists at the sight of her. Watching her, the ease with which she gravitates to me, always pulling me in—into her secrets, her family, her joy. She trusts me in ways I don't deserve. And I hate myself for keeping anything from her.

Declan clears his throat and lifts his phone. "Alright, enough chatter. We need some proper Christmas inspiration. Music."

A cheer goes up around the room because as much as everyone loves soccer, the muted drone of the match isn't exactly tree-trimming material.

We brace for Michael Bublé, maybe some Italian carols in honor of Declan's roots. Hell, I would've even settled for a little Motown.

Instead, the opening chords that come crashing through the Bluetooth speaker stop us all cold.

"My favorite Christmas album," Declan declares, grinning.

We all glance around the room, wide-eyed, trying to process what we're hearing—Justin Timberlake and the rest of the boys crooning *"Merry Christmas, Happy Holidays"* at full blast.

"NSYNC," Declan yells over the chords. "Don't you just love them?"

Chapter Fifty - One

CHAPTER FORTY NINE: MURDER & MOTHER WOUNDS

Declan

The call with my brother is quick, efficient, the way it always is. He talks, I listen. He doesn't mince words, never has. When I got really serious about soccer, he used to say I wasted my charm on the pitch when I should've been using it at the table. I told him I'd rather kick a ball than kneecaps. We still argue about it.

When he finishes telling me what I need to know, I exhale slowly and slip into the tongue that still feels like home, even after all these years.

"*Grazie per averlo gestito. Ciao.*" *Thank you for handling it. Bye.*

I hang up and turn to Marlow, who is perched on the edge of the sofa, eyes wide like she's bracing herself for some great revelation.

"Shaun Kennedy," I begin, "wasn't working alone. My brother found out he'd partnered with a hacker. A very good one. This man was tracking celebrity phones, pulling data, texts, even locations. But Niko sniffed him out." I allow a smirk. "Threatened him within an inch of his life. And suddenly, the man remembered how to sing."

Marlow blinks, slow. "That doesn't sound scary...or illegal... at all." The sarcasm drips like honey.

I shrug, leaning back. "Niko made sure to wipe all of the evidence he had against us and in the next forty-eight hours, Kennedy will be reassigned to Europe. Season-long coverage. Far, far away."

Her jaw drops. "How did you pull that off? Who are you people? And more importantly—who are my in-laws? Because, Declan Agassi, you all sound... pretty badass."

I can't help the laugh that escapes me. If only she knew.

So I tell her.

The version I've never put into words for anyone else, but for her, for my wife, I will. "I told Coach Saunders once about my mother. About how she left in the middle of the night, how we had to run. But what I didn't say—what I never say—is why. My father..." I pause, grounding myself, "...was the right hand to my uncle. The head of the Agassi Crime Syndicate."

She gasps, clutching her chest like I just confessed to burying bodies in the backyard. "Your family murders people?"

"That is *not even remotely* what I said," I reply, my tone flat.

She narrows her eyes. "Declan, when you put the words *crime* and *syndicate* in the same sentence, murder is always implied!"

I glance around like the walls might have ears. "Would you lower your voice? You want the neighbors thinking I'm hosting a Sopranos reunion in here?"

Her eyes widen, but there's a smirk tugging at her lips. "Fine. I'll whisper. Please, *Don Declan*, continue."

I shoot her a look but press on, pushing up from the couch. "Someone betrayed my uncle," I say, heading toward the kitchen like I need the movement to work this out of me. "And that someone was my mother."

She joins me in the kitchen, arms folded, perched against the counter as I pull the tray of dough I'd rolled out earlier. The motion of dusting flour on the board steadies me.

"Initially, everyone thought it was my father. That he'd staged the perfect power move—kill his own brother to take control of the Syndicate. It made sense. He was my uncle's right hand, his shadow, the one everyone feared he'd become if he ever got a taste of power. So when my uncle ended up dead, all fingers pointed to him."

I press the heel of my palm into the dough, stretching it, folding it over itself again. "But the truth was even more brutal. Because it was my mother. She slit the throat of the most dangerous man in Italy—and vanished before anyone could prove it. She left us there, in the wreckage, with a whole world of enemies convinced it was my father's doing. And when the whispers grew too loud, when revenge started circling our doorsteps, we had to run. Argentina...anywhere but home."

I glance at Marlow, her face a mix of horror and disbelief, and reach for the ricotta filling, spooning it into the dough. "Now, my mother runs the Syndicate. With Niko at her side. My brother may be charming, but don't let him fool you—he's sharper than anyone gives him credit for. Ruthless, when he has to be."

My hands still for a moment, pinching the dough into neat little pillows. "She and I...my mother," I let out a breath, shaking my head. "...we still don't speak. Haven't since the day she left. Niko was more forgiving."

The kitchen goes quiet except for the soft sound of my knife slicing the ravioli apart. A domestic picture, if not for the fact that I've just laid the truth of a crime dynasty at my wife's feet.

Marlow's voice softens, breaking through the silence. "And here I thought you were just being dramatic when you said you couldn't handle me leaving. But now I see. You've got a crime-boss sized mother wound and I'm sure that's not easy to mend."

I bark out a laugh. "That's one way of putting it."

She says it so easily—like naming my pain makes it smaller. A wound the size of a crime-boss mother. I laugh, but inside, the truth rolls heavier than I ever let on.

Because the second I knew Marlow was mine—the second I admitted I wanted her—fear dug its claws in. What if it happened again? What if she woke up one morning and decided I wasn't worth the fight? The same hollow pit my mother left behind threatened to open up all over again, and I wasn't sure I could survive reliving that kind of abandonment.

So I did what I've always done when the ache cuts too deep. I buried it. Layer after layer, I inked it into my skin, turned pain into permanence, pretending the art could hold me together. For a while, it worked—made me believe, made everyone else believe, I was fine. But when the ink dried and the sting faded, the fear was still there. Louder. Heavier.

Coach Saunders made me face it. Made me see that I can't control anyone else's choices. That my mother leaving wasn't my fault. That if Marlow ever left, that wouldn't be my fault either. People choose. Sometimes they choose wrong. Sometimes they choose to stay. But it isn't on me to carry the weight of their weakness if they don't. It isn't my fault if they don't have the capacity to love me.

And when I finally let go of that desperate grip on control, I found something better waiting in the space it left behind. Her. All of her. The chance to really learn her, love her, give her what she needed instead of what my fear demanded.

I take her hand, twining my fingers through hers. "I wish I could take you home to meet the family in Argentina. Let them see who you are, what you mean to me."

"I know. Me too," she says.

I kiss the palm of her hand, lingering there like I can seal the vow into her skin. "Once the season ends, we'll go. I promise. I'll introduce you to all of my family's Italian traditions."

The thought alone makes me smile. Because when I found out her mother had Italian roots, it was like puzzle pieces clicking into place. I knew there was something familiar about her from the start—something that pulled at me, something that felt like home. Something that felt like forever.

Her smile, warm and teasing, steadies something in me. "Until then, you're stuck with the Cinnamon Grove family traditions. There's plenty of them, trust me. Biddy Mason Charter School is hosting their holiday bazaar next weekend, and the Strikers are major sponsors."

I groan. "The bazaar, how could I forget? Games. Face paint. Kids."

"And prizes," she adds, lips twitching.

"And more children braiding my hair," I mutter.

She nudges me. "Oh hush, you've come to enjoy it. Admit it. Meeting the fans, being part of the community...it's good for you. And for them."

I exhale, but the truth is, she's right. At first, I hated it. The parades, the handshakes, the small-town carnival energy. But now, I look forward to the faces that light up when we show up. To the way, even the smallest kid feels big when we stop to listen. It isn't home, not Italy, not Argentina.

But with Marlow's hand in mine, it feels damn close.

I drop the ravioli into the pot, the steam curling upward like it's trying to carry all the heaviness of my confession away with it. Wiping my hands on a towel, I move to the cabinet, open it, and pull out a small blue bottle. Without saying a word, I set it down in front of Marlow.

She blinks at it, like I've just handed her contraband. "What's this for?"

I give her a look. A knowing one. "You fart in your sleep every time I feed you something with cheese. And lately, it's gotten ten times worse." I say, perfectly deadpan. "Leads me to believe you're lactose intolerant...or whatever you Americans call it."

Her gasp is so dramatic I almost laugh. She clutches the bottle to her chest like it's a personal attack. "I will have you know, I do not fart in my sleep!"

I shrug. "Fine, Americana. Let's say you don't. But why don't you take one, just in case one slips out in your sleep without you knowing?"

She bursts into laughter, cheeks pink, eyes sparkling as she gives me a playful shove. Then she actually pops the pill.

I let out a breath, leaning back against the counter as I watch her laugh—my favorite sound in the world. And I feel it again, the light she brings me, the way she makes all of this, all of me, bearable.

Chapter Fifty-Two
CHAPTER FIFTY: SPONSORS & SNOWFLAKES
Marlow

I love the holiday season.

I also hate the holiday season.

For me, it's always been a mixed bag of emotions.

Growing up, it was mostly just me and Daddy, and we never quite fit into those picture-perfect traditions people bragged about. Our holidays were pieced together—family friends who invited us over, Daddy's coworkers who let us crash their parties, the occasional extra seat at someone else's table. And while I was grateful, it never felt like ours. Never felt like those commercials promised—the ones full of big families, noise, love, and warmth spilling out of every corner.

So we started making our own. Just me and him. Little traditions stitched together year by year—the movies we watched every Christmas Eve, the way we stayed up to ring in the New Year by watching celebrations around the world. Every year Daddy would find something to add, something that made it feel like our holiday was designed just for us. For me.

And for as long as I can remember, that was enough.

This year feels different. This year...I actually feel cheer. I feel jolly. I feel like I have a family.

The holiday bazaar with Biddy Mason Charter School is one of the best partnerships Tatum and I have pulled off to date. The Strikers' logo is everywhere—on soccer-themed booths, stamped across discount tickets we've arranged with local businesses, even printed on flyers kids are waving around like trophies. But the part that makes me proudest is it isn't just a one-way sponsorship. The schools and shops actually get money poured back into them and their endeavors when they partner with us, creating a cycle that supports everyone. It's a win-win, and watching it all come to life makes me glow with pride.

The whole place is alive. Atlanta's own Dr. KAM in the Traffic Jam has the crowd hype from the stage, spinning Christmas tracks between his loud, booming jokes. Kids line up for the chance to belt out their favorite carols for prizes, and adults are out there challenging celebrity guests to dance-offs. The smell of kettle corn, cider, and funnel cakes fills the crisp winter air. Everywhere I turn, there's laughter.

When the Cinnamon Grove Sun reporter makes her way toward me with a mic, I tense out of habit. Old reflex. But I have to remind myself this isn't Shaun Kennedy. She's young, strikingly beautiful, her smile disarming in a way that feels genuine. She must be the one replacing Shaun, I realize. Thank God.

She asks me the usual—how I'm enjoying the bazaar, what it means to see so many families out here, how this event helps boost the Strikers' image after such a turbulent season. Her voice is warm, professional, but still I brace myself for the trick. For the hidden jab, the humiliating angle, the one line she'll twist into a headline that makes me look like a failure.

But instead, she just...smiles. Winks like we're in on the same secret. Then she congratulates me on pulling off something this big and tells me I should be proud of what we've done for the community.

I almost choke up right there, caught off guard by her kindness. I didn't realize how much it mattered—how much I needed this—but I'm grateful. Grateful the outlet finally put a woman in this position. For once, I don't feel like prey circling a shark. For once, I feel seen.

As I drift back into the crowd, watching from the sidelines, my eyes find him. Declan. He's sitting cross-legged in a circle, surrounded by little girls braiding his hair and squealing as they twist pink ribbons into it. Croix is right next to him, enduring the same treatment. Their mothers are snapping photos like paparazzi, and even the dads look like they're enjoying the sight. Declan catches my eye for a split second, winks, and my chest warms. I fall in love with him a little bit more, right here in the middle of this carnival of chaos.

That's when Eslin sidles up, eyes dancing. "Hey, boss lady. How do you feel seeing your stamp all across the city like this?"

I grin. "It feels pretty damn good," I admit, sweeping my gaze across the booths, the lights, the crowd. My husband. Then I look back at her. "And...I've decided to tell Daddy about me and Declan."

Her jaw drops, and then her whole body exhales like she's been waiting for this. "Oh, thank goodness! I hated keeping this secret from him!"

I frown. "Why would *you* feel bad about keeping a secret from my father?"

She laughs nervously. "Oh, you know how it is. I'm a therapist. I hold everyone's secrets, and sometimes it feels like my entire life is made of them. Having one about my boss's family, who I regularly have dinner with, you have to admit it would be a lot for anyone."

"I get it. I really do. Thank you for keeping my secrets, Es." And I mean that.

Maybe that's why it hits me in the chest—because the one thing I've never had to worry about was her keeping my secrets. Over these past few months I've learned I can trust her with anything. I lean in and hug her tight. "I appreciate you more than you know. I owe you big."

She laughs, even more nervous energy in her tone. "Glad to hear you say that because I have something to share."

I waggle my eyebrows. "Things heating up with Coach Jones? I saw the way he was looking at you at Thanksgiving!"

She waves me off. "No, nothing to do with Jones. Just meet me at Holly's when you're done being fabulous and making your rounds here, ok?"

"Yes!" I squeeze her again before pulling back. I look at the time on my phone. "I should be done here in about an hour. That ok?"

She nods and then heads off towards the stage where the team is doing the Cupid Shuffle with the kids, but Dr. K.A.M. has changed the music to match TLC's song, Sleigh Ride.

I look toward the cluster of news crews and spot my father, poised with that polished, camera-ready smile he's perfected over the years. Tatum arranged for a handful of specialized outlets to capture some father-daughter moments. And even though things between us aren't fully healed—he still refuses to tell me who that mysterious woman was, and none of Shaun Kennedy's footage gave me the answers I've been craving—I swallow the questions burning on my tongue. I push it all down, bury it deep where no one with a lens can see. For now, I let it go. And I lift my chin, step into place beside him, and smile for the cameras.

Because tonight is about family, in all its messy, complicated, beautiful pieces. And like it or not, Grant Mills is mine.

Eslin

Tonight's the night.

I told Grant since Marlow and I are friends, I should be the one to start the conversation about us. If she ever finds out she's poured her heart into me, trusted me with pieces of her life that she hadn't even shared with him, while I held back something this big...she'll never forgive me. I know I wouldn't.

So, tonight I'm going to make the first move. Tonight, I'm going to tell her about Grant. About Vegas. About how I fell in love with him that night and it's only gotten worse. Something I haven't even told *him* yet. But something about how this all came to be makes me feel like Marlow should hear it first. All of it.

Once it's done, when I've ripped the Band-Aid clean off, I'll go to Grant's cabin. The one tucked away in the pines, where the trees will muffle everything but the sound of our laughter. Where the fire crackles and the world feels small enough that I can breathe. Just me and him.

So here I am, sitting at the bar at Holly's, waiting for Marlow. The air smells like cinnamon and roasted nuts, the lights strung across the rafters twinkle in gold and red, and the speakers are crooning Donny Hathaway's "This Christmas." Holly's behind the bar, fussing with mugs and pretending she's not watching me worry a groove into the counter.

"Did she say what time she'd be here?" Holly asks.

"Soon," I murmur, looking at my phone to check the time. I've already filled her in—why this conversation matters, why this needs to happen tonight before me and Grant go away for the weekend. And Holly agreed her spot was the perfect neutral ground. She even promised to spike Marlow's cocoa with a little rum, just enough to keep her from going full nuclear if things went sideways.

We're half-joking about her annual *This Christmas* party—where she screens the movie and forces everyone to do karaoke to the entire soundtrack—when the door opens. I look up and Marlow steps in.

Then my heart drops.

She looks pale, clammy, her usually polished self nowhere in sight. Her eyes find me, and the sight of me seems to unravel her because she walks over, slumps onto the barstool, buries her head in her arms—and *cries*.

"Low, honey. Are you okay?" I reach for her, panic tightening my chest. "Is it Declan? Do I need to shank his Italian, tattooed ass?"

She lifts her head, eyes wet, face blotchy in a way I've never seen before. Then, like the words are trying to claw their way out of her, she blurts it—loud, raw, and shaking.

"Eslin! I'm pregnant!"

Chapter Fifty-Three

CHAPTER FIFTY ONE: PEPPERMINTS & POSITIVITY

Marlow

O kay. Something has been off with me. Wrong. My stomach's been tied in knots more often than not, I can't touch the food I normally crave, and the final straw—the one that really sent alarm bells ringing—was when I opened a can of diet soda and nearly gagged. Me. The girl who used to swear she had carbonated aspartame running through her veins. That's when I knew something wasn't right.

I'd planned to see my doctor next week, convincing myself it was just nerves from the job. But at the Holiday Bazaar, I ended up running to the restroom three times to throw up—and I hadn't even eaten since lunch. By the third time, my body felt hollow, my hands gripping the edge of the sink just to stay upright. That's when she walked in.

The new reporter. Shaun Kennedy's replacement.

At first, panic spiked—I was afraid she'd see me like this, unkempt and miserable, and spin it into a story. But instead, she offered me one glance, one sympathetic smile, and asked a single question that knocked the air out of me.

"First trimester or second? My sister's morning sickness lasted through both."

Her words slam into me like a brick to the chest. My throat goes dry, my knees nearly buckle, and before she can ramble on about ginger chews or pregnancy pops or Gatorade, I bolt.

Straight to the nearest drugstore.

I don't think. I don't breathe. I just grab every single brand of pregnancy test I can find, my hands shaking so hard I nearly drop them all in the checkout line.

I know I'm supposed to be meeting Eslin right now but I will not be able to sit through any conversations with this gnawing at me. And there's no way I'm waiting until I get home.

So I lock myself in the public restroom, rinse out an old coffee cup I had rolling around in my car, and use it as my makeshift sample.

One test. Then another. Then another.

By the time I stopped, twelve little sticks were lined up in front of me. Twelve glaring results. Every one shouting the same thing: Pregnant.

My life is about to change forever.

At Holly's, Eslin gently takes the mug I've been holding and swaps it for her own.

"Here," she says softly, "drink this one instead. That one isn't safe..." She pauses, and I swear I see tears threatening to spill in her eyes. "This one isn't safe for the baby."

I lift the cup, take a long sip, the peppermint cocoa warm and rich on my tongue, and glance back at her. Her face is frozen in shock—eyes wide, lips parted—like she still can't quite process the words I've just laid in her lap.

Leaning forward, desperation curling through my voice, I whisper, "Es, please. You *cannot* tell Daddy."

From behind the bar, Holly lets out a low whistle and mutters, "This shit just keeps getting better."

But Eslin isn't amused. Her voice is firm, almost pleading. "Marlow, you have to tell him. Please don't make me carry another secret for you. Not this one."

I shake my head, clutching one of the tests for dear life. "Just until I tell him about Declan. Once that's out in the open, then I'll...then I'll tell him about the baby. One secret at a time. Please, Eslin?"

Her eyes search mine, steady and unrelenting, but she doesn't push. Instead, she pulls me into her arms, holding me tight like she knows I'm unraveling right there in her embrace.

"Are you happy about this baby?" she whispers.

The question undoes me. A tear slips free, and I shake my head, then nod, then shake it again, my throat raw. Finally, the truth tumbles out, cracked and fragile. "I think I am. I'm having Declan Agassi's baby."

Eslin pulls out of our embrace and I remember she had something to tell me, too. "Hey! Didn't you say you had something to talk to me about?"

She goes stiff. "Uh. Um. I...Let's just save my news for later."

"Eslin, back at the school it seemed important. Are you sure? You know you can talk to me about anything, right?"

She nods. "I do. But, today, let's just keep this about you, for now. I want to know how you're going to tell Declan he's going to be a daddy!"

Eslin

A baby.

The word circles my brain like a storm cloud. Thank goodness Grant sent a car for me because I don't think I can focus enough to follow directions right now.

I thought keeping what I had with Grant from Marlow was already unbearable, but this...this is something else. Something fragile. Something that can't be risked.

If I pushed her too hard, if I told her about me and Grant now, would it shatter her? Would it put too much stress on her, on the baby? I can't do that. I won't. So, I tell myself—just a little longer. Just until she finds her footing. Just until she's ready.

The road to Lake Oconee unwinds before me, two narrow lanes flanked by tall Georgia pines that stretch toward the winter sky. Their branches sway in the breeze, whispering secrets of their own, and I can't help but feel like they're mocking me. Closer to the lake, the land opens wide. Expanses of water glint silver beneath the fading light, dotted with docks and the silhouettes of cabins mixed with luxurious estates nestled in the trees. It's beautiful. Peaceful. The kind of place that should quiet a racing mind. But mine refuses to still.

Because all I can think about are the secrets stacked inside me: Marlow's marriage to Declan. Her pregnancy. My affair—my love—with Grant.

Secrets and lies, each one heavier than the last. And now I'm heading toward the one place that feels like release: his cabin. His arms. The man who makes me laugh until I can't breathe, who touches me like I'm something precious instead of someone drowning in guilt.

I lean my head back against the seat and sigh just as the lake comes into full view, whispering to myself like a prayer: *Just a little longer, Eslin. Hold it together just a little longer.*

CHAPTER FIFTY TWO: PINES & PROMISES

Grant

I wanted this weekend to mean something. To show her that even if the world outside is clawing at us with its secrets, with its damn scandals, here—at the lake house—she is safe. So I came up early, made sure everything was ready, and sent the car to get her once she finished with Marlow.

The lake house isn't a simple cabin—it's three wings of luxury sprawled along the edge of Lake Oconee, built like a fortress dressed up in wood and stone. One wing belongs to Will, one to Xavier, and the other—mine. Floor-to-ceiling windows that stare out over the glassy water. A great room with vaulted ceilings and a stone fireplace tall enough to climb. Every detail is meant to feel both wild and indulgent, like the three of us wanted to stake our claim on the world and carve out a retreat no one could touch.

And even though it cost us an obscene amount of money to build this place, there's a peace here that money can't buy—a quiet that settles into your bones, that makes the world outside feel a thousand miles away.

But right now, even with the fire crackling and the candles I set out flickering low across the room, I can't stop pacing. Can't stop checking my phone, waiting for Marlow's name, or hers. Something. Anything. But the screen stays dark.

When the car finally pulls up, I nearly bolt for the door. And when Eslin walks in, frantic energy buzzing off her like static, the first thing she does is grab the glass out of my hand and down it in one gulp.

"Jesus, Es," I say, watching her chest rise and fall as she wipes her mouth with the back of her hand. "Did you tell her?"

Her eyes are wild, too bright. "It didn't come up," she says quickly, shaking her head. "I wanted to, but I couldn't. Not tonight."

"Then I'll call her—"

"No!" Her voice cuts sharp, desperate, and she catches my hand before I can reach for my phone. "Please, Grant. Don't. The secrets are already killing me, and tonight she told me something—something I can't tell you, and if I told her about us right now, it would only make everything worse. I just need... I just need the weekend. I'll tell her after this weekend."

Her words hang heavy between us, the silence broken only by the snap of wood in the fire. Finally, she stops, her frantic movements slowing as her eyes sweep the room. The candles. The roses scattered across the table, the mantle, the window ledge.

She blinks, then looks back at me, her lips parting. "You did all this?"

I shrug, feeling foolish, then grin like a boy caught with his hand in the cookie jar. "Saw it in a movie once. Thought I'd try it out."

She's speechless and I beam with pride. She likes it.

"It's amazing, Grant. No one has ever done anything like this for me."

"And to think," I say, drawing from a memory from our time in Vegas. "The night is just beginning."

She smiles, really smiles, then buries her head into my chest. "I can't wait to see what else you've got up your sleeve, Mister."

"Well, then I'm afraid you're going to be a little disappointed."

She looks up at me, frowning. "Why?"

"Because what comes next doesn't require sleeves. Or clothes, for that matter."

Her smile goes big. "Oh yeah?"

I lead her into the bathroom, my hand wrapped around hers, steadying her even though I'm the one who feels unsteady. It feels like it's taken so long to get her, so long for her to accept what's between us, that it doesn't feel real. But it is. She is.

And she's mine.

The candles throw soft shadows across the marble, the tub steaming, petals drifting on the surface like they've been waiting just for her. For a second she just stands there, staring, and I watch her eyes widen, her lips part like she's trying to take it all in at once.

"You're stressed, baby. Let me take care of you tonight."

She nods but no words come out and I can tell she's a bit overwhelmed. In the best way.

I go to remove her blouse, and I go slow. Each button undone feels like a vow I'm making, one after the other. My knuckles graze her skin, her pulse flickers under my touch, but I take my time. Because she isn't something to rush through, she isn't someone to consume and discard. She's everything.

The fabric slides from her shoulders, pooling at her feet, and I trace her with my eyes like I've never seen her before. Like I haven't memorized every line, every curve. I want her to know, in this moment, there is nothing missing in her. Nothing broken. She is whole. Perfect. Mine.

When her blouse falls fully open, lace framing her like some masterpiece meant only for me, I dip my head between her breasts. My tongue drags over her skin, slow and reverent, before I kiss each soft mound through the thin white lace. Her breath catches, her body pressing closer as though she can't help it.

Her hands are already tugging at me, pulling the sweater over my head, her fingers brushing my chest as I shake free of it. The moment I'm bare, I reach for her pants, slipping each button loose, savoring the way her body arches into my touch. I kneel as she steadies herself on my shoulders, her fingers buried in my hair as I guide her out of her pants, and then her panties—lace, matching, already damp.

I don't move. Not yet. I just stare. Jesus, she's glistening for me, every inch of her begging me closer. My throat goes dry. My dick aches. And still, I stay there, kneeling at the altar of her body, completely undone by the beauty of her.

One slow slip of my finger through her slick heat and I'm lost. I bring it to my mouth, eyes locked on hers as I lick her taste off, groaning like it's the first meal I've had in days. Her moan answers mine, soft and wrecked, and it lights me up inside.

"You taste fucking magnificent, baby. So damn good," I murmur, already starving for more.

She tries to protest, voice breathy. "The water's going to get cold, Grant."

I shake my head, grinning against her skin. "It won't. It's programmed to stay warm."

Her laugh falters into a moan. "Good to know."

"Now hold on to the wall for me, baby," I rasp, my hands gripping her thighs, spreading her open. "I need to taste you some more."

She obeys, pressing one palm to the wall while the other grabs my shoulder. She's offering herself up without hesitation. I loop my arms beneath her legs, locking her in place, her body mine to hold, mine to devour. Then I bury my face in her, tongue first, lapping into her like a man starved.

"Shit!" she cries out, the sound echoing off the tile, raw and unrestrained.

"Yeah, scream for me, Es," I growl, my mouth wet with her, my tongue driving deeper, circling, fucking her until she's trembling against me. "It's just you and me."

And she does—screams, moans, her body grinding against my face, her hands slamming against the wall as I take everything she gives. My tongue relentless, my fingers sliding inside her, curling just right until she breaks apart with a cry, shattering in my mouth, coating me in her release.

"Good fucking girl," I whisper against her, lips still pressed to the sweetest part of her. "So perfect."

Eslin

I came here dripping with panic, my nerves frayed and my chest tight from everything I've been holding back. But this man—this maddening, impossible, beautiful man—has managed to calm every worry and soothe every doubt with a single touch. And maybe a few flicks of his tongue.

And now, looking around at the candles, the roses, the steaming bath he drew just for me, I can hardly breathe. No one has ever done anything like this for me before. No one has ever thought to make me feel...special. Worthy. My heart clenches because the truth is, I've never known this kind of tenderness. Never felt it wrapped around me, burning into me.

I'm still reeling from the orgasm he's just given me, my legs trembling, my body loose and undone, when Grant rises. In one swift motion, his pants hit the floor, and my lips part as my eyes drink in the sight of him. He looks toward the tub, then steps in without hesitation. He holds out his hand for me, and I slip into the water with him, my skin instantly warmed.

As he sits back, he gestures for me to settle with my back to his chest. But instead, I grin and shake my head, turning to straddle him instead.

"Es," he whispers, his voice strained, "I had a whole massage planned for you."

"Well," I say, grinning wickedly, "you shouldn't have started with that explosive orgasm. Because now I'm eager to return the favor."

His laugh is soft, strained, his hands already sliding over my hips as I steady myself. And that's when I realize—I've never been on top like this before. Not in this angle, not in this way. My body hesitates, unsure, but he grounds me, strong hands anchoring me.

"Relax," he murmurs, guiding himself inside me, slow and steady, his hands keeping me in place. My body resists for a moment, but then I let go, let myself open to him, and he fills me—perfectly, completely.

I exhale, melting into the stretch, into him, and soon I'm moving, rocking against him, water sloshing around us, steam curling up to blur everything but him. My hands clutch his shoulders, my head tipped back as he groans beneath me, pulling my nipples into his mouth.

Every movement, every slide of him inside me, it's more than just physical. It's my body yielding to him as easily as my heart already has. And I don't want to stop. I don't ever want to stop.

His head tips forward, his lips brushing the swell of my breast, my throat, my ear. And then I hear it, faint but clear, breaking me wide open.

"I fucking love you, Eslin Saunders. Do you hear me? I fucking love you."

Chapter Fifty-Five

CHAPTER FIFTY THREE: EGGS & EVERGREENS

Eslin

The morning after, I wake to the smell of bacon and the soft crackle of a skillet. For a moment, I just lie there, cocooned in warmth, listening to Grant hum low under his breath as he moves around the kitchen. When I finally pull myself from the bed and wander into the great room, I pause.

The scene is like something out of a Christmas card—minus the snow. The lake glitters beneath the pale winter sun, pine trees sway outside the tall glass windows, and the house feels alive with the glow of the fire and the smell of breakfast. Even without garlands or twinkling lights, it feels like Christmas. Cozy. Magical. Mine.

I have never thought much about the kind of Christmases I'd have as an adult. I grew used to a patchwork of borrowed traditions—whatever hodgepodge of a celebration I'd been invited to, whatever table had room for me that year. But if I had dared to picture something for myself, something pulled straight from my wildest dreams, it would be this. This place. This man. This feeling.

Grant stands at the stove in nothing but a pair of low-slung sweatpants, spatula in one hand, coffee mug in the other, like it's the most natural thing in the world to be half-naked in this massive luxury lake house flipping bacon...*for me*. His hair is a mess, sticking up every which way, and I can't stop smiling.

It's perfect. For once, everything feels uncomplicated.

"Good morning," I say, smiling, and he greets me with that beautiful grin of his.

"Good morning, Sunshine. Sleep well?" he asks, lifting his mug for another sip of coffee.

"I did. Those pillows are magical."

"Glad you liked it."

"You're pretty magical too," I tease, stepping beside him as he flips an egg—over easy, just the way I like it.

He bends and presses a kiss to my forehead. "The magic only comes alive for you, Eslin Saunders."

"And you better keep it that way, Mister. I'd hate to have to cut a bitch."

His laugh rumbles through the kitchen. "I can't say I've ever had violence used as an expression of love, but I kinda like it."

The word love makes my gaze snap to him. My lips part, my heart stutters. "You know...you said you loved me last night?"

"I'm aware," he grins, eyes steady on mine.

"And that—" The words dry out, falling flat on my lips.

He leans down, fingers tilting my chin, and kisses me softly. "And I meant it."

Relief and joy flood through me, and I smile. "Good. 'Cause I think I love you too."

His brow lifts. "Think?"

I shrug, half nervous, half playful. "I can't say I've ever been in love before."

"And what makes you think you might be now?"

I sigh, checking items off my love list one by one. "The impossible pull you have on me. The way I feel instantly at ease with you, like I can actually be myself. And the fact that you cut a bald spot into my head and I'm still here, giving you my body like some weak-willed woman."

That makes us both laugh, the sound bouncing warm off the massive lake house walls.

"I love it here," I admit, my grin softer this time. "And...I love you."

He kisses me again, lingering. "Say it again."

"I love you, Grant Mills."

Another kiss, deeper. "I thought I was your mister?"

"You like sounding like my paid escort, huh?"

"No," he says, his lips grazing mine. "I like sounding like I've got something from you no one else does. My name. My claim."

"Fine. I love you too, *my* Mister."

And then it happens—the sharp crunch of tires against gravel outside. The sound slices through the air, shattering our fragile, morning-after peace.

I move toward the window just as the door bursts open, cold air sweeping inside. And there they are—Marlow, eyes wide and wild, and Declan, jaw tight, shoulders squared like he's ready for war.

And all I can think as I spin around is that Grant Mills is standing in the kitchen half-naked, frying bacon, while I'm still in his T-shirt.

Marlow's gaze sweeps the room, sharp and cutting, until it lands on me—then on Grant. Her whole face twists, her shock boiling into rage.

"What the actual fuck?!?" she screams, her voice sharp as glass. "This is where you've been? With him?"

Her hand flings toward Grant like an accusation before snapping back to me. "Daddy? Her?!"

The words hit harder than the cold gust of wind rushing in behind her. My chest caves, the air sucked right out of me.

I move past Grant, my hands half-raised, desperate to reach her. "Low, I can explain."

She jerks back like I've burned her. "Explain? He's shirtless. You're wearing said shirt. No explanation needed, Eslin!"

"Marlow, please," Grant says behind me, his voice careful, as if stepping closer to a wild animal on the verge of breaking.

But she only turns back to me, her eyes glassy, furious.

"Shaun Kennedy had one more trick up his sleeve before he was shipped off to Europe. My marriage to Declan is now splashed all over the fucking media. And you? You're here. Fucking my father?"

Grant moves closer, the weight of his presence shifting the room, his voice edged with both confusion and temper. "I'm sorry. Did you just say you were married?"

Marlow

I woke up at 4 a.m. to my phone buzzing off the nightstand like it's possessed. A barrage of calls, texts, emails—every single one of them screaming at me to look. Most from Tatum, others from PR staff, a few from numbers I don't even recognize. My stomach drops before I even swipe the screen.

I ignore all of them except Tatum and call her back immediately, tiptoeing out of bed so I don't wake Declan. My voice is barely a whisper. "What the hell is going on?"

"Go to *The Cinnamon Grove Sun's* website. Now."

"Shit. What is it?"

"See for yourself," Tatum says.

My pulse thunders as I scramble for my laptop. But of course, because irony is a bitch, my bladder decides now is the perfect time to remind me who's really in charge. So I end up in the bathroom, laptop balanced on my knees while I sit on the toilet and let go, multitasking like only a woman in crisis can.

Within seconds, the front page fills my screen and I feel like I've been punched in the face. Images from our wedding night. Our drunken vows. Video clips of the pop-up visit Chelsea Raymond swore up and down no one would see until next year.

I press play on one of the clips, my hands shaking. Chelsea's voice comes through, clear and cutting. "So, of course by the time this airs, people will have learned about your marriage, but as of right now, it's all pretty hush, right? What do you think your teammates will say when they find out?"

And then Declan—my sweet husband—pulls me into a kiss and says into the camera, "Fuck 'em. I don't care what anyone has to say or thinks about what we have."

They cut it there.

The next part—the part where I rush to clarify, where I tell Chelsea we can't be worried about what people think when we're still trying to figure out what this all means ourselves—gone. The soundbite leaves us looking careless. Reckless. Like Declan doesn't give a damn about the Strikers or his teammates, when that couldn't be further from the truth.

I try to three-way in Eslin. Straight to voicemail. Over and over.

"Yeah, she wasn't answering for me either," Tatum mutters, frazzled.

"Fuck!" My voice cracks. "My father! I have to get to him before he sees this or gets word!"

I hang up with Tatum and call Daddy. No answer.

By then Declan is awake, hair tousled, voice rough with sleep. "Marlow? What is it?"

That's when it all spills out—the video, the fallout, the timing, mother fucking Shaun Kennedy. My words tumble over each other, frantic, and my hands won't stop shaking.

"Declan, I know me and my father's relationship isn't the best right now," I choke out, "but he's my best friend. And he needs to hear this from me. From *us*. Before some reporter shoves a soundbite in his face and twists it into something worse."

He pulls me into his chest, arms wrapping around me with that unshakable steadiness that always manages to ground me. "We'll fix it, Americana," he says with quiet certainty, pressing a kiss to my temple. "We'll go to him."

And so we do.

***

Declan convinces me to wait for the sun to rise before ambushing my father, and I suppose he's right. Storming his penthouse in pajamas wouldn't exactly be the power move my image needs right now.

But when we finally make it to his building, the doorman greets us with an apologetic smile, letting me know my father left last night and hasn't come home since. Panic spikes sharp in my chest. Where the hell was he? And why, when everything is blowing up around me, is he nowhere to be found?

The proud daughter in me wants to believe maybe he and Malina Matthews finally hooked up—that my meddling had actually worked for once. But, unfortunately, this isn't the time to check in on the progress of my match-making endeavors. My life is currently exploding, and all I can do is try to keep the pieces from scattering too far.

By the time we walk back out onto the street, reporters are already gathering, cameras flashing, microphones shoved in my face. I duck my head, tugging Declan with me back into the building. There's no way we can drive ourselves without the risk of being followed. So, I call my driver to come get us and Declan calls Matteo to grab his car so we can make an escape.

"Let's head to the back entrance in the parking garage," I tell Declan.

"Okay, and then what?" He asks. "Where are we going?"

In nothing but the clothes on our backs, I have our driver take us to the lake house at Lake Oconee. No one will ever find us there. And since no one ever comes until Christmas, it feels like the perfect place for Declan and me to hide out while we figure out a plan—how to face the fallout, how to breathe through the mess that just detonated our lives. And maybe for me to tell him about the secret that is growing inside me, literally.

But the second we pull up, I notice it—thin curls of smoke rising from the chimney, blurring into the gray morning sky. My stomach twists tight, unease clawing up my throat.

"Weird," I mutter, more to myself than to Declan. "I wonder if Will or Xavier is here."

But when I push open the door, it isn't Will. It isn't Xavier.

It's them.

The sight hits me like a blade, straight through my chest. Betrayal and stupidity tangle together until I can hardly breathe. My best friend. My father.

And all I can think is—how could they?

How could she?

How could he?

CHAPTER FIFTY FOUR: RAGE & REVELATIONS

Marlow

"**W**hat the hell do you mean you're married?!" Daddy's voice booms through the house, and the headache I've been nursing all morning spikes like a hammer slamming into my skull.

"I'm sorry, excuse me?" The words spit out of me like venom before I can even think. "Don't you dare come down on me when I literally just caught you with your pants down—with my best friend! I mean, seriously, I should be in a goddamn institution with the amount of shit I've had to hide and cover up for you!"

"Okay, I think you're exaggerating—"

I cut him off, fire spiking hotter. "Exaggerating? Are you forgetting the time I had to bail you out of jail because you didn't realize the pretty lady at a fundraiser was a hooker? Or how about the time I walked in on you with my babysitter sucking your dick?"

Eslin's head whips to him so fast I hear the intake of her breath. "Excuse me?"

"Oh, come on!" Daddy throws his hands up, exasperated. "How long are you going to hold that over my head? It was after you were grown, and how was I supposed to know she babysat you in middle school?" He yells.

"Because you hired her!" I scream back, tears blurring my vision but not slowing me down. "More than twice! And because you're supposed to be a responsible parent!"

I've never let him see me like this—never let him hear my rage, feel the full weight of it. Until now, his antics were just...background noise. Embarrassing, yes. Frustrating, sure. But never personal. Never enough to cut me open. This time, though—this time it's different. This time it's close. Too close. And it hurts in a way I can't swallow down.

My chest heaves, my voice splintering with rage and grief all knotted together. "How long are you going to keep doing this reckless shit? Six months. That's how long you had to keep your promises, and you couldn't even do that! How long has this been going on?!"

"Marlow—" Eslin tries to cut in again but this time it's my father who keeps going, tumbling over her attempts at calming us down.

"This is rich coming from you, when you just said you came here to hide because of a secret fucking marriage—to a player, no less! How ridiculous could you be?"

Declan growls low, a sound that makes the air in the room shift. "Be careful. That's my wife you're speaking to...*sir*." Respect doesn't touch his tone; he's coiled and dangerous. And for a split second, I remember exactly who my in-laws are, what they're capable of.

"Okay," Eslin says quickly, gently, stepping forward like she's afraid the whole place might combust. "How about we sit down and talk this out?"

She turns to me, reaching for my hand, her voice soft. "Marlow, we didn't mean for this to happen. We really tried to fight it but—"

"Excuse me?" I snap, yanking my hand back like she burned me. "This is family business, and I need to speak with my father. Alone."

The words come out harsher than I intend, stabbing, cruel. And the way she recoils, like I've doused her in gasoline and lit a match, twists something sharp inside me. But I don't take it back. I can't. Not right now.

My dad catches my eye, jaw tight, and then nods toward the study. "In here. Now."

Without another word, we walk, the door clicking shut behind us.

It's just me and him now.

He drops into the chair behind the desk, running a hand over his face, and I stand there, arms crossed, my pulse hammering.

"Alright," he says finally, voice low but firm. "Let's have it out. All of it. Every secret, every lie. No more games, Munchkin. You want answers—I'll give them to you. But you damn well better be ready to hear mine too."

I nod while my dad begins.

Grant

I rub a hand over my face, pacing the study while Marlow sits there, arms crossed so tight across her chest I wonder if she'll leave bruises.

My voice is cautious, but there's no mistaking the weight of what I'm about to say. "Do you remember that story I told you about Vegas? About the woman I met there? The one I swore I'd never see again once I learned her age?"

Marlow cuts in immediately. "What does she have to do with anything?"

I don't let her tone derail me. "Everything. Because I was committed to that promise, Marlow. I kept it, even when that woman from Vegas showed up in Atlanta—as the new team therapist."

Her gasp cuts through the air like thunder. "Wait, what? I don't get it..."

"We agreed to stay away from each other, out of respect for you, out of respect for her job. But every time we were in the same room, every time we had to work side by side during team activities, it only got worse. The fondness grew. The wanting. Until it wasn't controllable anymore."

"So, you're saying Eslin was, *is*, the woman from Vegas that you couldn't stop thinking about?"

I nod once, firm. "Yes."

Her stare pins me in place, her jaw tightening. "And how long did you two wait before you let something happen between you?"

The air feels like it weighs a hundred pounds. I drag a tortured breath into my lungs, not wanting to admit to the months of near-misses, the brushes of temptation, the times I almost broke. "You have to understand, munch. Eslin really respects you. She loves you and—"

"How long, daddy?"

I shake my head. "Nothing *really* happened until..." The words scrape out of me, low, ashamed. I bow my head, because saying it aloud feels like betrayal all over again.

But Marlow—my girl has always been too damn sharp. Too quick at piecing puzzles together.

Her eyes go wide, wild, horror blooming across her face. Her voice rises, trembling but fierce, as she spits the words like poison. " Eslin was the woman from the gala?!"

"Yes," I admit without hesitation, because there's no point in dodging it. "It was her. And I know you're angry, but we planned to tell you. We wanted to do it right, sooner rather than later. Only—Eslin found out you were carrying another secret, and she didn't want to risk piling more hurt onto you."

"Un-fucking-believeable," she hisses, tears streaming down her face.

"I'm sorry, Low. You have to know how sorry I am."

She doesn't say anything. Silence stretches, heavy, until finally Marlow leans back, her jaw tight. "I don't know if I'll ever forgive you for this, Daddy. I don't know if I'll ever trust *her* again." She exhales hard, and for a moment, I think that's the end of it. But then her eyes flick to mine. "But I sort of understand."

And then, like she's dropping a grenade in my lap, she says, "That other secret Eslin couldn't tell you? I'm pregnant."

I blink. Twice. Unable to do much else.

Then my beautiful daughter launches right into how she ended up on a reality show that somehow resulted in her marriage, like this is just another catch-up.

Then she says something that makes me completely roll my eyes and even laugh a little inside. "But you can't tell Declan, Daddy. I haven't told him yet."

CHAPTER FIFTY FIVE: TREE TRIMMING & TRUCES

Eslin

M arlow has been on calls for the better part of the day, strategizing, pacing, snapping at people on speakerphone, then snapping at no one in particular. And even though she won't look at me or speak to me, I still make sure she's comfortable—keep her fed, press a glass of water into her hand, even prop her feet up on a pillow when she finally sinks onto the couch. She kicked me once for trying, but I'll take it.

I guess that's what they mean when they say, *love hurts.*

After I'm sure she's as relaxed as she can be, given the circumstances, I step back and let her breathe without me hovering like a mama bear.

That's when I notice Grant, lugging a box of Christmas decorations into the great room and I walk over to him. "Whatcha doin', Mister?" I tease, folding my arms.

He flashes me that grin that still melts me and leans down to press a kiss to my lips. Instinctively, I pull back, glancing over my shoulder.

"Uh, the cat is absolutely out of that bag, honey. Kiss me." His voice is low, playful, insistent. And then his arms are around my waist, tugging me flush against him before kissing me properly.

From the couch, Marlow makes exaggerated gagging noises. "Fucking gross!" she hisses, slamming a few keys on her laptop before returning her attention to the screen.

Grant chuckles, finally letting me go, and gestures to the open box. "Well, before we were barged in on, I had this plan for us to put up Christmas decorations. Just me and you. Start a tradition, maybe?"

The thought tugs at something warm in me, and I lean in for another kiss. He thought of everything that would make me feel special this weekend.

"I'd like that a lot. But...right now, the Christmas spirit feels a little lost. At least while..." I tilt my head subtly toward Marlow, not daring to say her name outright. "She's still mad at me. Jolly and cheer won't feel right until *we're* right. My stand-in."

Grant frowns, puzzled. "Your what?"

I shake my head quickly, brushing it off. "Nevermind."

That's the thing about my relationship with Marlow. While Grant and I have spent the last six months fighting every damn feeling clawing its way to the surface, Marlow and I were building something else. A collection of secrets, inside jokes, nicknames for our dysfunctional little friend-group—*my stand-ins.* Her and Tatum became family, in every sense that ever mattered.

And now, because I've never had this before, because I've never been allowed this kind of belonging, something inside me feels like it's splitting open. Like I'm the most selfish woman alive for choosing a man over my best friend. For choosing my happiness while hers is crumbling.

I glance out the window, spotting Declan on the dock, hands in his pockets, staring out at the water.

I turn back to Grant. "I'm going to go talk to Declan, alright?"

Grant pulls me close, presses his forehead to mine, grounding me. "She's going to be fine. I know my girl. She's stubborn and feisty and her feelings are hurt. But she'll come around. You just have to give her time."

I shake my head, resolve already knotting in my chest. "I don't like the idea of letting time pass where hurt festers. I'll get through to her. You just wait."

Grant laughs and drops a kiss to my temple. "Okay. Don't say I didn't warn you. And if her eyes turn red, just duck. She throws things."

I can't help but laugh with him, the sound easing the weight for just a moment. Then I pull away and head outside, the chill in the air biting at my skin as I make my way toward Declan standing alone by the lake.

"Hey, Declan. How are you? How are you holding up?"

He shrugs, casual as ever. "This is all media drama. I guess it'll blow over, right? I mean, I know Marlow's worried. But I don't understand what the big deal is. At least it's out in the open. We don't have to hide anymore."

I pinch the bridge of my nose, then sigh. "Okay, so, I'm going to drop my professional hat so I can speak as truthfully as I know how."

Declan nods, attention still on the water. "Okay."

"Declan, that is the dumbest thing I've ever heard you say. But you're a boy and you're pretty, so I'll give you a pass."

He frowns. "I don't understand."

"Exactly," I tell him. "This entire time, Marlow has been screaming about her image, about not being taken seriously as a woman in this field. It had nothing to do with you—or not taking things public—not specifically. It was always about protecting something men never have people question in her same position! Her respect. Her dignity. And now, her damn career."

Declan's shoulders dip, a rare humility in his expression. "I guess I lost sight of that."

"You think?"

"How do we fix it?"

I shake my head, helpless. "That's exactly what we're all trying to figure out. I just wish your wife would talk to me."

That's when he smirks. "Yeah, my wife is stubborn, I've learned. Whenever my brother and I were fighting, my nonna would lock us in a bedroom and make us stay there until we came out best friends again. Brothers."

A grin tugs at my lips. "Declan, I knew I liked you for my girl Marlow!"

Then I slap the man on the back and head back into the house.

***

When Marlow finally hangs up after another brutal round with her lawyers and PR team, I don't give her a chance to escape. I catch her arm, drag her straight into the study, and shut the door with a sharp click before locking it.

"What the hell, Es?" she snaps.

"We're doing this," I say firmly, planting myself in front of the door. "We're talking."

"Talking! You want to talk? Fine. I've got a lot to say!"

I nod, bracing myself for every word I know is coming, every sting I probably deserve. "Say it, Low. Say whatever you need to." I gesture toward the massive sectional in the study, and we sit—across from each other, opposite sides, like rivals instead of family.

For a moment, there's nothing but silence. Silence and tears. Hers and mine.

"I don't cry. I don't let shit get to me," Marlow starts, her voice breaking. "But these fucking baby hormones have me acting delirious!"

I bite back a laugh, though something about the mention of her baby pulls at my chest in a way I can't name. So I just give her a soft smile.

"But also," she goes on, "I've never let anyone this close to hurt me, Es. I loved you even before I loved Declan. And this betrayal cut me more than I ever thought possible."

My throat aches. "I'm so sorry, Low."

"And I hate that I let you call me that," she snaps, her words slicing clean. "Because that's always been reserved for family."

I bow my head, because that one...even though I knew she'd say some hurtful things, that one hurt deeper than I expected.

Her voice softens a fraction. "I'm sorry. I know I'm saying everything that comes to mind without a filter and I sort of don't care if it hurts."

I laugh through my own snot and tears. "Then why are you apologizing?"

She smiles through tears but it's a painful one. "Because I fucking love you! And even though I am mad as hell at you, you don't deserve my venom. But fuck—I'm so mad!"

The dam in me finally breaks. I reach across and pull her into a hug, holding tight as she shakes against me. "Shhh. I don't want you to upset the baby."

I pull back just enough to meet her eyes, and what I say feels like ripping myself open. "I'll stay in here with you until you yell, scream, curse me out for as long as you need. And I'll still love you. And then...I'll go out there and break things off with your dad."

Her eyes go wide. "What?"

"I choose you. I'll always choose you. Even though..." My voice cracks, my head bows, and the ache nearly swallows me whole. "...even though I loved *him* first. I loved him before I loved you but, Low, I'll still choose you."

Something inside both of us snaps, and suddenly we're clinging to each other, sobbing harder than either of us can control.

Declan's nonna had the right idea—lock us in until the fight burns out—because for a long while, we just *talk*. Voices rise. Accusations flare. Tears spill. But slowly, the poison drains. And when it's done, we're sitting on the floor, backs against the desk, legs stretched out like two kids who've cried themselves clean.

"Eslin?" Marlow's voice comes out small, almost childlike.

"Yeah?" I answer, wiping at my face, bracing myself for whatever comes next.

"I've never seen my dad like this. With anyone. Not since my mom. I watched you two from the corner of my eye earlier, when he was pulling out the Christmas decorations, and..." She lets out a shaky laugh. "It made me smile. To see him so smitten."

My heart stutters, caught between guilt and something dangerously close to hope. "Okay?"

"And I guess what I'm saying is..." She swallows hard, tears brimming again. "I love you both. And if you fought that hard to resist each other out of respect for me, I can't imagine how difficult it was. Because when I look at the two of you together—you're perfect."

The words hit me like sunlight after weeks of rain. Relief. Honor. Fullness. I can barely breathe past the lump in my throat. "Thank you," I whisper, voice trembling. "I love him so much, Marlow. I promise I do."

Before I can say more, the wall she's been holding up finally crumbles. Marlow collapses into me, sobs ripping out of her, raw and unrestrained again.

Every ounce of pressure she's been carrying—her marriage, her father, her career, the baby—it all spills out, shaking her from the inside out.

Her voice cracks, gutted and terrified. "Eslin. I may lose everything!"

CHAPTER FIFTY SIX: TINSEL & TRUST

Declan

I spot Marlow's father juggling boxes out of the back of the house while barking into the phone with Xavier Darcy and Will Huntley. All hands are in motion, which only drives home how big this really is.

I keep my head down, hoping to dodge him, but my new father-in-law has other plans.

"Hey, Dickless," he calls out.

My jaw tightens. "It's Declan."

"Any man who marries my daughter without so much as meeting me first? Dickless. Now get over here and make yourself useful."

Prick.

But I don't say it out loud. Because the prick's not wrong. Where I come from, marrying a woman without her family's blessing is grounds for exile. And while Marlow's dad isn't some old-school patriarch, I still wish I'd had the chance to look him in the eye. Tell him how much I adore his daughter before... well...defiling her.

So, I stand, cross the room, and take the boxes from him without complaint. They're heavier than he makes them look, but I don't give him the satisfaction of showing it. I follow him out toward the garage where he's stacking everything in neat piles.

After a beat of silence, he looks at me with that sharp, assessing stare of his. "What the hell made you think it was a good idea to join a reality show the week before signing on with the Strikers?"

I set the boxes down, dust off my hands, and square my shoulders. "Full transparency? I didn't realize how...*real* it would be. I thought it was for laughs, some light distraction before the season. But once I met your daughter—" I stop, shaking my head as a humorless laugh slips out. "Everything shifted. Everything became *realer* than I could've imagined. She was real. The kind of real I didn't even know I'd been waiting for...Sir."

I clear my throat. The word tastes awkward on my tongue, but I've heard American men like being called that—and if there's ever a man whose favor I need, it's his. Marlow might be mad at her father right now, but when she talks about him when he's not around, it's different. Like she forgets to be angry. Like she still sees him as her hero. I feel like I know him already. And it's clear—she thinks the world of him. So I try to build some semblance of a rapport with him. Because making her happy means trying.

The prick studies me, skeptical but strangely quiet, like maybe—for the first time—he's reconsidering the version of me he's already decided on.

Maybe I'll do the same. Because no matter how much Marlow adores him, I've always had questions. What kind of father parades women through the media like that? I know their bond is different. I get that. But still—I can't help but blame him for how long it took her to trust me. To lean on me. To believe in love. Us.

"I saw your interview," he finally says. "With that dumbass comment about the team. You've really gone and made a mess of things. The guys are pissed."

I drag a hand through my hair and shake my head. "I know. And I swear I'll fix it. I just don't know how yet."

"Xavier Darcy has ideas," Grant mutters. "But you're not going to like them."

I frown. "I don't understand."

"Exactly." He gives me that pointed look. "Just know this, those guys don't take kindly to being deceived. And they'll make you pay for it."

When it comes to being part of a team—this team in particular—I don't take it lightly. I show up. I make sure the new guys feel welcome, that no one's left behind, that everyone knows they belong. I've carried bags, stayed late, hell, I've even sat through hours in a high-end strip club just so Matteo could cram for his college entrance exams without feeling alone. That's what team means to me—sacrifice, loyalty, showing up no matter what.

So the fact that this—my mistake, my recklessness—has derailed the progress I've made, has put a crack in the trust I've been building with the Strikers, it guts me. And I mean it when I say I'll do anything to make amends. Anything to prove I belong here.

"Do you think they'll forgive me?" The words leave me quieter than I intend, heavier than I want my new father-in-law to hear.

The prick doesn't answer right away. Just studies me for another beat before finally saying, "If you tell them how you fell for my daughter—the same way you just told me—I think they might."

I nod, taking that in. Then we head back inside. Grant goes straight to the bar, grabs two glasses, and pours us each a drink.

"You like scotch?"

"I prefer red wine, but scotch is fine for the occasion."

He raises a brow. "What occasion is that?"

"That you didn't murder me for marrying your daughter."

He lets out a dry laugh. "Don't think I wasn't tempted."

He hands me the glass. I raise mine. "I hear congratulations are in order for you too?"

"Let's not celebrate just yet. Not until we see if Marlow let her live. They've been in the study for a while now, and it's gotten awfully quiet."

"Yeah. Your daughter's pretty violent when she wants to be."

"She throws things," we both say at the same time. That earns a laugh and a toast from my father-in-law—the prick.

Right on cue, the study door opens and my wife and Coach Saunders step out. Their eyes are red, proof they've been crying, but the smiles on their faces tell me it wasn't for nothing. Whatever happened in there, it mattered—and it worked.

Thanks Nonna.

And like a couple of idiots in love, me and the prick just stand there—grinning like fools at the women we call ours.

Marlow

When Eslin and I step out of the study, my chest feels hollow and full all at once. The tears dried on my face aren't pretty, but the smile tugging at my lips is real. She and I finally said the things we needed to say—the ugly, the honest, even the ones that hurt—and somehow, it stitched us back together.

My eyes sweep the room until they land on my dad. His expression softens the way it always does when he sees me. I square my shoulders and force the words out before I can chicken out.

"Daddy," I say, voice low. "I'm sorry. For making it seem like you were the only one who could derail my career. That wasn't fair. The truth is...I carry just as much responsibility for that. And, as luck would have it, it's my scandal—the mess I created—that could undo everything for me and everyone else."

Something shifts in his gaze, and before I can say anything else, Dad pulls me straight into his chest. His arms are solid, grounding, and for a second I let myself sink into it like I did when I was a little girl.

"No more secrets," he murmurs into my hair.

I nod against him, whispering back, "No more lies."

"Never again," he promises.

When he finally lets me go, he reaches for Eslin, pulling her close too. She startles at first, then melts against him, and I open my arms wide, stepping in so we're all wrapped up together.

It feels like a choice—his, mine, all of ours. A quiet promise that we're a family now. That no matter how messy or complicated it gets, Eslin belongs here too. She's home.

***

By Sunday, Eslin, Dad, and even Declan have all thrown themselves headfirst into crisis clean-up mode. But Saturday night felt like a different world—Eslin in the kitchen whipping up homemade hot cocoa, Declan pulling out his special biscotti recipe, the four of us ending the night with a ridiculous game of truth or dare just to peel back another layer and learn each other better. For a while, it felt...normal. Like we weren't patching together some messy, unconventional family, but stepping into one that had always been waiting for us.

And I love it here.

But Sunday isn't about cozy. It's about action. And the best thing about *my* family—and the ones who've stepped in when I've needed them—is that when it's time to get down to business, no one wastes a second.

We call Tatum and the rest of the PR team, settle around the dining table, and dive headfirst into strategy mode. Declan, suddenly the paranoid one about unsecured phones—a side of him that keeps peeling back more of who he really is—insisted everyone come to the lake house in person. Daddy didn't argue. In fact, he agreed right away, pointing out that Kennedy clearly had access to information he shouldn't, and until we figured out his source, we needed to keep everything close to the chest.

Even Daddy's blood seems to run cold when Declan mutters, "He'll be handled by morning."

None of us knows exactly what that means—and none of us dares to ask.

When the crisis team shows up, ideas fly fast—damage control statements, staged photo ops, spin tactics that might soften the scandal while keeping my job secure, my image intact, and my pregnancy hidden. Every option feels impossible, reckless, or both... until one finally lands.

"A Christmas wedding!" Tatum belts out.

I clutch my belly like I can already feel what's growing inside. "I'm sorry, what?"

"O.M.G. It's perfect!" Eslin claps, eyes shining.

I glance at my phone and the date, panic spiking. "It's less than two weeks away!"

"I'm sorry, have you met your Stand-Ins?" Tatum fires back. "We could run the world with a smartphone and a Google calendar."

"We're not talking about some Halloween party or back-to-school bash, Tay! This is my *life*. My career. And a wedding thrown together in two weeks cannot be how it all comes to a head."

Tatum reaches across the table and grabs my hand, steadying me in the midst of my spiral. "Look. I know you've only seen me pull off events that are all spectacle and champagne fountains. But I need you to hear me right now—this isn't just about optics for the Strikers. This is about *you*."

Eslin slides her hand on top of ours, grounding me with her calm as well. "If you let us carry this with you—" she glances at Tatum, then back at me, her voice soft but certain, "—we'll make it more than damage control. We'll make it beautiful. Intimate. Like it was always supposed to be this way. Like we've been planning it all along."

I look between them, my heart squeezing. My new best friend and the woman who feels more like a sister every day—standing shoulder to shoulder, ready to fight for me, for us. For the family we're somehow stitching together out of chaos.

It's the only plan that makes sense. An announcement obnoxious enough to drown out whispers, turning the conversation from shame to celebration. Not a scandal—an event. Something bold and impossible to ignore.

Eslin and Tatum throw themselves into the details, sketching out ways to weave the team into every part of it—photo spreads, behind-the-scenes clips, even small personal touches that make each player visible. Not props. Not background noise. Family. The kind that fights, messes up, but still shows up when it matters.

"The story shifts from scandal to unity, framing the Strikers not as fractured, but as something stronger than ever," Tatum adds.

Declan rubs a hand over his face. "A unit? How is that going to work if they're all pissed at me from that interview?"

Eslin just smiles, her confidence cutting through the doubt. "More on that later. For now, we have less than two weeks to pull off a wedding so beautiful, so magnificent, that your little secret looks intentional."

I glance at Declan, bracing myself. "And I know how much you hate doing interviews, but Tatum's already lined up a series. Stories about us. Our life. Behind-the-scenes visits into our home."

Eslin jumps in, practically glowing. "We're calling it *Sweet Home Americana*," she announces proudly. "After what you've nicknamed her."

"I'm aware," Declan deadpans, face flat, unimpressed.

Then his eyes find mine. "And you think this will help?"

I shrug, because what else can I do? "It's the best shot we have."

He exhales slowly, then shakes his head with the faintest smile. "I just want you to be happy. But if none of this works, I'm taking you to Argentina and getting you pregnant the first chance I get."

Daddy clears his throat, pointed and deliberate, reminding me that the secrets in this room don't belong to me alone. "I don't have any oaths to live by like Eslin does. If you don't tell him, I will," he warns.

Declan's head snaps to me. "What's the pr—" he stumbles, correcting himself, "What's your father talking about?"

I let out a long sigh, slip my hand into his, and tug gently. "Come on, husband. Let's take a walk by the lake so I can tell you about the birds and the bees."

Five minutes later, Declan is tearing around the lake, arms in the air, shouting, "Gooooaal!" before stripping down and cannonballing straight into the water.

Guess he's happy.

We're having a baby.

CHAPTER FIFTY SEVEN: CANDY CANES & SECOND CHANCES

Declan

T he cold shoulder has a way of sinking into your bones. The team hasn't said much to me since the announcement—my wedding to one of the owners making me public enemy number one in the Strikers' locker room. No outright blows, no screaming matches. Just silence. Cold, thick silence.

I can take a hit on the pitch, but this? This eats at me. Because I need them to trust me again. I need them to know I'm not here to screw them over.

Xavier Darcy and the Prick promised the guys had something planned. A way for me to earn my way back into their good graces. So far, though, the only plan I can see is pretending I don't exist.

It's December 16th, and Coach Saunders—always the genius at poking sore spots—asks us to share traditions from home. "Find the common ground," she says. "Build some shared experiences. Remember why you play for each other, not just yourselves."

Matteo's the first to step up. "Since we've all been so mad at Declan for keeping a secret," he says, his voice shaky, "I've been keeping one, too."

Croix London groans, thick Irish accent making him sound more wound up than usual. "Here we go. This bloody team and their bloody secrets."

But Matteo doesn't flinch. "I passed my college entrance exams. I'm going to be a teacher."

The room goes still and then smiles begin to form on the team's faces, one by one.

"Why the hell was that a secret?" Justice Trager blurts out. "That's amazing!"

Matteo shrugs, sheepish. "Because all you guys ever talk about is women, sex, and partying. Other than soccer, of course. I didn't think you'd care. And taking this step means I'll eventually have to step back from the Strikers. I didn't want you to look at me differently."

Justice claps a hand to Matteo's shoulder. "We're a team, no matter where you go. And shaping the minds of future Strikers—and Striker fans—sounds like the perfect job for you."

"Yeah, good for you, lad," Croix adds. "Nerd suits you much better anyway."

Laughter ripples through the locker room, breaking some of the tension.

But then Matteo turns, eyes landing on me and Luca. "But I couldn't have done it without Luca and Declan."

Silence falls again, sharper this time.

"They took me into one of their private suites, studied with me all night, ran practice tests until I was ready. I know we're all pissed at Declan for what he said, but I'm sure he didn't mean it. Because he's not that kind of guy."

I step forward, laying a hand on Matteo's shoulder, the gratitude heavy in my chest. For the first time in days, I feel like someone just cracked the door open for me.

Matteo clears his throat, glancing around the room. "Since it's December sixteenth, I wanted to tell you all about *Las Posadas*."

A couple of guys tilt their heads, curious. He brightens. "It's a Mexican tradition, from the sixteenth to the twenty-fourth of December where we re-enact Mary and Joseph's search for a room in Bethlehem. You go house to house, singing, until someone finally welcomes you in. Then you celebrate—food, drinks, piñatas. The whole neighborhood comes alive."

His voice softens, more personal. "When I was a kid, we'd start right at sunset. My siblings, my cousins, kids from down the street—we'd walk block after block, voices cracking from singing, until finally, someone opened their door. Then it was tamales, champurrado, laughter so loud you could hear it two streets over." He chuckles. "But everyone waited for one thing."

Justice grins. "The piñata."

Matteo nods, eyes glinting. "Always the piñata."

I glance around the locker room, confused. I know what a piñata is—we had them back home in Argentina too—but there's nothing hanging from the ceiling, no papier-mâché donkey in sight.

My frown deepens. "So...where's the piñata?"

That's when the smiles start spreading across their faces—slow, wicked, way too coordinated. And then Croix lifts a rubber bat from behind the bench, Justice follows, and suddenly half the team is armed. Some with rubber bats. Others with large, inflatable candy canes.

Oh, hell.

"You," Justice says, pointing his bat straight at me, "are the piñata."

Laughter erupts. Before I can protest, they've got me tied to a bench with rolls of athletic tape, arms stretched wide like some sacrificial offering.

"Alright, alright—easy now," I start, but the first *whap* hits my thigh.

Then another on my shoulder. Not hard enough to injure, just enough to sting.

"Shh! Ahh fuck!" I hiss.

With every tap, the guys let loose.

"Do you know what it felt like to hear you say you didn't trust us or didn't care what we thought?" Croix growls, giving me a smack on the arm.

"Not. What. I said," I squeeze out between hits.

Matteo follows, gentler. "It hurt, hermano. You're one of us." Matteo winks because he was in on the secret but I don't let the guys in on that piece. This is mine to carry. My mess to clean-up.

Then Justice. *Whack!* "Made me feel like I wasn't on your team. Like we weren't enough for you to lean on."

Each one takes a swing, each one letting me feel the weight of what I'd said. And then, slowly, the mood shifts.

"You work harder than anyone." A thump to the chest.

"You push us to be better." A tap on the shin.

"You always pick up the check when the rookies forget their wallets." Another whack, this one paired with laughter.

"You're a pain in the ass—but you're *our* pain in the ass."

By the time they're done, I'm bruised in body and ego, but my chest feels lighter than it has in days. They didn't just beat me down. They built me back up.

When they finally untie me, we're all laughing, the locker room buzzing with something that feels a hell of a lot like Christmas spirit.

And then Croix, never one to waste momentum, shouts, "And now it's time for caroling! That's on the Las Posadas agenda, right, 'Teo?"

Matteo's grin is wide enough to split his face. "That's right, hermano! You sing, you share joy—it's part of the tradition."

The locker room buzzes with sudden energy. Justice hops to his feet, clapping his hands. "Let's do it. Let's go caroling."

Matteo adds, "To the front office staff. They're the ones who really need to see we're united."

The suggestion lands like wildfire, spreading fast. Guys start whooping, tossing sweaty shirts across the room.

Croix raises his rubber candy cane in the air like it's a mic. "We do it shirtless. With Santa hats!"

The roar of approval nearly rattles the lockers. Someone digs into the equipment trunk, and I swear to God, out comes a box of Santa hats like they'd been planning this all along.

I shake my head, still half tied up. "I know the perfect song," I say, grinning despite myself. "But can someone untie me before I become the world's saddest Christmas decoration?"

Luca rips the tape free from my wrists, and before I can catch my breath, I'm swept up into the ridiculousness—twenty grown men, bare-chested, Santa hats crooked on their heads, buzzing like they've just won the damn championship.

Next thing I know, Coach Jones is at the front of the pack, strutting down the hallway with a radio hoisted on his shoulder like some old-school rap crew, only instead of N.W.A., he's blasting *Merry Christmas, Happy Holidays* by 'N Sync.

And the Strikers—God help us all—are caroling shirtless through the executive offices—half naked, sweaty, and off-key. All belting out the chorus while the front office staff doubles over in laughter.

And of course, everyone has a phone in hand recording us.

By the time we hit Marlow's office, Eslin and Tatum are in there with her, clearly scheming over wedding plans, I'm sure. The three of them look up, startled, as twenty half-naked Strikers crowd the doorway.

Coach clicks the radio, and the room shifts as the opening notes of *O Holy Night* swell through the hall.

Matteo steps forward, voice rich and steady as he begins the first verse in Spanish, his accent warm and reverent. Croix follows, picking up the next lines in his native Irish tongue, Gaeilge, his tone rougher but no less heartfelt, the old language giving the carol a weight that settles over everyone.

Then, one by one, the rest of the team joins in English, their voices uneven but full, echoing down the corridor. It's messy, imperfect, but somehow it feels holy all the same.

When the chorus rises— *"Fall on your knees"*—I drop to mine without thinking, my body moving before my mind can catch up. My head finds its place against Marlow's belly, her warmth grounding me as the world narrows to just this moment.

"Oh night divine," I whisper, the words sinking into her skin, into me, into the life we're about to build. And the one we're about to bring into this world.

Chapter Sixty

CHAPTER FIFTY EIGHT: HITCHED ON THE PITCH

Eslin

FOR IMMEDIATE RELEASE

Atlanta, GA — December 25 — Under winter lights and a sky clear enough to count the stars, the Atlanta Strikers' home field became a wedding aisle as **Marlow** and **Declan** were married in a private Christmas Day ceremony.

The pitch was transformed with winter-white tents, evergreens, and florals along the touchlines. In keeping with the couple's wish for an intimate celebration, the guest list included only the Strikers team, close family and friends, and one journalist granted exclusive access: **Zoey Sharpe**, the newly appointed reporter for **The Cinnamon Grove Sun**.

"This wasn't about spectacle," Marlow said. "It was about home. For us, that's this club, this field, and these people."

Declan added, "I've played on a lot of pitches, but nothing will compare to walking this one with her and leaving as husband and wife."

The ceremony highlighted the club's unity and the season's spirit—quiet, joyful, and close-knit—closing with carols and a small reception under the tents at midfield.

For the full exclusive story and photos, read **Zoey Sharpe**'s feature in **The Cinnamon Grove Sun**.

CHAPTER FIFTY NINE: MISTLETOE & MATCHDAY

Eslin

The field is still glowing from the wedding—strings of lights draped from goal to goal, white tents breathing out soft heat, evergreens threaded with ribbon along the touchlines. It smells like winter and sugar. The team is scattered in little clusters, balancing champagne flutes and plates of cake, ties loosened, cheeks pink from cold and relief. Family and a few friends fill the rest. Zoey Sharpe hovers near the edge of it all with her notebook, quiet and watchful, the only outsider invited in.

Their ceremony was elegant, simple—so Marlow. She wore an Italian lace gown with a chapel-length veil. Declan wore his Atlanta Strikers uniform, and the Strikers—his groomsmen—wore theirs. I've never been a part of something so liberating but welcoming at the same time.

Perfect.

I'm standing with Marlow and Tatum under a tent that looks like a snow globe cracked open. Marlow's dress catches every light; she looks like the best secret I've ever kept.

"You look ridiculous," I tell her. "In a good way."

"Stupid-level beautiful," Tatum adds, eyes wet. "And you can't even see your baby bump."

Marlow gasps. "Are you joking?"

"Yes," Tatum says with a straight face. "You don't look like you weigh more than a hundred pounds."

Marlow exhales, then turns to us, voice thick. "You two...thank you. For being my rock. For holding my secrets. I'm going to try not to ever put you in that position again."

"Noted," I say, bumping her shoulder. "But if you do, we know where the shovels are."

She laughs, wipes at the corner of her eye. "And you're one to talk!" She says, joking and we all laugh again.

Laughing with them has become my favorite pastime.

I glance around the tents, the corners, the shadows. "Whatever happened to Shaun Kennedy? Did Niko find him?"

Marlow scans the field like she's expecting him to pop out of a cooler, then shrugs. "No one has heard from him in a week."

That feels too heavy, too ominous for the moment, so I force a half-smile, add a little shrug, and let the words tumble out. "Damn shame what they did to that dog."

Tatum snorts, then full-on cackles.

Marlow blinks. "I don't get it!"

"Never mind," I say. "Next girls' night, we're watching *Coming to America*."

Arms slide around Marlow's waist from behind. Declan pulls her into his chest, mouth at her temple. "You ready to go, Senora Agassi?"

Tatum and I both swoon on cue, because we're not completely made of stone.

Marlow tilts her head up, kisses him, her eyes shining. "Sí, Señor Agassi."

His brows lift, his grin spreading wide. "Look at you, already sounding like a true Italian bride."

She grins. "I've been practicing on an app. Figured I should learn Italian."

Across the tent, Grant laughs at something Xavier says, then catches my eye and makes his way over to me. The look we trade says it all—we survived today, and somehow made it beautiful. I open my mouth to tell him how handsome he looks, but Xavier and Will call him back with that polite, no-nonsense tone that means *now*.

He groans under his breath. "They want to finalize things," he mutters. "Handing everything over to Marlow, for good."

"The control freak is finally giving up control, huh?"

His grin is easy, boyish. "Trading one addiction for another," he quips, then dips in, pressing a quick, certain kiss to my mouth.

Tatum clutches her chest dramatically, whispering, "Lord, have mercy," and I can't stop my smile from spilling wide.

"Well, yes, sir," Tatum says in mock approval, fanning herself as Grant squeezes my hand before heading back toward his friends.

I step away from the crowd, letting the music and laughter fade into a low hum. Out of the corner of my eye, I catch movement—Coach Jones, headed straight for me with that determined stride.

Tatum clears her throat at my side. "Heads up. Jones incoming."

I groan under my breath. Thanksgiving flashes through my mind, the mess I left behind. Since then, I've done everything possible to avoid him—took vacation days, worked from home, even camped out in Marlow's office when she wasn't around. Anything to keep distance.

And maybe he knows, because he brings the one thing I can't resist.

"Hey, Coach Rocky!" I yell, dropping down in my burgundy gown to greet our furry menace, grateful he's actually behaved today.

"Coach Saunders," Darren says, voice even.

I rise from petting Rocky to meet his gaze. "Darren," I reply, forcing myself to give him the name he's always begged me to. "How are you?"

"I'm well. You?"

I sigh, refusing to pretend. "Darren, you don't have to do this."

He tilts his head. "Do what?"

"Pretend like I don't owe you an apology. Like I didn't act like the biggest ass alive, leading you on like I did."

He grins, but it's softer than I expect. Gracious, even. "If we're honest," he says, that South African lilt giving the words more weight, "I played myself. Led myself on."

My brows pull together. "What do you mean?"

His eyes flick briefly across the room. Toward Grant.

"I knew—"

"You knew it was him?" I whisper, finishing for him.

"I knew it wasn't me," Darren says simply.

"Wow." My voice comes out low, heavy with guilt. "I'm sorry, Darren. I really—"

He lifts a hand, cutting me off before I can finish. "No hard feelings, Coach Saunders. Happiness looks good on you."

I smile, but both of us glance back toward the tent where the other players are gathered and tension is obviously building.

Coach exhales a long, weary sigh. "I need to go separate Luca and Croix again before they end up killing each other."

I shake my head. "I've got a joint session scheduled with them after the new year. Hopefully they can survive that long without drawing blood."

Coach groans as he and Rocky start heading toward the commotion. "From your lips to God's ears."

Grant walks over after he notices Coach Jones and I'm already shaking my head at his jealousy.

"Your spidey senses telling you someone was trying to push up on your girl?"

"My spidey senses told me I was about to have to come over here and kick someone's ass."

I laugh, loud. We both do. He's become one of my favorite pastimes, too.

"You ready to get out of here, Eslin Saunders? I hear the bride and groom are headed to Italy in the morning."

I frown. "In the morning? Won't he miss matches if he's gone?"

He grins. "Their last official match was earlier this month so he won't be missing anything."

"He's got some good bosses, I tell ya."

He kisses me and I melt into this man.

"Come on, Sunshine. I've got something special for you."

Chapter Sixty-Two

CHAPTER SIXTY: PRESENTS & PERMANENCE

Grant

M y palms are sweating, and that never happens to me.

I've spoken in front of thousands, faced down boardrooms full of sharks, but this? Planning out every last detail with Marlow, even down to the little white lie that she and Declan had already jetted off to Italy, has my stomach in knots. They are going—just not until after the next two matches—but I needed Eslin to believe they were gone so I could pull this off without interruption.

Tonight is hers. Her Christmas gift. A piece of magic I've been dying to give her.

I lead her through the glass doors of our building, her hand snug in mine, her eyes covered with the black silk blindfold I slipped over her in the car. She gasps, laughing nervously, tugging at my arm.

"What is going on, Mister?" she asks, her voice half a whisper, half a giggle.

"It's still Christmas," I murmur, brushing a kiss against her temple. "And I've got a surprise for my lady."

Her fingers tighten around mine as I guide her toward the elevator, the marble floors echoing beneath our steps. I can feel her pulse in her palm, quick and uneven, like she's bracing for something big.

"Relax, Es," I say softly, giving her hand a squeeze. "I've got you."

When the elevator doors slide open and we step out onto my floor, she stiffens again—but not with fear. With anticipation. I smile to myself, leading her into the penthouse, where the scent of pine and sugar cookies still lingers from earlier in the week.

I stop us in the middle of the living room. "Okay, sweetheart. Ready?"

She nods, breathless.

I pull the blindfold away, and her gasp nearly undoes me.

The entire room is a Christmas fever dream—the kind she confessed to me once she never really had as a child. Every piece of magic she missed, I brought to life.

In the corner, a full antique train set clatters cheerfully around the tree, the lights twinkling like stars. Near it, a towering Barbie Dreamhouse stands tall, flanked by rows of dolls—vintage classics side by side with brand-new ones, each one pristine, waiting for her. A bright-pink Barbie Corvette gleams beside a small boat. The Corvette scaled perfectly so she could climb in and drive herself around if she wanted. Ribbons of tinsel drip from the ceiling, candy canes dangle from garland, and stockings are lined up across the mantel with her name stitched right in the center.

Her hand flies to her mouth, and her eyes flood. "Grant," she whispers, her voice cracking. "Oh my God. What is all this?"

I move behind her, wrapping my arms around her waist and holding her steady as the emotion swells through her. "Every Christmas you missed, Es. Every unanswered letter from Santa—I wanted you to walk into them. They're yours now."

She turns in my arms, tears streaking her cheeks as she shakes her head in disbelief. "No one...no one's ever done anything like this for me."

I press my lips to her damp cheeks, to her forehead. "Get used to it. This is only the beginning."

I take her hand again and guide her down the hall to the master on the first floor, the heavy oak door swinging open into a space Marlow poured herself into—soft golds, creamy whites, a reading nook by the window, shelves already lined with books, and a bed draped in warm, welcoming quilts. It feels lived in. It feels hers.

"I'm not asking you to move in," I begin, my voice thick, careful. "At least not yet. But I am giving you a room of your own in my home. Marlow decorated it and everything."

She turns to me, tears streaming uncontrollably. "What?"

I nod. "She wanted you to have a home with us. *We* wanted you to have a home with us. Whenever you wanted. Wherever we are."

I dip my head to kiss her on the lips. Soft. "Because some people, Es...some people are meant to stay," I remind her. A call back from that magical night in Vegas. A reminder of her mother's words.

She looks around the room again. "It really feels like me!"

"That's what I said," Marlow calls from behind.

When Eslin turns, stunned, her tears spill harder because Declan and Marlow are standing in the doorway, Declan holding an oversized teddy bear almost as big as him. Marlow is holding a puppy.

Eslin looks at me and screams. "You got me a puppy?"

"Yeah," Marlow says sarcastically. "He's never given me a puppy when I asked for one."

Eslin runs over and takes the furry rescue from Marlow's hand. "And he has puppy breath!"

"I figure we can call him Nutmeg," I say.

Eslin looks up at me. "Why Nutmeg?"

"A call back to the day we first kissed."

She grins. "And the day I got hit in the head with a soccer ball from a nutmeg play?"

I laugh. "Exactly."

We all hug. The four of us. And I press a kiss to the top of Eslin's head and whisper, "Welcome home."

And just like that, my world—the one I never thought I'd get back—feels whole.

Chapter Sixty-Three

CHAPTER SIXTY ONE: NONNOS & NEWBORNS

Eslin

Seven Months Later

It's the middle of July, and even with the hospital's air-conditioning running full blast, it feels like we're all melting. Sweat sticks to the back of my neck, my scrubs cling to me in all the wrong places, and still—still—none of it matters. Because in Marlow's arms, the world has stopped.

Baby Maddy Mariana Agassi has arrived, a squirming, sticky little bundle of heat and perfection. Born the same month I moved to Atlanta last year, like God wanted to stitch our timelines together. She's all fire and olive, fierce even in her first cries, and I swear when she furrows her tiny brow, I see a little bit of me in her.

All the fights me and her mama had.

One by one, the players filter in. Big, brooding, larger-than-life men suddenly turned awkward and quiet in the presence of seven pounds of new life. None of them dare ask to hold her. But they all bring something. A miniature jersey, a soccer ball rattle, tiny cleats that won't fit her for years. A baby blanket embroidered with the Strikers' crest. Each gift, clumsy and perfect in its own way.

I lean against the wall, arms folded, and take it all in. My family. My crazy, wacky family that came together one insane night in Vegas and somehow, against all odds, turned into this. A team. A tribe. A home.

And as Maddy lets out another cry, strong and steady, I can't help but smile.

"Welcome to the world, little one. You have no idea the love you've just been born into."

Grant

It's the middle of the night, and yet none of us can bring ourselves to sleep. We're all wide awake, eyes fixed on this tiny little miracle who's stolen the show—and our hearts—in less than twenty-four hours. Baby Maddy.

Declan's family is up on the big screen, all crammed together in some living room half a world away. Their voices spill into the hospital room in a mix of English and Italian, laughter tumbling over one another, faces shining with pride.

We'd all already made the trip to Italy during Marlow's pregnancy. The first time it was just Declan and Marlow, and the second time, Eslin and I joined them. That second visit is the one I'll never forget, because it's where I proposed.

We were wandering the streets of Italy late at night when Eslin decided she had to have real Italian pizza. So we stopped, grabbed a slice, and sat on a corner like a couple of teenagers. She took one bite, and when a string of cheese slipped from her lips and landed on her chest, she laughed like only she can—loud, unrestrained, beautiful. And right then and there, I knew. I knew I wanted her in my life forever.

We'd never talked about it before. I didn't even know if she actually wanted to get married. But call me an old romantic, I had to try. So there I was, dropping to one knee with nothing but that ridiculous grin of hers to hold onto and a grease-stained napkin in my hand, asking her to marry me.

And thank God, she said yes.

Then, with cheese still dripping down her chest, she laughed and told me not to say anything to Marlow. Not until after the trip, because it was Marlow's time with her new family. I agreed, because that's Eslin. Always thinking about everyone else before herself. But the second we landed back home, she went and spilled it to the girls at one of their "stand-in happy hours."

So the secret lasted all of three days. Fine by me. By then she had a ring.

On the screen, Marlow lifts little Maddy toward the camera, introducing her to the other half of her family. Declan's father leans in, squinting like he's trying to memorize every detail through the pixels. His English is broken, but I get him all the same. We've already found our common ground—our shared irritation over Declan's tattoos, and the fact we missed Christmas together, thanks to that dumbass reality show wedding. He's a good man, Declan's father. Solid.

I'm still deciding on how I feel about his son.

Then Nonna bursts in, her words flying fast and sharp in rapid-fire Italian. I don't catch a single word, but I don't have to. The rhythm, the warmth, the way her hands flutter toward the screen like she could pluck Maddy right out of Marlow's arms—it's pure love. And damn it, I inwardly cringe at how soft this has all made me.

Declan's brother, though...that kid is something else. Quiet in a way that isn't just shy. Quiet in a way that makes the hairs on the back of my neck rise. There's something brewing in him. Something I can't place. But tonight isn't the night for worries. Tonight is for joy.

But I put it in the back of my mind to ask about him later.

And then it all crashes over me like a fresh wave, sharp and unrelenting. I'm a grandpa. The word feels foreign on my tongue, but it settles heavy in my chest, stilling me. My Maddy isn't gone. She left something else behind for us all. A piece of herself woven into every one of us, a reminder that this messy, tangled, unlikely family we've built is real. Forever.

And it will keep living on.

I clear my throat, calling out to the kid who somehow became my son-in-law. "Hey, Dickless."

"Yeah, Prick?" Declan fires back without missing a beat.

I smirk. "How do you say grandpa in Italian?"

Declan starts to answer, but it's his father who leans in from the screen, his voice rich and proud. "Nonno."

I look straight at him, and something passes between us. An agreement. A joining of families. "Ok," I nod. "We'll both be called nonno."

His nod seals it.

I bend and kiss the soft crown of my granddaughter's head. Then the temple of my own baby girl, grown now, but still mine.

And finally, I lace my fingers through the hand of the woman who's turned my life upside down in the best way possible—my fiancée.

I exhale, the weight of everything—the scandal, the secrets, the chaos—melting away. "Welcome home, Maddy-girl. Welcome home."

THE NEXT MATCH
The game is far from over!

First came the loyalty. Then came the betrayal. In *Hook, Line + Star-Crossed*, the next gripping installment of the Atlanta Strikers Series, Croix and Luca's legendary friendship is officially dead. Once attached at the hip, they are now driven by a fierce, unspoken hostility. What happens when teammates become strangers? Find out what ruined everything. **Click Here** for the next match!

ABOUT THE AUTHOR

Taccara Martin, writing under the pen name **T.L. Martin**, is a contemporary romance and romcom author, as well as an award-winning fiction podcast producer. She's becoming known for crafting emotionally immersive experiences across the page and the mic. Whether she's setting hearts racing with high-stakes suspense or making readers laugh through the life and love, her stories always strike a delicate balance between desire, danger, and depth.

A proud lover of dark romance, T.L. Martin thrives in the shadows—where every secret has consequences, every kiss threatens destruction, and vulnerability is the ultimate weapon. But just when the stakes feel too heavy, she wields sharp wit and well-timed comedy like a blade, offering readers a jolt of levity that makes the emotional gut punches land even harder.

While both pen names reflect her passion for storytelling, it's under **T.L. Martin** that she invites readers into the most unfiltered corners of her universe, where unforgettable characters navigate passion, peril, and the pursuit of truth. If you're looking for emotionally raw, sensually charged, and fiercely entertaining stories that dare to toe the line between pleasure and pain, you're in the right place.

Married to her "forever book boyfriend," T.L. openly shares how finding safety and security in Kenyon fuels her endless romance inspiration. For booking, tour and mailing list info, visit TLMartinWrites.com. To take a virtual tour of her fictional small town, Cinnamon Grove, visit TLMartinWorld.com.

ALSO BY TACCARA (T.L.) MARTIN

Whether you're diving into stories by Taccara Martin or T.L. Martin, the world of *Cinnamon Grove* was designed to bring these characters together in ways that feel interconnected and alive. It's a place where heartfelt, emotional journeys meet lighthearted banter and unexpected connections.

If you're drawn to the emotional depth and complexity of Taccara Martin's stories but also crave the humor and charm of a good rom-com, I encourage you to explore the romantic comedies by T.L. Martin. There's something for everyone in this shared universe, and I can't wait for you to discover all the ways these characters' lives intertwine!

Contemporary Romance by Taccara Martin:

- **Day One,** Love Stories from the Unmasked Podcast, Book 1

- **This Time It's Love,** Love Stories from the Unmasked Podcast, Book 2

- **So Into You,** Love Stories from the Unmasked Podcast, Book 3

- Become "Us," Coming 2027

Rom-Coms with a Dark Romance Edge by T.L. Martin

- **The Black Wife Effect**

- **My Filthy Rich Valentine,** The Black Wife Effect, Book 2

- **The Seven Day Hitch,** The Black Wife Effect, Book 3

- **Captured by the Canadians,** A Standalone Black Wife Effect

Spin-Off

- Ms. Lorraine's Late in Life Love, Standalone Novella from the Black Wife Effect Series

- **Nutmeg & Mistletoe,** Atlanta Strikers Series Book 1

- Hook, Line & Star-Crossed, Atlanta Strikers Series, Book 2

- Header Over Heels, Atlanta Strikers Series, Book 2 (Fall, 2026)

Dark Romance by T.L. Martin
- **Fury's Embrace,** Friends of Fury, Book 1

- Friends of Fury will return in 2027.

To learn more about Taccara, her fiction podcasts or upcoming projects, visit **TLMartinWrites.com.**

JOIN THE FLIGHT CREW

I've said it before and I'll say it again: **The Cockpit Chix** are the heartbeat of everything I build. You all are the reason **Cinnamon Grove** exists, and you're the reason my career exploded the way it did.

But as I look at what's coming in 2026, I realize I need an elite team by my side. I'm looking for the ones who are ready to go beyond being a passenger and step into the flight deck with me.

I'm officially opening applications for my ARC team: The Flight Crew.

Being part of **The Flight Crew** isn't just about getting a free book. It's about being the first to see the world as it's being built. It's about having a direct hand in the success of the stories that mean the most to us.

As a member of The Flight Crew, you'll get:

First Access: Read my upcoming releases (starting with the new heat coming to the Grove) before they hit the shelves.

The Vault: Exclusive "Flight Crew Only" sneak peeks at covers, character art, and those spicy deleted scenes I can't post anywhere else.

The Blueprint: Direct updates from me on how we're growing this empire.

What I need from my Crew: I'm looking for readers who are ready to show up. That means honest reviews on Ama-

zon and Goodreads during launch week and help-
ing me spread that "scorch the earth" energy across social media.

If you're ready to help me navigate the next chapter of Cinnamon Grove, I want you in that seat.

Scan the QR code below to fill out the application, and let's get ready for
takeoff.

See you in the air,

T.L. Martin *Architect of Cinnamon Grove*

www.ingramcontent.com/pod-product-compliance
Lightning Source LLC
Chambersburg PA
CBHW030550020726
47494CB00005B/1553